ONLY THEIRS

A MMF ROMANTIC SUSPENSE NOVEL

ANCHOR BAY
BOOK 3

KENNEDY L. MITCHELL

Cover Design: Bookin It Designs

First round editing: Kristin Scearce

Second round editing: The Picky Bitch

Proofreading: All Encompassing Books

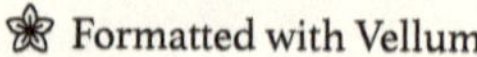 Formatted with Vellum

ABOUT THE AUTHOR

Kennedy L. Mitchell lives outside Dallas with her son, goldendoodle, and giant puppy. She began writing in 2016 and has no plans of stopping.

She would love to hear from you via any of the platforms below or her website www.kennedylmitchell.com You can also stay up to date on future releases through her newsletter or by joining her Facebook readers group - Kennedy's Book Boyfriend Support Group.

Thank you for reading.

To those left devastated by someone who claimed to love you. Our scars prove what we've been through; they don't dictate our future. Some are physical for all to see, others hidden, deep slices in our heart and soul. Both are proof of what we've survived and the trauma we continue to carry. Yet still we smile, we carry on because we choose every day to embrace the difference between being alive and actually living.

PROLOGUE

UNKNOWN

A sharp hiss whistled through my clenched teeth as I prodded the swollen area around the open wound. The slight pressure made the surrounding muscle twitch, sending a bolt of fiery pain shooting from the vicious bite mark.

"That damn mutt," I grumbled under my breath as I plunged the unused needle into my hip. As I pressed on the plunger, injecting the much-needed antibiotic, I hoped it worked the same on humans as it did the animals and I wouldn't die suddenly from some strange reaction. Antibiotics were antibiotics, and I wasn't in the position to not take the risk, considering it was the only medicine I could get my hands on without drawing questions about the massive dog bite.

Paper rustled as I lifted the unopened gauze package to my mouth and used my teeth to rip it open. Careful not to touch everything I'd just cleaned, I placed the gauze over the missing chunk of flesh and muscle, gently wrapping it to keep bacteria from contaminating the wound.

Jaw tight, I ground my teeth, remembering that night

and how my perfect plan went to hell in a split second. Heat flooded my veins as my anger rose, mixed with the consistent burning throb radiating from the damn bite, causing sweat to slick the back of my neck and drip down my bare chest. Now I not only had the fucking headache of making sure I didn't get gangrene or rabies or some shit but was also one product short to deliver to the buyers.

How was I supposed to know that woman had brought her demon dog to hike the trail alongside her?

A frustrated huff escaped as I thought about all the extra work that oversight would cause me. Now, there'd have to be a last-minute trip to Anchorage to find a replacement. I rolled my eyes, knowing it was less work taking those women off the streets, but they also weren't worth as much to my buyers as the healthy ones I procured on the Soul Trail. But at this point, meeting my promised quota mattered most.

The heavily armed Russian assholes who bought stock from me didn't give a fuck about excuses, only results—in this case, young, pretty women. Plus, even if they didn't shoot me after finding out I was short, how would I explain what actually happened? It sounded made-up even to me, and I was there that night.

Everything had gone to plan, exactly how I'd done it dozens of times before, until that damn wolf dog lunged out of her tent when I unzipped the door. To keep from getting my jugular ripped open, I wasted a round on the mutt. Between the commotion of me fighting with the animal and the gunshot, the woman had woken up and bolted into the woods, making me chase after her.

Which put me in an even worse mood since I fucking hated running.

It didn't take long for me to catch up with her enough to

get a shot in. Of course my aim was perfect. Sure, the night-vision goggles helped, but it was still fucking difficult to hit someone right between their shoulder blades while running through the trees. Disoriented, it was easy to drug her and then haul her slight frame to the mine, which was when I thought the plan was back on track.

Not by a long shot.

Setback number two happened while I was hauling her back to the mine where I was holding the others. Out of nowhere, completely taking me off guard because I'd gotten far enough away, came her damn dog. With her over my shoulder, I couldn't react fast enough before his sharp-ass teeth sank into me and tore out a chunk. The shock and pain made me drop her, and on such a steep slope, she just kept on rolling.

And rolling.

And rolling.

The good part was that the dog followed her down, which meant the demon wasn't attempting to eat more of me; the bad, he stood over her like some damn bodyguard. Without real bullets in my gun and not wanting to get close enough to use my knife, there was no way for me to know if she was still unconscious or dead.

Guess I would never know if she was dead from the fall or died later from her injuries. Hell, she could've even drowned from the amount of rain that came in the days following the shit show. I wanted to return to kick her body into the ravine after the rain stopped, knowing it would take her far away from anywhere close to the mine, but it was too late.

The fucking righteous cavalry had swarmed and recovered her body, and bonus, Anchor Bay's favorite vet had made best friends with the hellhound. I wasn't too worried, as the rain would've washed away any evidence that could point to me, but there was still the unknown threat to my operation.

What did they find?

How much did they know?

Was I now a suspect?

Ignoring the swirling questions, I snatched the fresh change of clothes off the floor, knowing I needed to hurry. Tugging on the rough cotton, my wince reflected back at me in the smudged, cracked mirror over the sink as I dragged up the pair of black pants and matching long-sleeve T-shirt. The clothing was overkill considering the warmer late-summer temperature, but I couldn't risk drawing attention to the obvious injury when I went to work later.

Jerky movement in the mirror brought my gaze to the reflection of a woman attempting to escape. Watching her futile efforts had the corners of my lips curving upward. The drugs in her system, which I had an ample supply of courtesy of my buyers, kept her like the others, barely lucid and too weak to escape their cells or even yell out for help. The heavy sedation was key to keeping them from hurting themselves, but not so out of it that they couldn't move, which could lead to bedsores and faster muscle deterioration.

Those helpful insights were all detailed in Dad's journals. They were the perfect step-by-step guide for almost all circumstances revolving around the procuring and selling of women. It was important to keep the stock waiting to be sold as healthy as possible in an old, drafty mine to maximize profits. It was almost an art form, balancing the perfect type and amount of drugs, food, hydration, and of course timing. The living product needed to be moved often, not only to make room for more, but the longer you held on to a product, the higher the potential of them getting sick, hurt, or worse, dying. That always sucked. Not only was the money you would've made lost, but you also wasted valuable resources keeping them, as well as the effort to procure them in the first place.

A soft moan had me focusing back on the woman rolling along the worn mattress.

"Thanks for the quick fuck," I said to her reflection. "Not that you had a choice. I have to go out, so be a good pet and get your rest while I'm gone. I'll be back for more of you tonight."

Her pitiful whimper echoed off the walls of the small cell.

"You know, all this could be over if you told me where you hid your journal." A deep chuckle vibrated in my chest. "Well, not over—you're way too much fun for that—but I might be inclined to be more gentle."

I waited, hoping that this time she would finally tell me. At her slight headshake and mumbled words, I whirled around to face her, fingers curled into tight fists at my sides. Fiery anger flooded my veins. My feet slammed onto the worn dirt floor as I stormed to the edge of the tattered mattress. My knees popped when I squatted low to grip her dirt-streaked face in a bruising grip, forcing her to look at me.

"Where the fuck is that journal, Caroline?"

Her cracked lips pressed into a tight line.

With a frustrated curse, I shoved her back, her head clipping a portion of the uneven wall from the force.

Not only did I need that journal to keep my operation safe, but I was curious about the contents too. Had she really put two and two together somehow, confirming her suspicions about her mom not running off but being one of Dad's early success stories? And if she *had* tied her mom's disappearance all those years ago to my operation, how the hell did she put it all together when no one else had?

If she didn't tell me where it was, I would never know, and that annoyed the shit out of me. I had thought that fucker Jasper might have a clue where she hid the journal, but he was a bigger idiot than I realized. Either way, if he knew anything, it all died with him.

Standing over her frail frame, I scanned the scrapes and bruises marking her pale skin, the layers of dirt and blood from her tumble all those weeks ago. I should've bathed her at some point, but it wasn't like I needed her face or body to be clean to use her the way I liked.

"Did you know your so-called friends are still looking for you?" Her lashes fluttered as she attempted to open her lids, a barely there moan escaping her parted, dry lips. "And unfortunately, after finding that bitch's body in the woods before I could get rid of it, they're getting too close." Reaching out, I ran my fingers through her ratty hair, tugging carelessly at the tangles and clumps of mud. "Which means it might be time for me to use you as a distraction."

Caroline's lips moved, but only ragged breaths escaped.

"Don't worry, pet. I'll make good use of what little time we have left together."

I smacked my palms against the sides of my thighs to rid them of the dust and grime. Snatching the glowing lantern off the floor, I exited the makeshift cell, closing the ill-fitted door behind me. Dirt clouded the air and bits of rock rained down from the carved-out doorframe as I secured the latch as best I could. The stench of mold, body odor, and piss flooded my nose, tainting the inside of my lungs as I shuffled along the worn path made by miners years prior.

Pausing outside a deep divot along the rocky wall that

I'd turned into the first holding pen, I peered through the rusted metal bars to check on the first of the current batch. Holding the lantern up high, it took a moment with the low light to catch the slight rise and fall of her chest. She'd been held the longest, and it showed. If I didn't get this batch sold soon, she might be a waste, putting me down two instead of just the one.

A soft chime echoed through the narrow tunnel, alerting me to an incoming call on my satellite phone. Knowing the signal sucked inside, I continued toward the mine entrance, not bothering to look in on the others in their cells as I passed. Pushing open the heavy wooden door, I stepped out into the fresh air. Blinding sunlight cut into my eyes, making me squeeze them shut, leaving me to blindly secure the door behind me.

Dad had mentioned this place in his journals, more than once appreciating the happy accident of stumbling on the long-forgotten, abandoned mine as a child roaming the wilds of Alaska alone. It was the perfect place to keep both his stock and now my own hidden until the exchange with the buyers. While I mostly followed Dad's road map and tips, I'd made a few adjustments, maximizing today's available technology to make it easier on myself.

Tugging the satellite phone free from the side pocket of my cargo pants, I took a second to inhale a deep breath, allowing the crisp mountain air to cleanse the cave stench from my lungs. Tapping the button to accept the incoming call, I held the ancient device that the Russians insisted I use to my ear as I scanned the dense trees surrounding me.

"I'm here," I stated. The fuckers who bought from me didn't believe in pleasantries.

"Is the exchange still a go?" The deep rumble of his voice and thick accent made it difficult to understand him, but thankfully this conversation was basically a repeat of the ones before.

"Yes—same place, same time."

"And the special one? You get her for the boss?"

The phone slid in my sweaty palm as I tightened my grip around the device. "I told you," I gritted out, "it's too risky to take her. What about the money and drugs? Like always?"

His raspy, condescending chuckle added to my growing agitation. "*Da*. You bring girls; we bring money and drugs."

The following stretch of silence signaled he had hung up.

"Fucking typical," I grumbled as I pocketed the phone.

Scrubbing a calloused palm over my face, I sighed, knowing they wouldn't let that "special one" shit drop until they had her. Which complicated things, since she was basically untouchable. Ever since their boss saw her picture on the updated Uplift Adventure and Rescue website, there hadn't been a single call where they didn't ask about her. He wanted her badly for his personal collection and was intent on getting her.

Good fucking luck with that was what I wanted to tell him but mouthing off to a Russian mobster was a quick way to die a slow, painful death. It was too great of a risk to even consider it, though. There was no way in hell I could sneak into their compound and take her without anyone noticing.

The insistent burning throb pulsing from the damn dog bite had me spinning on my heels toward the mine. I needed to feed and water the stock before heading to Anchor Bay. Everyone was a suspect, their actions and whereabouts monitored now that the asshole detective Brandon brought from LA was sniffing around. Everything was easy to cover and hide until he showed up and started asking too many damn questions, being a little too observant and rallying that whole fucked-up community together to stop my lucrative business.

Maybe he needed to be taught a lesson. Needed someone he loved, like his wife or kid, to be threatened because he was here. That would send him running back to California, and he would leave me the fuck alone.

Yes, that was a great idea.

Now to figure out what, how, and when. Which would be easy. It took me all of a few hours to come up with Jasper's "suicide" and execute the perfect plan, after all.

That detective would regret the day he moved to Anchor Bay.

1

JUNO

The stench of sweaty socks and other odors I didn't want to identify permeated the air as I studied my reflection in the locker room mirror, inspecting each flaw, cataloging them to run on repeat tonight while tossing and turning in bed. All the imperfect features in the mirror staring back at me were recognizable except for the light brown curls framing my full cheeks. After several failed attempts to find someone in Anchor Bay who could continue to successfully highlight my natural brown locks to the brilliant blonde I was used to, I threw in the towel and dyed it back to my original color myself.

It wasn't a bad dye job, but the brown wasn't doing my fair complexion any favors. Which was why I went blonde years ago, hoping the lighter hair would help maximize my only striking feature—my large aqua eyes framed by naturally long dark lashes.

Or at least that was what that asshole ex of mine convinced me of.

A boom of vibrating metal echoed through the locker room from a fist beating on the door from the other side.

"Let's get to it, Juno," came the deep voice of my self-defense trainer, Oliver. "I don't have much time this morning. Hell of a lot going on in my day job."

I snorted in agreement. That was an understatement. As our deputy sheriff, he was overwhelmed with everything going on in our small town, even with the LA detective that Brandon, the owner of the adventure and rescue company I worked for, had asked to come assist.

"Be right there," I shouted back before returning my gaze to my reflection for one more critical pass.

Full round cheeks, a tiny, upturned nose, thin upper lip offset by a full lower one, wide forehead—*ugh, is that a fucking wrinkle?* Hips pressed against the cracked sink, I leaned toward the mirror for a closer inspection. A finger pressed on each brow, I pulled them apart, making the faint line disappear.

"Guess that's what I get for being in the dreaded mid-thirties," I grumbled. "Getting old sucks ass."

My loose hair shifted side to side with a disapproving headshake as I turned from my reflection that reminded me I wasn't and never would be enough. Careful not to snag the wild curls, I pulled the unruly strands into a high bun and secured it with a tie on top of my head.

Passing the single bench in the middle of the row of lockers, I grabbed my gloves and bag, not wanting the clothes inside to absorb the stink, and shoved open the door, eager to escape the stagnant stench of sweaty men. Out in the main area, Oliver glanced up from his phone where he stood by the mats, giving me a quick assessing once-over before tossing the device onto the top of his training bag along the wall.

"You're seriously wearing that to spar today?" With a

furrowed brow, he gestured to my hot pink biker shorts and matching top. The punch of insecurity his comment delivered to my fragile ego must have registered on my face, because a panicked expression overtook his. "Not that you look bad. You look great. Sexy as fuck, actually. I just mean —" Oliver cut himself off and tipped his face to the ceiling. "Are you trying to get me killed? If Langston walks in and sees us sparring with you wearing that, I'm a dead man."

Him mentioning that asshole cut off the voice in my head telling me my legs were too thick, too flabby, too... anything but gorgeous in the shorts I daringly purchased the last time I was in Anchorage. Forcing a smile, I waved off Oliver's worry and began strapping on my gloves.

"First, you're being overly dramatic, which is concerning for someone who's our first line of defense in Anchor Bay. We need someone calm, not dramatic."

The corners of his lips twitched upward. "The second line of defense, technically. I'm only the deputy sheriff, so my dad is the first."

I grimaced. "That doesn't make me feel any better."

"Me neither," Oliver grumbled while swiping the training pads off the floor. "And second?"

"Second, why the hell would Langston care about what I'm wearing if he comes in to work out today?"

Oliver paused what he was doing to shoot me an incredulous look that said I was the one being an idiot here.

Gloves on, I tossed both hands in the air in exasperation. "It's obvious we can't stand each other. Why does everyone here seem to think we're faking the heated arguments—"

"Sexual tension," he said around a fake cough.

"The death glares," I added, narrowing my eyes at the back of his head.

"His way of saying he loves you," Oliver countered like it was obvious.

"Or the way he critiques my every damn choice or move," I snapped, putting both hands on my hips.

He turned with a sigh. "That's the only way an overprotective, slightly obsessed asshole like Langston can show he cares."

"Whatever," I grumbled. "And third, I will wear what I want to wear, and you will say nothing about it. I swore to myself that I'd never allow a man to dictate what I can or can't wear again. Or let someone's opinions make me self-conscious about how I feel in clothes I believe I look good in—"

Two calloused palms settled on my shoulders and squeezed, pausing my rambling. With his lips pressed in a tight line, Oliver's dark gaze scanned my face.

"Juno, who the fuck said that shit to you that you had to make a promise like that to yourself?"

Realizing I'd accidentally allowed a peek into my shitty past, I quickly sealed my lips shut to keep from divulging more.

"Juno Jones."

With a huff, I gave him a dramatic eye roll and stepped out of his hold. "Drop it, Oliver. I'm wearing this no matter what you say. Now, are we training or what?"

He studied me as I distracted myself from the heavy conversation, stretching both arms overhead and leaning to one side, then the other. "You know, when you came to me asking to learn basic self-defense moves, I thought it stemmed from the missing women cases. Now I'm wondering if that's the actual reason or if you need to protect yourself from something or someone else."

I lifted both shoulders in an exaggerated shrug. "Does that change your willingness to train me?"

"No." He shook his head. "But please don't take this training and kill some dumb fucker from your past who doesn't know his dick from his ass. Because that's what he is if he ever even hinted at you not being perfect no matter what you wear. Because you are, Juno."

Unshed tears burned behind my eyes. If Oliver only knew half the degrading lies and comments that were flung my way at one time. He was the type of man who would not only encourage me to seek Eric out to set him straight but would probably arm me with weapons too. Which was why I hadn't mentioned him or anything in my life pre–Anchor Bay to anyone. Those shitty years and people needed to stay in my hometown of Banks, Alaska, where they belonged, allowing me the chance at a new life here.

I'd never heard of the quaint bay town where I ended up until I came across a job ad for a social media and scheduling coordinator posted by Uplift Adventure and Rescue Company. Needing a quick exit from my old life—as in I packed up my shit and bolted without telling anyone—I accepted the job sight unseen and moved my meager possessions to Anchor Bay. Little did I know it would be the best rash decision ever. I not only got away from the emotional abuse, but it led me to meet an amazing group of people who quickly became the family and friends I'd never had but always wanted. Being introduced to the poly community created by the owners of Uplift—Brandon, Amy, and Carl—was a shock at first, but now the thriving and happy throuple relationships seemed a lot more stable than traditional ones.

Everyone in the community was amazing, even the infuriating bastard Langston. Though that was mostly because he was so attractive that I forgot how to breathe around him, if he didn't open his mouth and remind me why I named him Captain Asshole after that first meeting. He was well over six feet tall, with dark, almost black thick hair, a chiseled jaw, full sleeves, and jade-green eyes that I swear could see into your soul. Which sucked because the man was annoying, rude, instigating, and, for some reason, hated me.

Why?

Hell if I knew. Since that first meeting when he picked me up in Anchorage after I was hired, the man had a cactus up his ass when it came to me. Other than him, and the female hikers and our friend Caroline going missing—oh, and the recent murder of a local—life was great now in my new home.

"Earth to Juno."

I blinked and flinched at Oliver waving the practice mitts in front of my face. With a huff, I batted them away and went back to stretching. "By the way, while I love changing in a locker room with a urinal that was last cleaned in the sixties and metal lockers teeming with tetanus, when are you renovating this place?"

He spun in a slow circle, inspecting our surroundings with a grin. "What do you mean? It's functional, right?"

The corners of my lips curled upward as I took in the mostly empty space. Other than the new sparring mats and punching bags hanging from the ceiling, plus the ancient treadmill I was pretty sure he'd found while dumpster diving, it barely looked like an actual gym. He never explained why he leased the dilapidated building six months ago, and maybe he never would. We all had our secrets, and I, for one, was glad he never pried into mine, so I offered him the same courtesy.

Similar to our previous sessions, I took my time warming up, making sure my muscles were loose before putting power into my punches and kicks. Oliver never touched me, preferring to coach from behind the mitts on my stance or posture. Soon, his deep voice and the pounding of my fists connecting with the firm pads were all I heard, offering me a few precious moments of peace from the relentless negative thoughts that constantly ran on a loop in my mind.

Almost half an hour had passed when he dropped the training pads and inclined his head toward my water bottle. "Take a break."

Sweat dripping down my temples and breaths coming in quick pants, I dropped my fists and stepped back, ever grateful for the breather.

"You're getting better. You take verbal correction well and put effort into our training time. You've come a long way from the woman with two left feet who asked me to train her."

"Thanks," I breathed as I downed some water. With the back of my forearm, I wiped at the few drops that clung to my lips. "At first, I just wanted to feel capable of defending myself, but now, being here, going through the movements, it's freeing in a way. The movements, the sounds echoing around the empty space, help me zone out. It's helping me feel strong, not just physically but mentally too. Not sure how that works."

Oliver nodded. "I don't know how it works either, but I feel the same way when I train. Which is why I'm here working the bag most of my days off." Hands on his hips, he turned in a slow circle, admiring his gym. "I guess that's one reason I rented the building and started putting together the small boxing gym. The place has turned into my haven from all the messed-up shit going on outside those glass doors."

"It just needs a women's locker room," I commented with a grin as I checked the time on my phone. "Shit, I need to get going. I have a meeting with Brandon to update him on the scheduling software I'm creating and don't want to go in there smelling like ass."

Before he could respond, the front door opened with a grind of the metal hinges, allowing a gust of morning air to sweep through the space as his brother Kale stepped inside. The man froze when he saw me before continuing deeper into the gym.

"Hey, what are you doing here?" Oliver called, dropping the training mitts to the mat. "I thought you were laying off the workouts until your knee healed?"

Kale hooked a thumb over his shoulder. "Yeah, I am, but I saw your car out front and just wanted to stop in, say hi or some shit."

"Liar," I snorted.

Releasing a frustrated groan, Kale ran a hand through his long, wavy hair. "I might have stopped in to see if there were any updates on that Jasper thing. Everyone in town is freaking out. Old man Murray thinks a bunch of devil worshippers possessed Jasper and made him kill himself."

A soft laugh escaped as I started unwrapping my gloves. "That man needs to stop watching so much TV. Devil worshippers? In Anchor Bay?"

"'That Jasper thing' being his active murder investigation?" Oliver said. "You know I can't discuss the details of an ongoing case and—"

Kale raised both hands in surrender. "I'm not asking for details. Just give me something, anything that will calm people down. Do you know how many theories and conspiracies I've had to hear since it happened? With being your brother and the best bartender in Anchor Bay—"

"So modest," I chimed in with a wink while pulling on a pair of sweats over my tight shorts. It was one thing to wear the shorts while working out; a totally different level of confidence was needed for stepping outside the makeshift boxing gym.

Kale rolled his eyes and flipped me the bird before continuing. "Help me out. Give me something to tell them and...." He trailed off as if recalling something before pointing at Oliver. "Did you say *murder*? Fucking hell. I thought it was suicide or a stupid accident or something like that. Murder? Are you serious?"

Oliver pressed his lips in a tight line, clearly frustrated with himself for letting that detail slip. It was a known theory within the Uplift community that he suspected Jasper's suicide was staged, but most of the Anchor Bay community still thought he'd taken his own life.

"Well," I called out, making the two men look my way, "I'll let you two handle this drama between yourselves. I have to go if I want to shower before that meeting."

Mid-stride, I lifted my gym bag off the cracked concrete floor and headed for the front door. Pausing next to Kale, I shoved his shoulder, making him stumble to the side. "So, self-proclaimed best bartender in town, how about next time all of us girls are at Dave's, please, please, *please* do not allow us to order duck fart shots. Last time nearly killed me."

I dodged his return shove. "That had to do with the quantity of alcohol you and your friends consumed, not the type of shot, Juno. Next time, don't order seven rounds."

Just remembering that night, and the following morn-ing, made my stomach roll. I was hungover for days following the emergency book club meeting Baylee had called.

Running out of time to get my much-needed shower, I waved goodbye to Oliver and stepped out into the fresh morning air. Inhaling deeply, I allowed my eyelids to close for a few seconds, absorbing the peaceful moment before stepping up to my bike. Gym bag secured in the small front basket, I wheeled it away from the wall where I had parked it earlier and hopped on.

Loose strands of hair fluttered along my neck as I pedaled down the nearly empty street. Smiling wide, I tilted my face upward, appreciating the sun's warm rays on my skin. Summer in Alaska was stunning but short-lived. Normal days were cloudy, misting and gloomy, which meant I needed to savor every second I could of the gorgeous weather. So today, instead of driving my small SUV to the gym, I opted to bike even though it took twice the time to get there and back home to the Uplift compound.

The term *compound* made it sound like a cult, but the community was far from anything like that. We were a tight-knit found family who all worked for Uplift in some capacity and also lived within the self-sustaining community. It was its own small town with a main street lined with cabins that Brandon and Carl had built and continued to build as the company and community grew. There was even a small general store that their wife, Amy, ran along with a farm with horses, cows, and recently added goats. Everyone had their part, not only in helping the community run but in their jobs at Uplift.

We had Miles and Aiden, whose adventure specialties were anything ATV or dirt bike related. Liam was our resident cowboy, taking clients out on trail rides that ranged from kid-friendly to advanced riders only. Ethan was our survivalist who took clients off-grid for days, teaching them how to live with only a knife and flint. Langston ran everything that was water-based, while Dax and Finley were our resident pilots for rescue missions and client expeditions.

There were also others who lived outside the community but were one of us, like Oliver, Anchor Bay's deputy sheriff, and the recent addition, former LA detective Hudson and his family.

After spending the first thirty-two shitty years of my life never feeling like I belonged or was wanted, this place and these people were exactly what I needed to feel alive. But I couldn't complain too much, because if my early years weren't so terrible, I wouldn't have been as reclusive, turning to computers and online gaming as refuge, which led to my career as a programmer and web designer.

Was I a computer geek? Yes, I was. Did I love playing online video games? Again, guilty. But since living in Anchor Bay, I'd not only balanced that isolation side of myself by socializing with my new friends—and liking it— but had come to understand that my geeky side wasn't bad.

Hell, it could be worse. I could be addicted to drugs or online gambling, right?

Since settling into my new home, I no longer lost hours consumed in an online role-playing game or coding a website for a client.

I was happy and actually living a real life, not a virtual one.

And that terrified me.

Guiding my bike onto the road that ran through the quaint downtown area, I couldn't help the heavy dread that settled in my stomach despite the colorfully painted buildings I passed. If I could count on one thing in my life, it was that nothing good lasted, which meant this amazing chapter of my life, the first one where I actually smiled more than cried, would end.

And I really, *really* didn't want that to happen.

But considering how the past usually predicted the future, my luck would run out.

Soon.

2

LANGSTON

That woman was going to get herself killed.

An annoyed grunt rushed past my lips as I leapt over a waterlogged pothole, all while monitoring Juno up ahead. Pieces of her newly colored hair whipped in the wind as she casually pedaled down the street, seeming to have zero cares in the world.

Which was a big fucking illusion.

She was a lie; I just hadn't figured out the why yet despite my best efforts. Though if I suspected she was here to harm any of my Uplift family and their connected partners—because damnit, that woman Aspen and the new hipster Memphis had wormed their way into my dark heart too—Juno wouldn't have made it from Anchorage to Anchor Bay still breathing.

I chuckled to myself as I weaved around a parked car, keeping pace with Juno easily despite that I was jogging and she was on two wheels. Hell, was she even pedaling? There was a bit of worry blooming in my chest that the bike was going so damn slow it would just tip over, sending her tumbling into the street, in front of a car, and—

I sucked in a sharp breath as my heart rate picked up at that visual. No, Juno was fine and would stay that way. I'd make sure of that while I continued my investigation into what the hell she was hiding. At least until I uncovered her past; then I could move on to my next obsession, something to hyper-fixate on until I peeled it apart to understand every micro-detail.

A happy, feminine laugh trilled through the morning air, causing goose bumps to rise along the inked skin of both arms. Jaw clenched tight, I ground my molars as she waved at Ches, the owner of our favorite dive bar, Dave's, who stared a little too long in her direction after she'd passed the weathered building where he stood along the walkway.

He was still staring at the way her plump ass molded around the bike seat when I jogged past, startling him.

"Get inside, Ches," I snapped. "Unless you want to lose those eyes."

Why I cared that he was staring at her perfect, full ass, I had no idea.

Ches grumbled something under his breath after I passed. The urge to turn around was strong, but not stronger than the insistent need to ensure Juno made it home safely.

That wasn't the reason I followed her whenever I could, though—or at least that was what I told myself. I needed to protect my family by uncovering her secrets, exposing what she was hiding so I could finally be done obsessing over the obnoxious, feisty, brilliant computer programmer who looked like a blonde—now brunette—version of my baby sister's Strawberry Shortcake doll from when we were kids.

What? I was a good older brother who entertained his kid sister while our mom worked two jobs just to keep us fed and a roof over our heads. Memories of dark nights, the electricity being shut off again because of nonpayment, and sleeping on the floor in front of Mattie's door slithered through my thoughts, infecting me now with all the bad from then.

My breath hissed through my teeth as my stomach cramped, the worst memory flashing like a horror film on repeat of that awful night that triggered my insistent resolve to always protect Mattie.

Stretching my neck from side to side, I forced those memories back into the box stuffed in the back of my mind where they belonged and recentered my focus on the current threat.

Juno Jones.

The background check Carl begrudgingly ran at my request—for security reasons only, obviously—came back completely uneventful, so I had zero clues as to why she was here. On paper, she was the innocent, introverted though smart-mouthed programmer she claimed to be, but there was something that just didn't sit right with me. She was hiding something, but not some weird fetish or hobby. I'd noticed it the moment she boarded the boat in Anchorage after accepting the social media job with Uplift. It was almost like she was skittish, haunted even, but not in grief like our resident veterinarian, Baylee, had been when she moved to Anchor Bay.

No, Juno Jones was running from something. Or someone.

And I was determined to find out what or who. All in the name of protecting the community, of course.

It took twice as long to get back to our community outside of town as it should have. The woman must love the nice weather, because there was no way she could've pedaled any slower—hell, my cat GG could've made it here faster, and she was the laziest cat I'd ever known.

After making sure Juno made it into her cabin safely—which pissed me off since I'd followed her from Oliver's gym all the way here and she didn't even fucking notice; she needed lessons in surveillance and awareness instead of that boxing shit—I headed home to get cleaned up.

And maybe jack off in the shower.

Which also pissed me off. I couldn't even look at her from a distance without getting a hard-on. It didn't help that ever since she signed on with Uplift and moved into one of the single cabins three down from mine, I hadn't been with a woman, alone or with West. There was plenty of opportunity, sure; West and I never had issues finding someone who was down for a night of fun with us. But since Juno arrived, I hadn't found anyone who could distract me from my weird obsession with her.

Hand wrapped around the back doorknob, I stilled at the muffled grunts and heavy breathing from the other side. Licking my lips, I quietly turned the knob and pushed the door open without making a sound. The sounds, no longer distorted by the heavy wood, along with the erotic visual playing out in the living room had me adjusting my hardening cock as I watched my best friend and roommate.

West was butt-ass naked, pumping out one-arm push-ups over and over with his injured hand resting in the center of his back. The colorful sugar skull tattoo that covered the full expanse of his muscular back moved and shifted with every rep.

Either feeling the breeze from the open door or sensing my stare, he popped up and spun around, a knowing smirk on his lips. Swiping his thick, black-framed glasses off the kitchen island, he slid them on and strode to the fridge.

West and I were... complicated. Until him, I was never attracted to men. And I still wasn't—just to West. Though we weren't in a relationship in the conventional way. Hell, nothing we did around here was what most people considered "normal." But I wasn't sleeping with anyone else, neither was he, and we hadn't done anything together, just us two, in a while either.

And of course, my abstinence coincided with the arrival of that woman.

I was glaring at the floor, wondering why in the hell I allowed Juno to mess with my sex life when she wasn't a part of it, and almost missed the question West tossed over his shoulder as he scanned the refrigerator shelves.

"How did your early-morning stalking go?"

Rolling my eyes, I flipped him the bird while shutting the back door. "It's not fucking stalking; it's intelligence gathering."

He scoffed, taking out a bottled water and slamming the fridge door shut. Twisting the cap off, he lifted the water to his lips, downing half before responding. "You say recon, I call it what it is, and that's stalking. Though I guess it's the same thing—the biggest difference is that one of us isn't lying to themselves about the underlying reason for it."

Ignoring him, I ripped my thin T-shirt over my head, tired of it sticking to my sweat-slick back. Balling it up, I launched it at his face, which he dodged easily with a grimace.

"What the fuck is that smell?"

"I had to wait next to the dumpster while she worked out," I grumbled, cheeks heating at the admission. "It was the best vantage point to see through the front windows without being noticed. Speaking of which, how important do you think Oliver is to this town and the ongoing investigation? Would anyone really miss him?"

The water bottle froze, hovering just over West's lips as his eyes widened. "Fucking hell, Langston. I swear I'm your ride or die, brother, but digging a shallow grave with one hand will—"

"Fuck, I didn't kill him." He waited, motioning for me to say the next part out loud. "Yet," I groused.

He threw his hand in the air in obvious exasperation. "And there it is. What did he do now? Actually touch Juno while he was training her how to protect herself?" He pointed an accusing finger at me. "You should be thanking the bastard, not plotting his murder."

"You should've seen what she was wearing, though." *Fuck, did I just whine?* From the shocked expression on West's face, that would be a definite yes. "He shouldn't have let her—"

"Fuck no," he snapped, pushing his glasses higher up the bridge of his straight nose with a single finger. "If Juno wants to work out fucking naked, that is her prerogative. Just because you have this weird fixation with her—"

"Fixation?" I scoffed and crossed both arms over my chest. "Then what are you calling *your* obsession with her?" He blinked those long dark lashes, acting all innocent, like he didn't know what I was referring to. "Don't give me that bullshit. You make up any excuse to be around her, and you watch her every move, just like me."

"But with less hostility. You glare, I observe," he grumbled. "And yeah, of course I watch her. Who wouldn't? She's sweet yet feisty and stubborn—the first part of which I obviously bring out, and the other is all you, my friend. And then there's that...." He waved the hand in a cast, like that helped me understand the word he was searching for. "You know."

"Clearly not," I deadpanned.

"I just want to hug her. There's something sad and scared about her when she lets her guard down. It makes me want to protect her."

"Right," I joked. "Protect her with your dick in her pussy."

He waggled his dark brows suggestively. "I wouldn't say no to that kind of cuddle comfort." A sly smile pulled at his lips as he stared at my bare chest. "You know that firsthand."

I did know that.

Not recently, though. I was still attracted to West and wanted him, but the idea of following through felt empty, almost like something—or someone—was missing and it wouldn't be right.

"Whatever. I need to shower, and you need to take care of that situation." West chuckled, nodding at the outline of my hard cock beneath my shorts. "And shower that stink off you before it permeates the fucking paint. We have a meeting with Brandon in an hour."

I twisted to see the clock on the microwave, cursing. Damn, West was right. If I wanted to make the meeting with our boss without a hard-on and smelling like garbage, I needed to hurry.

Walking through the kitchen, I swiped my dirty shirt off the floor mid-stride and went to my room, heading straight for the shower.

Under the warm spray, I slapped a palm to the tile wall and wrapped the other around my stiff cock, squeezing until my hiss sounded over the streaming water. Remembering Juno in those tiny shorts that made her ass and thighs look fucking squeezable and that top that had her full tits spilling out had my hand pumping faster.

A dirty fantasy played out, of me pinning her to the wall with a hand around her throat while the other stripped her naked. I would take my time with her, teasing her to the breaking point like she had me these last few months before hiking her leg over my hip, giving me the perfect angle to slam into her warm pussy. Eyes sealed shut, I thrust into my fist, imagining it was her tight cunt squeezing me to death, not wanting me to ever pull out.

That image faded to the three of us on the bed, me taking her from behind while West stuffed his long cock down her throat, entranced by the way mine disappeared inside her. We'd watch each other, both of us taking her hard and fast, her muffled screams piercing the air with every soul-shaking orgasm we wrung from her as we chased our own.

Peeling my lids open, I gazed at my dick, fantasizing a different scene of West taking Juno hard on my bed with me right behind him, fucking him into her.

"Fuck," I grunted, slamming a fist against the tile hard as a violent orgasm raced through me. Both knees shook and my thigh muscles spasmed, threatening to make my legs give out under me. "Fuck, fuck, fuck," I repeated as I thrust into my hand, wringing out every drop of cum and watching the evidence of my obsession swirl down the drain.

So I found her sexy as hell. That meant nothing. Juno Jones was trouble, I just knew it, and there was no way in hell I'd let my defenses down around her long enough to see those fantasies come to life.

Forty minutes later, I no longer smelled like I'd swum in a dumpster full of rotten fish and piss, and I'd relieved enough of the earlier tension that I wasn't a walking hard-on, which would've made the coming meeting awkward as hell. After locking up the cabin, I leapt down the front porch steps, eager to find out what this impromptu meeting was all about. In stride, West and I walked along the main road that cut between the row of cabins, heading toward the building where Brandon held all his meetings since his office was tiny and he shared it with Carl.

As we walked past Miles, Aiden, and Aspen's place, the former SEAL raised a hand in greeting, and I returned the gesture with a nod. Not that he noticed, as his focus was already back on Aiden and Aspen, laughing about something while they rocked back and forth on their front porch swing.

"Careful there," West murmured with that knowing smirk of his that made dimples pop in both cheeks. "Keep watching them with that longing look in your eyes and people will think you're jealous of their little family."

A huff escaped, sounding more like a scoff, as I jerked my attention to the opposite side of the street, forcing myself to look away from the idyllic scene. My heart squeezed painfully at yet another reminder of the type of relationship I didn't have now or ever before. Well, except Mattie, but she was my baby sister and didn't count. And West, but what we had didn't fill that family need that had grown over the last few months.

Sure, everyone here in our community was the family I'd never had in the way of love and support, but I wouldn't admit how much I had wanted a family of my own, a solid unit that was mine to protect and I could depend on in return. That need made me feel weak, to want a committed relationship with someone who accepted me and stood by my side. West was my best friend, and I could count on him always, but there was still something missing there that no amount of support, love, or fucking him could manifest.

I cleared my throat. "I'm not jealous of them. Just watching to make sure everyone is good."

"Right," West drawled as he marched up the steps to the meeting room ahead of me.

Opening the door, he walked in first, then spun around with a mischievous grin, which had me groaning in return. With a hard push, the door swung fast toward my face. I slapped a hand to the center of the flimsy wood right before it could smash my nose.

"Stop being a fucking toddler," I snarled, pushing it open so hard that he stumbled back to keep the edge from clipping his side.

"Fucking make me," he joked with a middle finger raised high in the air, taunting me to finish what he'd started.

I knew what he was doing, and I hated to admit that it was working. West noticed everything about those around him, and this was his immature way of cheering me up—distracting me by being a brat, which made me want to dominate him, naked, like I had in the past.

A low growl vibrated in my chest as I stormed into the meeting room, my only focus on West, determined to put the sassy fucker in his place. Passion-filled heat slithered through my veins as I pictured slamming him against the wall and reminding him exactly who the fuck he was taunting. He wouldn't walk right for days after I was through with him, and he would love every fucking second of it like he had before.

"Fucking hell."

Chest heaving from the building frustration, I turned a death glare at the man following me into the meeting room, just now realizing he had been right behind me.

The former SEAL just glared right back, not giving two shits about my foul mood, as he passed. "You two need to sort your shit out."

"What shit?" I grunted, working hard to slow my breathing.

Hudson huffed an incredulous laugh, like *I* was the idiot missing something. "Between the two of you, plus you and Juno, the constant fucking sexual tension around you three is annoying and distracting. Hell, Calista makes a joke about it when I come home worked up, knowing exactly who I'd met with."

I shook my head. "Juno and me, sexual tension? I don't think so. We're more likely to strangle each other than fuck it out."

I swallowed hard, knowing those words were a lie as I turned to find a chair far away from West's antics and froze, finding a pair of big aqua eyes glaring at me from the doorway. My narrowed-eyed gaze slid to West, whose loose fist hovering over his lips did nothing to conceal the mischievous grin.

"What are you doing here?" I grumbled like the asshole I was.

Entering the space after Juno, Brandon rubbed his temples. "Langston," he sighed, like I was trying his patience. "Stop being an asshole for two seconds. I asked her to be here for this."

My gaze cut to Juno, who shot a smile over her shoulder at Brandon only for it to disappear when she noticed me watching her.

"And, West," he continued, "stop fucking instigating his foul mood, because then we all have to deal with the result."

"I think that's just his perpetual mood. Grumpy asshole with a chip on his shoulder," Juno said under her breath as she found her seat, setting the laptop she went nowhere without on top of the table in front of her.

"I'd rather be that than...." *Fuck.*

I adjusted my backward black Golden Knights cap in frustration. I couldn't think of a damn thing negative to say about her, because as much as I didn't trust Juno and knew she was trouble, the woman had no flaws. From the way the loose curls framed her face to the unique color of her eyes, that little nose that fit her other petite features, and those fucking suckable, kissable lips.

Lips I wanted everywhere.

"Care to finish that statement for the class?" West questioned, grabbing a chair with his good hand and twisting it around to plop down into the seat backward.

I flipped him off and jerked a chair out, praying it didn't break as I carefully sat. At six foot three with a solid-muscle frame that came from a lot of hard work in and out of the gym, I'd broken a few cheap chairs just by sitting in them. It hadn't happened only to me either. Miles and Liam both had chair legs fold out from beneath them in the past, so I tried not to let it bother me too much.

Gripping the sides of my hat with both hands, I twisted it back and forth while glaring at my best friend. Instead of responding to his comment, since I had none, I rolled my eyes and crossed my inked arms over my chest. Out of the corner of my eye, I caught Juno studying me, gaze locked on the word *ARMY* stretched across my gray T-shirt.

A single corner of my lips twitched upward. Maybe Miss Trouble wasn't so turned off by my asshole personality after all, or at the very least she liked what she saw physically. If I trusted her more, we could fuck out the simmering aggression between us, possibly curing the rolling tension that hadn't faded since she stumbled into my life.

Our gazes clashed, and a spark of thrill raced through my veins as we stared at each other. It was then that I saw a glimmer of what West mentioned earlier. I didn't see deception or malicious intent behind her gorgeous eyes, rather sadness mixed with fear and reservation.

Blinking her long black lashes, she jerked her attention to West, who instantly softened, a slow, shy smile curling his lips, which he knew was sexy as hell. He was upping his game, popping the dimples at her.

Brow furrowed, she studied his injured hand, resting on the table, before reaching across the worn surface to take it in hers. "How's your hand healing?" Chewing on her lower lip, she carefully brushed the tips of her fingers along the soft cast. "I have nightmares from that day." Her throat worked with a hard swallow, skin paling. "Remembering how much pain you were in and that there was nothing I could do about it but hold you."

All the annoyance and frustration from earlier drained away. My arms went slack at my sides as I studied each gentle stroke along his cast. Hearing her mention that day, how it affected her, was like a punch to the gut with a dull sword. I wasn't there for either of them like I should've been.

It happened weeks ago. West, our company's resident fixer of anything with an engine, was working on the helicopter when something in the engine shifted, smashing his hand and fingers. I wasn't there to offer my medic training help, but Memphis, Baylee's new guy, had been an EMT back in Orlando and handled the situation, maybe even better than I could have.

Juno's resulting trauma from the accident was from holding him as he screamed between going in and out of consciousness.

West's was a memory of the intense pain, which had caused night terrors.

Then there was mine, even though I wasn't there to witness it all or experience the debilitating pain. My distress came from being out on a run for The Nest's doctor instead of with my best friend when he needed me most. I should've been there for him, but I wasn't, and it ate me fucking alive every time I thought about it. About my friend in pain while I was out on the fucking boat without a damn care in the world.

"Langston," Hudson said, voice loud and commanding, like it wasn't the first time he'd said my name.

Fixing a blank expression on my face to hide my inner turmoil, I turned his way, arching a single dark brow.

"Did you hear *anything* Brandon just said?"

I slid my gaze to my boss, instantly grimacing at his annoyed expression that was aimed at me. Clearing my throat, I shifted in the seat uncomfortably. "You were saying, boss?"

He held me hostage with his glare for a few more moments before repeating what I had missed, too lost in my own thoughts. "I was telling everyone about the new feature Juno created for the client booking system, then asked if you would sit down with her tomorrow to go over the details she needs for the fishing and boating options." He studied me and then her with a weary expression. "Without it ending in a yelling match."

"I don't yell at women," I said through gritted teeth. "Any man who does deserves to be eating through a straw the rest of his life."

Juno looked shocked by my response, eyes wide and lips parted.

Hmm, that was interesting.

Interesting and concerning.

Well, concerning for whoever made my statement seem shocking to her.

Studying Juno while she explained the new addition to the program, I wondered if maybe it was time to do more than just watch her to uncover her secretive past. Maybe West was spot-on when he said she'd been hurt and was running from someone rather than from trouble that might follow her here to Anchor Bay and put my family at risk.

Absentmindedly, I traced the many scars decorating my knuckles while plotting how I could learn more about Juno Jones and uncover her darkest secrets without letting my guard down and falling for the mysterious, yet amazing and beautiful woman.

How hard could that be?

3

WEST

"I'll make these few tweaks to the website and then send a link over with the changes for you to approve," Juno murmured, face in her phone as her thumbs flew over the screen. Without looking up, she tucked her laptop under her arm and weaved around Brandon's desk and past Hudson, blindly slapping at the door for the knob until her small fingers wrapped around the metal. Without even a goodbye or "see you later" tossed over her shoulder, she tugged open the door and strode out into the bright afternoon sunlight.

"Ten bucks says she sends over those changes for the site and more ideas for the scheduling system before we're done with our meeting," I commented with a wide grin. Juno was hyper-focused when it came to her job and an absolute badass with anything computer related. Which was good for Uplift, but I worried about her because of it too.

She would lock herself in her cabin for days working, not once coming out for air or food. Sometimes Finley or one of her other friends would pop in for a wellness check if we hadn't seen her in a while. And if it wasn't work, it was her online gaming obsession that kept her inside, staring at a screen for hours. That couldn't be good for anyone.

"We're lucky to have her," Brandon said, rubbing a hand along his scruff-covered jaw. "Carl was always too swamped to do anything with the site, and that new system she built from scratch has streamlined our process, which benefits you all as well as our clients."

"Lucky," Langston grumbled while he rocked the chair back on its two back legs. The big fucker was on the verge of breaking another one if he wasn't careful. Then again, he deserved to be sprawled out on the floor with a sore ass considering his foul mood. "Pain in the ass more like it."

Though the way his green eyes kept finding the door she just disappeared through gave his grumpy ass away on how he really felt. Not that I was any better. It was hard to stay in my damn seat to find out why Brandon had called the meeting when all I wanted to do was follow her.

Langston stalked Juno for his own misguided reasons. I didn't disguise that I wanted her. Well, that was a slight lie. She didn't know that friendship was not all that I hoped for with her. That while we joked around and talked, or spent hours together while she played those crazy video games, I desperately wanted more. All of her time, focus, energy, attention—everything about her if I were brutally honest with myself. The fact that Lang wasn't there yet had me holding back for now, but soon he would get over his irrational issues with her unknown past, and then we could both be all in on convincing Juno that she was our perfect match.

My attention dropped to my wrapped wrist and hand. Maybe it made me a sick bastard or just as delusional as Langston, but I'd offer something else to be crushed if that meant I got more of her time and gentle comfort like she'd offered the past few weeks.

"...with that evidence, Oliver and I agree it wasn't a suicide like someone staged it to look like, but murder." Realizing they had stopped talking about the website and shifted to Jasper's death, I turned my full focus on Hudson as he paced in front of Brandon's desk. "We just don't know the why."

"It has to be tied to the missing women cases. He was connected to Caroline, who's still missing," I stated tentatively, hating saying her name because of the devastated expression that flashed over Langston's face. Yet another person he felt like he'd failed, as if the man could be everywhere at once protecting everyone from the unknown dangers in life.

"That's where we landed too," Hudson commented, coming to stop at the edge of the desk, tapping the firm surface with a single knuckle. He eyed Brandon for a moment as if debating his next words. "I'm thinking this is bigger than what Oliver and I can handle on our own. It's time to pull in people with more resources and experience dealing with serial cases."

"Do you have someone in mind?" Brandon asked, leaning back in his chair and interlacing his hands behind his head. "Because you're the only connection I know who had the experience to help Oliver."

Hudson slowly nodded. "I have a contact in the FBI who I'd like to reach out to."

The corners of Brandon's lips pulled downward before he pressed them into a tight line. "And how will Oliver's dad feel about us bringing in the feds?"

"Who gives a fuck," Langston cut in, allowing his chair to fall forward, slamming the front two legs to the floor.

"This is bigger than *anyone* in this town can handle. We need help if we want it to stop and catch the bastard behind it all." I nodded in agreement, drawing his attention across the small table. "I, for one, can't stomach anything else happening to our family because of all this."

His green eyes bored into mine, making my heart race.

The part about the accident that almost cost me full use of my hand and fingers that no one really talked about was that it wasn't actually an *accident*. After investigating why the engine was nonoperational, the evidence pointed to someone sabotaging the helicopter engine, which was why I was working on it when it crushed my hand. That's why Langston was giving me the no-nonsense glare—which was sexy as hell, if you asked me—and on board with Hudson calling his FBI contact.

Most people would think his getting this worked up meant he felt more about me than he let on, that we were more than friends who fucked when tensions were high and we both needed an outlet. One thing was certain, though: No one fucked with his family, blood or forged, or they would see a side of Langston that even I was slightly scared of.

That dangerous side turned me on in a disturbingly dark way.

What could I say? I had issues—a whole fuckload of them.

"What the hell are you smiling about?" Langston asked, resting his tattooed forearms on the table.

I met his stare, letting him see all the dark, dirty thoughts now swirling through my mind after that sexy display of "touch him and die."

Arching one dark brow, he pointed at me. "Careful," he commanded in that tone that had my dick twitching.

"This is the shit I'm talking about." Hudson gestured between me and Langston. "Enough."

"What shit?" I asked, breaking off Langston's heated glare that had him grunting in annoyance.

"Nothing," Langston cut in. "I vote he calls this FBI contact—"

"And maybe his wife too," Hudson added, staring at the far wall. "Rain's a medical examiner and helps their profiling team with tough cases. She could review the autopsy results on the body we found off the trail and Jasper's, plus the others. If anyone can find new clues, it's her. And her husband, Jameson, the FBI profiler can help us get into the mind of the fucker terrorizing Anchor Bay."

"Maybe even help with a motive and what the hell he's doing with the missing women," Brandon mused, rubbing at his jaw. He paused for a moment before dipping his chin in agreement. "Do it. If they need an invitation from the local police force, I'm sure Oliver will help with that."

"Why the hell would you know that?" I asked, running my good hand over my shaved head. It still felt strange not having hair, but the upkeep was fucking amazing compared to how long and thick it was before.

Brandon's lips curled in a slow smile. "Our Amy loves that show *Criminal Minds* and mentioned the 'invitation from the local police' technicality during an episode once. I assume it came from some writer's research and not something they randomly made up."

"I'll reach out to Jameson today, get his thoughts on all this and ask about Rain's help," Hudson said. "Until then, I'm waiting on the autopsy results from the woman Memphis, Baylee, and Liam found in the woods and will keep digging into Jasper's life. Maybe he got too close to something since he's the one who told us about Caroline's missing journal and how she was attempting to connect the recent missing women cases to those from years ago. He could've found something that got him killed."

With a clipped nod to Brandon, Hudson left, slamming the door shut behind him, leaving just me, Langston, and Brandon.

"Now." Brandon shuffled some papers around on his desk and pulled a Post-it free. "On to why I needed to talk to you both." Between two fingers, he held up the yellow note. "I received a call requesting transportation from Anchorage to here for a couple. They called instead of booking online because they didn't want to alert the very person they're coming here to surprise."

Hell, that could be any of us—well, except me. No one outside of this community would come see me, much less as a surprise. The fact that I didn't have any family used to weigh me down when I thought about it, but not anymore. Not since coming to Anchor Bay and finding a genuine family working with Uplift.

My thoughts crept down a dark path, memories of my childhood and years on the street doing whatever was necessary to survive, only to be ripped back to the present when Brandon mentioned who the mystery couple wanted to see.

"They grew up with Juno and want to surprise her in person with some kind of good news."

Suspicion mixed with dread sat heavy in my gut as Langston and I shared a confused look. Clearing my throat, I twisted in my seat to face Brandon, not wanting to piss him off by questioning him.

"Don't take this the wrong way, boss, but that sounds shady as shit," I stated bluntly. "Right?" I turned to Langston, hoping he'd back me up.

His nod was slow, as though unsure if agreeing with me conflicted with his feelings about Juno. "She hasn't mentioned a single person—hell, any details about her life before coming here." He adjusted his backward ball cap, his tell when he was agitated.

"And how would you know that?" Brandon asked, trying and failing to hide a smirk.

"Research," Langston grumbled. He paused and looked at me with a wince, telling me I wouldn't like what he was about to say. "Shady or not, it would give us insight into her past."

I smacked a palm on the table. "A past she clearly doesn't want to mix with what she's building here," I stated. The demanding tone in my voice had both men staring at me, clearly surprised by my outburst.

Out of the many dominant, aggressive, and overprotective assholes employed by Uplift and its owners, I was the least assertive of us all. Not that I was a pushover or passive, just not as "I'll prove my point with a fist to your throat" or "let's see you say that to my gun" like the others. *All* the others. So that bit of bite in my tone no doubt took them off guard, because that wasn't me.

But what *was* me was understanding her desire to leave the past exactly where it should stay—buried in the back of your fucking head where it couldn't taint the good you were currently living. Cutting everyone off and leaving it all for a clean start was what some of us needed in order to move the fuck on from the trauma and hate that darkened our past like an ink splotch seeping through a sheet of white paper.

Hopefully, Juno's past wasn't as dark as mine. My good hand curled into a fist beneath the table just thinking of her scared or hurting with no one to rely on or turn to for help.

A surge of protectiveness swelled in my chest, burning through my veins unlike anything I'd felt before.

Breathing deeply through my nose, I tried to calm down, slow my heart rate to a non-stroke-inducing level. Damn, was this how the other guys felt all the time, this need to kill anything or anyone who dared harm someone they cared about? No wonder all my friends were tense as hell if they constantly fought this urge to wipe out the existence of anyone who even remotely hurt or upset their girl.

I stilled at that thought. Juno wasn't my girl, not technically. Just like Langston wasn't technically mine either. Unless you were of the school of thought that if you licked it, it was yours.

"What the fuck are you thinking about?" Langston said, humor lacing his tone.

I shot him a sly grin—one I knew drove him nuts because it made my dimples pop. His green eyes darkened like they did when he was either super pissed or turned on.

"Fuck, you two," Brandon grumbled, exasperation in his tone. "They already paid, and I said yes, so this is happening. Langston, you'll pick up—" His gaze flicked to the note. "—Eric Adler and Stephanie Wilson the day after tomorrow at 10:00 a.m. Their plan is to stay one to two nights at The Nest before heading back to Anchorage. And they emphasized multiple times that we not ruin their surprise by telling Juno they're coming."

My lips parted, ready to comment again on how shady it all sounded, but Langston beat me to it.

"I don't like it," he muttered. "If I get a bad feeling about them, I'm turning the fucking boat around and kicking them off."

"Don't you have a bad feeling about everyone?" I said tongue in cheek.

"Well, most people are shady assholes, so yeah. What I mean is, if it feels like them being here will hurt her or anyone here, then I'll make sure neither makes it to Anchor Bay."

"You make it sound like you'd toss them overboard," Brandon joked. When Langston didn't deny it, Brandon sighed with a headshake. "Get the hell out of here before I start to believe you." The chair legs screeched along the floor when Langston and I both stood. "And, Langston, don't forget about getting with Juno about the details and specifics she needs from you to finish up that add-on to the scheduling system."

With a clipped nod, he strode to the door and yanked it open, storming out and slamming it in his wake.

"He's so worked up over that woman and denying the real reason why that I'm worried he'll do something we'll all regret," Brandon mused. "We can't lose her because he's an idiot who can't see he wants her. She's not only streamlined our systems but been an excellent addition to the community we've built here. Amy loves her and would be upset if she left, and I fucking hate it when she's sad, so help him figure his shit out before it's too late." His gaze slid to the soft cast. "How are you healing?"

"Good. The surgeon thinks I'll gain full mobility in my fingers and hand if I don't rush the recovery and keep up with my physical therapy." I stared at the closed door. "And I get what you're saying about Langston, but I don't think it will become an issue."

He leaned forward, pressing both forearms against the edge of his desk. "Oh really? And why do you say that?"

A slow grin pulled at my lips. "Because I'm going to do everything I can to break the bastard down until he sees that she's his lobster."

Brandon blinked at me a few times before responding. "His fucking what?"

I tossed my good hand in the air. "Really? Have you never seen *Friends*?" I waved off his confused expression. "Never mind. Just know I have a plan."

With a nod, I left the small office, but instead of heading home, I altered course just slightly. Maybe the word *plan* was a slight exaggeration; *outline* or *sticky note ideas* was a better description for what I'd pieced together to get those two on the same page.

Well, the three of us, because you better fucking believe my non-plan plan had me in the middle of a Juno and Langston sandwich.

Good hand tucked into the front pocket of my favorite jeans, the ones that were so worn the material was butter soft and fit me perfectly, I meandered down the street, smiling to myself at my brilliance as I passed the cabins.

Raised in the foster system, if someone had told me I'd grow up to live in a place that looked like it belonged in a picture-perfect family sitcom, I would've laughed in their face, then knocked them out for making me hope for a second that my life would ever be anything more than shitty. Langston definitely wasn't the only one with anger issues. Even though our childhoods were different, our anger, resentment, and distrust were the same as a result.

Those dark memories tried to push through, ruining the rare, beautiful, clear-blue-sky day, but before I could let them sink their claws in and pull me under, three dogs tore around the corner of a cabin. Yipping and barking in utter carefree joy, they raced toward me, tongues hanging out of their open muzzles and flapping with every bounding step. They looked like they were smiling.

"No, Bacon," yelled a soft voice, making me twist to

find Samantha, Hudson's daughter, racing after their small dog, who was desperately attempting to catch up with the first three. "You stay here with me. It's teatime."

As if he understood her words, the small dog slowed his pursuit of Jubie, the Bernese mountain dog; Hank, the large husky; and Elvis, the yellow lab. I couldn't help the laugh that bubbled up as Samantha scooped the small dog up and marched back toward their cabin where Calista, Hudson's wife, waited on the front porch with a wide smile on her face.

Our gazes connected, and I was engulfed with the kindness and joy that poured through hers. You would never know the woman had a rough childhood like mine, and adult life too. That was how she and Hudson met, after she was attacked in LA and he was the detective who worked the case.

"I bet I can guess where you're headed," she called out, angling her head toward Juno's place.

"Guilty. I can't seem to stay away," I responded with a single shoulder shrug, not caring that I was predictable at this point in my obsession with Juno.

"You should just ask her out already." Tracking Sam along the front path and trotting up the steps, Calista patted the top of her daughter's head as she passed and headed into the house. "See you around, West."

"She's not wrong, you know." I whirled around on my boot heels, finding Aspen and Baylee standing behind me, the former with the camera that never left her hands and the latter wearing her lab coat, signaling she'd come from the barn or her veterinary clinic in town. "Juno needs you and Langston to make it obvious you want her, not this dumb stalking and overprotective bossy shit the men around here do in some weird adult version of pulling our pigtails."

I arched a dark brow at Aspen. "Tell me what you really think. Trouble in paradise?" My chest felt tight as I waited for her answer. Her, Aiden, and Miles's relationship was one I hoped to model one day. The three of them worked as a unit and seemed happy—really, really happy.

She waved me off. "What? No way. But I remember Miles's version of flirting and showing he cared at first was trying to protect me from...." She looked at Baylee, who just nodded, no doubt understanding, considering her former Army Ranger and MMA fighter partner Liam. "Well, everything, including myself."

"So, what should I do?"

The two women shared a long look I couldn't read. Then they both nodded as if they'd actually said something, though the conversation was completely silent.

Women were curious creatures.

"Juno needs to know you won't leave when things get hard or mundane. That you want her for who she is, computer-geek side and all."

Brows pulled in tight, I studied Baylee like the words she'd just spoken were a puzzle and I needed to decipher the meaning. "Wait, how do you know that? Did she say she thinks I'll walk away from her if things get hard?"

Both women just shook their heads while smiling.

I frowned. "Okay, I'm confused. How do you know that's what she needs from us?"

"Because that's what all women want—to feel safe. To be free to be yourself and know the person you're trusting with the real you won't leave."

A skeptical scoff escaped as I crossed my arms, eyeing the two women doubtfully. "How can someone not feel safe surrounded by all of us here? We're more protective of the family we've built than a damn mama grizzly bear, and with all the guns, maybe more deadly."

Baylee's lips split in a wide grin while Aspen just bit her lower lip, attempting to smother hers.

"You're such a guy." Aspen laughed.

"I don't understand that response," I drawled. "How does me having a dick change how someone feels safe?"

"Everything," both women said around a laugh.

I rubbed a hand over my head, wishing like hell I could tug on the long strands that were now gone. "Women are confusing."

"Men are too literal and focus only on the physical aspect of safety," Aspen explained. "There's a difference between feeling emotionally protected and physically. Emotionally safe is knowing you can fall apart, release all your deepest fears and worries and the whole damn mental load that weighs you down daily, and know your guy will hold you, love you, and support you. Not fix it but ease your worries and just be there."

My attention slid to Juno's place. "And how do I do all that?"

"That's for you to figure out, West. There isn't a manual that you can read and know how to fix it all."

Well, fuck. That was how my brain worked. If something was broken, I studied it and then figured out how to fix it.

Guess I'd just have to wing this plan of getting me, Juno, and Langston together based on that little bit of insight.

I just hoped I didn't mess it up.

4

JUNO

S weat slicked my palms, causing the controller to slip in my tightening grasp as the fight escalated. My fingers shifted, adjusting the movements of my avatar on the screen as I fought for our lives. Well, not exactly hers, since she was computer-generated, and I guess not technically mine either, but the anticipation and excitement were real. My heart hammered in my chest as if I were the one wielding the magic toward my opponent while darting around thick trees and leaping behind jagged boulders to evade the asshole hell-bent on taking me out.

"Not today, motherfucker. I need this win after running into *him*," I grumbled.

Without taking my focus off the flashing screen, I peeled one hand off the controller, blindly searching for the large metal bowl filled with popcorn and M&M's sitting some-where beside me on the couch.

Munching on the perfectly popped kernels, savoring the mix of salty and sweet, I recalled the earlier meeting. I wasn't actually upset from the encounter with Captain Asshole and his sweet, adorable best friend West, more confused, which was why I couldn't stop thinking about it. I'd hoped that playing my favorite online game would help distract me, but somehow it didn't. There was that intense stare-off that felt like he was looking directly into my soul and excavating all my secrets, and then there was that super-random comment about what should happen to a man who yelled at a woman. It was all slightly concerning.

Concerning because I liked it—really liked it, to the point that his aggressive show of legit masculine protectiveness, not the toxic shit spewed to men nowadays, made me so wet I thought I'd peed myself. I legit checked my boy shorts when I got home to make sure I didn't.

Also concerning because, well, I was raised by and dated men who 100 percent did not agree with Langston on that point. Or maybe it was just my headstrong personality that made men feel the need to raise their voice and get in my face on several occasions to get their viewpoint across.

At least that was the lame excuse they used for screaming at me until I gave in or faked understanding where they were coming from. I was a stubborn child, knew what I wanted and had my own opinions on things, but somewhere along the way while growing up with my asshole stepfather, I allowed him and others to shrink me. I either became less so they could be more, or, at the very basic level, I realized if I was quiet and didn't have my own opposing opinion, then things ran smoothly. Everyone was happy.

I figured if my shrinking made everyone around me better off, then it was worth it, right?

Shoving another handful of deliciousness into my mouth, rogue pieces slipped through my fingers or didn't quite make it between my parted lips and tumbled to my lap, adding to the small pile of discards. Needing both hands to keep fighting, I wiped my palm on a dishcloth and gripped my controller, ready to give it all I had in this ultimate battle.

Even as I bobbed and weaved, tossing spells and fireballs at my enemy, all those years of being smothered kept running on a loop in my mind. "Never again," I bit out. "Never again will someone tell me what to do, who to be, what to wear. Never again."

"That's an excellent motto. Stitch that on a pillow," said a deep voice directly behind me.

I froze, as if my character's wand was real and had directed an immobilization spell right at my chest. Nothing functioned the way it should, not my lungs, not my brain; everything had suddenly gone offline.

Damnit. What good was the self-defense training with Oliver if I froze up when surprised?

My vision blurred with the need to blink, but I couldn't even do that. The air shifted as the person behind me moved around the couch and stepped into my line of sight.

The moment recognition weaved its way through my sluggish brain, all the tension drained out of me. With a grunt, I slumped against the couch, my energy zapped from those few intense moments. Hand over my pounding heart, I narrowed my eyes at the smiling hottie blocking the TV, where I was almost positive I was getting my ass kicked based on the sounds vibrating through the surround-sound speakers I installed last week. It made the gaming experience that much better when you could feel the sounds in the air.

"West O'Donnell, you fucking asshole," I griped. Grabbing a throw pillow, I launched it at his head, which he dodged easily.

He looked at the pillow on the ground and then back at

me like I'd just offended him somehow. "What did I say?" he asked innocently.

My breath caught for a second. He was just that good-looking in a sweet, sexy way with his glasses and shy smile. Loose, worn jeans hung on his hips but were snug around his thick thighs—making it very clear that even with his injury, he was keeping up with leg day—and pooled into a pair of untied work boots. Large work boots. It made me wonder if the saying was true about big feet meaning a big—

"Earth to Juno," he laughed, waving his good hand in front of my face.

I blinked, only now realizing I was in fact staring at his crotch.

Fuck a walrus.

"What the hell, West?" I snapped, hoping he didn't catch me mentally measuring the size of his dick based on his boot size and.... My focus zeroed in on his good hand. *Big hands too. Thick fingers....* I shook my head hard. What the hell was going on with me today? Maybe my assortment of toys and I had not spent enough quality time together lately because, holy fuck, I was horny. "You scared the shit out of me, sneaking up like that. Did you forget to knock?"

That mischievous smirk that showed a sexy dimple disappeared, replaced with a serious expression. The sudden shift in his mood had the previous heat filling my veins turning to ice.

"I scared you, and you just sat on the couch, frozen in place?" He crossed both thick arms over his muscular chest and shot me a disapproving look.

I picked a piece of popcorn off my lap and tossed it into my mouth, giving me a second to come up with a decent answer that wouldn't make him even more frustrated with me. "Um, yeah. I was deep in battle here, and I wasn't expecting someone to just barge into my home unannounced."

Shitty excuse, but that was the best I could come up with to defend my inaction while distracted by him.

His head tilted to the side with a quizzical expression. "Um, no one ever expects to be attacked."

I arched an eyebrow at him, stifling a chuckle. "But you're not attacking me, right?" Fuck, why did I phrase that as a question? And did I want him to say yes or no? The good kind of attacking, obviously. Not the hurtful... well, sometimes that was the good kind too. Just not the "I want to leave you dead" kind of attacking.

He looked at me like I'd lost my mind. Maybe I had.

"I know you're working with Oliver on self-defense, but you need reactive help too."

"I do?"

He nodded with a calculating expression.

Waving a hand in the air, I gestured to his face. "I don't like that look, whatever it is."

"You and me."

"Go on," I blurted before slapping a hand over my mouth. His lips curled upward in a slow smile. "I mean... fuck, what were you saying about you and me?"

"I'll help train you on your reaction time, faster reflexes for when you're surprised."

I wiggled my fingers in the air. "Yay," I mocked, despite loving the idea and knowing it would be helpful.

The way his grin fell made me feel like an asshole.

"Sorry, I don't mean to sound ungrateful. Your help would be great, thank you." I plucked a few pieces of popcorn off my lap and tossed them into my mouth. "I want to be ready for anything, anyone, just in case."

That stony expression came back in full force.

"Anyone, or someone in particular?" I shrank into the couch, sinking deeper into the cushions as he stepped around the small coffee table, cutting the distance between us. "That isn't a rhetorical question, Juno."

I blinked up at him, heart racing at the way he loomed over me. What would it feel like to have him reach down, scoop me off the couch like I weighed nothing, and toss me over his shoulder? To have his strong, protective arms wrapped around me in a way that made me feel so utterly safe, I could let my guard down for a few minutes, knowing nothing could get to me?

"Juno?"

Soft brown curls shifted along my shoulders with the sharp headshake it took to clear those crazy thoughts.

"Yeah, yeah, reactive training would be great," I muttered, picking up the discarded controller. "Thanks, West. You're a good friend."

His responding annoyed huff as he fell into the armchair by the couch had me eyeing him in confusion. With a shrug, I fixed my attention on the screen, where the other player's character was celebrating his victory by dancing over my dead body.

Classy.

"I can't even win virtually," I muttered under my breath, tossing the controller back onto the couch.

"What was that?" West asked, leaning forward as if actually waiting for my answer.

"Nothing. So, did you guys get everything worked out with Brandon in your meeting?" Out of the corner of my eye, I caught him stiffening as if he was uncomfortable with my question. "What happened? Wait, did Langston put up a fight about helping me with the information for the scheduling software?" An annoyed groan vibrated past my lips as I shoved off the couch. "He is such a raging asshole, you know that? I know you guys are"—I waved a hand in the air while I paced from one side of the room to the other—"whatever you are and—"

"You can ask me for details, sweet cheeks. I'll gladly tell you all about our relationship and all it entails."

My toe caught on the edge of the rug, sending me stumbling forward. Or at least I blamed the rug and not me being so caught off guard by the dirty visions his sultry voice and words created that I forgot how to walk. My palm slapped against the wall, keeping me upright before I fell face-first to the floor.

West's deep chuckle filled the small living room. I glared at the sexy bastard, but he just smirked in return and leaned back in the chair like he was enjoying teasing me.

"That's not what I was getting at," I rasped, throat dry as those visions of them together continued to play out in my mind.

"Wasn't it?" he asked, arching a dark brow.

"Fishing," I blurted, shoving off the wall to stand up on my own.

That cocky smirk fell, taking his dimples with it. "What?"

"That's what I need from Langston. My idea is that when clients book online, they'll also have to choose from a drop-down box on their experience level. That would help Langston when he's preparing for the group, or I assumed it would."

West rubbed at his jaw, studying me. "It would. I can't tell you how many times he's come home ranting about not having the right gear for the experience level of the person he took out. That's good thinking, Juno—*if* the person booking self-selects their experience level correctly, of course."

I nodded and tucked a piece of dark hair behind my ear. "That's why I need Langston's help, so no one has to guess where they land on a 1-10 scale. The drop-down will be specific, and I can make it very clear why this information needs to be accurate to ensure a great outing for everyone."

Excitement about the program thrummed through me. Hurrying over to my laptop, I swiped it off the couch and perched on the arm of the chair West occupied. The laptop wobbled on my knee when I opened the screen. Holding it with one hand and typing with the other, I didn't expect West's move until his arm curled around my waist and tugged.

A loud, surprised squeak escaped my lips as I toppled onto his lap. Eyes wide, I twisted around and blinked at the grinning man.

"This seemed easier for you," he said. The arm around my waist tightened when I shifted to get up. "You wanted to show me the changes, right?"

I looked at my laptop, my gaze slowly sliding lower to where my ass sat on his thighs. Heart hammering, breaths suddenly shallow, simmering heat pumped through my veins, making sweat slick along the back of my neck. I wet my lips and tried to swallow to relieve my desert-dry mouth. I took a deep breath to calm my crazy hormones and erratic pulse, then quickly realized that was a huge mistake when West's masculine scent filled my lungs, ramping up the steady throb between my thighs.

With a single finger, he shifted my hair to one side in a gentle caress and pitched forward, resting his chin on my shoulder.

"Everything okay?" His words whispered along my neck, causing goose bumps to rise in their wake.

Not trusting my voice, I nodded, jerking my focus back to the laptop. I gazed at the screen, working to get my rapid breathing under control.

This was insane. I had never reacted to a man like this, in such a physical, demanding way. It had to be more than me simply needing an orgasm or two; I felt the vibrating energy between us deep in my very being rather than just in my needy core.

"Juno," West whispered. "You're safe with me."

"I know that," I answered softly. "I know I am with you."

"And him too."

My lips parted to deny his statement about his asshole friend, but no words came out. I knew he was right. Even though Langston and I butted heads and drove each other up the wall with his overbearing attitude and me pushing back, not daring to allow another man to have a foothold over my life, he was safe.

I was safe with everyone in our community despite the dangers and mystery encompassing Anchor Bay. But the comprehensive safety I felt when West and Langston were around went deeper than with the others. If they were close, I knew without a doubt that one or both had an eye on me, which I cherished—even though I pretended to hate it to piss Langston off.

Like that embarrassing night at Dave's a few weeks back when he literally manhandled me out of the bar. I was drunk as hell, and he went and tossed me over his shoulder, completely ignoring my demands to be put down. I hated it and loved it in equal measure.

Damn, this was confusing.

How could I hate everything about the controlling man

but be borderline obsessed with it too? I craved his focused attention and overprotective demands. Which was dangerous.

Both he and West were. Case in point: how I was now relaxed back against the sexy man, his arm snug around my waist, and I liked it, knew I would miss it the second the moment was over.

This was all too dangerous. I would not open myself up to be hurt again by another man, allow myself to lose the parts of me I was just finding again. I'd just found my freedom to be unapologetically me and needed to cling to it with everything I had to keep the forward progress moving.

"West," I sighed, sitting up straight to put some much-needed distance between us. Closing the laptop, I held it to my chest like a shield. "I can't—"

Both our heads snapped toward the front door when it flung open so hard it slammed against the wall and bounced off, almost hitting the person walking in like they owned the place. Finley took one step into my cabin, mouth open, no doubt about to call out my name before her gaze landed on us. Motionless, eyes wide, she gaped for a solid five awkward seconds before clearing her throat and kicking the door closed behind her.

"Am I interrupting something?" she asked, waggling her brows. Striding across the living room, she fell onto the couch, grabbed my popcorn bowl, and began tossing pieces into her mouth.

I narrowed my eyes accusingly at my friend, which only made her damn smirk grow into a full-on smile.

"I was just showing West something on the laptop."

Finley hummed a noncommittal response and leveled a pointed expression at the closed laptop pressed tight against my chest.

My eyes rolled to the ceiling as I held in a frustrated scream. "Did you need something, Fin?"

"Need something, no. But...." She tossed the bowl aside and dusted off her hands before sitting forward. She practically bounced on the couch with excitement. "I have the best fucking news, and I wanted to tell you first."

Using the armrest instead of West's hard thigh, I stood, though the arm around my waist tightened a fraction as if wanting to keep me there before slowly loosening, allowing me to escape. I didn't dare look back to see if he was as disappointed as I was at the loss of his touch. Carefully setting the laptop on the coffee table, I perched on the couch arm, facing my friend.

"So, spill it. What is the best fucking news that I get to hear first? And I'm honored, by the way." Digging around in the bowl, I picked a few candy-coated chocolate pieces from the popcorn and tossed them all in my mouth. A cheerful hum vibrated in my chest as they melted on my tongue. "Also, when did you stop knocking?"

"I only knock on cabins where I might walk in on something I can't unsee, like a friend's va-jay-jay or one of the guy's hairy asses. Your cabin is safe from all that." She cut her eyes to West and then back to me. "For now."

I flipped her off at the same time West's deep chuckle sounded behind me. Rolling my eyes, I used the other hand to flip him off behind my back.

I snapped my fingers, drawing her attention from the popcorn bowl. "Fin, what is this news?" Keeping that woman on track was difficult; she got distracted by, well, everything.

Brushing both palms along her black leggings that accentuated her long, lean legs, she shot me a megawatt smile. "I have a date."

At the disbelieving scoff, we both turned to glare at West.

"Have something to say?" I snipped.

"I...." He shook his head, rubbing his good hand over his shaved hair. "Nothing, never mind. But the question is, does Dax know about this date of yours?"

Finley shrugged and picked up a discarded gaming magazine to flip through the pages. "Not sure. Like I said, I wanted Juno to be the first to know."

West hummed. "And does this guy know he's risking his life by taking you out?" he hedged, looking partly worried but also entertained.

"Oh, come on. You guys wouldn't mess this up for me on purpose, would you?" she said with a dramatic pout, falling back against the couch with her lower lip stuck out. "It's my first actual date in what feels like forever."

"*We* wouldn't, as in me or Langston," West muttered under his breath. "Now, if someone *else* in our community might lose his head and plot this poor unknowing bastard's murder? Yes, that is a concern I have."

While they bickered back and forth about how Dax would react to Finley's date, an idea hit me. This thing building between me and West, tipping our friendship closer to the "more than friends" category, was terrifying. Add in how my body reacted around him and Langston both, and I needed a distraction.

"Does this guy you're going out with have a friend?" I blurted before I lost my nerve.

The cabin went silent. It was so quiet I swear I heard West's blood pressure as it ticked higher and higher, a flush creeping up his neck and face, reddening his naturally tan skin.

"A friend?" Finley asked, drawing my attention from

West. Her lips pulled into a wide, playful grin as her gaze bounced between the two of us. "I'm sure he does. A double date is a great idea. Are you sure?"

I blew out a raspberry, lips tingling with the vibration. "Honestly, it's been a while since I've been on a first date, so that part sounds horrible, but I think I need the... after part."

"You mean you need to get laid," Finley laughed. "You don't want a date; you just want the fun that comes with it."

Muttering a string of curses, West shoved out of the chair, sending it careering backward a few inches, and stormed out the front door, slamming it shut behind him.

I blinked at the solid wood, shocked at his palpable frustration and that he'd left without even saying goodbye.

"He'll be fine, Juno. He probably just needed to leave before he said something to mess up"—she gestured between me and the direction West vanished—"that."

"What does that mean?"

"Come on," she sighed. "We all know it's only a matter of time before you three figure out you're absolutely obsessed with each other and start bumping uglies."

Picking up a piece of discarded popcorn, I threw it at her face. "Do you really want to talk about unspoken obsessions, Finley Jane?"

She swallowed hard and shook her head. "Had to toss out the middle name, did ya?"

"I'm just saying, I'll stay out of your complicated mess if you stay out of mine. I don't know what's going on between me, West, and Langston. All I know is...." I blew out a breath.

"You're scared of what it could be," she whispered.

"And losing myself in it."

"And what would happen if it didn't work out?"

We sat in silence, both mourning relationships we wanted but knew could never happen. She and Dax, me and the two men who made me feel alive and all me.

"So," I said with a clap to redirect our thoughts, "when and where is this double date?"

I was playing with fire, going on the date with West—and undoubtedly Langston, soon—in the know.

Only time would tell if it was them, or me, or all of us who would get burned.

5

LANGSTON

The skin around my knuckles pulled and burned with every slam of my fist against the punching bag I'd been working for the last thirty minutes. The muscle-memory motions combined with the sound of skin slapping the red leather and the smells of the gym soothed me in a way no amount of running or other cardio could. It was also a perfect outlet for my mounting frustration, which made coming to Oliver's gym a necessity after West's announcement yesterday.

Several feet away, in the far corner among the dust bunnies and spider webs, my best friend's feet pounded on the ancient treadmill, glaring at the cracked wall like it was the one who asked Juno out on a date. It took a lot to make him this angry, but somehow she'd accomplished it. We both had pent-up frustration that needed to be worked out before we exploded on each other or someone else, not only because of Juno's date, but for me the two hours I'd worked side by side with her earlier, helping her with the information she needed for the scheduling system.

It was hell sitting beside her, her gorgeous eyes

squinting in concentration, her naturally soft scent wafting off her fair skin every time she moved or flicked her hair. When she spoke, I couldn't help but stare at her lips, wondering how they would feel on me. Plus, watching her work, her fingers flying over the keyboard and the determined focus she had while coding, was sexy as hell. Not only was the woman feisty in how she pushed my many buttons and turned me on, but she was also a computer genius, funny, and the most strikingly, naturally beautiful woman I'd ever seen.

Our size difference made me want to pick her up and carry her around. Almost a foot shorter than me, with wide, sexy hips and thighs, and an ass that I wanted wearing my handprint on both cheeks, she was soft and feminine in all the perfect ways.

The subtle shift beneath my shorts from just thinking about Juno had me grunting in annoyance and slamming my fist harder into the bag. It wasn't smart to think about her while wearing nothing but a pair of thin shorts; everyone in the gym would get an eyeful of my massive dick standing at attention.

Even as a horny teenager, this never happened to me. Juno was the only woman who could make me hard as steel just by thinking about her. But even if my body reacted to her without my permission, it didn't mean I was ready to let my guard down, not yet. I still had to uncover what she was hiding from her past. And now with the mystery couple coming to surprise her tomorrow, I needed to be more cautious than ever around her.

The sunlight pouring through the glass front door shifted when it opened wide, bringing in a gust of cool fresh air to the musty space along with the object of my obsession.

Earbuds in, head bobbing to whatever song she listened to, Juno didn't even notice me or West as she headed to the locker room, too focused on whatever she was typing on her phone.

I dropped both throbbing fists to my sides, shocked at her oblivious concern for her surroundings and safety. Had she biked the entire way here distracted and unable to hear someone if they came up behind her?

Anger and fear swirled in my chest at her complete disregard for her safety. How dare she put herself in danger like that, especially with everything going on with the unsolved missing women cases?

The soles of my trainers were slamming against the concrete floor before I even realized I was moving toward the locker room. Somewhere, West yelled my name, the sound echoing off the bare walls, while Oliver's barked curses and demands for me to stop went in one ear and out the other.

I smacked my palm to the center of the door and forced it open, storming into the locker room, ready to lecture her on being aware of her surroundings and safety. Inside the small room lined with lockers and a single bench between them, she stood at the opposite end, her back to me, earbuds in and eyes focused on her phone. She didn't even notice my presence until I wrapped my fingers around her ponytail and tugged. Her soft gasp had my dick waking back up, ready to hear that sound again. Bending low, I hovered my lips along the shell of her ear, fighting the urge to wrap her hair around my fist and tug, arching her back and forcing her round ass to press against my twitching cock.

"What the hell do you think you're doing, Juno? You—"

I didn't get to finish. The feisty woman caught me off guard. Instead of freezing like West said she did when he surprised her, Juno folded to the ground like a sack of potatoes. Her soft brown hair slipped through my fingers when she twisted around to slam a fist behind my right knee. Any other time, I would've expected the attack, prepared for it by balancing my weight, but I was too stunned by her quick movements. The hit had my leg buckling, sending me toppling forward.

Seeing the inevitable, Juno's eyes went wide. She clearly hadn't counted on me falling directly on top of her. Vibrations shot from where my palms connected with the floor, stopping my full body weight from slamming into her. Nose to nose, our quick breaths mingled as we stared at each other, both in shock at the quick turn of events.

"What the fuck was that?" I growled, my voice shaking from the effort to keep my weight off her.

"You first, Langston," she snapped, not dropping my glare. With a huff, she shimmied along the floor, attempting to slip away, but only succeeded in shifting her core beneath my hardening dick.

"Stop moving," I hissed. Both eyes sealed shut, I inhaled deeply to cool the liquid heat pumping through my veins.

Fuck, this was bad. She was trouble, dangerous, and unknown. I couldn't let my guard down around her. This was just to teach her a lesson about being aware and taking her safety into consideration, nothing more.

"Then get off me," she demanded. When she moved again, I knew the second she lifted and shifted just enough to be very aware of how turned on I was. Stilling, she blinked those long dark lashes up at me. "Langston."

"Juno," I breathed, scanning her petite face. Fuck, she was even more beautiful this close. I folded my fingers into my palm until the nails bit into my skin to keep from stroking them along her jaw and throat.

I imagined my hand wrapped around her neck while I took her hard, West's dick stretching her pretty lips wide as he fucked her throat.

"Lang." My eyes slowly lifted from where they had fallen to her parted lips. "What are you doing?"

My throat worked with a hard swallow as I tried to figure that out myself. What the fuck *was* I doing? Yes, there was attraction there—fine, obsession—but she was still an outsider, someone keeping secrets that could harm the family I'd found here in Anchor Bay.

With one last look, committing her faint freckles to memory, I pushed off the floor with a grunt and leapt to my feet.

Her hooded gaze tracked my hand when I adjusted my hard cock, attempting to make it less obvious.

"Just don't go walking around town so fucking distracted again," I barked. "It's not safe."

I spun around to leave the locker room when she stopped me in my tracks.

"I took you down just fine," she called out with so much sass in her tone it was almost a taunt.

The fact that she took my warning as a joke, that she took her safety as something to make light of, sent that earlier frustration roaring through my veins once again, pounding in my ears. Which only made my dick stiffen more, emphasizing how fucked up I was in the relationship department.

Dropping to my knees, one on either side of her waist, I gathered her wrists in one hand and pinned them to the floor above her head.

If I were a smart man, I would've realized this was a terrible decision, considering our position, and aborted the safety lesson, but apparently I was a masochist and liked to test my limits.

Juno didn't move a muscle, just kept her heated aqua eyes locked on me as I leaned in close.

"There are women being snatched off the fucking streets—"

"I'm not on that trail. There were people around, and—"

Her dismissive tone, the complete disregard for the danger lurking all around us, had me doing what I'd fantasized about a dozen times since meeting Juno. I gently wrapped my long fingers around her throat, squeezing just enough to ensure I had her full attention so she would hopefully grasp how serious I was about keeping her safe, even if that meant from herself. Her throat moved beneath my hot palm when she swallowed.

"I don't give a damn if you're on the trail or even walking the main road in front of your cabin. There is a sick fucker out there taking women and doing who the fuck knows what with them. Take your safety seriously, Juno." I flex my fingers, making her breath hitch. "Or I will."

That did it; those last words of warning pushed the independent woman too far. All the heat in her glassy gaze vanished, replaced with anger I could almost feel burning into me.

"Fuck you, Langston," she rasped, barely getting the words out around my hold on her throat. "I'm not an idiot, or helpless, or incompetent, or—"

The passion and conviction in her tone had me locking in on her choice of words. "That's not what I'm saying, Juno." My eyes flicked between hers. "Did someone say that to you, that you were?" I demanded.

A blank mask took the place of her shocked expression,

and she pressed her lips together, clearly not wanting to answer.

"I'm not saying you are any of those things, more just careless. You walked into the gym, face in your phone, listening to the new Swift shit you love—"

Her hair slid along the concrete with the tilt of her head, her confusion clear. "How do you know I'm a Swiftie?"

"Not the point." She didn't need to know how deep the stalking—I mean recon—went and that I knew a disturbing amount of details about her. Well, except for what she left behind when she moved here.

The corner of her lips quirked upward. "Kind of is...," she teased.

"Juno," I said with a frustrated sigh. How could I make her understand what knowing she was potentially in danger did to me? "Our friend is missing. We're all at a loss on where she is, who has her, or if she's even still alive." I slid my gaze to the dented and rusted row of lockers to avoid the pity in hers. "And there is nothing I can fucking do about it. She's missing, and...." I swallowed hard. "Please be more careful. I can't...."

"Okay," she whispered when I trailed off, unable to utter the next words around the lump in my throat. "I promise to be more careful. Hey, look at me, Langston."

Swallowing hard, I reluctantly shifted my watery gaze down to her.

"I'm worried about her too, but you guys were family. I can't imagine how hard it is on you, West, everyone at Uplift. Do you have someone to talk to about it?"

Seeing the compassion in her soft gaze had me forcing all those emotions down. Feeling too raw and exposed, I peeled my fingers free from around her throat. That was enough of opening up about the things eating me alive inside.

Sitting back, I crossed my arms. "Who said you were ignorant or incompetent, Juno?"

"And back comes the caveman," she muttered with a sigh. "No one, okay? Can I please go work out now?"

"Not until you tell me who spewed those lies at you."

Her teeth sank into her lower lip, a swell of unshed tears suddenly filling her lower lids as she shook her head. "Please, Langston, not now. Maybe never, but not now."

"Why?"

"Because talking about it means remembering, and remembering means feeling all that shame and self-loathing all over again. Once I do, it's hard to stop, and I don't want to go down that path today, and especially not with you."

I bristled at the last part. "You actually believed that shit you just said about yourself? How?" *Idiot, incompetent,* and anything else similar were not words I'd ever even think of using about the amazing woman.

Focusing on something just over my shoulder, she slowly nodded. "At one time, yeah, I did. But I'm working to undo it all, little by little."

"Why did you believe it?" None of this made any sense. She was so strong and self-assured with me, never backing down. I couldn't imagine her believing any of that, much less listening to someone else say it to her.

She blew out a shaky breath, and I steeled myself for her answer, knowing I wouldn't like it. "Because when it constantly comes from someone you love and who you think loves you just as much, it becomes your truth."

Bloodlust pumped through my veins, making me vibrate with unfiltered anger. Someone who said they loved her filled her mind with those lies, which made it worse somehow.

"Who?" I demanded. "Give me a name, and I will rip out their throat so they can't say that bullshit to you or anyone else again."

"No need to kill someone and end up in prison for the rest of your life on my behalf," she huffed with a small grin. "But thanks."

I angled my head to one side and then the other, stretching out the building tension in my neck and shoulders. "Juno, I would gladly die there with a smile on my face if it meant ending the person who made you question the truth of who you are."

Her eyes widened in obvious shock. Before she could respond, the locker room door flung open.

"Okay, you two, that's enough time alone to figure your shit out." I snarled at the intrusive asshole over my shoulder, which only made West's smile widen. "Hey, don't give me that look. I've held Oliver back from barging in to check on you two, so turn that scowl into a smile and a fucking thank-you." His gaze shifted down to Juno, his features instantly softening. "You okay, sweet cheeks?"

Her soft laugh eased some of the tension making my muscles twitch. "There's that term again."

West bit his lower lip and nodded. "What can I say? It fits you. Now." He clapped his hands together before pointing at me. "Answer the question. Are you good, or do I need to kick my friend's ass?" He arched a dark brow my way when I huffed out a laugh. "I was going to offer to let her watch."

"Fucking hell," Juno groaned with a slight whimper.

"Is that a yes?" West asked, moving to my side, shifting to angle his crotch right in front of my face. The knowing smirk he shot down at me said he was well aware he was being a fucking tease. "I see you already got him all riled up. He might take that out on me." Running the tip of his thumb along his lower lip, he looked between us. "But don't worry, Juno. That's how I like it."

"Fuck," I snapped and shoved off the ground to stand. West's heated gaze stayed locked on my tented shorts. "Fucking watch it, West."

"Oh, I am," he joked.

"Help me up before you two attack each other," Juno grumbled.

I extended a hand, and when her tiny one slid into mine, I carefully lifted her off the floor. We eyed each other for a second before she carefully weaved between me and West for the exit.

"Juno," I said, making her stop with a hand on the door. She didn't turn, but I knew she was listening. "I'm serious about taking your safety more seriously, and that includes that fucking date of yours. You're not going out with a stranger tonight, or any night, until we catch the sick bastard."

"Oh, fuck," West muttered under his breath, looking to the ceiling like he might find more patience there.

Juno whirled around, the tip of her ponytail smacking her in the face with the violent move, and pointed at my chest.

"You can't tell me what to do, Langston. I will go out with who I want, when I want."

I studied her flushed cheeks and heaving chest. "Fine." I shrugged as if it didn't matter to me. "It's his fucking funeral."

Her high-pitched screech of pure exasperation echoed off the lockers, making me wince. The door slammed shut behind her, cutting off her detailing all the ways she wanted to murder me.

"Well, that went well," West snapped. He smacked his good hand between my shoulder blades. "Way to prove to her that we are, in fact, just a couple of overprotective assholes."

"We are," I muttered indignantly. "Why hide it?"

"Um, so we don't piss her off like you just did." He turned, running a hand over his head. "I know you're still lying to yourself that you aren't utterly obsessed with that woman, but I'm not." He turned and stabbed a finger in my chest. "And since we're a package fucking deal, I need you to calm the caveman shit down, get your shit together, and help me convince her she's ours."

"Oh, we're a package deal, are we?"

Mischief sparked in his dark eyes, and I knew I was going to fucking love and hate whatever he said next.

"If you don't think so, maybe I'll take a play out of Juno's book and find a date tonight and—"

In a swift move, I pinned him against the lockers with his chest and cheek pressed to the metal. After a few half-assed attempts to buck me off him, he relaxed with a deep, guttural groan.

"You are not going out with anyone, not without me," I snarled in his ear. Unable to stop, I ground my painfully hard cock against his firm ass, making us both suck in a hissed breath. "But you want Juno, that's fine. I'll be the levelheaded one and stay the fuck away from her until we know she's not trouble."

"Oh, she's trouble," he said over his shoulder. "The best kind."

"That woman is hiding something, and until I know

what it is, she's all yours to fuck around with. And about that date—we *are* going tonight."

He strained to look over his shoulder, eyes wide with surprise. "What?"

I nodded, easing up on my hold. "Recon only. We hang back to see if she reveals anything and to make sure she's safe."

"Safe, right," West laughed, his entire body trembling against me. "And if she goes home with this guy or he goes back to her place? What then?"

I thought for a moment before responding. I was a stubborn idiot for not admitting what everyone else knew. Hell, even I did too, deep down. The truth was, I didn't trust her not to hurt my best friend, my Uplift family, or me. What West didn't realize was that when I said "safe," I meant safe for us, not just Juno's safety.

"Then I guess you'll have to step up your game if you want her to come home with you instead."

West flipped around to lean back against the lockers. "Really?"

Arms crossed, I shrugged. "You want her, you figure out how to get her. I won't stand in your way."

A slow smile pulled at his lips, making his dimples pop. "Fuck, you're stubborn." He sighed. "Fine, I'll figure something out."

Stepping back, I adjusted myself, the discomfort making me grimace, which of course he noticed.

"I can help you with that, you know."

"Don't fucking start," I grumbled. But holding her down, then pressing against West had me so fucking hard I could feel my dick leaking.

"You really need to figure your shit out so you don't die from fucking blue balls."

"Maybe I'll find some random, then," I snapped, moving to the locker where I'd stored my keys and wallet. That was a lie, and he knew it, which was why I made it a point not to face him.

"Damnit, Langston. Stop lying to yourself. Enough is enough. You're not going out tonight or any other night to find some random woman to fuck and leave." West dropped his head forward, making my chest pinch at his obvious disappointment with me. "And here's a thought: Maybe if she knew *why* you were overly protective and concerned about her safety, she would open up about her past and understand your tantrums a little better." He peeked up through his dark eyelashes. "Someone hurt her, Langston, and she needs to trust that we won't too."

"She wouldn't tell me who," I practically pouted, making West swallow a laugh.

"You no doubt did your whole 'who hurt you?' growly bit and demanded it."

"So?"

"Well, it obviously didn't work."

"You walked in before I could get it out of her."

He slowly nodded. "Baylee and Aspen said we need to gain her trust, show her that we'll protect her not only physically but in every way."

My brows pulled in tight. "I don't follow."

His damn wide smile appeared once again as he shook his head and ran a hand over his short hair. "I know you don't, and honestly, I don't either. Something about being emotionally safe, whatever that means. Either way, we'll figure it out and be that for her. Which means you need to tone down—" He gestured up and down my body. "—that."

"You gestured to all of me."

"Well, not the physical parts of you, because you know how fucking hot you are, but more what's on the inside."

"Thanks, fucking asshole." I hitched my chin at him. "Grow your hair back out. I liked it long, and I can tell you miss it."

He shot me a wink and headed for the door. "You just enjoyed having something to grab. But just think, if you ever pull your head out of your ass when it comes to Juno, her long ponytail would easily wrap around your fist."

Once he was gone, I slumped against the locker and rested the back of my head on the cold metal. I was in so much damn trouble with those two. West could handle himself, so I shouldn't worry about him, but he was mine, so I would. Juno surprised me earlier, but her being out alone on the streets or even alone in her cabin scared me to death as much as the woman herself did.

She was practically a stranger with how little we knew about her background, and I knew all too well how strangers could quickly destroy someone if I wasn't careful.

First, I failed Mattie.

Then Caroline.

West, when he was hurt.

None were my fault, but I wasn't there when they needed me to protect them.

I wouldn't let that happen again.

Not to them or anyone else I claimed as my family.

And if that meant Juno hating me for a little longer until I uncovered her secrets, then so be it.

I was trapped.

Sweat coated my forehead and slicked my back, totally negating my earlier shower. Struggling against the unforgiving cotton, I gave up attempting to push the soft cast through the armhole, ripping the whole shirt off and flinging it across the room with a barked curse instead.

Hand on my hip, chest heaving from my mounting frustration, I glared at the few shirts hanging in my closet, debating which one I should—and could—wear for our stalking mission.

"What the hell is going on in here?" Langston leaned against the doorframe with his inked arms crossed over his chest. My glare zeroed in on his two fully functional hands. He tracked my focus and huffed out a laugh. "If you need help, just ask."

"Right, like either of us are good at that," I grumbled, grabbing a looser-fitting shirt off the hanger so hard that the thin plastic flung around the metal rod and crashed to the bottom of the closet. "And I'm fine. Everything is just ten times more work. Hell, getting dressed is a fucking challenge with this thing."

"Again, all you have to do is ask." Langston strode to the corner where I'd tossed the black long-sleeve T-shirt I almost suffocated in when it incarcerated me in its buttery softness and snatched it off the floor. He shot me a knowing smirk. "You really need more than one 'good' shirt, West."

I shrugged. "One is fine if I could get it on."

Motioning me closer, he helped me slip it over the recovering hand first, the soft fabric catching on the cast, before helping me thread the other arm through. After pulling it over my head, he stepped back and nodded.

"Was that so fucking hard?"

I gave him the bird and moved to the dresser to find some socks. I swallowed a groan, knowing that would also take me three times as long with only one working hand.

"You're not the one actually going on the date, you know. No need to put on your Sunday best." Which was hilarious coming from him, because I knew for a fact that Langston chose his current clothes because the jeans hugged his firm ass and thick thighs the best and the shirt was practically painted on. Plus, the color made his green eyes even more entrapping. "The plan is to stay hidden and see if we can learn more about Juno."

Scoffing, I rolled my eyes. "That's *your* plan, not mine, remember? And honestly, you lie to yourself way too much for it to be healthy. Do you actually believe you'll stay hands-off if I somehow find the opportunity to convince Juno that I'm a better option than whoever she's with?"

"I told you, I don't trust her." Langston shifted to lean back against the wall, watching me struggle to pull on a tall boot sock.

"Why the fuck not?" I snapped. "So she's keeping something from you. Big fucking deal. You don't get to know everyone's darkest parts of themselves right away. Maybe try being nice to her and talking to her for once without arguing about every damn thing. Then maybe she'll open up." I dropped my head in exasperation. "I want her, Lang, and I won't let your stubborn ass get in the way of the three of us being together."

Langston's lips parted, ready to respond, when someone pounded on the front door, the sound echoing through the cabin and shaking the walls from the force. We shot each other surprised and cautious expressions before filing out of my room to see who was attempting to beat down the solid wood.

With a white-knuckled grip, Langston yanked on the handle and opened the door wide, barely shifting in time to miss the fist aimed for his nose. He snatched it out of the air and used the hold to shove our friend Dax backward onto the porch.

Dax stumbled, arms pinwheeling as he attempted to stay on his feet and not tumble down the porch steps. Once he had his footing, he tossed both hands up in the air with an expectant expression.

"What the fuck was that for, Langston?" he demanded, storming up to the door.

"For almost hitting me and your annoying knocking," Langston snarled before turning around and stomping back into the cabin. "I'll get the supplies we'll need for tonight."

"Supplies? What supplies?" I questioned as he stalked past me.

"Guns, duct tape, zip ties...."

"I brought a shovel." I followed Dax into the living room with both eyebrows high on my forehead. "What?" he said with a wicked smirk. "You never know what you'll need."

"I think he was kidding," I sighed, rubbing at my temples to ward off the headache I felt coming on. "At least I fucking hope he was."

"It's Langston, going to stalk Juno—"

"Recon, not stalking," Langston corrected from the kitchen.

"Right," Dax drawled. "Anyway, I want in."

"In on what?" I headed back to my room to grab my glasses and came back to find Dax pacing the length of the wide stone fireplace. "In on what, Dax?"

He shot me an incredulous look. "Sabotaging their date, obviously."

I slid my glasses on while contemplating finding new, less violent friends. "Who said we were sabotaging it?"

He scraped a hand along his neatly trimmed beard. "Everyone who knows you and that stalking asshole."

I froze halfway between standing and sitting on the worn leather couch. "Does Juno know we're planning to follow her?" I cleared my throat. "For her safety, of course."

"Of course. Safety first." With a dramatic sigh, he fell into Langston's favorite chair.

I stifled a smile when a gruff "Get the fuck out of my chair" came from the kitchen.

Rolling his eyes, Dax shoved out of the recliner and plopped down beside me on the couch. "I don't think so, but I wouldn't know. Hell, Finley didn't even tell me who she's going out with."

"Probably to protect all innocent parties involved," I muttered under my breath. "Do we even know where they're going, or are we just searching around town until we find them?"

"That fancy restaurant at The Nest." Langston rounded

the couch and sat in his chair with a pointed look at Dax. "My chair."

"Fuck, you're even possessive of furniture," I chuckled.

"I hear no complaints from you, Westly."

I swallowed hard at hearing my full name in his deep voice. He normally only used it behind closed doors, just us two, which meant he'd intended to trigger the passionate heat flowing through my veins straight to my dick.

Asshole.

It also further proved my point that there was no way in hell he would let me pursue Juno alone. He was too possessive of me, of our relationship, not to be a part of what I hoped to build with her.

His comment about the restaurant had me sitting forward. "Langston, how do you know that's where they'll be?" I asked. It was the first I'd heard that bit of information since he got back from the store earlier. "Who do you have spying on them?"

"Informant," Langston remarked, studying his phone.

"You know, switching out words to make your actions seem more credible and less illegal doesn't actually change what you're doing." He just smirked, ignoring my earlier question. "Who, Lang?"

"My source would prefer to remain anonymous." He tossed his phone onto the coffee table.

I stared at him. "Langston, I'm not dropping this."

"Fine, it's Kale, Oliver's brother. That's who told me where they're going because...." His green eyes slid to Dax, and a sharp smile split his lips. *Fuck, that's not good.* "He's Finley's date."

Dax leapt off the couch with enough force from his lean six-foot-two frame that it slid along the hardwood. I cursed, shifting to the side to stay seated. His boots thumped against the wooden floor as he stormed to the door. "Of course it's that fucking cocky bastard. Thinks he's so fucking untouchable because of his brother and dad, and his fucking great hair."

Langston and I shared an amused expression at that last comment. Before Dax could leave, Langston called him back.

"Sit the fuck down so we can discuss how to handle tonight."

Releasing a frustrated groan, Dax slammed the door shut and stomped back to the living room.

"And yes, it's Kale, but that's good for you."

Dax scoffed. "How is that good for me? Have you seen the guy?"

Langston sighed. "Right, but have you ever heard of him dating anyone local?"

Dax's lips parted before he paused, his brows pulled in tight as he thought over Langston's question. "No, I don't think I've ever seen him do anything other than work and hang out with Oliver."

"Exactly, which means tonight won't end with anything serious. The guy goes to Anchorage to get laid; he knows better than to fuck where he eats."

"I don't think that's the saying," I drawled. Pushing the thick frames back up the bridge of my nose, I cautiously asked the question I needed the answer to but was also terrified to find out. "Who's the guy taking Juno?"

A Cheshire cat grin spread across Langston's face before he smothered it.

"What did you do?" I demanded, stomach sinking with dread.

"Nothing."

"Langston." I shoved off the couch and moved around the coffee table to stand over him. "What. Did. You. Do?"

"It's some guy who Kale works with," he said, hiding his smile by rubbing a hand across his lips. "And after I found out his name, I looked up his address and stopped by earlier."

I tossed both hands up in the air. "You said you were going out for fucking eggs."

He pointed at the fridge. "Which I did, but I also made a detour to check the guy out."

"Oh shit," Dax chuckled. "Is he still alive?"

"That is way out of line, Lang." I moved to pace in front of the fireplace. "Juno will be fucking furious if she finds out you investigated her date. All she wanted was a date and—"

Langston stood and stopped me with a hand to the center of my chest. "No, you said she mentioned not looking forward to the date part, only what came after."

"So fucking what, Langston, you—"

"I said nothing to the guy. Calm your ass down. And this is good for you too."

My jaw dropped. "How? How is this good for me?"

He waved me off. "He's no competition to you. Just get Juno alone, and you'll both get what you want."

Well, fuck, that sounded good. But also orchestrated, and I didn't like that.

"It has to be her choice," I demanded. "And how do we even know that she'll be okay with me being her...."

"Orgasm donor," Dax chimed in.

"Good-time bringer," Langston added.

"How the hell am I friends with you two?" I grumbled. Running a hand over my head, I sighed. "I don't mind her using me; that's not the issue here. But what if she doesn't want me over this guy?"

"If you'd let me finish." He shot me a pointed look, like I was the annoying one at the moment. "I initially stopped by to check up on him since I had never heard of the guy, but while I watched him—"

"You really have a stalking problem." I jabbed a finger at him, which he batted away.

"I didn't get a good vibe from him."

Dax sat forward on the couch, full attention on Langston, while all I could do was not wrap my hands around the asshole's neck. He didn't like anyone until he got to know them, so his perspective on this guy wasn't concerning.

"His name is Stew Walters he continued, "and he's a barback at The Nest's restaurant and Dave's."

I ran that name over and over, coming up blank. "Who?"

"Exactly my damn point. He's lived in Anchor Bay for the last five years, and no one even knows his name."

"That sounds suspect," Dax mused. The leather groaned as he leaned back, draping one arm along the back of the couch. "Should we tell Oliver and Hudson? Maybe they can detain and question him about the missing women."

My jaw went slack. "You can't be serious."

He just shrugged. "Langston here is an excellent judge of character."

"I'm going to need Tylenol before we head out tonight." I pinched the bridge of my nose. "Just because he's an introvert or antisocial does not make him a serial killer."

"But it is one of the checkboxes," Dax added, as if that proved his theory.

"Besides him being shy," I groaned, "what else made you not get a good vibe from him, Lang?"

He sealed his lips together, making me more nervous. *Shit, what else did he do?*

"Okay, here's what we will *not* do. We will not accuse a man of being a serial killer just because we don't know him." I eyed Langston with suspicion. "What else happened?"

He avoided my eyes. "While he was taking out his trash, I may or may not have made sure he saw me, and I did the whole eye-point thing to let him know I'm always watching."

My lips in a tight line, all I could do was stare at my friend in utter exasperation. At least he didn't tie the guy up so he couldn't go out on the date at all.

He shook his head. "None of that matters, though, because he's not her type, and nothing will happen between them."

I scoffed. "So now you're a stalker *and* clairvoyant?"

"Careful," he muttered with a dark look my way. The heat from earlier came roaring back to life, making my cock twitch beneath my boxer briefs. "Your Juno wouldn't go for someone that weak."

"My Juno?" I arched a brow.

"Are you denying it?"

"No," I drawled. "It's just...." I wanted to hear him say "our Juno," but baby steps. He would get there. Eventually. Hopefully.

"She needs someone like you." Langston shot a look at Dax. "And you need to get your fucking act together and make a move on Finley before it's too late."

"Whatever," Dax grumbled. "I'll handle my own shit; you handle yours. Fin and I have been friends for too long. Making that shift to more isn't in the cards for us, and—"

Whatever he was going to say next was cut off by his high-pitched screech as he leapt up and bolted around the coffee table. Eyes wide, Dax gaped at the couch.

"What the fuck was that?" he panted, the burst of adrenaline having made his heart race.

Brows pulled in tight, I tried to figure out what the hell just happened when a fluffy white tail whipped out from beneath the couch. With a loud laugh, I pointed to where the tip still peeked out.

"Ah, that would be GG."

Dax looked at me in utter confusion. "What do you mean, GG?"

I could feel Langston's stare burning into the side of my head.

Here was the thing with Langston. He wanted everyone to think he was this tatted-up hard-ass who didn't give a shit about anyone but himself, but that wasn't even remotely true. He cared about the people he considered family almost to the point of his own downfall. Most importantly, he didn't want anyone to know that his weakness—other than cookie dough, Mattie, me, and I guess Juno now—was his precious GG.

His fucking prissy-ass, all-white Persian cat.

Her name was Gorgeous Girl, or GG for short, though mostly because I refused to call her by her full name—it just inflamed her ego. Anchor Bay's notorious asshole Langston Allen gave the name to the entitled feline after his sister gifted him the cat.

And like her owner, GG had a massive attitude problem and didn't like anyone, hence Dax screaming. She'd either bitten or swiped at his ankles while he sat on the couch.

Knowing Langston wanted to keep his favorite pussy a secret, I told the lie I had used before.

"My cat," I sighed, hating my fucking life at the moment.

Langston's shoulders dropped from around his ears.

"She's yours?" Dax asked. I slowly nodded. "Why do you

own a demon cat? Nope, scratch that. Why do you own a cat at all?"

I shrugged, not really having the energy to come up with some elaborate lie to help conceal Langston's furry friend. Eyeing the stuffed pack on the kitchen counter, I headed toward it, curious to see what supplies he'd actually packed.

"Binoculars?" I chuckled as I pulled the heavy Army green item free and reached inside to find more. "A big-ass knife—"

"Always be prepared," Langston muttered, plopping back down in his chair. GG immediately slid out from beneath the couch and leapt up into his lap. Dax watched the white fluffball with suspicion, like it might attempt another attack.

I held up the roll of silver duct tape. "Seriously?"

"You never know what you'll need while out on a mission." GG's back arched as Langston stroked his wide hand along her spine, and a soft smile that rarely appeared curled at his lips. The man was the epitome of pussy whipped.

"Let's hope it doesn't come down to that, because the last thing I need is to bail one of you out of jail." I slid my hard gaze to Dax. "Again."

"I told you, that tourist was asking for it. It wasn't my fault that we started a bar brawl. And besides, I'm different now." He hitched his chin in the air. "More mature."

"That was just last year," I deadpanned.

"Exactly. People change, West."

I just rolled my eyes and stuffed everything back into the pack. Maybe Dax had grown up a little since then, but I wasn't sure about that. The man loved to fight, and he sought any opportunity to do just that. Why, I wasn't sure. He seemed happy-go-lucky, all jokes and carefree, especially when Finley was around, but when no one was watching and his mask dropped, you could see the simmering anger that sat just below the surface. It was almost as if Finley was the only cure for his rage.

"We need to get going." Back against the wall, Dax eyed GG with a mix of fear and disdain as he shifted toward the door. "Bye, devil cat."

He jumped a foot in the air when GG hissed at him and, I swear, fake-lunged in his direction just to freak him out. I was still laughing when the door slammed shut behind him.

"Good girl," Langston cooed as he scratched behind GG's soft ears.

I chewed on my lip, debating how to bring up my concerns without Langston getting defensive or blowing off the effects of us following her.

"Out with it," he groaned. "I can hear your mind working on overdrive from here."

I pushed the thick frames back up my nose and leaned a hip against the counter.

"I feel like I actually have a shot at something happening between her and me, and I'm afraid tonight is going to fuck it up." My dark eyes collided with his green ones. "I like her, Lang. A lot. She's beautiful, funny, brilliant, kind—everything I never knew I needed or wanted in a woman."

"What's your point?" He carefully picked up GG and set her in the spot he'd just vacated. Coming to the kitchen, he paused directly in front of me. "What are you worried about?"

"That I'm going to fuck it up before I even have her." He scanned my face, searching for what, I wasn't sure. I sighed. "I want her. All of her, and not just for tonight."

He adjusted his backward hat, shifting it side to side

before settling it back over his dark hair. "Is that all you want?"

"You know it's not," I whispered. "I want us too."

With a clipped nod, he moved to grip the counter on either side of my hips and leaned in until our noses almost touched. My breath hitched at the dark sparkle in his gaze.

"Good, because I won't lose you, or us. I won't fuck this up for you tonight. I'll even go as far as helping make sure it all works out. Whatever you need from me, I'm there for you. Always."

"Understood," I breathed.

"Good. Now go get your other sock on and let's go. We have your woman to stalk."

7

JUNO

Before the night was over, I had grand plans of strangling both Kale and Finley.

My glare bounced between the two across the table, both trying and failing to hide their amusement. Assholes. The candle's flickering flames wavered with my heavy sigh, the silverware and dishes rattling when I set my elbow on the white tablecloth, resting my chin in my palm.

All I had wanted out of tonight was to get laid, but that was absolutely, 100 percent not happening with the man sitting beside me picking at his nails. The "friend" Kale set me up with was just a random guy he knew from work. Hell, Kale even admitted that he thought the guy was slightly strange.

Strange and in desperate need of a shower.

When we met them here, I instantly regretted putting in the effort to look nice. I'd even put on a real bra—the one that was currently poking the shit out of my right boob— and cute panties that were currently up my crack so deep the lace was on the verge of cutting me in two.

Releasing another bored sigh, I cut my eyes over at my date, Stew Walters. His long, greasy, dark hair, which he clearly didn't wash for tonight's date—or anytime in the last few days—was pulled back in a low bun, and his muddy eyes had only met mine once the whole evening. Which was fine with me. That split second we made eye contact sent a shiver slithering down my spine at what lurked in his blank stare.

It almost made me wonder if I was safe with him even in a room full of crowded people. If he abducted me and used me as a skin suit, I was so haunting Finley. She would never get laid again. I'd use my ghost mojo to give any guy she was with a limp dick.

Pretty sure that was how it worked when you were a ghost.

"So, what do you do for fun?" I asked, forcing a smile and directing the question to Stew.

His large frame shivered at my voice, making me shoot a worried expression at Finley, who appeared just as concerned for my safety.

"Hiking," he muttered.

That was shocking. The guy didn't really give off the outdoorsy vibe.

Not for the first time tonight, I glanced down at his bandaged wrist. "What happened there?"

He quickly tucked it under the table, hiding it beneath the white tablecloth, and shot me a sharp look that had me sucking in a tight breath.

"Nothing." He turned his face back to his empty bread plate, shutting me out.

A soft buzzing in my purse had me searching inside for my cell phone, thankful for the unexpected distraction. It was rude to check it, but it was clear this date wasn't going anywhere, and I honestly hoped someone needed me so I could excuse myself and head home to my pajamas and video games.

Tapping the texting app, a pulse of excitement made me suck in a breath at seeing West's name.

West: You look bored.

Licking my lips, I quickly sealed the phone screen to my chest, carefully searching the restaurant for him. How else could West be spot-on about how utterly bored I was?

"What's wrong?" Kale questioned, shifting to lean closer to Finley, draping an arm across the back of her chair.

I shook my head while still scanning the various tables and packed bar. The phone buzzed again in my hand, but I ignored it in my search.

Coming up empty, I slumped against the seat back. Disappointment hit me hard, making unshed tears line my lower eyelids. He was probably at home just messing with me—he knew I was on a date, after all. It was dumb even to think West would care enough to be here watching.

We were flirty friends, and his best friend hated me.

Well, I thought he did, until earlier when he had me pinned to the floor with his hand around my throat. Just remembering the feel of his hot palm wrapped around me, the control he had over me, sent desire flowing through my veins, settling between my thighs. The moment was hot, and it definitely didn't feel like he hated me.

"Juno?" Finley asked. "Everything okay?"

I nodded, clearing my throat of the emotions clogging it. "Yeah, fine," I rasped. "A wrong number, I guess."

Needing to know what the other incoming message said, I tipped the screen away from my chest just enough to see the alert. Tapping the text, I sat frozen in place, reading and rereading his words.

West: Want to make the night more interesting?

Palms sweaty, I dropped my hand to hold the phone beneath the table so no one could read my response.

Me: How do you know I'm bored?

West: Because we're watching you.

My heart leapt into my throat.

Me: We?

West: We.

Me: You mean you and...?

I almost choked on my tongue when a new text popped up, this time in a group chat with *him*.

West: Him.

*****Captain Asshole has left the group*****

West: Asshole. He's here too. He even brought binoculars.

Me: WHAT?

Me: That is so creepy.

West: But not me... right?

Me: Debatable.

West: I'll take it.

West: So back to my question.

West: Want to make the night more interesting? With me?

West: I'll make sure tonight ends the way you hoped.

West: Let's be honest, could you say the same about the guy beside you?

I peeked out of the corner of my eye at Stew, who was glaring at his empty plate.

Me: What do you propose?

West: Excuse yourself to the bathroom.

Me: Then what?

West: Come find out.

Me: Will he be there too?

I chewed on my lip, unsure how I wanted him to respond. On one hand, I'd love Langston's palm sealed around my throat again while West devoured my mouth. But then again, I'd have to actually deal with his asshole attitude, which would really kill the mood.

West: He's promised to be a good boy.

A soft snort escaped.

Me: I know that didn't happen.

"Juno," Finley said, making me jump. The phone landed on my lap as I jerked my attention up to her and Kale. "Are you feeling okay? You're looking all flushed."

"Yes," I rasped. "Is it hot in here?"

Kale's slow smirk told me he knew exactly what was going on. "Oh, I think she's just fine. Care to share those texts you're reading with the table?"

"No," I blurted too quickly, making him and Finley chuckle. I dared a look out of the corner of my eye at my date and blinked in shock at the empty chair. "Where did he go?"

"He didn't say. Just got up from the table and walked off." Finley shoved Kale's arm off her chair. "And you, how could you set up my friend with that guy?" She crossed her arms in frustration and shifted in her seat to face Kale.

He held up both hands in surrender. "It was kind of a last-minute request, Finley."

While they bickered back and forth, I turned my attention back to my phone to scan the missed texts.

> West: Perfect time to break away, sweet cheeks.

> West: I'll make it worth your while.

> Me: Where?

> West: That's my brave girl.

Brave or horny was up for debate. Though I couldn't deny that the idea of sneaking off with West, Langston somewhere in the shadows watching, and getting out of this situation all at once was too good to pass up.

West: Head down the hall toward the bathroom.

West: I'll find you.

I wet my lips and peeked over my shoulder toward the hall that led to the bathrooms. Heart racing, breathing shallow, I tucked the phone back into my purse and set the heavy bag on my lap.

"I need to go to the bathroom," I murmured, shooting Finley an apologetic smile. "Be right back."

"Juno."

Standing by the chair, I gripped the back, knuckles going white with the nervous and excited energy coursing through me and blinked at Kale.

"Be careful. I know I brought Stew." He ran a hand through his long, wavy hair. "I just want you to be safe, you know. I don't think he'd hurt you or anything, but I just wanted to warn you, I guess. I feel responsible."

I smiled at his concern. "I'll be okay, Kale. I'm not going after him or leaving. Just headed to the bathroom."

"It's just, with everything going on...," he said with a sigh. "And add in Jasper being murdered. We all need to stay on high alert everywhere around town, not just on the trail." He turned his attention to Finley. "What were you saying about hearing that guy Hudson is calling someone he knows in the FBI?"

While Finley dove into that bit of gossip, I eased back a step, then another, before turning on my wedged heels. The short hem of my sweater dress brushed against my thighs with every quick step, the heels clicking on the polished floor. Slowing my pace, I sucked in a fortifying breath and cast a last look back at Finley and Kale only to stumble in surprise.

What the hell is Dax doing in my seat?

Paused, I debated what to do. Continue my crazy, exciting adventure to find West, or be a good friend, return to the table, and make sure she was okay?

Except I didn't have to make the choice, because Finley made it for me. Standing so fast that her chair clattered to the floor behind her, she leaned over the table and dumped the full contents of her beer over Dax's head.

And then stormed off.

Kale sat frozen while Dax said something I couldn't hear despite the full restaurant going silent at the drama. Then he called Finley's name and hurried the way she'd disappeared. Knowing she had her car here—we'd ridden together to meet the guys—I pulled out my phone and shot her a quick text to let her know I was good and that she could leave without me.

How did I know that?

Because West and the asshole were here, and they wouldn't let anything happen to me. Langston was a jerk, but not cruel, never putting my safety at risk, and West wasn't the type of guy to do all this as a prank or joke. And if I was with those two, I would be safe— from everything, not just the person haunting Anchor Bay.

My phone buzzed in my purse again. I pulled it out and opened the message.

> West: Fin is okay. Dax overstepped tonight, but he'll make sure she gets home safe.

> West: Langston says Dax should've stuck to recon like him.

A soft snort escaped, and I tossed the phone back into my hobo bag. Hefting the heavy contents higher onto my shoulder, I moved down the hall, gaze flicking from side to side, searching for any sign of West.

With my pulse pounding in my ears, I worked to slow my shallow breathing with every step. I jumped, hand flying to my chest to keep my heart from leaping out of it, when the bathroom door swung open, casting bright fluorescent light into the dimly lit hall.

Hand in the middle of the heavy wooden door, Stew stood as still as a statue.

"Did you follow me?" he accused.

I stumbled back, the wall catching me before I fell on my ass. "What? No."

His thick brows furrowed. "Then what are you doing? Are you really that desperate for attention? First, you have to ask for someone to take you out, and now you follow me?"

My jaw fell open and my brain froze, unable to come up with a response to his cruel words and condescending tone. Tears gathered in my lower lids as humiliation simmered inside me.

A distortion of the light from movement down the hall had me peeking in that direction. Looking like an avenging villain, face and body cast in shadows from the light behind him, Langston stood with his muscular chest puffed out and his dark glare narrowed on Stew.

"Who the hell are you?" Stew questioned. "Wait, you're that big guy who was hanging out around my apartment earlier today. What the fuck do you want?"

"For you to watch your fucking tone when you're talking to a woman like Juno."

I could've pissed my pants at the anger in Langston's tone because of how Stew spoke to me. *Am I in some kind of dream or twilight zone?*

Stew hooked a thumb in my direction. "Her?"

Langston nodded. "Her."

Stew scoffed. "Whatever, man." Turning to me, he hitched his chin toward the dining room. "Be ready to order. I'm starving." With that, he shuffled down the hall, avoiding Langston, who refused to move from blocking most of the path, and headed back to the table.

"I'll make sure he doesn't come looking for her."

I cocked my head to the side, not understanding Langston's words until a soft touch stroked along my hand, jerking my attention to the man now standing beside me. West's shy smile had my shoulders dropping and the tension from seconds ago draining out of me.

Interlacing our fingers, he urged me to follow him deeper down the hall. Which I did willingly. He shot a mischievous look over his shoulder when we paused outside a closed door before guiding me into the dark storage room. Once we were both inside, he turned the lights on. The fluorescent bulbs overhead flickered before buzzing to life, highlighting racks of shelves and the boxes stacked along them.

The purse strap slid in my sweaty palms as I adjusted my grip, gaze bouncing around the small room to avoid looking at West.

What the hell was I doing? Sneaking off with West O'Donnell while I was on a date with another guy? This wasn't me. I wasn't adventurous—or that rude.

"West, I—"

A pair of soft, full lips pressed to mine, cutting off my next words and erasing all thoughts and reservations. He urged me back a step, then another until my spine pressed against a shelf beam, holding me up as I lost all sense of reality. Before I could deepen the kiss, he pulled back just enough that when he spoke, our lips barely brushed.

"You do not know how long I've wanted to do that," he rasped, dark eyes searching my face. "Please, Juno."

"Please what?" I whispered.

"Please let me kiss you." I sucked in a startled breath at the feel of him brushing a single finger along the inside of my bare thigh, inching the hem of my sweater dress higher with every stroke. "Let me touch you."

"West."

"Sweet cheeks."

The corner of my lips curved upward only to slip, remembering all the sweet things Eric had said to me in the beginning. It was too risky for me to hope for more than this moment with West, to think this passion and sweetness from him would be something that would last.

What terrified me the most about the man staring at me like I was the air he needed to survive was that I could easily look at him the same way.

"This is just for tonight." He blinked at me as if processing my words. "Tomorrow we go back to how things were, just friends."

"Why?" he questioned.

"That's just how it has to be. I can't be anything more than that, West."

His dark eyes bored into me as if trying to uncover all my secrets. "What if I say no?"

My heart sank. "Then I go back to my so-called date, and then tonight, when I go home, I take care of my needs alone."

The fire that flared in his gaze rekindled the one burning in my lower belly.

"And who would you think about while you took care of your own needs?" West leaned in close, gliding his lips along my throat before nipping at the delicate skin.

My purse thumped to the floor. Grabbing his neck, I held him close as he sucked and licked down to my collarbone. Desire leaked from my core, no doubt soaking my panties, making me cringe. Eric had told me on more than one occasion that it was gross how wet I got when turned on.

A sharp bite just beneath my ear snapped my attention back to West.

"Answer me, Juno. Who would you be thinking about while you played with yourself?"

I wouldn't lie to him. Couldn't even if I wanted to, with the need thrumming through my veins making my thoughts fuzzy.

"You," I breathed.

"What about my friend? Would you think of Langston too?"

A soft brush of air and a faint creak of hinges had my lashes fluttering open. Langston's green eyes were locked on me as he closed the door behind him and leaned back against the solid wood. My chest rose and fell in shallow, rapid breaths.

"Yes," I whispered, not looking away from Langston. "I'd think of him too."

"Good girl," West murmured in my ear. "I can't wait to feel you." The tip of his finger brushed along the edge of my lace panties before dipping beneath. His guttural groan vibrated along my skin as he stroked my soaked seam. "Fucking hell, you're drenched."

My spine went ramrod straight and I squirmed, trying to move away from his touch. "I'm sorry. I know it's gross and—"

"The fuck did you say?" Langston demanded.

West pulled his hand free, holding the single glistening

digit between our faces. Embarrassed, I turned away, cheeks heating.

"This is not gross," West rasped, gaze locked on his fingers. Slowly, I turned back to him, cautiously studying the two men for any sign of deception. "It's fucking sexy as hell. It makes me want to drop to my knees and lick it all from the source. I bet you taste as good as you smell."

"West, you don't have to—"

"Why don't you believe him?" Langston asked.

I rolled my lips inward to keep from blurting out the truth.

"Show her how much you like it, West."

"Yes, sir," he chuckled.

Before I could protest, he slid those fingers into his mouth and sealed his lips around them. Dark eyelashes fluttered as his lids closed and a deep, lust-filled moan rattled in his chest.

"I need more. Please, Juno."

All I could do was nod, too shocked and confused to do anything else.

Reaching his hand beneath my dress, he pushed my panties aside to drag three fingers through my soaked slit, gathering up more of my desire, then licked it from his fingers.

"Holy shit," I breathed.

Hand between my thighs once more, West leaned forward. "I'll show you how good you taste." Pressing our lips together, he pushed his tongue between my lips to stroke my own. A sweet flavor that was all me filled my mouth. My nails dug into the back of his neck as I sucked my desire off his tongue.

Our desperate kiss broke apart when he slid two fingers into my core. Gazes locked, he pulled them free only to thrust back in, grinding the heel of his hand against my swollen clit. Shifting to put my thigh between his, West ground his hard dick against me.

"West," I begged, dropping a hand to grip the top of his jeans. "Please."

Before he could respond, Langston did it for him.

"She doesn't get rewarded with your dick after calling her drenched pussy gross."

A pitiful whimper escaped me at the same time a desperate grunt came from West.

"But...." Langston pushed off the door and came to stand behind West. "How about I take care of my friend while he takes care of you with his thick fingers deep in your cunt?"

"What?" I said at the same time West said, "Yes."

"Your call, Juno," Langston said. I followed his hand as it slid down West's taut stomach and dipped inside his jeans. A sharp hiss whistled through West's teeth while Langston just smirked. "His other hand is out of commission, or he'd be doing this himself right now. I'm just being a good friend."

That was a lie.

He knew it.

I knew it.

West knew it.

The blasts of sexual tension thrumming off him, his hooded gaze as he watched West's hand moving beneath my dress, and how his own hand had gripped the front of his jeans were confirmation. But for tonight, I wouldn't call him out on it.

For tonight, we would all ignore the truth of us three.

Including me.

With bated breath, I followed Langston's fingers as they worked to pop the top button of West's low-slung jeans.

"I need an answer, Juno."

Peering up through my dark lashes, I found his eyes already locked on me. "Yes."

"Yes, what?" he demanded as the grind of the zipper teeth releasing filled the small storage room.

"Yes, sir."

"Good girl."

Holy fuck, there was no chance in hell I would ever be the same after this.

But ask me if I cared.

8

LANGSTON

I'd never been so close to coming in my pants as I was now, not that I would tell either of them that. West shifted back, pressing his ass to my crotch, and ground against me. My grip tightened around him in warning, making a depraved groan vibrate in his chest.

Juno watched as I worked his jeans over one hip and then the other, never releasing his cock. Her desire-filled gasp had me watching her parted lips; the way she licked the lower and then top made me want to grip my cock to ease the pressure.

"What are you waiting for, Westly? Your girl needs your fingers filling that needy pussy of hers."

Pumping my hand up and down in slow, tight strokes, I watched his hand dip beneath that damn dress that hugged her luscious curves. I knew the moment he touched her, even though I couldn't see it. Juno's lashes fluttered shut as her head fell backward, hitting the shelving keeping her upright.

"Tell me what she feels like," I whispered in West's ear as

I brushed a thumb over his head, swirling the cum leaking from the tip down his shaft.

"I don't know how I'll ever fit," he rasped. "She's so fucking tight, I can barely get two fingers in. And she's squeezing so damn hard too. Fuck, that will feel amazing."

"But not tonight." I pinched his head just enough to make him twitch, his knees giving out before he caught himself. "Tonight, it's just your fingers working her soaked cunt and you fucking my hand."

"Please," Juno whispered, peeling her lids open to level her glassy-eyed gaze at me.

"Please, what?" I pumped my hand faster, making West's hand move faster beneath her dress.

"I want to see."

I hummed a contented response. "You want to watch me jack off my best friend?"

"Fucking hell, do it, Lang. Fucking show her," West ground out, barely holding it together. This was more worked up than he'd ever been when we shared women before.

"Only because you said please," I said with a grin as I tugged his boxer briefs down with my free hand. I had to hold back from sliding beneath her skirt to add my fingers with West's in her pussy.

Juno whimpered as she watched my hand move up and down West's thick cock.

He trembled against me while she writhed from side to side, head rolling against the shelves. I knew they were both close, but I wasn't done with them yet. I had one more order to hand out to ensure this was a night neither of them would forget.

"Flick her swollen clit, Westly. Make her come so hard she needs those fingers in her pussy to keep her standing."

With a string of pleading and mumbled words, Juno came hard, her whole body shaking. Her whimpers were still echoing in the space when I lifted her dress high enough to expose her creamy white thighs and bit down where West's neck and shoulder met.

He came with a barked shout, his cum spurting right where I wanted it. It dripped down the insides of Juno's thighs; her ragged breaths matched his own as I carefully rubbed it into her skin.

No one said a word, both of them staring at me until I was done and licked what remained off my fingers.

"There," I said after popping my fingers free from between my lips. "You marked her; she's yours now."

Stepping back, I tried to hide my wince of pain. *Fuck, maybe West was right and I will die of blue balls.* Turning to the door, I paused with my hand on the knob to look over my shoulder.

"Don't you dare clean up, either of you." They both gaped at me, and I shrugged. "I'll go make sure that fucker is long gone and get us a table."

"A table?" they both repeated at the same time.

I hitched my chin at Juno. "She didn't have time to eat earlier, and neither did you," I said, sliding my gaze to West, who was attempting to pull up his jeans one-handed. "And I need a fucking drink."

Leaving the room, I waited outside the door, listening to see if they did as I'd instructed. And to my surprise, their combined laughter filtered through, making my lips quirk upward. Now to get them fed, me a drink, and then get home to take care of my own needs, because fuck, that was hot.

I just wished I trusted her enough to join in.

We would see how tomorrow went. Hopefully, the

mystery couple would shed some light on Juno's past and help me see her as someone I didn't have to suspect.

And if that happened, if I could trust her, then Juno Jones was fucking mine.

Well, ours.

All ours.

HEAVY WAVES SMACKED against the hull, attempting to shift the boat off course. The rough seas weren't uncommon but were annoying as hell. Looming gray clouds hung low in the sky, giving the early morning an ominous feel, which didn't help my mood one damn bit.

No matter how many times I jerked off in the shower to the erotic memories from last night, I still woke up pissed at the world, edgy and horny as hell. Even now, despite the soothing lapping of the waves and peaceful silence, their combined groans and moans that had echoed in the closet were like a damn song that I couldn't get out of my head no matter what I tried.

And I had tried everything, even turning on some old Taylor Swift music that Mattie had downloaded on my phone forever ago. It was catchy, sure, but even Taylor couldn't drown out the memory of their passion.

Downing a gulp of lukewarm coffee, I aimed the boat toward the docks outside Anchorage, where I was to pick up the mystery couple. Soon, I would have over an hour alone with this Eric and Stephanie, giving me ample time to crack the Juno mystery. Then maybe I could finally find relief—deep inside that soaked pussy that smelled so good last night in that small room, I almost dropped to my knees and forced my face between her thighs just for a taste.

Not yet though. But soon.

At least I fucking hoped so.

After last night, my restraint had worn paper thin, the need to make Juno mine making me desperate.

By the time I pulled the boat alongside the dock, I'd shaken off my foul mood and slipped into my normal skeptical-asshole persona. An overdressed man and woman stood on the weathered planks, clearly waiting for me. Like I'd done hundreds of times, I tossed the guy a rope, which he caught midair with a wide smile that instantly put me on alert, and killed the engine. While he secured the boat, I slid my phone free to check for any missed texts now that I was back in cell service range.

Mattie: I told you she was prickly. That's why I gave her to you. Even though Trace was disappointed.

Mattie: Nothing has happened with my #1 fan recently. I think he or she has given up.

Me: You'd tell me if I need to come to Vegas and help, right?

Mattie: I would, but I'm good. We're good.

Me: How is that asshole ex of yours? Has he signed the papers yet?

Mattie: No, the fucker. He keeps fighting over more time with Trace, which we all know he's only doing to make himself look like a good dad.

Mattie: Which anyone who actually knows the situation knows he wasn't.

> Me: If his team wouldn't miss their goalie, I'd take him on a boat ride he wouldn't come back from.

> Mattie: But they would, and the cops would subpoena these texts, and you'd go to jail. Forever. I can't have Trace's uncle in jail. Gotta run, going on the air in 10.

Swiping to a missed text from West, I tapped on the picture and choked on my spit. It was of him, in bed with the sheets tented by his massive, hard dick.

> West: Last night only made this fucking worse.

> West: You need to get on board with us three fast, asshole. That was so damn hot I'll be hard for the rest of my fucking life.

> Me: You have one good hand. Use it.

> West: Come home and make me.

"Excuse me." I slid my glare up to the asshole interrupting me. "Are you Langston Allen from Uplift?"

A somewhat confirming grunt escaped as I pocketed my cell phone. *Time to work and earn my pay.* I moved to the front of the boat and leapt off, rubber soles slamming onto the wooden planks.

"All this is yours?" I hooked my thumb toward the four bags waiting beside them in a neat little row. "For two days?"

"We overpacked just in case we decide to stay longer. I'm Eric Adler."

I eyed the man's extended hand before running an assessing eye over his pressed khaki shorts, wrinkle-free polo, and wide fake-as-shit smile. There was something behind the overly friendly mask he wore that I couldn't read, which only added to my suspicion.

Smile faltering, he slowly lowered his hand, realizing I wasn't the hand-shaking type. At least not with this asshole.

Grabbing their luggage—all matching, of course—I tossed it onto the boat with little care and gestured for them to climb on board. He cautiously stepped onto the bow before heading to the cabin, finding a spot along the row of seats protected from the elements by the surrounding glass. With a disgusted headshake, I turned to the woman attempting to board the boat without help, one wrong step from slipping into the freezing water.

"Here," I grumbled, jumping onto the bow and extending a calloused hand to help her board.

She offered a soft smile before sliding her much smaller hand into mine. A squeak of surprise sounded over the lapping waves as I hauled her off the dock and safely onto the boat. "Thank you. I'm sure he would've helped; he's just distracted."

I cast a dubious glance at the man who clearly didn't give two shits about anything other than the phone in his hand.

She shrugged. "Work is busy right now. You know how it goes."

Not waiting for an answer, she ducked into the cabin and sat beside Eric, who quickly tucked his phone away. Seemed suspicious as fuck if you asked me.

After untying the boat, I climbed into the cabin and cranked the engine, eager to get back to Anchor Bay. I debated how to talk to them, ask the questions about Juno I needed answers to, but came up blank. I wasn't the outgoing, friendly type, and actually starting a casual conversation was way outside my comfort zone.

Not far from Anchorage, my plotting was put on pause when the two behind me started talking, their voices barely carrying over the engine's whirling hum.

"I'm just not sure this is the best idea. You know she hates surprises," Stephanie said.

"You're overthinking this, babe. She loves surprises. Remember, I know her a little better than you." I tilted my head to the side at that remark, hoping to get a better angle to hear more clearly. "And I know it might be a shock for Juno, but she'll understand. We deserve to be happy, Steph."

"It's just the way things ended, how she found out about us and how hurt she was—"

My knuckles went white around the wheel. What the fuck were they talking about?

"Steph, we've talked about this. You know things between her and me weren't great, neither of us happy. I don't understand why we have to keep coming back to this. We're together, and happy, and I bet she's fine now. Can you let the past stay there and stop bringing it up? It's done."

"Okay, yeah. Sorry, you're right."

Anger thrummed through me at not only the asshole's words but the condescending tone he took with her. Those bits and pieces of their conversation consumed my thoughts the rest of the ride home, making me wonder what the hell they did to Juno.

And if it was as bad as I assumed... what would I do to them in return for hurting my girl?

9

WEST

I was an asshole.

Not as much as Langston, but nevertheless, what I just did, the text I sent, firmly set me in that category. Though technically it wasn't an outright lie, more of a fudging of the truth.

Could I get my clothes on without help? Yes, I could.

Did I want to do it alone when I knew all I had to do was shoot a desperate, pleading text to Juno, knowing she would come over? That would be a firm hell no. Not when I was eager to see her again. Last night, that small taste of her, not just what I licked off my fingers and her lips but the intimacy of that moment, lit a fire inside me I knew would never burn out. It had been there before, a small flickering flame in my gut when I saw her, but now it was an inferno eating me alive with the insistent need to be around her, see her, touch her.

All my thoughts and needs revolved around Juno now.

Grabbing a T-shirt out of the closet, I headed for the front door, knowing she would be by any second. Her response to my pitiful text came only a few minutes ago, and her place was only a couple down from ours. Tapping the screen, I scrolled to Langston's text, smirking at his response just like I did the first few times I read it.

He was so close to breaking. I could feel it. Last night pushed him even closer to the edge of joining me in the glorious free fall toward Juno. All he needed now was the last bit of confirmation that she wasn't a threat to his family here in Anchor Bay. How we would get that, fuck if I knew, but it needed to happen soon.

Staring at the short list of ongoing texts, my stomach flipped. What if Juno found it weird that I only had the family I'd made here at Uplift as friends? What if she couldn't accept the life I was forced to live to survive before I moved here?

Or found me damaged if I opened up about those horrible years of bouncing around foster homes that each ended up being worse than the previous? A violent shiver racked my whole body just thinking about those dark, lonely moments. But before those shame- and pain-filled memories could take root, taking me down a black hole that I wouldn't emerge from until Langston could pull me out, a knock on the front door jerked me out of my head.

Hand slightly shaking, I palmed the knob and pulled the heavy wood door open. My heart literally skipped a beat and my lungs stopped working at the sight of a sleepy Juno on my front porch. Fuck, what it would be like to have her look like that in my bed, all soft and rumpled, hair a little crazy, lids still heavy.

"You play dirty," she grumbled.

I started to respond that it wasn't dirty, that I really needed help, only to snap my lips shut. It wasn't my needy text she was referring to; it was how dressed—or undressed—I was, based on how her eyes were now wide open and scanning every inch of my bare chest, stalling at where my unfastened jeans rode precariously low on my hips.

"Fuck." Rubbing a hand down her face, she closed her eyes and inhaled deeply.

"I just need help from a friend." I emphasized the word, remembering what she'd said last night, that it was a one-time thing and after, we would go back to normal. I knew there wasn't a chance in hell for that to happen for me, though, and from the way she was eye-fucking me, it wouldn't be possible for her either.

When she stayed rooted on the porch, I gently wrapped my good hand around her firm bicep and guided her inside, then shut and locked the door. Even though it was my place and not Juno's, I didn't want to leave Finley interrupting us again to chance.

"Shut the front door," Juno exclaimed.

I eyed the closed door and then her. "It is."

Those aqua eyes rolled while a smile pulled at her lips. "It's an expression, a less aggressive way to say 'shut the fuck up.'"

Still utterly confused, I pushed the center of my black frames up and pulled both brows in tight. "But I wasn't saying anything—"

"Oh my goodness, you're adorable. I'm talking about that."

I followed where her blue-painted nail pointed. GG sat on the back of the couch, staring at Juno like it was love at first sight, her fluffy white tail twitching back and forth in utter excitement.

"Who in the heck is this beautiful kitty?" she gushed.

Before I could warn Juno that GG was actually a secret assassin—at least that was the way she acted around strangers—she marched over to the couch and scooped the cat into her arms.

And yet the meanest, surliest pussy ever born didn't attack or look two seconds from reaching down Juno's throat and tearing out her heart. No, GG actually sighed and relaxed in Juno's arms. I couldn't help but gape at the sight as Juno whispered in baby talk while rocking GG back and forth around the room.

When Juno's excitement-filled eyes met mine, she froze. "What?" Clearly, my astonishment and fear that GG was waiting for the perfect moment to strike were written all over my face. "I won't hurt her if that's what you're worried about. Oh, and I'm not allergic. Genetic lottery if you ask me."

"It's more the other way around." Now that the shock had worn off, I was slightly pissed at the attention-seeking cat. She'd stolen Juno's focus from me.

Asshole, just like her owner.

She carefully set GG down onto Langston's chair, which the cat protested, swiping at Juno's hand to pick her back up. With one more soft swipe behind the ears, Juno turned her attention back to me. If I were a lesser man, I would've stuck my tongue out at GG in a taunt, but I wasn't about to stoop to that level with a fucking cat.

Instead, I flipped her off. Which I swear she returned with a sassy meow, flicking her tail aggressively as she pranced away.

"Sorry. If you can't tell, I'm more of a cat person than a dog person, and I couldn't resist. How did I not know you owned a cat?"

I shrugged and tossed the T-shirt over my shoulder. "Doesn't really come up in meetings, I guess, and this is the first time you've been here. Thanks for coming over to help,

by the way. Lang is on a run to Anchorage to pick up—"
Remembering Brandon said to keep our mouths shut, I cut
myself off with a cough. "I just need some help with all
this."

I pointed to my bare chest and unfastened jeans. Which
was where her gaze stayed while chewing on the corner of
her lower lip.

"West... I...." Groaning, she turned, gaze searching until
it landed on something in the kitchen. "I need coffee for
this." She gestured over her shoulder at me.

"Did you just wave at all of me?" I chuckled, following
her. "If you're going for the coffee, I think it's still hot.
Langston always makes enough for me when he has to leave
early."

Rather than asking for a mug, Juno started opening one
cabinet after another until she found them. Inspecting each,
she carefully chose the one I knew was Langston's favorite
and filled it to the brim with steaming dark liquid.

"Did I wake you up?" I reached around her, snagging a
mug and setting it beside hers.

She nodded while filling mine.

"It is ten on a Saturday, and we got in late." Biting back a
smile, she tried to hide it behind the cat-shaped mug. "I had
fun last night, and not just what happened in the closet."

Her mentioning it had flickers of those few minutes
flashing in my mind, making my cock twitch. Considering
my pants still weren't secured, that would be a problem fast.
Clearing my throat, I took a sip of coffee, burning my tongue
but welcoming the distraction.

"It was nice actually being out, having dinner somewhere other than Dave's. Did you know that was my first
time there? That restaurant?"

Leaning a hip against the counter, I shook my head.

"What have you been doing since you got here other than work and working out with Oliver?"

"Book club." Her smile grew. "Hanging out with the Uplift girls. I've babysat for Hudson and Calista once or twice while they went out. And I've played a lot of video games. *A lot.*"

The way she said it made it sound like she didn't know how to feel about that.

"But you like doing that, the online gaming stuff, so why does it sound like you're ashamed or embarrassed by how much you play?"

"Because... I don't know. It's a waste of time?" she said. I arched a brow. "At least that's what others think."

"Others?" My mug thumped on the counter when I set it down with more force than necessary.

But instead of giving me a direct answer, she just waved me off and avoided my questioning gaze. "And I feel guilty. I'm in this beautiful place with people who go outdoors to do fun things for a living, and all I do is stay inside and play video games. And eat snacks. Can't forget the snacks."

"What kind of gamer would you be if you did?"

A timid smile pulled at her lips. "Exactly. But I just get lost in the online world. Sometimes it feels easier than reality."

I took a sip of coffee, the steam fogging the lenses of my glasses. I couldn't see her, but her soft giggle filled the small kitchen. Taking them off, I used the soft cotton T-shirt to clean off the lenses.

"I guess I can relate. It's why I love motors and fixing broken things as much as I do. I get lost in the problem, trying different tricks until something works. I can lose hours while problem-solving an issue, but it keeps my mind off other things."

Juno nodded and tucked a piece of light brown hair behind her ears.

I reached out and tugged at a loose strand. "I love the new hair color, but why?"

"Needed a change, I guess. While I enjoyed being blonde, it was never my first choice." She peeked up through her long dark lashes, which only made her unique eye color pop even more. "You know what would be?"

I angled my head to the side, contemplating my answer. "Blue?"

Her tiny nose scrunched up. "Pink. Rose gold, more specifically. It fades so beautifully." Her wistful sigh made my heart clench. "But that would require a lot of work and constant maintenance for the color."

I twirled the loose curly strand around my finger while keeping my gaze locked on hers. "I like this color, and I liked the last one, and I know I'd feel the same about the pink. Everything looks good on you, sweet cheeks."

Her lips parted with a quick inhale. "Except right now, right?" she whispered. "I mean, I rolled out of bed after a shit night's sleep, weighing the pros and cons of being more than friends with you, and—"

Unable to take another second of being so close to her lips and not feeling them against mine, I sealed them together. Her soft moan had her lips parting, opening up enough for me to tease my tongue against the tip of hers. Heat flooded my veins while my cock instantly stiffened. Her hand wrapped around the back of my neck, urging me closer.

Mine slid down her spine, over her perfect ass to palm one firm cheek.

Pulling back, Juno sucked down several deep breaths. "Fuck, you're good at that."

"So are you," I murmured, leaning in close to brush my lips against hers again, unable to resist. "I don't know if I've ever been this turned on from a kiss before."

Her eyes slid down my chest and widened at my very obvious stiff cock desperate to escape my boxer briefs.

"West." Her hand trembled as she reached between us to brush the tips of her fingers along my taut abs. "I wish we could be more than friends. You don't know how bad I want that." When she looked up, tears filled her lower lids, making my stomach drop. "But I'm too broken for someone like you."

"What are you talking about, Juno?" I stepped back, needing the distance to focus on her words and figure out what the fuck was going on.

Grabbing the edge of the counter, she lifted herself up and sat beside her nearly steaming mug. With her head drooped forward, her hair hung like a curtain, keeping me from seeing her face.

The tension radiating off her pulled me closer. Knuckle under her chin, I tilted her face until her sad eyes met mine.

"Talk to me," I murmured, scanning features that were filled with joy just seconds ago, now replaced with hesitation and fear. "What do you mean, for someone like me?"

"It means I'm broken, West. In all the ways that matter in a relationship, a good relationship. I'm broken here and here." She tapped the side of her head and then over her heart. "You don't deserve someone who has scars this deep, ones that will never, ever heal." A single tear slipped down her round cheek. "I want you. I want to be more than friends with you, but I know it won't work, and I can't risk losing what we do have."

"Juno, I'm not following. Risk losing what?"

"That I'll lose you as a friend when it doesn't work out or risk the chance that you'll re-break the little parts of me I've spent the last several months trying to piece back together." More tears leaked from the corners of her eyes, dripping down her chin. "I can't go through that again, West. I barely survived it once; a second time would destroy me forever."

I'd never hated my bandaged hand more than I did in that exact moment, desperate to hold her damp cheeks between both palms. Cradling one, I brushed a thumb over her soft skin, wiping away the tears.

"You're scared." She nodded, teeth sunk into her lower lip to keep it from quivering. "Of me?" I asked softly.

"Of what you could do to me, and the chance that even with someone like you, someone amazing, sexy, funny—"

"Hell of a kisser," I added with a wink.

"—that I'm too broken to be worth anything to anyone." Her voice cracked, making my heart do the same. But at the same time, vengeful rage spiked my pulse, knowing someone made the amazing woman in front of me question her worth.

"You keep using that word. What makes you think you're broken, sweet cheeks? Who lied to you enough times that you actually believed it?"

"It's not a lie. After...." She squeezed her eyelids shut. "After him, what he did, it broke me on the inside even more than I already was. Now, bonus, I don't trust anyone on top of my other issues." She sniffed and wiped at her nose. Grabbing the roll of paper towels, I ripped one off and placed it in her trembling hand. "I lost so much of myself for years, not realizing I was becoming someone I didn't recognize, and then when he betrayed me in the worst way possible, I broke. I don't even know where the parts of myself, my true self, are anymore. I'm trying to find them little by little, but I might never be whole, West."

"Why do you feel you have to do that alone, Juno?" Her eyes fluttered open, and a faint line formed between her brows. "Why do you feel you have to do all the healing by yourself, with no support?"

"Because...." She leaned forward, pressing her forehead to mine. "I don't know how to trust you, or anyone, really. I did that before, put complete blind faith in someone who promised me the world, and then one day they decided that promise didn't matter to them anymore, only what made them happy. And all those years of conforming and molding and trying and giving suddenly meant nothing. There is no undoing or healing that deep a scar, West. It's just there, a permanent fixture on my soul reminding me that everyone leaves, no matter what they tell you."

"Doing that kind of healing alone, with no one to talk to or be there with you in the silence so it doesn't feel so dark and soul-absorbing, I agree." Pulling back, I grabbed her hand and interlaced our fingers. Seeing her smaller hand, the blue nails resting on my scarred knuckles, had a soft smile forming. "I agree because I know what feeling like you can't trust anyone again is like, that you'll never be truly happy again. And then I came here, met Langston—" I huffed a laugh when she rolled her eyes. "He's a really great friend and man, Juno. I know you two butt heads, but his hypervigilance about protecting everyone in his life comes from something that happened when he was a kid."

"Oh, I...." She bit her lower lip. "I don't know how to respond to that."

"When I came here, I was alive but not living. Do you understand what I mean?" She nodded. "And then I opened up to Langston, the other guys, and even to Amy. They've helped me realize I didn't have to fight my past and demons alone, and that with their help, I could move past what happened. Those scars are still there, and the memories sometimes dig their claws in, refusing to let go, but it's a process, a long process that I'm glad I don't have to walk alone."

"I'm not sure I'm there yet," she admitted. "And I don't know when I will be."

"That's okay. I'm guessing it hasn't been that long since… it happened?"

I couldn't even say the words out loud. The idea of someone hurting my Juno on purpose, knowing the pain their actions would cause her, made me so fucking angry I knew I wouldn't be able to keep that out of my tone. And while I wasn't sure what happened in that relationship she was referring to, I assumed expressing my anger right now wasn't smart.

"Almost a year ago," she whispered, looking down at the floor. "I wanted to make it work so bad. I loved him." When she looked back up, fresh tears had fallen. "But when I realized he didn't have any intention of putting in the same effort, that I wanted us more than he did, I left. I started looking for a job away from my hometown the next day and found the Uplift posting."

"So brave," I whispered, stroking a knuckle down her cheek. "So fucking brave and strong." She rolled her eyes and huffed. "You don't see it yet, sweet cheeks, but you are, and I have every intention of making sure you see it in yourself too."

And I would.

No matter if she wanted to stay just friends or more, I would be there for her.

Everyone deserved someone they could rely on while

they healed and found their way through the darkest parts
of their lives.

Or I guess, in this case, two someones.

10

JUNO

I was a fucking mess.

And the worst part was, I wasn't even a *hot* mess. Maybe that made me a tragic train wreck everyone watched, knowing what would happen but couldn't turn away from. That had to be why West still stood in front of me after I gave him a small peek at the damaged parts of me I was desperately attempting to heal from. There was no way he would stick around for any reason other than sheer macabre fascination.

Right?

Last night with him and Langston was one of the best nights I'd had since arriving in the tiny town. Which shocked the hell out of me, making me wonder if it was all just a dream. Of course, what happened in the supply closet was fantastic, but what came after was just as great. The three of us ate delicious food and had a few drinks. The easy conversations and cheek-hurting laughter, mixed with heated looks, made the night one I would never forget. After they had walked me to my door, staying rooted on the porch until I firmly secured the handle lock and deadbolt—and even then, I swore the handle twisted as if one of them had tested it to make sure I actually did—I literally fell into bed but couldn't sleep despite the exhaustion and late hour.

I'd lain there for hours, mind racing, contemplating the pros and cons of putting my heart back out there with West. There were so many caveats to consider, such as his best friend, who treated me like the enemy he didn't trust as far as he could throw me, and potentially ruining my friendship with West. But the chemistry between the two of us—and Langston too, even if I didn't want to admit it—was seventh-level-of-hell hot.

Of course, then my messed-up brain cut through the lust fog, bringing me back to the reality that it was just me feeling the connection and chemistry, that for them, it was normal, average, mundane. That was the real reason Langston stepped in. It had nothing to do with West's injured hand and everything to do with me not being sexy enough or expressive enough to turn him on. That rang more true than actually believing they thought last night was as hot as I did.

"Juno." I jumped at the volume of West's voice, almost shouting in my face. "What the fuck was that?" he demanded.

I shrank back against the cabinets, wishing like hell I could disappear into them.

With a frustrated groan, West ripped the glasses off his face and rubbed his eye with the heel of his hand. "I'm sorry. I didn't mean to startle you like that, but you were just..." His dark eyes bored into me as if trying to read my thoughts. "Blank, stuck in your head, I guess, and I didn't know how to pull you back to me."

"No, I'm the one who's sorry," I apologized quickly. "I didn't mean to zone out like some weirdo while we were talking. Sometimes I do that when I'm overthinking something, and I know it's rude. I'm sorry—"

"Fucking hell," West grunted under his breath while situating the thick frames back on his too-handsome face. "I swear, if I find the asshole who messed with your head this much, I'll...." He considered me for a second before smirking. "Tell Langston everything, and he'll make sure they disappear."

A soft, disbelieving huff brushed past my lips. "Right," I scoffed. "He wouldn't care."

West's full lips pressed together as he looked to the ceiling. "I swear, you two are equally blind and stubborn. But back to you zoning out. You don't need to apologize for getting lost in your thoughts, sweet cheeks, but I would be honored if you would share those deep thoughts with me so you don't have to figure out whatever it is alone."

My lips curled in a stiff smile as I gave a dismissive wave. "You wouldn't want to hear all that. It's just me being me."

Desperate to avoid his determination to unravel me further, I shifted along the counter to hop down, but West stepped between my spread thighs, sealing his body against the concrete top, pinning me in place.

"And that's bad?" My lips parted, the word *yes* ready to slip off my tongue, but I snapped them shut at his disapproving expression. "Let me set something straight right now so you never have to question when we're together. I always want to hear what you're thinking, Juno. Always. I wouldn't ask if I didn't."

"Okay." That was all I could say, knowing there was no way I would ever feel comfortable verbalizing my circling thoughts. No man actually wanted to hear what was bothering a woman. Men only listened with fake interest and connection to lead to the real reason they pretended to care, which, in my experience, was always something sexual.

They listened during date night? Oh, then they should be rewarded with sex.

They stopped by the grocery store to pick up something he wanted? He should totally be rewarded with a blow job.

They planned a weekend getaway, so they should totally be rewarded every hour of that trip with sex, and if they weren't, then they could pout and complain about how mistreated they were.

"You're killing me, Juno." It was the desperation in West's voice that pulled me out of my head. "Please open up to me."

"I need to go," I whispered. "Please let me down."

With a sorrow-filled expression, he stepped back enough for me to hop down and squeeze past him. With the needed cold distance between us, the earlier desire fog that had muddled my thoughts lifted. Inhaling deeply through my nose, I turned to him with a stiff smile.

"Okay, so back to why I'm here so early. You needed help to get dressed, so let's do that."

Clearly frustrated with the steel wall I'd erected between us, West ripped the super-soft cotton shirt off his shoulder and held it out for me to take. Rolling the shirt just so, I situated the head hole over his short hair and carefully slipped it down, making sure it didn't snag his glasses.

"You're too good at that."

"Well, I have been dressing myself for a while," I remarked.

"I meant deflecting, shutting down what you're thinking

or feeling, and shifting the conversation away to something safe."

Humming a noncommittal response, I helped him thread the shirt sleeve over his injured hand, followed by the other.

"Thank you. Way easier with help." A small smile tugged at the corners of his lips, popping both adorable dimples on his scruff-covered cheeks.

"Those dimples should come with a warning label," I grumbled as I situated the shirt so it wasn't twisted and awkward. My fingers itched to brush against his rippled abs, to dip beneath the thick band of his boxer briefs.

"Ah, yes, I've been told that a time or two."

I huffed out a laugh and rolled my eyes at his cocky tone. "I'm sure you have." The back of my knuckles skimmed along his skin as I fumbled with fastening his jeans' button. Peering up through my lashes, I found him gazing down at my hands with a heated look. "Can you do the zipper?"

Fuck, did I want him to say yes or no?

Those dark eyes met mine. "I mean, I can, but..." He lifted his injured hand. "I really shouldn't." And as if he wasn't playing dirty enough with bringing attention to his injury, he stuck his lower lip out in a dramatic pout.

"I hate you."

Lies. All lies.

"No, you don't. You just don't like how you're feeling."

"And how is that?" My fingers trembled as I secured the denim in one hand and pinched the zipper with the other, careful not to brush against the very large and obvious bulge.

"Vulnerable, exposed."

"Whatever," I whispered and backed up a step, then

another and another until I was as far from him as possible without racing out the door.

Back sealed to the far wall, I stood frozen in place as he stalked forward, following me every step for step until he paused inches from me. Pitching forward, he pressed his forearms on either side of my head. Steeling myself, I slowly tilted my head back to meet his gaze.

"You can be both with me, Juno. I'm not afraid of what's in here." The tip of his finger tapped my temple. "Or here." That same finger traced down the length of my neck and oh so softly pressed to my sternum, right over my hammering heart. "And I'm willing to wait for you to understand that I'm telling you the truth. I'm not going anywhere just because you seem to think you're not worth fighting for."

Warm tears flooded my lower lids and my nose burned as I fought the urge to break down, finally give in to the exhaustion that was my daily life. "Why?" The word was more of a rasped breath that I somehow got out around the emotions clogging my throat. "Why would you? You're really not understanding this, West, how leavable I am. I'm not fun or outgoing; I'd prefer to stay in most nights reading or playing video games than going out with friends. And of course, because I'm not lame enough, I don't like the physical side of relationships. Sex is a chore, a payment that's exchanged for a good mood or a job well done on something. Which is probably why I'm bad at it and—"

He gently sealed his palm over my lips to make me stop. Dark brown eyes bored into mine. "We're going to circle back to all that false bullshit in just a second, but first, let's clear up the answer to your why. I will fight for you, every piece of you you're willing to give me, because you're an amazing woman who deserves to be fought for, Juno. I don't know who made you believe differently, but you deserve someone who will actively listen, work to understand what you're going through, and work every damn day to be there for you. Not because of what I'll get out of it, but because I want to, because I care about you."

A few rogue curls brushed against my cheeks with my disagreeing headshake. "You don't know me, and once you do, you'll quickly realize I'm not worth that kind of effort. I'm not," I begged, wanting him to believe me now before I got my hopes up that he was actually different. "I swear to you, I'm not."

That was the ugly truth that tainted me from the inside, souring anything good in my life. I had nothing to offer a partner that would make the energy and effort to break past my walls worth it.

Because deep down, I'd always known I wasn't worth keeping.

"But what if you are?" he whispered, leaning in until our noses almost brushed. "What if what I see in you, this amazing woman who I am desperate to know inside and out, the good and the bad, is actually the truth, and everything else is only the lies someone made you believe?"

"Maybe, but I know me, West. Better than you do. And what if you don't like the actual truth? What if you realize everything I've said is true?"

His long eyelashes fluttered closed as he sealed his forehead to mine. "You know little about my past, and I'm terrified that you'll discard me when you finally find out. It's not pretty, Juno."

I inhaled, lips parted to deny that I would be the one to walk away, but my stomach growled, sounding like a hungry bear was in the cabin. I grimaced, cheeks warming as an embarrassed flush spread across my face.

With both brows nearly at his hairline, West slid his gaze

to my abdomen before peeking back up with a smirk. "How about we put this super-deep conversation on hold until I feed you as a thank-you for helping dress me. We have nothing here, so how does heading out to Sips sound?" At the mention of the little coffee shop in town that had the best fresh-baked pastries, my stomach spoke up again. West's cheeks bunched with a wide smile. "I'm taking that as a yes. And thanks to you, I'm ready to go."

I gaped down at the off-the-shoulder T-shirt and loose sweats tucked into my old Uggs that I threw on before leaving the house. Oh, and I couldn't forget about the bare face and unruly hair tied back in a crazy bun.

"Sure, that sounds great, but I need to change first. I can't go out looking like this."

West shrugged like he actually didn't care that I looked hobo-ish. "That works, but only if you really want to. I think you look great without changing, though. Adorable, actually." Popping a quick kiss to the end of my nose, he stepped back, giving me some space. "But if we head there now, we'll get there before all the good pastries are gone. You know the best ones sell out fast."

Teeth gnawing on my lower lip, I debated between looking put together and mouthwatering pastries. I didn't actually mind going out dressed as I was. Sure, it was slouchy, but I was comfortable, and everything matched, with no holes in inappropriate places. Was that really so bad?

Old Juno would've said yes. I needed to hurry home to shower, change, and fix my face just to grab a chocolate croissant and coffee in town. I would put on flattering jeans, cute boots, fix my hair and face enough to look nice but not overdone. Just the way he liked me to present myself out in public.

How *he* liked me to look in public.

Thankfully, new Juno said, *Fuck that.*

"Actually, if you're good with being seen with me like this—"

"I'm happy as fuck to be spending time with you, Juno, no matter what you're wearing."

"Oh." I paused, studying him with narrowed eyes, looking for any deception. "Really?"

"Really, really. Now, are we walking or walking?" I couldn't help the way my smile grew at his shy grin. "I'm not comfortable taking you on the bike with only one good hand, and Langston took his 4Runner to the docks."

I lifted one hand and then the other, like I was weighing my options. "I think walking sounds great. It's a little cloudy out but still nice, so yes, that sounds perfect."

His shy grin grew into a genuine smile so wide his joy practically radiated off him.

Me.

I made him that happy simply by agreeing to walk to breakfast with the incredible man.

Was that normal? Or was it part of this newish thing between us and would soon fade? That seemed more likely. Which scared the shit out of me, because that meant every relationship was doomed, the spark not sustainable, and in the end, it left you more hollow and lost than you started. But there was only one way to find out, and I needed to figure out if I wanted to take that risk.

West was right. I was scared. Terrified, really, of opening up to another person and them leaving again like I never mattered. Then there was also the chance that I wouldn't be able to trust anyone like that again no matter how hard I tried. At least not without a little shove from the universe, forcing me to open up and let new people in.

Like that would happen.

"Again," West begged. "Show me again the look on Langston's face when you took him down in the locker room." With both elbows pressed on the table, he leaned in with an expectant expression.

With a dramatic eye roll at his persistence, I reenacted Langston's shocked expression for the third time since we sat down at the two-person table on the walkway outside Sips's large glass window.

Like the previous time, West barked out a loud laugh. "Damn, I wish I could've seen it firsthand. That bastard is hard to surprise."

"Probably because he knows everything, or am I the only one he follows?"

He stilled at that revelation, the coffee mug hovering halfway between the metal table and his lips.

I shrugged and popped another bite of buttery croissant into my mouth. "Yes, I'm aware he's sometimes there watching what I do and where I go. I just can't figure out why."

His mug landed on the table with a soft clink. "Why haven't you called him out on it?"

I slid the paper napkin between my fingers as I focused on folding it instead of looking at West. "I don't know." Lie. "It's annoying." More lies. "But I'd rather ignore him and hope he stops than confront him." Oh, so many lies.

I felt his focused stare as he studied me as if he could see straight through the false words. "Do you have any theories about *why* Langston is obsessed with stalking you?"

It was my turn to freeze. I blinked in disbelief and utter

confusion at the man now smirking at me like he was in on some secret. "Um, I did not use the words *obsessed* and *stalking*. What the hell are you talking about?"

"You clearly haven't noticed *all* the times he has," West grumbled into the almost-empty mug.

"That's... disturbing." Yeah, that was the right word, which explained the swarm of butterflies fluttering in my gut and the thrum of excitement that heated me from the inside out. "He's such a weirdo. But for a theory, maybe it's that he doesn't want me here and is trying to find a reason for Brandon to fire me?"

West fixed his gaze on the chocolate muffin he'd barely touched. "I could see why you would think that, but no. Langston...." He blew out a breath and looked up at the cloudy sky. "Lang has some major trust issues that stem from a bunch of shit in his childhood, but one instance in particular. So when someone new comes into his life, he likes to make sure they're safe, not a threat to his family. Which is exactly what he considers all of us at Uplift. He hasn't been able to get a read on you, and that scares him, hence the stalking to figure you out."

I slow-blinked as I processed that information. "Langston, the big-ass man who could squash me with one arm, is scared. Of me."

West's expression softened. "Of what you might do to his family if he's not careful, yeah. I think we've all learned through life that there are a lot more ways to harm someone than physically, so his strength or yours doesn't really come into play."

"No truer statement has ever been said," I muttered. Slouching back against the chair, I twirled the empty mug along the tabletop. "Obsessive stalking, huh?" I shot West a smirk at his own smile and nod.

"I would take it as a compliment. You're the only one he's gone to this length to understand."

It made me feel special, though I wasn't sure what that said about my mental state. Maybe our book club's recent selections were a little too dark and had me thinking the idea of being stalked and maybe kidnapped was sexy rather than terrifying.

"I get it. I hate surprises, like really, really hate them. So I guess along those lines, I get where he's coming from, not knowing my background—what?" My heart dropped to my stomach at his panicked expression. "West, you're scaring me. What's wrong? You look like you're about to throw up."

Head on a swivel, I searched up and down the street for whatever had freaked him out to the point that all the color had drained from his face. Not finding a monster or knife-wielding crazy person, only a man and a woman walking past the row of shops in the distance, I turned back to West. Unable to stop myself, I looked back over my shoulder at the two meandering our way, squinting to see if I recognized them, but I couldn't make out their features. At that familiar feeling tingling in the back of my brain, my stomach tightened, twisting with nerves, forcing bile to creep up my throat, but for the life of me, I didn't understand why.

"Juno." I twisted back to West, brows raised at the shake in his voice. "I have to tell you something."

A fresh rush of nerves flooded through me, spiking my pulse so fast that I gasped down air as if I'd just worked out.

"West, what's going on?" My voice trembled with the building fear. Something was wrong. Very wrong.

He reached across the table and grasped my hand, squeezing it hard. "Believe me, Brandon said we couldn't say anything. It was what the client wanted." He swallowed hard, his throat bobbing. "Langston should be here any minute with them, but I feel like I need to warn you—"

Each sharp breath felt like shards of glass lining my throat. "Who is 'them'?" I somehow got out.

He ran his good hand over his shaved head and offered me a pleading look. "Two people—a couple, maybe. I don't know all the details. They're coming here, to Anchor Bay, to surprise you. But you just made it very clear that you hate surprises, so I think—"

My stomach revolted, swirling the coffee and croissant as my fear and dread mounted. I pressed my palm against it, hoping that would keep its contents down, as I stared at West with a pleading expression. "Who?" I breathed.

West shifted in his seat, his own rising panic making the movement jerky. "Fuck, I can't remember their names. I just... fuck. Okay, one was Edward or Easton or—"

"Eric." I dropped my unseeing gaze to the empty plate. Damnit, what was he planning to—

Realization that he'd said a man *and* a woman knocked the air from my lungs like a punch to the gut. I twisted in my seat, frantically searching for the people I'd seen earlier. There they were, close enough now to see exactly who'd decided to surprise me like the assholes they were.

"And Stephanie."

Without waiting for a response, knowing I was right and needed to get far, far away from them, from him—hell, from everything—to fucking think, I shoved out of the metal chair, careful not to make a scene and draw their attention. Then I bolted. Heart hammering, I walked as fast as I could without running, heading down the wooden walkway that lined each side of the storefronts before dipping into the first alley I came to. Stumbling forward, I caught myself on a dumpster. Knees wobbling, I used it as support, making my way to the other side to block the view from the street. The moist mold that grew along the older brick building cooled my heated back when I fell back against it and squeezed my lids shut.

This could not be happening. Not here. Not when things were separate, my old life totally behind me where it couldn't contaminate this new hopeful one.

Thoughts spiraling, I jumped when a gentle hand gripped my shoulder, but I still kept my eyes closed, not ready to accept the last few minutes as reality. Maybe if I hid here for a little while, then I'd wake up and this would all be a nightmare.

"Juno," West pleaded. "We didn't know. Fuck, believe me, we didn't know you'd react like this. I don't even really know what's going on, just that...." When he trailed off, I peeked a single lid open to see what stopped him. "It's him, isn't it?"

"Who?" I asked, opening both eyes to search his face. There was no way he just put two and two together that fast. Fucking hell, why did I open my big mouth earlier? Why did I give him a peek into my past instead of keeping it shoved down deep where it belonged, where I had kept it hidden from everyone here?

I blamed his fucking dimples.

"Everything you told me earlier, the reason you're afraid to open up, of being vulnerable. It's because of that fucker who's here to surprise you." I only blinked, face blank, not giving him anything. His brown eyes narrowed as if he saw right through me. "That's the bastard who hurt you, who lied to you." West stood tall and shifted to stare down the alley. "Who made you think you weren't worth anyone's effort."

I gripped his arm when he started toward the road.

"West, don't. Please," I begged. "I need to get out of here now. I can't see them like this."

His lips pressed into a tight line, he slid his gaze back to the open alley as he debated ignoring my plea and going to find Eric.

"Please," I whispered, finally allowing the tears that had built up to fall. "I can't let them see me like this. I want to go home. Take me home, please."

11

LANGSTON

My gut told me something wasn't right with them. It was their reasons for coming to Anchor Bay that had the suspicious feeling strengthening through the quick trip from Anchorage to home. It didn't seem as if they wanted to harm anyone, yet the heavy weight of shame and guilt had ballooned in my chest, making it hard to breathe.

Why?

Hell if I knew.

I had a feeling the elephant sitting on my chest had to do with how the woman they were here to surprise would take them showing up unannounced. The word *surprise* had a positive spin to it; what they were doing seemed more like a sneak attack, but I still hadn't found out why. Neither seemed the type to plan all this to attack Juno, but that wasn't the only way to hurt someone.

Maybe that was just guilt hanging around my neck like a noose. I prided myself on protecting my family and friends, and somehow Juno too, yet I allowed the two people who were obviously conspiring about something to walk off the boat with no interrogation about what that surprise encompassed.

Surprise her with an apology? Not likely, based on that douchebag Eric.

Surprise her with a knife in the back? Not their type.

Surprise her with news that wouldn't feel like good news to Juno? That felt closer to the truth.

I ripped off my ball cap and slapped it on my thigh, cursing myself. I'd fucked up big-time. I'd allowed my frustrations with Juno to cloud the black-and-white guidelines I kept to, in order to keep those around me safe. Hopefully, it wasn't as bad as the massive weight crushing my chest, slowly suffocating me, made it seem.

But why did it feel like I'd betrayed her just by being their water taxi?

The coarse rope slid across my calloused palms as I secured the multifunctional boat Uplift purchased for ferrying clients between here and Anchorage, plus other water activities that I guided. Both knees popped as I stood, dusting off my hands on my thighs before waving back at the captain as he pulled out into the bay. The docks were quiet at this time of day, most of the boats out fishing or out with clients. Uplift Adventure and Rescue wasn't the only adventure company in Anchor Bay, but we were the biggest —and the best, if you asked the locals.

Brandon, Carl, and Amy handpicked everyone who worked for them, which was why the small community had grown from a place to work to a family. A genuine family. One that had one another's backs and wanted the best for everyone. Sure, I had Mattie back in Vegas—she was my only living blood relative I had left—but the men and women at Uplift were just as much family as she was.

The water-swollen wooden planks groaned beneath my

weight as I marched down the narrow walkway, the icy waves splashing beneath me and slapping against the poles, making light showers of spray sprinkle across my jeans. Nostrils flaring, I inhaled the comforting aroma of salt water and diesel fuel, holding it until my lungs burned, hoping that would chase away the pressure in my chest.

"I didn't know," I grumbled to myself as I exited the dock, slamming the wire gate behind me with more force than necessary. "It was a job. Brandon said we couldn't tell her." Hand shoved into the front pocket of my jeans, I wrapped my fingers around the 4Runner keys, tightening until the metal bit into my skin. "Going against a direct order goes against everything the Army taught me."

Reaching for the door handle of the late-model SUV, I paused to pull the ringing phone out of my pocket. A sigh of frustration blew past my lips at yet another delay. The insistent need to see Juno and make sure she was safe—from a distance, of course—rode me hard, making me almost twitchy.

I frowned at West's name flashing on the screen. With a finger on the green circle, I answered the incoming call and tucked the phone between my ear and shoulder as I pulled the driver's side door open. "I just got back, headed home now—"

"We have a problem."

It was the tremble in his voice, the fear and worry leaking through his words, that had me freezing halfway inside the SUV.

"Who?" I asked as panic surged. Once again, I wasn't there, and someone got hurt. That was the only explanation for why West sounded like he was about to shit his pants.

"Juno."

I would've thought hearing her name, not one of the

other members of Uplift, would've offered a sliver of relief considering everything, but the opposite happened. Sweat instantly slicked my forehead as a fresh rush of guilt and dread pumped through me. Heart slamming in my chest, I slumped into the driver's seat, death grip on the phone with one hand and the wheel with the other.

"Is she hurt?"

He paused.

He fucking hesitated.

It was bad, then. Each knuckle turned white from my tightening grip on the wheel.

His shaky breath blew across the mouthpiece. "Physically hurt, no. But she's not okay, Lang. Like, really not fucking okay. I think she's having a panic attack. Come help me. Help us."

Shoving the key into the ignition, I cranked the engine and slammed the door shut.

"Where are you?"

"In the alley next to Sips."

That was the last damn place I'd expected him to say, but that didn't matter right now. All that mattered was getting there and helping them both. I knew West—seeing Juno upset or whatever she was meant he needed help too. With his background, he didn't do well in high-emotion situations; they made him shut down. But it sounded like he was actually holding it together okay. For now.

"On my way." I shifted the SUV into reverse and pressed down on the gas pedal without looking behind me. "You okay?"

"Yes and no." The tremor in his voice had me cursing under my breath. "We fucked up, Lang. We really screwed up."

"How?" The tires screeched along the pavement, trying

to get traction as I peeled out of the parking lot and turned the wheel toward Sips, the sign already in sight.

"Them, him. She saw them walking down the street and...." He trailed off, gasping for breath as if he was the one having a panic attack. "I think you just brought the reason she's been hiding her past from us—hell, from everyone, I think—to Anchor Bay."

My heart stopped before kicking back up again and banging against my chest. "It was my job."

"But we both knew better, both thought it sounded shady as fuck. We should've pushed Brandon so she could've had some warning and not been caught off guard." He paused. "What if she never trusts us again, Lang?"

The heartbreak in his tone had me sucking in a sharp breath and holding it. Not knowing how to respond to that —the idea of losing Juno's trust had unfamiliar desperation welling inside me—I told him I'd be there soon, then hung up and focused on not hitting pedestrians in my race to them.

The alleys between a few of the brightly colored buildings weren't big enough for a car, the narrow gaps mostly for the business owners to place their trash and accept walk-up deliveries. The tires all but smoked when I slammed on the brakes, the SUV coming to an abrupt halt directly in front of Sips, uncaring that I took up three spots in my hurry. The slam of the door echoed, followed by the pounding of my boots on the wooden walkway.

The stench of garbage mixed with the sweet scent of baked goods filled my nose the moment I turned the corner into the alley. Gaze bouncing, I searched the area for the two people who were responsible for my near-stroke-level blood pressure.

I was about to call West when he stepped out from

behind a dumpster. I was already moving toward him before he finished waving at me. Stepping back around the metal bin, he dropped low, balancing on the balls of his feet in front of where Juno sat on the broken pavement, her back pressed to the brick building, holding both knees tightly to her chest.

Seeing her like that, curled up so small, like that could protect her, I understood the heartbreak in West's tone on the phone.

The feisty woman who could hold her own with me verbally, put me in my place daily, had the balls and strength to take me down, was gone, and this trembling, small, terrified woman was left. She shifted, slowly lifting her head to peek up at me, lashes and cheeks wet from recent tears, before burying her face behind her knees once again.

She looked utterly destroyed.

"Juno." Stopping beside West, I gripped his shoulder to help him up, allowing me to take his place. Kneeling, I ran a palm over her wild hair in slow, repetitive strokes. "Hey, shortcake, I need you to look at me."

I bit the tip of my tongue, hating that in my moment of weakness, I let the nickname I'd been calling her in my head slip out.

Juno responded with something that I couldn't understand with her face buried in her knees.

"You have to look up for me to understand you," I admonished, giving a strand of her brown hair a slight tug.

Ever so slowly, she unfolded, her tear-streaked face tipping up until her aqua eyes met mine.

"I hate you. I hate you so much right now."

I shot West a dirty look, knowing he was the one who told her exactly who brought the mysterious couple to

Anchor Bay. The asshole just shrugged, his worried gaze locked on Juno.

"Why did you bring them here? Do you want me gone so badly that you'd dig into my shit past and bring the two people who—"

I pressed the pad of my thumb against her lips to stop her.

"I don't want you gone," I said steadily. Her eyes narrowed. "And you don't hate me."

She huffed in annoyance, but a gleam shone in her gaze, warning me that I'd better watch out half a second too late.

"The fuck?" I jerked my thumb back and studied the slight teeth indentations. "You bit me."

"You were silencing me."

"You were accusing me," I snapped.

"You brought the two people I ran from, desperate to leave them in my past, to my somewhat happy present."

"I didn't fucking know—"

A loud clap rang through the alley, bringing our attention to West.

"Now, children, if you'd please stop fighting." He glared at me.

"She started it by biting me," I huffed.

She reached over and shoved my thigh, sending me toppling to the side. My palm scraped the pavement as I caught myself right in the middle of a suspicious sticky substance before I face-planted. I cut her a "you'll pay for that later" look, which she returned by sticking her damn tongue out at me.

"Careful." If she weren't, then the sliver of restraint I hung on to would snap, and I'd tell her exactly how I wanted her to use that tongue of hers. Seeing her so vulnerable and upset had broken through the remaining doubt I had about Juno Jones.

Blowing out a steady breath through pursed lips, I looked up and down the trash-filled alley. "Listen, I'll give you answers, but we need to move somewhere that doesn't smell like garbage with questionable liquids soaking the pavement."

Her frustrated gaze dipped, her little nose scrunched up as if she was just now realizing how disgusting the alley was. "I want to go home," she whispered.

"How about I make you a deal?" I shifted my hat side to side a few times, coming up with a quick plan. "I'll give you answers if you come home with us." I inclined my head to West, who looked happy as fuck at my suggestion. Which was why I made it. I knew there was no way in hell he'd be able to drop her off at home, alone and this upset, and walk away. And honestly, neither could I. The guilt at knowing I was part of the reason she was distressed was eating me alive. I needed to repair her trust and explain everything.

She studied me for a few seconds. "Why do you care?"

I huffed and dropped my head forward. "I care way more than I should, Juno."

"Is this a trick?" At the rasp in her voice, I looked up at her pale face. "Please don't take me to them or—"

"You have my word that this isn't a trick. You will get in the 4Runner with me and West, and we will go to our place, just the three of us, to talk this out."

"I don't know if I trust you."

Those words out of her mouth were like daggers to the fucking heart. "I promise, Juno."

"So do I," West added, coming to stand beside me. He rested his good hand on my shoulder and squeezed. He knew how badly her words wounded me just now.

I turned back to her. "Take it or leave it, shortcake. But we have to get out of here before this stink sinks into our fucking skin."

"What's with the shortcake name?" she grumbled. Palms to the pavement, she pushed herself up to stand, only to crumple back to the ground. I caught her with a barked curse before she could hit the pavement.

Blush stained her cheeks, and she avoided my gaze. "Guess my legs fell asleep from sitting like that so long. Just give me a second and I'll—"

Fuck that. Without warning, I hauled her against me. "Arms around my neck and legs around my waist as best as you can."

"What the hell? You do not have to carry me, Langston. Put me down. I can walk on my own in a few minutes."

I'd had enough of her not letting me take care of her when she needed it. Maybe I needed it just as much, but like hell would I admit that to even myself.

Slapping her round ass hard, I shifted her in my arms so her shocked face was inches from mine. "You don't have to be strong and do this on your own right now, Juno. Let me help you." West's cough was loud and very fake. "Let *us* help you. For this afternoon, let us be the ones you lean on."

She gnawed on her lower lip, looking uncertain. "I don't know how to do that."

"Try for me. I promise we won't let you down. You're safe with us."

Her chin wobbled, and unshed tears filled her lower lids, threatening to spill over.

"I've been an asshole to you, and you have every right to believe I'm not being real with you, but know that I would never intentionally hurt you."

"Wow," she rasped, though a small smile pulled at her

lips. "You finally admitted that you're an asshole." Knowing this was not the time to correct what she heard versus what I said, I sealed my lips shut. "Okay."

"Okay, what?"

"Okay," she drawled, "we can go to your place. But, Langston?" I arched a brow at her dramatic pause, as if waiting to make sure I was really listening. "Me going with you doesn't mean I've forgiven you for not telling me who was coming to surprise me, or for being an asshole—"

"Don't forget the stalking," West added with a little too much fucking glee in his tone. "So much stalking, remember?"

Juno pointed at West and nodded. "Oh, right, that shit too." She swung that pointed finger my way and stabbed at my chest. "Which we will discuss later. And don't worry, I won't expect anything from you. We can go back to being enemies as soon as I'm done with my little breakdown."

My throat worked as I swallowed down my response, choosing to nod instead. I had no intention of things going back to the way they were between us. Everything had changed in the way I saw Juno. With the curtain of suspicion keeping me from trusting her lifted, she was no longer a potential threat to my family. Which meant all the pent-up desires and dirty fantasies I'd had about the stunning woman the last few months could finally be more than just a wet dream.

All I needed to do was help her see I wasn't actually an asshole just because I acted like one sometimes.

Okay, fine, most of the time.

After her perceived betrayal today, combined with our fighting the last few months, it would take time and a lot of constant effort to build her trust, which was reasonable.

Juno Jones was a woman worth me giving it my all for.

Once she was secure, arms looped around my neck and thighs clutching my waist, I spun on my heels and started for the SUV when the sound of a door opening had me pausing. Glancing over my shoulder, I saw the side door that led to Sips had swung open toward us, blocking my view of who stood on the other side.

"I understand delays, but that shipment should be soon, right?"

Recognition hit the moment the voice filtered through my ears. Even without seeing the man, I knew it was Paul, the owner of the coffee shop, who was talking to someone either inside the shop or on the phone. Either way, he clearly didn't know we were standing in the alley hearing his conversation. "No, I don't think anyone knows. Listen, I've kept my end of the—"

The clanking of an empty soda can rolling along the cracked pavement echoed through the alley, cutting Paul off instantly. Over my shoulder, I rolled my eyes at West, whose grimace quickly turned into an apologetic smirk that forced both damn dimples to pop. An exasperated huff shook my chest. The manipulative bastard knew I couldn't stay pissed at him when he showed those bitches.

Alerted to our presence, Paul popped around the edge of the door, narrowed eyes searching before finding me and widening in surprise.

"What the hell are you three doing back here?" His face flushed red when they landed on Juno wrapped around me. "Get the hell out of my alley. I don't allow that kinky-ass shit you and—"

"Watch yourself, Paul," I said in an eerily calm tone that promised pain if he finished that statement. Whatever he read on my face made him flinch. Shifting Juno so she couldn't see Paul's disgusted expression, I tilted my head toward the mouth of the alley. "We were headed out anyway, so finish that conversation."

His face paled, and he stammered something about a flour shipment before disappearing behind the door. It slammed shut behind him, the loud bang making Juno tense in my arms.

"That was weird," West said, and I grunted in agreement. "Come on, let's get her out of here."

Digging into the front pocket of my jeans, I pulled out the keys and tossed them to him. The fucker gave a pointed look at Juno curled around me, then glanced back at me with an "I told you so" grin before heading down the alley.

Arms tightening to keep her secure, I followed him, ready to get the woman who was becoming more precious to me by the minute back to our place.

Maybe then, with Juno there, it would finally feel like home.

12

WEST

The front door closed behind me with a faint click, but even that made me flinch and check over my shoulder to see if the small sound woke Juno. The stingy bastard I called my best friend beat me to carrying her inside after she'd fallen asleep in the SUV during the short ride home.

Even now, Langston refused to set her down. Instead, he figured out a way to keep Juno in his arms and sit in his favorite chair all without waking her. For a big bastard, I had to admit it was an impressive accomplishment.

Movement in his bedroom doorway drew my attention to GG, who pranced across the hardwood floor and gracefully leapt up onto the armrest beside Langston.

"They met this morning," I murmured softly as I rounded his chair to lower slowly onto the leather couch.

Langston's only response was an arched brow, which somehow I understood was a silent question, wondering why she had come by earlier. How the man conveyed what he was thinking without uttering a single word was beyond me. Or maybe I was the talented one who could read his expressions so well that he didn't need to speak.

We had been friends for so long that it was probably a mix of both. When I started at Uplift, Langston did his normal asshole routine, but I saw right through it. It didn't take long for me to break down his walls, for him to see me as a friend, not a foe.

"I needed help to get dressed." Avoiding eye contact, I shrugged innocently, but from his chuffed response, he knew I was anything but innocent. "You were away, so I called Juno." I rubbed my palm over my head, the spiky ends of my short hair scraping the calloused skin. "I couldn't get last night out of my head. I mean, you saw how I woke up. I needed to see her, so yeah, I exaggerated the truth a little." I tossed my hand in the air, frustrated with myself. "I couldn't help it. My fingers texted without my approval, like they had a mind of their own."

"One body part did that for sure," Langston murmured.

I shot him a dirty look. "You don't understand. You didn't taste her last night, feel her squeezing the hell out of your fingers. I'm a damn addict for her now, and honestly, I don't give a fuck. I'm perfectly fine staying hooked on her."

Jade-green eyes bored into my soul, but Langston didn't utter a single word. Maybe because he was afraid of waking Juno or just didn't know how to respond to that. Either way, I wasn't finished.

The leather groaned as I sat forward, legs spread and forearms resting on top of my thighs. Things had escalated between last night and today. He needed to get on board now.

"Please," I whispered, tone slightly begging but forceful too. "Please tell me you're done questioning her, that after the last twenty-four hours, you see she's not a danger to us."

Jerking his gaze away, he sealed his lips shut, toeing the line of shutting me out.

"Fine, not a danger to us in the way you were protecting us from. And, Lang, she's not a danger to you or me in any other way either." His gaze cut to Juno, features softening just a fraction. "I want this to happen." I pointed at her, then him before tapping my sternum. "You feel it. I know you do, or you wouldn't be holding on to her like you're afraid someone might take her from you."

"So?" The single word rasped past his lips, barely a sound, but I heard it loud and clear.

I huffed in a mix of annoyance and disbelief. "So, you want her, but you're not sure how to take that next step. Last night was the most fun we've had on a date in months, maybe ever, and I'm not just talking about what happened in the storage closet. You haven't smiled that much in years, Langston. *Years.*"

The corners of his lips turned down. After a few moments of silence, they parted to respond when the most adorable squeaking noise pierced the silence, stopping him.

Our focus turned to Juno as she shifted against Langston, slowly waking up. Those long dark lashes fanned up and down, blinking several times as her beautiful eyes took in her surroundings, stilling when they focused on me, then widened when she tipped her face upward at Langston.

"Um, what's going on?" she murmured, pushing off his chest, clearly confused. "What happened, and why am I on Langston's lap?"

When she attempted to slide off his thighs, Langston tightened his hold around her waist, keeping her in place. Mouth hanging open, Juno gaped at his smug expression like he'd grown two heads.

I choked back a stifled laugh at the hilarious scene playing out in front of me. "Juno, you fell asleep on the way here, and the big guy currently holding you hostage on his lap carried you inside and has since refused to put you down."

"It would've woken her up, asshole," he growled.

"And how about now? I mean, she *is* awake, so why not let her go?" I asked, gesturing to Juno, whose wide-eyed gaze volleyed between us.

"Shut the fuck up." Turning his attention to Juno, his eyes narrowed. "Do you make it a habit of falling asleep in cars with strangers?"

"I, um...." She shot me a pleading look for help.

Leaning back with an exasperated sigh, I pointed at my friend. "Langston, stop being an asshole. We're moving past that phase, remember?" I emphasized the last word, making him huff in disagreement. "We are not strangers, especially after last night." I waggled both brows suggestively. Juno's cheeks reddened before she twisted to bury her face between Langston's shoulder and jaw, hiding her embarrassment. "You should take it as a compliment that she felt safe enough with us to fall asleep instead of chastising her for not being on high alert."

The color bled from his lips with how hard he pressed them together as he considered my words. At his slow nod, the best I would get to him agreeing with me, I tossed both hands up in the air in victory.

Fucking hell. Making this work between the three of us just might kill me.

"You're not very comfortable." Juno pushed off Langston's chest and poked at his thick bicep. "Not soft at all."

"Sorry?" I snorted a laugh at his confusion. "Why are you so tired?"

My chest tightened uncomfortably at the clear worry in Langston's tone. *So he does care.*

"Um...." Juno chewed on her lower lip until he pressed the tip of his thumb against it and tugged, releasing it from her teeth. "Well, I don't know. I've never actually done that before. I'm normally not that...." Her disheveled hair shifted with the tilt of her head as she considered her words. "Comfortable."

"Well, then I am definitely taking you napping with us as a compliment." I smirked, and shot her a wink, but it was short-lived knowing the heavy conversation ahead. "Are you ready to talk about who that was in town, the two coming to see you?"

Her responding groan echoed around the room as she dropped her head back to stare at the ceiling. "No, not really. But I guess we need to so you understand why I freaked out. But first things first, I have to pee, which means I need you to release me before I wet my pants."

Hands around her waist, Langston cautiously lifted her and stood, not releasing his hold until he was positive she wouldn't crumple like she had in the alley. At her first retreating step, he countered with a step of his own, hands extended, ready to steady her if needed. Brows pulled in tight, Juno shook her head in utter confusion and took another step back, Langston again matching it.

"Seriously? I'm okay. It's not like I suffered a head injury or anything. I can make it to the bathroom." She gave Langston a pointed look. "By myself," she added. She whirled around and took one step only to pause and look over her shoulder at me. "Um, where is the bathroom?"

"I thought you could make it by yourself," Langston said

in a playful tone I rarely heard. "Come on, I'll show you." When her lips parted, he held up both hands in surrender. "And will leave you there, alone."

Stepping to her side, he pressed a large palm to her lower back to guide her toward his bedroom and the adjoining bathroom. A few seconds later, he emerged, leaning a shoulder against the doorframe of his room. "We have a serious problem."

"What the hell happened in the five seconds it took you to show her to the bathroom?" I exclaimed. "Giving directions works too, by the way. She didn't need an escort."

He just shrugged as if what he did was normal and not oddly possessive. "The problem is that I need to know who that Eric asshole is to her, but if I find out he hurt her...." His jaw worked back and forth while his chest heaved with deep breaths. Once he had his anger controlled, he continued. "How much bail money do you have saved up?"

My laughter trailed off when I realized he was serious. "Not enough to get you out for first-degree murder."

He nodded as if agreeing with me, but that was not the case. "That means I can't get caught."

"Caught doing what?"

Langston straightened as Juno squeezed past, eyeing him with suspicion. I winced when she flopped down into Langston's chair, but he didn't say a word. Pink cotton pinched between her fingers, she lifted the front of her T-shirt to her nose and fake gagged. "I smell like trash."

"Great, and you're sitting in my chair," Langston grumbled under his breath.

"Oh, this is your chair?" Juno shot me a conspiring look before wiggling all over the seat, her smile growing with every twist. "Oh, I'd hate to rub this deliciously rotten stench off on your favorite chair."

"You're a brat," he said, fighting a smirk. "And you know what happens to brats in this house?"

"They get grounded?" she sassed back.

"They get their perfect asses spanked, that's what."

Juno froze, her eyes so wide it would almost be comical if I wasn't worried she was about to bolt.

"Alrighty then."

The way she said it had me sitting up straight and pointing at her in excitement. "Did you just quote *Ace Ventura*?"

She nodded with a skeptical expression, like her quoting that movie didn't make me fall for her a little more just now.

"I love that movie. Please tell me you love stupid comedies as much as I do."

Her lips curved in a slow grin. "I may or may not indulge in the occasional brilliantly clever film when I need a break from battling it out online."

The cushion adjusted beneath me as I shifted on the couch to lean in closer. "All-time favorite, go."

"*Napoleon Dynamite*. Duh," she scoffed, as if it was a dumb question. "You?"

"I'm old-school. *Monty Python and the Holy Grail*."

Juno nodded, tapping her lips with a single finger. "Solid choice. I approve." A mischievous look overtook her features. "Did we just become best friends?"

My smile couldn't have been wider. "Yep. And I love that you just quoted my other all-time favorite, *Step Brothers*."

"Of course. You set me up for that one, really."

"Oh fuck," Langston griped. "There are two of you."

Juno and I turned to him with our tongues sticking out. When his gaze darkened, I snapped mine back in fast, Juno doing the same.

"Let me guess, you're a *Rambo* or *Die Hard* fan," Juno

teased. When neither Langston nor I commented on her guess, she studied me and then him. "What? What am I missing? Am I wrong?"

"Just slightly," I chuckled under my breath, holding in the truth.

"West," Langston growled, stalking over to where we sat. "Don't you fucking dare."

Juno's gaze volleyed between us before she scoffed. "What, does he like romance movies? Wait, nope, he's totally a Hallmark guy, right?"

There had never been a more silent silence in the history of silence.

Even GG slowly backed out of the room, though I swear one paw covered the cat's teasing smile.

With a loud gasp, Juno leapt up, pointing an accusing finger at Langston's chest.

"Shut. The. Front. Door. You do not." She whipped her head toward me. "He does not. Not the grumpiest, snarkiest asshole in Anchor Bay."

"I'm not grumpy," Langston pouted, crossing his arms over his chest.

"I mean, she's not wrong. You are—" The unamused expression Langston shot at me said I would pay if I finished that sentence. "And he's a cat daddy." I slapped a hand over my mouth, shocked the truth had slipped out. "I'm sorry," I cackled.

"Oh, you're going to get it now." He lunged toward me, anger and heat burning in his darkening gaze.

In a desperate escape attempt, I jumped over the coffee table, barely missing Langston's outstretched fingers, and ducked behind Juno. It might make me a coward, but I grabbed her around the waist to use as a human shield.

"You can't hurt the already injured," I shouted from behind her back. "It goes against the bro code."

"So does calling me out on owning GG, you fucker," he snapped.

"I think I'm dreaming." Reaching down, Juno pinched my arm, hard.

"Ow!" I yelped. "You're supposed to pinch yourself, not someone else."

"Yeah, but that hurts, so...." She shrugged.

Turning to face Langston, she reached out to pinch his chest, but he snagged her hand out of midair. In a move I'd been on the receiving end of before, he carefully twisted her around, pinning her back to his chest.

Juno's lashes fluttered, her brain attempting to catch up to recent events. A deep chuckle vibrated in my chest at her confusion. Closing the distance, I stopped in front of her, sandwiching her between us.

"What just happened?" Her whispered breath brushed against my throat, making goose bumps spread in its wake. "And why am I not freaking out?"

"Because you know you're safe with us." I stroked a single finger along her jaw. "And it's hot as fuck."

Her plump lips parted in a sharp inhale. Flicking my gaze to Langston, I found his green eyes already on me, hooded and blazing with heat. Not dropping my own heated stare, he leaned down, brushing his lips against the shell of Juno's ear.

"No more distractions, shortcake. Tell me who they are and why you're hell-bent on avoiding them."

Juno chewed on the corner of her lip. "Are you sure you don't want to talk about Hallmark movies—" With an almost growl, Langston dipped lower and nipped at her neck. "Hey," she exclaimed. "That hurt."

"Not as bad as my palm against your bare ass if you don't answer me right now, Juno."

"Fucking hell," I groaned, sealing my lids shut. "Can we not say shit like that when my dick is already so hard it fucking hurts." At her soft giggle, I peeked one eye open. "It's not funny."

Juno cleared her throat. "Right. Sorry, it's just...." She looked over her shoulder at Langston. "What the actual hell is going on right now? Why are you being nice to me?" She looked back at me. "And why are you suddenly very comfortable talking about your dick and touching me and talking dirty and—"

"Because I'm done pretending that I don't want you," I whispered. "After last night, there's no going back for me, sweet cheeks."

"And your bossy friend back there?" She arched a questioning brow, but I could see the confusion mixed with interest in her eyes.

I eyed Langston. "He's done seeing you as a threat to his family and can finally admit what you really are and have been since you arrived in Anchor Bay."

"What's that?" Juno rasped.

"Ours," Langston growled.

She swallowed nervously. "I'm not so sure about that. I told you earlier, West, I'm broken. I'm really not someone either of you should want. And on top of that, I don't think I can."

"Why?" Langston asked.

"I'm scared, mostly."

"We'd never hurt you. You have to know that."

I nodded, agreeing with Langston's statement.

"Physically, yeah, I know, but... what if I trust you both and you break me all over again? Or worse, you smother the part of me that makes me Juno Jones just when I've finally found those lost parts of me again."

Silence filled the small space. I started to respond, but Langston beat me to it.

"That's it." Juno's sharp squeal had me wincing as Langston picked her up by the waist and carefully set her down in his chair. Gripping the armrests on either side, he leaned in, brows pulled in tight. "You tell me everything that fucker did, and I swear to you I'll give it back to him a hundred times over. He fucked with you, which means he's a dead man walking in my book. Tell me, Juno, or I swear on my damn cat that I will turn your ass red until you do."

With a wince, I adjusted myself to relieve the pressure. His bossy, protective nature had always been a turn-on, but when it was directed at Juno, someone I was also attracted to and wanted to keep safe, it was almost too much. Just imagining her over his knee, bare ass in the air, had precum soaking my boxer briefs.

"Okay," she whispered, cheeks flushed pink as she blinked up at him. "But you have to back up a little. I'm fighting the urge to either smack you or beg you to follow through on that punishment."

Langston stood tall and crossed his arms. "Have you ever been spanked before for punishment or pleasure?"

Her head rolled from side to side against the back of the chair. "No, but I've lived a thousand different lives in the books I read." The pink staining her cheeks darkened. "Fuck, what am I even saying right now? You're putting some kind of lust-induced spell on me or something."

"Same, shortcake. Now." He reached behind him, pulled the coffee table until it was a foot away from the chair, and sat, his knees encasing hers. "Talk."

Blowing a raspberry, she looked at the ceiling. "The two

people I never wanted to see again, ever, who you so rudely brought to my little sliver of Alaskan paradise—" She cut a frustrated look at Langston, who just shrugged like it didn't affect him, but I saw the stiffness in the movement, the downturn of his lips. "—are Eric Adler, my former fiancé, and Stephanie Wilson, the woman I caught him cheating on me with." She paused, her gaze flicking between us. "Oh, and bonus, she's my sister."

What. The. Actual. Fuck.

13

JUNO

My stomach rolled saying those words out loud. My fiancé cheated on me with my sister—well, stepsister, if we were technical about it. Mom married Stephanie's dad after mine left us high and dry. Apparently, he wasn't "happy," and that meant it was okay for him to bolt. So for almost two decades, Stephanie had been my sister. We were opposites in every way, but we had loved each other like biological sisters would.

Had being the key word. Though I guessed I did still love her—I just didn't like her after catching her kneeling on our kitchen floor giving Eric a blow job when I came home early from work. Why did I do that? To get an early start on my birthday dinner, which I had planned to cook like I had done years prior. That was how it worked with Eric and me. Anything that was special or important to him was important to us both equally, but if it was something for me, well, then it was only special or important to me.

I realized the absurdity of that now, months removed from the somewhat emotionally abusive and controlling relationship. Eric was as selfish as selfish could be, and our entire relationship was about him.

It shocked me that Stephanie would go behind my back like that or do anything that soiled her reputation. Between the two of us, she was the sweet one, the naturally beautiful, submissive one, the... everything opposite of me. I knew that because my stepfather loved to remind me how perfect she was while I wasn't, not by a long shot. After hearing that so many times, I attempted to mold myself to mimic her, but it never stuck.

"Can you repeat that last part?" West stood from the cozy leather couch, crossing his arms over his chest, and I couldn't help but stare at the way his shirt sleeves stretched to the max around his thick biceps. I bet he was that buff everywhere, and I desperately wanted to find out for myself. And there was this frantic need crawling under my skin to touch him, to wrap my hand around his cock just like Langston had last night.

I jerked in the chair at that thought. There had been something very wrong with me lately. Those kinds of thoughts, desperate sex thoughts, were not me. Even when I was with Eric, I didn't enjoy being touched all that much, and I for sure was never excited for sex. Though, considering the two men in front of me could make me wet with a heated look, I wondered if the problem wasn't with me but Eric.

"Juno," Langston snapped, directing my blurred gaze at him. I shook my head to clear my thoughts and focus on him. "Did you really say she's your sister?"

I nodded slowly. "Well, stepsister. I'm sure you noticed that already, though, since she and I look nothing alike. She was always the pretty one," I murmured.

"Like fuck she is." With both hands, Langston shifted his

ball cap from side to side. I noticed he did that a lot when he was really agitated, which meant constantly when I was around. "She's a fucking beanpole with zero curves and so much of that shit on her face that I bet I wouldn't even recognize her without it. Oh, and that nasty fake hair." He huffed while I just gaped at him.

"If you can't tell, Lang and his sister, Mattie, are very close." I blinked up at West, who didn't notice, too busy smirking at his best friend. I wondered what it was like when they kissed. *Did* they kiss, or was it just sex? "Which is why he has a cat, a gift from her, why he loves Hallmark movies, her favorite, and how he knows about hair extensions. Because of her job, she's surrounded by fake people and complains, in detail, about their fakeness."

"Don't fucking distract her," Langston sighed, but I caught the curve of his lips, an almost smile. "I need more detail than that, Juno. Your reaction earlier was sheer panic."

Staring at my lap, I pulled at a loose thread on my sweats. "Besides catching them in the act, on my birthday," I griped, disdain dripping from my tone, "it was more about what I came to realize after I left that makes me panicked to see him. I'm not sure if I'm strong enough yet to face him."

"Did he hit you?" Langston asked, so gently it took me by surprise.

"No, which was why it took me so long to realize...." I took a deep breath. "No, he didn't hit me, but he was controlling, manipulative, and so selfish that he was a borderline narcissist. Everything revolved around him: what he wanted to do, what he liked, what he needed. For the longest time, I thought that was normal, how every relationship worked. It didn't start out that way, though. It was great at first, but then the little things I'd do here and there were never good enough.

"Like, the food I made wasn't flavorful enough, or I didn't have enough food on the table. Or I wasn't presentable enough to go out with him unless I was totally put together; anything less, I heard about it the entire time we were out. Or if he was unhappy, then he made sure I knew about it, so then I started pouring all my energy and time and focus and own happiness into keeping him happy because, well, things were just easier that way. And then after I found him and my sister, he said I caused him to cheat."

"The hell?" the two men said in unison.

"He blamed his cheating on you?" Langston asked, completely confused. "How?"

"Because we weren't having enough sex, of course," I stated bluntly, staring just over Langston's shoulder so I didn't have to see his reaction. "And it was true, we didn't, and that was on me. I've never really been an overly sexual person anyway, but I needed a deep connection with him to *want* the physical aspects of the relationship, and it wasn't there. I tried to like it—"

"Juno, you know that's utter horseshit, right?" West moved to sit on the armrest, concern swirling in his dark eyes as he stared down at me. At least it was concern and not pity.

Pieces of my disheveled hair brushed my cheek with my confused head tilt. "Which part?"

"All of it," Langston snorted. "If I found out my girl, much less my fiancée, wasn't getting what she needed from me in or out of bed, I'd figure that shit out in a hurry."

"Yeah, well, Eric didn't feel the same way. It was easier for him to blame me for what was wrong instead of focusing on himself. After I found them, he cut it off and said he was sorry, that he loved me. And like the idiot I was, I wanted to fix it, us. Maybe if I could do better, be more of what he needed, then we could work it out. There was just so much history between us...." I paused, wondering how to explain the initial infatuation I had with Eric, how I felt special for being noticed by him. "His parents are wealthy, and mine weren't, so when he asked me on a date, I felt honored, I guess. It didn't help that my mom and stepdad liked to remind me how I should have been grateful that someone of his caliber would want me—"

Langston ripped off his hat and twisted it between his hands. "My 'strangle with my bare hands' list is growing longer by the fucking second. Your stepfather and *mom* said that to you?"

I nodded.

"That's messed up, sweet cheeks," West said softly.

My throat worked as I tried to swallow, throat scratchy and dry. "Then Mom got sick." Unshed tears burned behind my eyes. "That was when most of my time and energy shifted from Eric and our relationship to taking care of her, visiting her at the hospital, then hospice."

Langston's massive hand reached for mine, thick fingers intertwining with my much smaller ones. "Losing a parent is an awful thing to go through, especially alone, which it sounds like you were with that bastard as a partner."

He wasn't wrong. Eric wasn't really there for me like I needed him to be, more worried about how it affected him instead.

"I mean, my stepfather helped some, but yeah, you're right about Eric. Looking back, I realized he actually made me feel guilty for spending that time with her. He would complain about how I wasn't around as much. He said it was because he missed me, but when I was home, he was frustrated at how exhausted I was, making me the bad guy for taking care of my mom. I honestly think he was relieved when she died," I whispered. A fraction of the tension in my chest eased at that, having never said that suspicion out loud before. "That's what I mean by history. He was there through so much, and we'd been together for so long, that I didn't want to give up easily. So I tried, I really tried to fix me—"

"Damnit, Juno," Langston snapped, cutting me off. "There is nothing to fucking fix." He leaned in close, freezing me with his intense stare. "You hear me, Juno Jones. There is nothing about you that needs to be fixed or changed."

"You don't know me," I rasped, wishing like hell he was right. "It's why I prefer computers and online games. I'm better virtually than I am with actual people—"

"Tell that to the people here you've become friends with since you arrived. I know most of the women here would disagree with you," he countered.

"Fine, I make female friends okay, but as far as relationships go, I suck. I'm not what a guy wants. I'm introverted, not very affectionate, and then there's the not liking sex thing, which every man needs—"

"From what I've heard, that was more of an Eric problem than something wrong with you, Juno," West said, stopping me. "From our perspective, it's easy to point out what was messed up in that relationship, but everything you've said points to him being the issue, not you. He sounds like a selfish asshole who only cared about himself, and that's not a relationship." He paused, scanning my face as if trying to figure me out, then sat back with a curse. "I get it, and I don't blame you."

"What do you get?" I said warily.

"You believe that's how all relationships function," he mused, rubbing a hand over his jaw as he studied me. "That's what you meant by being broken. You think all the dysfunction in that relationship was your fault, which means every other relationship will be the same."

I lifted both shoulders in a minuscule shrug. "It's easy to think that when that's what you've been told"—a single tear escaped and slipped down my cheek—"your whole life."

"Look at me." With a small headshake, I lowered my gaze to Langston's boots. "I said look at me, Juno, now." The dominant command in his tone had me raising my head just enough to see through my dark lashes. "Fuck them."

I jerked back, startled at the intensity in his loud voice.

West reached over and patted Langston's thigh with a wince. "I think what my not-so-eloquent friend is trying to say is, who cares what they think? They were wrong. You see that now, right?"

I angled my head from side to side in a so-so gesture. "It's ultimately why I left like a damn thief in the night. I realized he wasn't trying to save us, or at the very least putting in the bare-minimum effort, and I had to stop disappearing into the idea of saving us or there wouldn't be anything left of the real me to salvage. So I ran, had a few great, peaceful months making friends and healing from all that trauma, and then boom." I gestured to Langston. "Captain Asshole ferries my worst nightmare straight to my little sanctuary." Brow arched, I shook my head in disapproval. "I'm still confused about how all that came about. West tried to explain, but I wasn't really listening at the time—panic attack and all that."

Langston grabbed both of his knees in a white-knuckled grip. "I didn't do it on purpose. They called Brandon, booked a trip from Anchorage to here like any other client would. The caveat was that they were coming here to surprise you, and since we didn't know any of this until now, we didn't see a problem with it. It did sound suspect, yeah, but Brandon took their money and ordered us not to say anything to you." His voice trembled with frustration, no doubt aimed at himself.

"Well, they got what they wanted. I was surprised all right, but thankfully without them knowing. If I would've panicked like that in front of them...." I trailed off, not even wanting to think about that level of embarrassment. Pressing a loose fist to my sternum, I rubbed to release the pressure. "It has to be more than just showing up together. What do they want? Why are they really here to see me?"

"No clue," Langston grumbled, looking anywhere other than at me.

"Are you serious?" I glanced between the two men. "No one asked when they booked? And you didn't interrogate them on the ride from Anchorage like you do to everyone, Langston?"

He just pursed his lips in response. *Guess that's a no.*

West smirked, those damn dimples popping, as he shook his head. "All the information they gave Brandon fit on a Post-it note—not much."

"Great," I whined in frustration. "Guess that means I'll just have to wait for them to blindside me face-to-face to find out why they're here. That sounds fun."

"Well, maybe not. They needed dinner options and asked where the locals go. I suggested Dave's," Langston said. "We go tonight, stage the meeting so you know it's happening—no being blindsided—and you can find out what they want. We get the information and then bounce. I tell them to leave Anchor Bay first thing in the morning or I'll do it for them, with them in body bags."

I blinked at him, trying to figure out if he was kidding.

And if I was good if he wasn't.

West sat up straight, excitement practically vibrating off him. "It could be a date. The three of us. Kind of like a dinner theater type of thing, but real life."

I shook my head, biting back a smile, but it slipped into a flat line when the word *date* registered. "West, did you not hear everything I explained about myself? Broken, not exciting, hates sex, trusting no one ever, ever again?"

West shrugged like my words went in one ear and out the other. "I heard you, but I like a challenge. I'll make you see that bullshit for what it is, sweet cheeks."

"I'm not so sure about that," I murmured under my breath.

"Nope. That's it." With a gentle grasp around my shoulders, Langston hauled me out of the chair, spun me around to face it, and pressed between my shoulder blades, bending me over. My slick palms slapped the armrests, fingers digging into the soft leather to keep me from face-planting into the seat he'd just stolen from me.

Before I could get a word out about his manhandling, a fiery sting bloomed from my right ass cheek as the spanking sound filled the room. "We will not allow that horseshit here. What you say about yourself is what you believe, and we're correcting that right the fuck now. Do you understand?"

Jaw slack, maybe a little drool sliding out of the corner of my mouth, I gaped over my shoulder at Langston. "You spanked me," I accused.

He offered a clipped nod in response. "That's what happens when you talk badly about yourself."

"You spanked me," I repeated like an idiot, because apparently, spanking not only turned me on in ways I didn't want to examine at the moment but knocked my thoughts loose too. "You really did it."

"I always follow through, Juno. Remember that. Especially when it's mutually beneficial." Face pinched in discomfort, he reached down and adjusted the very large bulge behind his jeans. "Fuck, I can't wait to do that to your bare skin, see how pink I can make it."

"Fuck," West and I rasped at the same time. We exchanged heated looks that turned into wide smiles.

"So, what will it be, Juno? Dinner at Dave's tonight, hoping those two fuckers show up, or avoid them until they come to find you?"

I blew out a controlled breath, debating West's question.

The last thing I wanted to do, ever, was see either of them, much less together. My stomach knotted just thinking about having to confront them, but it would be better to get it over with on my terms instead of giving my anxiety time to create horrible, embarrassing scenarios while waiting for them to find me.

"We can go tonight, but I have one rule." I stood and turned, crossing my arms and flicking a no-nonsense stare between them. "We go as friends, not a date. I don't want the pressure, and I really don't think you two are grasping what I'm saying. I'm not who you think I am, and I honestly don't want to end up even more damaged when you do."

"That's borderline talking badly about yourself," Langston said with a single dark brow raised.

Rolling my eyes, I stuck out my tongue.

"Careful, shortcake. My restraint only goes so far before I snap and show you exactly where I want that tongue on me." His gaze flicked to West. "Or him while mine is inside your drenched cunt."

"Um, friends don't say that to friends," I whispered, not sure what else to say.

"No, they say it to their girl."

Before I could correct him, Langston turned, stomping to his bedroom and closing the door behind him.

Arms slack at my sides, lips parted, I stared at the closed door, wondering why I felt the need to correct him for labeling me as "their girl" at all. Despite my best efforts at warning them away, they were persistent and, from what I could tell, genuine in their interest of me—and not just for sex. Each heated glance, every smile and laugh they pulled from me was like stripping away layers of protective film I'd carefully placed over my heart.

"We'll win you over, Juno." West stepped close, his hands gently gripping my waist in a way that was hot and protective at the same time. "Now, if we're doing the staged encounter bit, you might want to go shower."

My lips pulled down in a frown. "But you said I looked fine earlier."

A shy smile grew, making only one of his dimples pop. "You look beautiful as always, but remember the smell you mentioned? It's less about appearance and more about the unique aroma wafting off you that needs to be addressed."

Oh, right. I'd forgotten about that with the whole Langston and West sandwich. But even as my cheeks heated, the normal embarrassment felt different somehow, not as gut-wrenching. It was West's tone, more joking than accusing or disgusted, not making me feel like I didn't live up to some high standard like Eric would.

It hit me what I didn't feel.

Shame.

I wasn't thrilled about the animal-urine stench wafting off me, but there wasn't that added icky feeling of shame tagging along with it. Odd. Almost as if I was okay that I wasn't perfect because West didn't expect me to be.

"What are you thinking so hard about?" He tapped between my brows.

"That maybe, with someone like you, like Langston, I don't have to hold myself to a crazy-high standard that I could never meet. That when I make a mistake or smell like garbage, it's not the end of the world."

Now it was his turn for a deep line to form between his dark brows. "I'm understanding just how deep the emotional abuse went with that dipshit. We'll expose the lies he made you believe about relationships and a true partnership little by little. That's for us to figure out together —us three—not just on you to undo alone. You will need to be upfront and honest with us as we work through it together, though."

"As friends," I added slowly. "That's all I'll ever be good for, West. I know myself, and I know what I can offer. I don't want to disappoint you and Langston—"

The stomping of boots on the hardwood floor cut me off.

"Run," West whispered out of the corner of his mouth. "Save your ass. Literally, Juno."

With a squeak of surprise mixed with excited thrill, I turned on my heels and bolted for the front door. Grappling with the handle, I yanked the heavy wood door open and dashed down the front porch steps, not stopping until I was standing in the middle of the main road.

Chest heaving with every heavy breath, a wide smile spread at finding Langston in the middle of the doorway, tatted arms crossed over his chest, looking sexy as hell and making me question running from him.

"Your time will come, shortcake. You can't hide from my palm forever." He started to turn but paused. "We'll come by around seven for our date." The last word was emphasized with a smirk.

Before I could correct the misused term for tonight's meeting, Langston retreated into the cabin and slammed the door shut.

Shaking my head at his stubborn ass, I started walking home, mind racing with a thousand thoughts a second.

Why was I hell-bent on pushing them away? I warned them I wasn't what anyone wanted in a girlfriend, so why keep forcing the issue? Granted, I could just let everything play out between us until they truly understood how broken I was and they dropped me like a bad habit. I was absolutely certain that would happen at some point.

There was a seed of worry that kept me from going all in and enjoying the attention from the two men—that I wouldn't survive them leaving, solidifying the fact that I'd never be enough for someone to truly love.

14

LANGSTON

Hands dangling at my sides, I flexed my fingers, attempting to ease the ache in the stiff joints as we walked to Juno's cabin to pick her up for the "not a date" date. West tracked the movement with his brow furrowed.

A chuff puffed past my lips. The man was almost as observant as me. I was only slightly more from the two tours I served in the Army, needing to tune those observation skills to stay alive. Plus, during Mattie's teen years, I monitored everything to ensure she was safe and taken care of at all times—which of course, like any teenage girl, she hated.

She thought I was overprotective for no reason, but she didn't know, nor would she ever, about all the "talks" I had with boys from her school to make sure she was respected. Mattie just assumed they were good guys and I expected the worst in everyone.

"Shouldn't it be your forearm and wrist that are sore?" West teased, but it was a cover for his concern about the old injury he of course knew about. "Unless your grip is so tight around your dick that your fingers are sore too."

"Funny, I've never heard complaints about my grip from

you." I shot him a smirk only for it to slip, my thoughts circling back to the pain in my fingers. "If she finds out, or I ever tell her, do you think Juno would care about my hand, the story behind how I broke it?"

West rolled his eyes, as if I was being ridiculous. "Find out that you shattered your hand while beating a man almost to death when you were twelve and it didn't heal correctly?"

"You know what I mean," I grumbled. But yeah, exactly that.

"I don't think she's the type to shy away from overprotective-asshole gestures." At the next flex of my fingers, I only straightened the middle one and pointed it at him. "But it's something you might want to talk with her about," he continued, ignoring me. "If we want this to work, then we should be up-front about everything from the start. I don't want to give her any reason to think we're anything like her ex."

I'd shoot myself in the fucking balls as punishment and ensure I never reproduced if I was anything like—or was even adjacently compared to—that manipulating jackass.

"We need to make sure she doesn't feel like she's stepping between us. Let her know we're not *together*, together. She knows we do our thing, whatever that is, but I don't want her to think she's a third wheel. Does that make sense?" he asked.

I paused at the steps that led to her small front porch. "Do you think she'll be okay with us, with what we do, as long as she's involved?" A lead weight settled in my stomach thinking about having to choose between the two of them.

West just shrugged. "No fucking clue."

"Good to know I'm not the only one feeling clueless in all this," I grumbled as I leapt up the stairs, boots slamming to the top, making the entire porch shake. After pounding on the door, I took a large step back to not crowd her when she opened it.

Before we left, West sat me down, looking serious as hell, and told me to calm my shit down or I'd scare her away with my overbearing antics. Which I called utter bullshit. It wasn't like she was one of our one-night stands. She knew I was intense and high-strung, and I saw the way her gaze heated when I pulled the dominant card. She might not be ready to admit it, but Juno loved my protective, slightly obsessive, asshole side.

He may have played it off that me being overbearing would make her bolt, but I knew better. Juno wasn't the only one afraid of someone leaving after they found out the darkest parts we all kept carefully hidden. The worst of our pasts had yet to be exposed, which was the way we both liked it. I never wanted Juno to know about the times I'd failed, while West kept his abusive childhood memories buried so deep that he'd only mentioned it once when he was piss-ass drunk.

You'd think someone like me would hear what happened to him and go on a murderous rampage, but— and I blamed it on the tequila—I went to my room and fucking cried.

He never mentioned it again, either not remembering he told me or preferring to act like it didn't happen. Either way, I followed his lead, because what kind of asshole would I be if I made him talk about his trauma when he wasn't ready?

The dark-stained wooden door swung open. I started to ask if she was ready, but all words vanished, zero thoughts flickering through my head except two little words that said it all.

Holy fuck.

I slow-blinked at Juno, who was gripping the edge of the door with an expectant expression. Still unable to speak, I dropped my gaze, inspecting the gorgeous woman inch by inch, starting with her brown ankle boots, then up her bare legs to where the black skirt hit mid-thigh. Fuck, her legs looked perfect to wrap around my head while I ate her cunt clean. My brain again short-circuited when I got to her chest, the sweater material stressing her large tits and the deep V-neck showing more of the soft, fair skin I wanted to taste.

With light makeup, just enough to make her eyes pop but not look fake, and her brown hair styled in gorgeous loose curls, Juno Jones was jaw-droppingly, brain-freezingly gorgeous. She was every day, but tonight, she was stunning.

"Are you going to say something or just keep staring at me with...." Her head tilted to the side. "What is that look exactly?" Juno gestured to my face while looking at West with an arched brow.

"I think you broke him," West said, poking a single finger at my shoulder.

"Come on, I don't look that different." Juno laughed, a faint blush now staining her cheeks. My breath caught at the sweet sound, so pure and carefree, everything I was not. "It's just a little makeup and actually taking the time to blow-dry my crazy hair into submission."

"You look great," I mumbled, finally finding my words. "Do you want a jacket?" Or a parka... anything to hide how fucking delectable she looked in that outfit. All I could imagine was sitting her down on the kitchen counter with that skirt around her waist and my cock buried deep inside her soaked pussy.

"A jacket?" she asked. Stepping around me, she stuck her

hand out as if testing the temperature. "Why would I need a jacket?"

West's chuckle had me turning to him with a dull look. "I think my friend here is concerned about all the men he'll be forced to blind for staring at you in that outfit. It's already a problem, and looking like that, there will be no man in Anchor Bay with eyes after tonight."

Juno scoffed and rolled her eyes as if she didn't believe him. Did she really not notice the way men watched her wherever she went, no matter what she was wearing?

"But now that you're ours—"

"Friend," Juno cut in with a pointed look at West. "Your friend."

"Special friend?" West countered.

"Friend who is special?" she responded with a smile.

"Special-to-us friend, who is also ours?" West leaned in close, putting his nose near her neck, and inhaled deeply. "Damn, you smell good."

"It's just soap," she replied, her voice shaky.

"Nah, I know that smell. Its taste is ingrained on my tongue from last night. And I would bet that if I snuck my hand beneath that skirt and stroked your pussy, my fingers would be drenched." Juno's lips parted, her gaze fixed on where West stroked a single finger along her hip. I desperately needed to adjust my cock but stayed frozen to not disturb whatever the fuck was happening. "And I would lick up every drop you'd give me, sweet cheeks."

"West," I practically growled. "What the fuck are you doing?"

"Getting us all ready for tonight," he responded innocently.

"For me to get dick chafe and Juno to walk around with wet panties all night?" A thought hit me like a lightning bolt to the chest. With a single step, I pinned her against the doorframe. Chest heaving, I stared down into her aqua eyes. "You *are* wearing underwear, right?"

If she said no, then there would be no holding back from pushing her into the cabin and begging her to let me fuck her until the sun came up.

"Yes," she rasped. "Yes, I am."

"Good girl."

Juno straightened. Palm to my chest, she pushed me back and fanned herself with the other. "Damnit, Langston, you can't go saying shit like that. Give a girl some fucking warning first."

West and I eyed each other in confusion. "Okay?" I said warily.

Huffing, she tossed both hands in the air. "Well now, thanks to my so-called friends, I need to go inside and change underwear." When she stepped back into the cabin, I followed, but she stopped me cold with a single hard look. "Alone."

"But I can help," I offered. Help her get out of them— that was for damn sure.

"You and your friend's help are why I need to change. Give me a minute." Her gaze darted over her shoulder. "Or a couple."

Before she could close the door, I slapped a palm to the center of the thick wood. "If you do anything other than change your soaked panties, like play with that delicious cunt to take the edge off, I will know, and you won't like the consequences."

"I wasn't," she whispered, but I heard the lie. It was in that single glance she gave to her bedroom that was filled with indecision and longing. I arched a brow silently, calling her out on it. "Fine, maybe, but it's your fault." She waggled a finger between me and West.

"Then let us take the edge off for you," he suggested, coming to stand beside me.

"No, that would make this"—she gestured between the three of us—"even more complicated and confusing."

"Oh, shortcake, there is nothing confusing about it. We want you, and you want us. You're the one holding back, making this complicated." I hovered so close that she had to tip her head back to maintain eye contact. "We're consenting adults. We're asking for a chance to show you we're different. Not a marriage proposal, just a chance."

"But what if you don't like who I really am?" she asked. The fear in her eyes made my heart clench.

"Then you'd have gotten hundreds of orgasms out of it and the solid answer that we're piece-of-shit humans, because that is the only type of person who wouldn't see your value." Unable to stop myself, I leaned in close and pressed a kiss to the corner of her mouth. "Go change those soaked panties, Juno. We'll be waiting."

Standing tall, a soft chuckle vibrated in my chest at her frozen, confused expression. After a few seconds of her gaping at me, I gently grasped her shoulders to turn her into the cabin, smacking her ass lightly to get her moving.

I choked on a stifled groan at feeling her cheek jiggle with the light smack. Hopefully soon I would get to see my pink handprint on each ass cheek, or the plump globe mold around my fingers as I squeezed tight.

"You're so fucked," West chuckled.

I shook my head and turned to face away from her cabin before I broke and followed her.

"No, asshole—*we* are."

Shoulder pressed against the porch post, I stared off into

the distance, savoring the pleasant evening. After a few seconds, I gave voice to what I'd been thinking about all afternoon. "Knowing he didn't physically hurt her doesn't make me want to kill him any less. That shit she's talking about is the same bullshit Mattie's ex spewed at her."

"But Juno didn't have you, or anyone, to counterbalance the lies with truth. I know what that feels like."

The heat pumping through me from earlier, warming my skin to the point of sweating, cooled at his sobering tone. Twisting around, I found his unfocused gaze fixed on the porch's white-painted boards.

"Maybe, since you both being alone is similar, that's something you two can work out together," I hedged.

West shook his head. "No one needs my fucked-up past in their heads. It's bad enough that it's in mine."

I wasn't a sensitive guy, but seeing him looking so distant, hopeless, had me swallowing hard to clear the emotions clogging my throat. I couldn't protect him from his past, but I sure as hell would do anything for the man to help him process the awful things he'd survived.

West was loyal, dedicated, brilliant when it came to anything with an engine, and soulful when you least expected it. He deserved a full life without assuming he didn't because of what was done to him as a kid.

"That's your call," I murmured. "But she might be more understanding than you think. Sounds like her childhood wasn't great either."

"Neither was yours," he added with a bit of bite to it, telling me we were edging into an uncomfortable territory for him.

"Yeah, but I had Mattie, and when she was home, I had Mom. We were poor as shit, but we had each other, and Mom, for all her other bad qualities, tried to be a good mom." I grasped his shoulder and squeezed. "Just think about it."

Before he could respond, the door swung open and Juno stepped out, ending the conversation. West's pinched features transformed into a wide smile, though I noticed it looked stiff, unlike earlier.

Hell, if she could help him heal from his past, then I'd give her whatever she wanted. My best friend deserved to be happy, and so did she. Which was why this had to work between the three of us.

Juno eyed us after closing the door and locking up. "Everything okay out here?" She arched a questioning brow in my direction. "Lovers' quarrel?"

West huffed. "You're confusing lovers with fuck buddies."

I trailed behind the two as they descended the steps, heading toward the parking lot.

"I think I'll need a little more insight into that comment," Juno hedged, looking over her shoulder with a shy smile.

"Or a demonstration?" I offered with a smirk.

Crimson bloomed on her cheeks and down her neck. "You're the worst, Langston."

"When it comes to fucking, I can guarantee he's not." West chuckled, the memories that had been dredged up earlier long gone.

"How did this conversation swing back around to sex already?" Juno groaned. "Let's talk about the weather or birds or computers."

West responded with something that made them both laugh, but I didn't hear their words. They continued on, but I'd paused in the middle of the street, eyes locked on the woman standing in her small front yard, staring at her cabin with a worried expression. My feet were carrying me toward her before I even realized I was moving.

"Calista." She jumped slightly and swung around, hand on her chest like I'd spooked her. "Everything okay?"

"Um, yeah, all good, Langston." The fake smile she forced only solidified that she was absolutely not okay.

"Hudson home?" I paused beside her, gaze sweeping over the house for what was causing her obvious distress.

"No, he was in Anchorage for something regarding the case, then went to the trail with Oliver and Ethan. I think they found something belonging to the hiker who died."

I scanned the yard. "Where's Sam?" My heart rate spiked, blood thundering through my veins at not seeing the vibrant and demanding girl running around after her dog like she always did. "Is she okay?"

"What? Oh yeah, I just dropped her off at Amy's for a bit. She offered to watch her for a little while so I could get some stuff done around the house." This time Calista's smile was genuine. "Cleaning with Sam in the house is nearly impossible. She pulls everything out that I'd just put away."

Enough bullshitting. If I didn't find out what was wrong, I'd jump out of my skin. "Why are you out here, staring at your cabin?"

Her slim shoulders rose and fell. "I don't know exactly. Something just feels off." She paused, but I didn't say a word, knowing she had more to add. "And after everything back in LA, when something feels off, I've learned not to ignore it."

"That's smart, trusting your intuition. What exactly feels off about the house that's making you not want to go inside?"

"I don't know. When I walked up, everything was fine,

but when I went to open the door, I froze. Like my muscles locked up. I don't even know what caused it to happen."

Motion behind me had me whirling around, hand going for my sidearm that I was only without when I was naked, only to pause when I recognized Juno and West. They watched me with curiosity, gazes bouncing between me and Calista.

"What's going on?" West asked. "Everything okay?"

"I'm going to check out something inside for Calista. Why don't you go on to Dave's?" I reached into my pocket, palmed the keys, and tossed them to West, who caught them midair. "I'll be right behind you."

"Do you want me to stay with you, Calista?" Juno cut the distance between them and wrapped her up in a tight hug. "If you don't want to be alone while he does whatever he needs to do, I'll stay with you."

"No," I barked before taking a deep, calming inhale. There was no way in hell I wanted Juno anywhere around if Calista's feeling was correct. I locked gazes with West and inclined my head toward the parking lot. "Get her to Dave's. I'll be right behind you."

With a clipped nod, clearly understanding my concern, West wrapped an arm around Juno's shoulders and dragged her away from Calista.

"Come on. Let's go get you some of those amazing nachos while we wait for the two douchecanoes to show up and ruin our night."

It took a few promises from Calista that she'd stay safe before Juno reluctantly backed out of the yard, calling over her shoulder to reach out if we needed anything before disappearing around a cabin. I waited until I was positive they were gone before sliding my sidearm free of the holster, palming the grip as I marched up the porch steps.

Not taking my eyes off the front door, I shouted over my shoulder, "Was Brandon or Carl home when you dropped off Sam?"

"Carl was. Brandon was out doing something in the toy shed."

I nodded more to myself than her. "Good. Go back over there, have them call both Oliver and Hudson and tell them something is going on at your place."

"But what if I'm wrong?" Calista whispered, wringing her hands. "It could be nothing."

"What if you're not?" I inclined my head toward Carl, Amy, and Brandon's cabin. "Go. I'll check out inside, make sure things are secure here. I'll come find you when I'm done."

I waited until she was halfway down the street, just a few cabins down from her destination, before stepping up to the front door. Inspecting the edges of the wooden frame, I scanned every inch for tool marks or signs of forced entry. The cool metal slipped in my hand as I turned the knob, slowly inching the door open to step inside.

The aroma of something savory cooking in the crockpot on the counter filled the room, and my stomach growled in interest. Taking in the small living area, I couldn't help the smirk that tugged at my lips at the array of toys scattered across the floor. In the corner was a child-size round table with a little tea set on top, dolls in three of the four small chairs. Adjusting my hold on the gun grip, I moved around the room, stepping over Sam's things and weaving around furniture while monitoring my surroundings. It didn't feel off like it did for Calista, but I sure as hell would not let my guard down.

After a clear sweep of the kitchen followed by the two bedrooms and bathrooms, I holstered my gun. Standing in the middle of the living room, arms folded over my chest, I found my gaze falling on the small table again, something drawing my attention. Steps light and sure, I crossed to the corner, squatting low to inspect the play set.

My harsh curse echoed in the quiet room. A note sat perched against the pink plastic teapot, the writing clear and the spelling correct, which instantly told me Sam was not the author.

Mindful not to leave prints, I used one of the doll's creepy plastic hands to adjust the note so I could read it. As the words processed, boiling anger filled my veins and pulsed in my ears while dread sank in my gut like a hundred-pound weight.

"Keep your friends close and your enemies closer. But which am I? Leave, or your girls will be the next ones needing missing person flyers."

Holy shit.

This was bad. Really fucking bad. First Caroline went missing along with all the other women on the trail, and now the sick fuck had broken into someone's cabin here, leaving a threat without any of us noticing.

Which made one aspect of these cases very clear.

The person responsible for everything evil in our town was someone we knew.

15

———

WEST

E xcited chatter and loud laughter filled the bar around us. Like usual around dinnertime, Dave's was packed, all the locals coming out for their few hours of social time before heading back home. We had scored a four-person round top toward the back with a decent line of sight to the front door so we could watch for Eric and Stephanie. A roar of laughter from my right had me twisting in the seat with a grin.

Seemed everyone was having a great night. Well, everyone but the gorgeous woman across from me. I studied the way she sat up straight, shoulders back, gaze locked on the large front door, jerking every time it swung open. It was clear she was nervous, but like we'd discussed on the way to Dave's, it was her best option to gain control of the situation.

Disgust and rage burned in my gut, stealing my appetite, the longer I thought about the deceptive way the couple went about blindsiding Juno. They knew she wouldn't want to see them, especially here together, yet they staged the surprise visit, which was a total asshole move and made me wonder what they were hoping to achieve by doing all this.

Though after hearing Langston's perception of them, the whole messed-up plan had to be that dipshit Eric's idea.

Not that her stepsister was innocent by any means, but the more Juno talked about Eric, the more I understood that he wasn't just a selfish asshole but a manipulative one too.

"How long do you think we should wait?" Juno asked, focused on the empty water glass she spun along the table-top. "I'm worried."

Brow furrowed, I pitched forward, pressing both fore-arms to the edge of the round table. "About what?"

"What if he got hurt or something went wrong? You should call him to see if everything is okay."

No clue why she thought I would have Eric's number, but also, why did she sound upset at the thought of him being injured? "I don't have his number, but I have to admit, I wouldn't care if he did get hurt, or hell, fell into the bay on his way here. It would solve a lot of problems, if I'm being honest."

Juno's head popped up where it had dropped forward, shock written all over her features. "How can you say that? He's your best friend, and you two being a package deal is not a problem. I'm fully aware that you're a buy-one-get-one type thing, and not just because of how hands-on he was with you last night. Plus, we live in a multi-partner commu-nity. Did you actually think I would want to split you two up? And of course you have his number, so why are you lying—"

My heart swelled with her ramblings. Reaching across the table, I threaded my fingers through her thick hair to pull her lips to mine, ending her speech with a demanding kiss. It only took a second for her to melt into me, lips moving against mine and parting, allowing me to tangle my tongue with hers.

I pulled back a fraction with a smirk. "I thought you were concerned about that dipshit ex of yours being hurt, not Langston." Her nose scrunched in the most adorable disgust. "But good to know that you understand Lang and I are what we are and you're not interested in splitting us up or asking us to stop. One thing is certain: You either get both of us or neither, sweet cheeks. But it sounds like you already knew that." I shifted to brush my lips against the shell of her ear. "And I think you like the idea of him and me together. Of having two men worship you, yes, but the thought of us together turns you on, doesn't it?"

Her sharp inhale and hissed breath confirmed my suspicions.

"What are you two to each other?" she asked, bright eyes searching mine. "Boyfriends? Friends with benefits?"

An ache built in my cheeks from the wide smile splitting my face. "We've never labeled ourselves, but I guess you could say friends with benefits who would kill for each other but are exclusive with men." I chuckled at the way her lips parted in surprise. "You can ask any of the questions you want about us; we're not shy about who we are. But I want Lang involved in the conversation, so maybe we put a pin in it for now."

As if saying his name reminded her of his absence, Juno's gaze jerked to the door. "Can you call him, please. I didn't like leaving him there alone."

Warmth swelled in my chest at the genuine concern in her tone. Though she didn't need to be. Langston could handle almost any situation with his military background, anger management issues, and sharpshooting skills. The man was a badass in every sense of the term, but it was sweet that she was worried—it meant she cared for the asshole.

Teeth sunk into my lower lip, attempting to smother my wide grin, I reached into the front pocket of my jeans to slide my phone free. Tapping his number, I pressed the smooth screen to my ear, her eyes tracking each movement like a hawk. It rang several times before going to voicemail. Staring at the screen, I called again but had the same result.

The earlier grin had dimmed, my concern mounting. "I'm sure he's fine," I placated with more confidence than I felt. Opening our ongoing text string, I shot Langston a quick message for him to call me and set the phone down, face up, to know immediately when he responded. "Langston can handle himself. I'm sure he's busy updating Hudson or something like that."

No longer focused on the night's plans, hoping to see Langston's picture flash on the phone screen, we stopped watching the door and monitoring who entered. Which had to be how Eric and Stephanie came in and weaved through the tables with us completely oblivious until they appeared next to Juno.

"Juno Bug."

Juno went unnaturally still; she didn't blink or even look like she was breathing. The preppy douche standing next to her chair smiled, clearly loving her discomfort. She refused to look at him, instead fixing her stare on the table in front of her.

Not me. I needed to catalog every inch of the asshole who'd fucked with our Juno.

A sneer pulled at the corner of my lips at his perfectly styled short blond hair, his clean-shaven face, and pressed polo that he'd tucked into a pair of loose-fitting khaki pants tailored to hit right at his loafers.

This guy made Juno question her worth?

Her throat worked with a hard swallow, gaze finding

mine before she straightened and turned to the soggy sandwich. "Eric," Juno rasped. Nostrils flaring with a deep inhale, she twisted to see behind him. "Stephanie."

At Juno's blank tone, Stephanie's skin turned a sickly green. Good. I hoped she puked all over herself and Eric for doing this to Juno. Other than looking so nervous that she was about to vomit, Stephanie was unremarkable, forgettable if you asked me. Perfectly put together just like Eric, everything was ironed and fit her slim frame like it was tailored for her specifically. Only a sliver of pale skin showed between the hem of the ankle-length skirt and her short black wedge boots. A thick coating of makeup covered her entire face, meant to highlight her cheekbones and make her brown eyes pop, but it only made me wonder what she hid beneath the perfectly done mask.

Desperate to give Juno all the support I could without overstepping, I shifted in the hard wooden seat until I could drape an arm over the back of her chair. One soft curl pinched between two fingers, I slowly twirled it around, never dropping the stony stare leveled directly at Eric. He tracked every movement, nostrils flaring when I planted a reassuring kiss to her shoulder.

Calculating blue eyes met mine, and it was in that moment that I saw the fucker for what he was: a selfish asshole who thought the world owed him something. Maybe it was how he was raised, or he was just that damn arrogant because of what he thought he offered the world. I would need to ask; I had zero doubt she knew.

"Surprise," Stephanie said with a stiff smile, cutting through the awkward silence.

"Yes, yes, it is. A big surprise." She glanced at me and winked. "What are you two doing here in Anchor Bay, let alone together?" When neither of them responded, Juno gestured to Eric. "I never took you as much of an outdoor lover, Eric."

His fake laugh grated on my nerves. "You know I love to hunt, June Bug. Though that isn't why we're here."

"Sending someone out to track big game and then radio you to come shoot it is not hunting," Juno corrected in a bland tone. "That's just killing."

"I guess we see it differently. You'd know if you ever cared enough to come out with me." Eric turned to me. "She's not the outdoorsy type. I don't know how she can stay inside all day playing games with other losers."

"Watch it," I ordered, tone so commanding it surprised me.

"Who's your friend?" Eric asked, turning back to Juno with a tight smile.

Call me possessive, but that question combined with the disgust in his tone had me gripping the back of Juno's chair and sliding it until our seats bumped.

"Oh, I'm more than a friend, but I have no damn clue who you are." I twisted to Juno with fake concentration. "Who is Captain Douchecanoe, sweet cheeks? I don't remember you mentioning an Evan."

"Eric," the asshole snapped.

Juno's teeth sank into her lower lip in a failed attempt to stifle her widening smile. "Yeah, I don't think I ever mentioned him. It wasn't important."

"We've been too busy doing more... physical activities rather than talking." I planted a kiss to the corner of her lips and turned to Eric with a dull expression. "She can't get enough of me, and I'm worse." I twisted to lock eyes with her. "I'm addicted to her taste."

A rosy blush bloomed along her cheeks, and for a passionate moment, it was only her and me, utterly lost in each other and wishing we were somewhere more private. Like a supply closet. Or maybe I was dreaming, because I would do anything, even sell a vital organ, to get her alone for another taste of her pussy. This time, though, I wanted to lick it straight from the source.

"You look good, June Bug." Annoyed that Eric's nasally voice broke our moment, I faced him only to find his focus all on Juno, smiling like he actually meant it. It was there and gone in a flash, but the calculating spark in his gaze had me sitting up straighter, preparing for whatever bullshit he was about to spew. "Though I loved you blonde. It really highlighted your only striking feature."

"The fuck did he say?" I practically growled. A hand squeezing my thigh stopped me from leaping over the table and ripping out Eric's jugular.

"I like it back to my natural color, actually," she stated evenly, but I heard the vibration of tension in her tone.

"Well, I guess you always had questionable taste." His following laugh had me fisting my good hand beneath the table as burning rage pumped through me. "Remember when we first met, and you were always wearing those awful shoes you thought were still in style and thrift store clothes?" His calculating gaze swept down to her chest. "You actually look put together tonight. Must be a special occasion to get you out of your sweats without a fight."

"Juno," I hissed through gritted teeth.

Her sad gaze met mine. "Please," she whispered. "Don't make a scene. I'm fine."

"This isn't fine," I murmured. "It's fucking degrading and openly cruel."

Her forced smile and shrug spoke volumes. These were the types of pointed jabs she'd endured while she was with the bastard. No clue what she saw in the asshole in the first place; surely he had some redeeming qualities that made her want to be with him at one time.

Pasting a fake smile on, I turned to the asshole. "I love her sweats. They make her ass look absolutely spankable."

"Oh my," Stephanie gasped.

Eric whipped her way, suddenly remembering she was there, with a condemning look.

"Well," he stated as he snaked an arm around Stephanie's waist, pulling her toward him in a controlling jerk. "We were planning to surprise you tomorrow, but since we ran into you tonight, we might as well tell you the exciting news."

My stomach sank with dread; nothing good would come from whatever he said next.

Eric dropped his hold around Stephanie to harshly grip her left hand and thrust it across the table so hard the woman stumbled forward to stay on her feet.

"We're getting married."

I shifted to seal my side tighter to Juno's. Scanning her features, I studied the unshed tears welling in her lower lids, the slight tremble in her chin as she fought them back. Ever so slowly, I lifted my gaze to the asswipe, ready to murder him in the middle of the busy bar for making my girl cry. Only Juno shoving back from the table, the chair legs screeching across the sticky floor, stopped me before I could lunge forward.

"That is exciting news." Her smile wavered. "Congratulations. If you'll excuse me, I need to use the restroom."

"I need to go too," Stephanie called out and started to follow Juno, but Eric gripped her bicep, stopping her cold.

"No, you're fine. We need to get drinks to celebrate." Reaching back, he pulled out a thin wallet and slapped a shiny black credit card onto the table. He paused, glancing at me and the card as if waiting for me to comment on it.

I snorted and leaned back in the chair, *very* unimpressed with his flaunting.

Lips pressed in a tight line, he twisted back to Stephanie, inclining his head toward the packed bar. "Go grab us a decent bottle of whiskey—surely they'll have something I'll like—and three glasses."

A low, dark chuckle vibrated in my chest. "Oh, make it four glasses. I'm staying for this so-called celebration, especially if he's buying." I tossed him a wink. "Thanks, Edgar."

"Eric," he snarled.

"Same thing," I sang.

Out of the corner of my eye, I tracked Juno as she weaved through the packed tables, hurrying for the hall that led to the bathrooms. My muscles twitched with the need to push out of the chair and follow her. Unable to resist, I stood, only to pause, noticing a familiar hulking frame bulldozing through the crowd, gaze locked on the bathroom hall.

A relieved breath fanned across my lips with a slow exhale. Langston was here, clearly fine after whatever happened at Calista and Hudson's place, and would take care of Juno if she needed someone.

Then I swallowed a groan. Fuck, that meant I had to entertain the asshole across the table.

"So... I didn't catch your name." I just stared at him until he grumbled something about me being an asshole. Clearing his throat, he fixed a pleasant smile on his face. "Okay, well, what do you do? You do work, right?"

I arched a single eyebrow at the condescension in his annoying tone. Of course that was his first question. Shrugging, I relaxed a fraction, no longer muscle-trembling tense with Juno out of his line of sight, his carefully cruel words unable to reach her.

"Murder for hire," I deadpanned. "I normally only accept contracts for taking out cheating assholes." I relished the way his face paled. "You have to get creative, you know; there are so many out there. If I'm not careful, I could get bored, but thank fuck for Google. What about you? What does an arrogant prick like you do for a living that makes you think you're above everyone else?"

His thin lips pressed into a tight line, and crimson spread from the base of his neck up to his face.

"You're fucking with me." I shrugged and gestured for him to keep going. "Well, not trying to brag." *Riiight.* "But I run the full account team for my dad's company. It's easy mostly, and everyone loves me. Our clients have stayed with us for years because of me and what I bring to the table. I'm just that good at my job."

"Wow, and humble too." I gave him a thumbs-up. "Great job."

He smirked. "Why be humble when you know you're right?"

Scanning the bar, I started counting the number of people I recognized to keep from having to hear the other aspects of his job that he was so exceptional at. I'd only been in the guy's presence for ten minutes and was already about to murder him.

A slow, knowing grin grew, bunching my cheeks.

I was the patient one between me and Langston. I wondered how long he would last before he put his fist through the asshole's chest.

Guess I'll have to wait and see.

16

JUNO

The loud chatter and clinking of glasses muffled the moment I rounded the corner, dipping into the dimly lit hall that led to two single-stall bathrooms. While all the locals loved Dave's, it was well known around town that you came for the food and drinks, but if you needed to pee, you held it until you got home thanks to Ches, Dave's owner, not putting cleaning the bathrooms high on the priority list.

My thigh muscles twitched from either the stress of the day or adrenaline, making me unsteady. Halfway down the hall, I spun, pressing my spine against the dark paneling for support. I tipped my head back to stare at the water-stained ceiling. Heart racing, pulse fluttering at an unhealthy speed, I squeezed both eyelids shut and inhaled, my nostrils flaring with each deep pull of oxygen, hoping that would calm my body down before I stroked out.

Engaged.

My former fiancé was, in less than six months after I called off the wedding and bolted, engaged, and to my *step-sister*, who he cheated on me with and then swore up and down it was over.

Not caring about my perfectly fixed hair, I rolled the back of my head along the wall, wishing like hell I would wake up from the nightmare already. This was what soap operas were made of, not real life, so why the fuck was it happening to me?

My thoughts raced, none of them finishing before moving on to the next, as every imaginable feeling swirled and fought for dominance. It was difficult to unravel how I really felt about the two of them being in Anchor Bay and finding out about their engagement, but there was one overriding emotion that I didn't expect: worry. You'd think rage or grief would be prominent considering the circumstances, but no, it was concern—for Stephanie.

I couldn't give two shits about him moving on. I'd rather tickle a shark than be with Eric again, even in a friend capacity. But his moving on with my stepsister, someone who I cared about despite the whole cheating thing, had dread weighing heavy in my belly, making me nauseous. Eric wasn't a good person and was an even worse romantic partner. When we were together, I knew deep down that the way he treated me, his selfish nature, and impossibly high expectations weren't normal, but what relationship was, right?

He never hit me, so it wasn't abuse. So what if the relationship revolved around him? It wasn't like I had it as bad as others who showed up at the ER every other month.

Right?

The last few months far away from Eric and his constant belittling comments had helped me see the actual truth, not his version of it. I didn't want any of that for her. No one deserved to be trapped with someone like that for life, to have your own wants and dreams dismissed so many times that you began to do the same.

It was scary how close I got to losing years of my life tied to that man. He almost had me convinced that I had it good, that the little effort he put in was so much more than other men. All those years of chipping away at all the pieces of me that made me Juno Jones, he almost made me believe that his lies were the truth. Then I came to Anchor Bay, saw how real men treated their partners—hell, even their friends—and realized that while it wasn't physical abuse, it wasn't healthy either.

A roaring laugh echoed down the hall followed by a group cheering, snapping me out of memory lane. *Time to wrap up the mini breakdown and get back out to the table, hopefully before West murders Eric with his bare hands. Well, with him being down one, I guess it would be bare hand?* I shook my head, smirking at that random thought.

I needed a few more minutes to secure my walls again so Eric's jabs wouldn't hit home, at least not like they used to. As long as he stayed on the topic of degrading me, everything would be fine, but if he started after West, all bets were off. Though murder was off the table. I liked Oliver and wouldn't want him to feel bad about arresting me.

Exhaling a loud sigh through my nose, I rubbed my lips together, still unable to process how I felt about him and Stephanie. Sure, we weren't blood-related, but she was my sister. Yes, I was still hurt that she went behind my back with Eric, but did that mean she deserved a lifetime of being degraded and minimized? Incurable crabs or IBS where she pooped her pants every time she sneezed, sure, but a life with a man like Eric? That felt like too much for even my worst enemy.

"What the fuck did that asshole say?"

The deep voice and harsh tone had my lids popping open, finding a pair of emerald-green eyes gazing down at me, an inch from my face. I sucked in a breath, scanning his furrowed brow and the tight line of his lips.

"You're here," I whispered, more to myself than to him. Without thinking, I rose onto my tiptoes to wrap my arms around his neck, drawing me flush against his chest. Cheek pressed to his sternum, the steady thump of his heart soothed my frayed nerves, easing the stress flowing through my tight muscles.

"Are you okay?" Langston asked. "What do you need?"

His arms wrapped around my shoulders and tightened, squeezing me even closer. I couldn't help the small smile that pulled at the corners of my lips. Who would've thought that being in this man's arms, Captain Asshole himself, would be exactly where I needed to be during one of my most stressful and emotional moments.

"I was worried about you."

His scoff sent rogue locks of my hair floating.

"*You* were worried about *me*," Langston stated in utter disbelief. My hair rasped against his long-sleeve T-shirt with my slow nod. "Why in the hell would you be worried about me?" The confusion in his tone made my smile grow.

Pulling back, I gazed up into his searching green eyes. Fuck, he was so damn hot. Tan skin, dark hair, muscles for days, tattoos—

"Juno?"

I blinked a few times and shook my head, realizing I was just staring at him instead of responding. But when you were in the arms of someone like Langston, who would blame me?

"I was worried because West and I just left you alone in an unknown situation. We shouldn't have done that, should maybe have stuck around—"

"No. I needed you away from the danger and somewhere safe."

"But aren't I safe with you?" I arched a sassy brow, which made him chuckle.

"Me or West. Don't let that injured hand fool you; the asshole could still win most fights, and if he was protecting you, I know he'd die before letting anything happen to you."

My heart hammered in my chest at his admission. How was that even possible? This, between the three of us, wasn't anything, yet they were still beyond protective.

I'd be lying to myself if I said it wasn't a turn-on and also made me want to cry.

"I was worried something had happened to you when you didn't show earlier."

He nodded but still looked unsure. "Things are handled for now. But there is a lot to discuss with the others. I think Brandon plans to call an all-Uplift community meeting to talk about what was found and our next course of action."

"Are we in danger?" I probed, not liking his hesitant tone.

The way his lips sealed shut told me everything I needed to know.

"Back to me questioning you now." He inclined his head toward the busy bar. "What did they say to you to make you come hide back here, alone?" he asked, a slight growl of disapproval on that last word.

"I needed a minute after their big surprise." I wiggled my fingers in fake jazz hands. "Which I'll spoil for you. They're engaged." I shrugged as I diverted my gaze to the wall behind Langston. "Why they couldn't have told me over email, or carrier pigeon, or never, I don't know."

That was a lie, though. I knew Eric wanted to see my reaction when I found out the news.

Fuck, he was such an asshole. Maybe I should strangle him just to rid the world of his pompous ass. Oliver would understand; he wouldn't really arrest me for murder. I'd just updated the main emergency services website for free, so surely that gave me a literal get out of jail free card.

"Are you fucking with me right now? Their surprise was to tell you that bullshit?" Langston spit.

I slowly nodded, in awe and a little turned on at his anger on my behalf.

"I can definitely see it being more of Eric's idea than Stephanie's. But yeah, they're here to tell me the joyous news of their engagement." I paused. "Come to think of it, did he give her my old ring? Surely not, right?" The shape and size had looked similar now that I thought about it. Then again, I only got a flash of it when Eric shoved it in my face as he made his dramatic announcement.

"A guy like that?" Langston scoffed. "I bet he recycled the ring. It would be too inconvenient for him to find another one."

I tapped the end of my nose. "Spot-on. I've described him accurately, it seems."

"You still haven't told me why you're back here alone." His features hardened. "I don't want you going anywhere without me or West until we catch the sick fucker who's out there hurting women."

I huffed and shook my head. "Considering I'm a homebody, that won't be a problem. And I'm back here because I needed to process, you know. I was prepared to see them, but to hear that... I was caught off guard."

Langston grunted a noncommittal response. Pressing both hands to the wall behind my head, caging me in, he scanned my face. "And now?"

"Now," I breathed, "I'm better, thanks. You're a pleasant distraction."

"Is that all I am?"

"No," I drawled. "You're an asshole too."

The corners of his lips twitched upward.

For several seconds we stood there, lost in each other's gazes while the world went on around us. It was strange, but with each moment with him, it felt like I was absorbing his strength. The memory of the last time we were in this bar together flashed in my mind, making a slow smirk appear.

He leaned in even closer. "What's that mischievous look on your face for?"

"I was just remembering the last time we were here together, and you hauled me out over your shoulder like a damn caveman."

A slow grin grew on Langston's face, transforming his normal stony expression. "I remember that night too. And if I remember right, I hauled you out of here, smacking your ass because you were being a mouthy, drunk-as-shit brat."

"I was not! You came in and ruined all our fun."

He arched a dark brow, clearly not agreeing. "You girls were hammered. Way too many duck fart shots, plus a mix of other drinks based on the glasses piled in the middle of the table."

I started to deny it but snapped my lips shut.

He was right. Most of us were nearly black-out drunk after the emergency book club meeting to discuss Baylee's love life crisis. Our advice clearly worked. She was happy with her own little harem, who loved and protected her with their every breath.

I turned my gaze to Langston, finding him already staring down at me. "Okay, fine," I relented. "Maybe I acted a little bratty in my drunken state, but I was just annoyed at being manhandled." And also annoyed at myself for liking it a lot. "I apologize for saying I wanted to fillet your balls and feed them to you."

He barked out a laugh. "I don't remember hearing that or I would've spanked your ass again."

I shrugged. "Maybe I just said it in my mind, then." I chewed my lower lip. "I don't think I ever thanked you for that night and getting me home safe. Even though I didn't expect you to show up and save me from myself and the terrible decisions that could've happened, I'm thankful that you were there. Even when I didn't know I needed to be saved, you were there." Emotions constricted my throat. "I've never had that, you know. It's nice to know that there's someone out there looking out for me, without me even having to ask."

"Always, shortcake." Knuckle under my chin, he tipped my face up to his. "You've been under my protection since the day you arrived in Anchor Bay." I arched a brow, making him chuckle. "Okay, yeah, I was suspicious of you and why you showed up here like you were running from something. But you were—that's clear now. Understand, I would do anything to protect my family here, and I didn't know you. I didn't trust you."

"Do you now? Or do I still need to pass some kind of screening process? Maybe get fingerprinted later?" I joked only to stop short. "Wait, if you trust me now, does that mean you'll stop being an asshole?"

"Doubtful," he grumbled as he adjusted his backward ball cap.

"You're not being one right now. You're the opposite actually, and it's kind of throwing me off a little."

His responding chuckle was deep, vibrating in his chest.

"Oh, I'm still an asshole, Juno. Don't you worry about

that. But West warned me to tone it down a little so I didn't scare you off before we showed you how good it could be with us."

"Oh," I breathed, face heating.

"I think he's afraid once you find out how deep my need to protect you goes, and the lengths I'll go to make sure you stay safe, you'll run."

That seemed sweet for West to say to him, but I'd kind of fallen for Asshole Langston over the last few months. This side of him was just as hot, but I enjoyed bickering and fighting with him. It made me feel alive, strong even, because I stood up for myself against him.

"I don't want you to stop being you," I said after a few moments. "Maybe it would help if you explained the why behind your obsessive protectiveness?"

His throat bobbed with a hard swallow. "One day. It's not a story I enjoy telling, the first time I failed someone. There's not a day that goes by where I don't think about that one oversight and what it cost the other person. And me."

"I'll take that. But don't change who you are, Langston. If this is going to work, being more than friends, then I want to know the real you and be with the real you. Not you holding parts of yourself back just because you're afraid I'll be scared away. Because I could do the same. I could put on this perfect façade, the person who Eric wanted me to be, instead of the quirky computer geek who would rather be in her sweats and Uggs than designer clothes. Who's an emotional train wreck most of the time and also needs constant reassurance. But then that wouldn't be fair to you guys.

"You need to know what you're getting into from the start, so hopefully when you decide I'm too much, it's sooner rather than later, so I can protect myself from even more heartache—"

"I swear, woman," he growled, "you and that mouth of yours. How you talk about yourself is a fucking problem. One I plan to fix by spanking your perfect ass pink from now until it stops."

"Langston," I groaned. "I'm just telling you the truth. You'll get tired of—"

His lips sealing to mine cut me off in a demanding, passion-filled kiss.

Pressure wrapped around my throat, making me gasp. Thumb beneath my chin, he tilted me to just the angle he wanted, allowing him to command the kiss. Roaring voices and bursts of laughter from the bar faded. The entire world ceased to exist; it was just the two of us lost in each other.

Never had I had a kiss like it. One that made me lose all sense of reality because it was that good, not to mention who was kissing me. I could let go of the worry and fear, let my guard down because I knew Langston's was up. Regardless of the situation, he had it under control.

I could lose myself because he had me, us, no matter what happened.

My lips followed his, not wanting the kiss, our first actual kiss, to end. A soft expression eased the normal tension in his features as he gazed down at me. Gone was the cocky asshole, the demanding jerk, leaving a man who almost looked like a lovesick boy in front of me.

"That's your final warning, Juno. You watch how you talk about my girl."

"Um, okay, but I'm not your girl." He hummed a noncommittal sound, making my temper flare. "Are you saying you'll make me yours and West's no matter what I want?"

That loose grip around my throat tightened just a little in warning, turning me on way more than it should have. Hell, this whole possessive bit he pulled turned me on more than my independent-woman side wanted to admit.

"No, I'd never make you do something you don't want to do, and I'd murder someone with my bare hands if they ever did." Again, why was that level of violence on my behalf so fucking sexy? "I'm saying if you're not convinced—" He leaned in close, our noses almost brushing. "—then my buddy West and I need to step it up to make sure there is no doubt in your mind or anyone else's whose you are."

Zero sassy comeback left my lips, because who the hell in their right mind would say anything but "yes, please"?

Adjusting his hat, he shifted his focus down the hall that led out to the bar. Sighing, he released my throat, trailing his hand over my shoulder and down my arm to interlock our fingers together.

"Come on, let's go before West takes matters into his own hands and murders that son of a bitch before I get my shot. Plus, I have a feeling they aren't done."

"What do you mean by 'not done'?" My stomach soured as I shuffled behind Langston, who led us toward the bright lights and loud sounds.

His wide shoulders rose and fell in a shrug. Looking back at me, he searched my face, lips pressed into a tight line. "Just a feeling I have about that fucker. He's the asshole who doesn't stop at one blow."

"Great," I grumbled, making Langston smirk.

They'd already announced their engagement, came here specifically to surprise me with that little nugget. What else could they have to say? What could be worse than that?

17

LANGSTON

The way her tiny hand fit into mine, my large one engulfing hers, had unknown emotions stirring in my chest. She was so small, tough but wounded, and in more danger than any of us realized. What I'd discovered earlier had me more on edge than normal, and that wasn't good for anyone.

Especially not the fucker we were walking toward. Deep in my gut, I knew they weren't done revealing all the "surprises" they came here to blindside Juno with. There was more to it than making her face them when they broke the engagement news. No, the asshole would want to do as much damage as possible while he was here.

While it was true that I didn't like many people, I had a deep hatred for men like Eric. The type of man who bullied, manipulated, and degraded the woman who loved them all because they thought lording over someone made them powerful. Women in love could overlook glaring red flags, and some fuckers used that to their advantage. They would manipulate and twist the gentleness women naturally offered until there was nothing left, just a hollow shell of themselves, and they were so used to doing everything on their own, they forgot what it was like to have a proper partner, leaving the man free to do whatever he wanted while the woman carried the emotional and mental load of the entire relationship.

Not that I was an expert on covert narcissists, but I understood from an outsider's perspective from watching Mattie go through the entire cycle with her asshole soon-to-be ex-husband.

Thankfully, she made the tough decision, leaving the controlling bastard before I resorted to killing him. It was hell not following through on all my murderous fantasies, but the asshole was my adorable nephew's father—not that I wanted him anywhere near the chunky, cheerful kid or my sister ever again.

Worried my hold was too tight around Juno's delicate fingers, I flexed my own to adjust my grip and to remind myself she was still there, close behind me as we weaved through the full tables. I glared at those filling the seats, pissed that they had chosen tonight of all nights to come out to get their socialization needs fulfilled alongside Dave's famous nacho fix.

A slow grin spread when Eric stiffened at my approach, no doubt remembering my less-than-pleasant attitude during the boat ride from Anchorage. Good, maybe this wouldn't end in bloodshed if he was already intimidated by me from our short time together.

His gaze slid down to where my hand was wrapped around Juno's. Confusion registered first before a deep line formed between his brows and his lips dipped in a disapproving frown. The scars lining my knuckles popped as I wrapped my hand around the back of the chair beside West, using my other to guide Juno into the seat. Needing one of my own, I stole one from the table behind us, shutting their protests up with a hard glare, and slammed it down between Juno and Eric. Falling into the seat, I spread my long legs out wide, forcing him to move to keep us from touching.

"Those should be illegal." I broke off my bored stare from the douche to see what Juno was referring to. All the tension drained out of me at seeing her and West grinning at each other.

"What should be?" West laughed, his dark eyes brighter than I'd seen them in too damn long.

My heart clenched at the sight of how carefree he seemed, and happy—genuinely happy. Fuck, this had to happen between the three of us, for him, for me, and hell, for Juno too. So she could see and know exactly how she was meant to be treated, like a fucking gift, and maybe West and I could finally find someone who we could spoil rotten and love every second.

Juno playfully pressed the tip of her index finger into one of West's dimples.

"Those dimples should be illegal. I bet they allow you to get away with murder."

His smile grew wide, making the other dimple pop. "If that were the case, then I wouldn't be holding back from making this table one person lighter."

My chest rose and fell with a loud huff. "They don't get him out of murder, but they help him get away with more shit than he should."

"What's going on here?" Eric asked, cutting into our conversation. Clearly annoyed at being left out, he flicked his hand between the three of us. "How do you all know one another?"

Wanting to follow Juno's lead, I kept my mouth shut, but I dropped a hand to her bare thigh and gave it a reassuring squeeze. My gaze slipped to where I touched her, imagining how easy it would be to slide my fingers up her inner thigh to brush a finger along her slit.

I swallowed a frustrated groan. It either meant I had restraint of steel or was a blind dumbass for how I'd held myself back all these months. It made me want to kick my ass at the time lost from not trusting her and giving in to the mouthwatering temptation that she was. All this time, she could've been with me and West, but I couldn't get past those lingering thoughts of needing to protect my family.

The only way to pay penance was doing whatever she needed to feel safe with me and spending massive amounts of time between her thighs. My attention kept finding the faint red marks along her throat from where I'd wrapped my hand around it in the hall. Seeing her chest rise and fall, my gaze slid down, my thoughts instantly going to fucking her full tits one day soon, or letting West do it while I fucked her or him. We should probably try both ways to see which was better for all of us.

"Langston." The amusement in her voice had me shaking out of those dirty thoughts and focusing on her smiling face. "My eyes are up here."

"Oh, he knows," West laughed. "I'm sure he's just coming up with fun activities for later, sweet cheeks. By the way, take notes, Lang, so you don't forget. I can't wait to hear what you just came up with."

"Enough," Eric snapped. The few tables around us fell silent, a few locals turning their attention to Eric, who shot them a fake apologetic smile. I noted the muscles along his jaw twitching as he ground his teeth. "What are you doing here, boat guy, and what are you both doing touching my June Bug?"

Juno snorted with an eye roll. "First, I'm not your

anything. Second, stop calling me that. I hate it. I've always hated it. And third, what's going on here"—she gestured to the three of us—"is none of your business. Oh, and 'boat guy,' really? He has a name. And *Langston* is here because I want him to be."

"Unlike you," I added under my breath, just loud enough for him to hear.

Palms to the table, he leaned in as if that would make him seem intimidating. Maybe to a woman, but with me, it just poked the fucking bear. "Watch your tone, Juno. And do you know who the fuck you're messing with?" Eric sat back and rolled his shoulders, glaring at me. "I could get you fired for how you're treating an Uplift client."

"I think you're asking the wrong question. Do *you* know who you're messing with?" West stated in a menacing tone that had my lips curving upward. Seeing him so protective and aggressive on Juno's behalf was hot as fuck. West wasn't a dominant guy, unless you went after someone he considered family; then a very dark side of him came out.

Stephanie approached the table, carefully clutching four glasses filled with amber liquid. I shot Eric a disapproving frown. Had he really sent his girl to the bar to fetch drinks?

Her timid smile dropped as she took in the tension radiating from the table. After setting a drink down in front of everyone, giving me what I had to assume was supposed to be hers, she moved her purse out of the seat and eased into the chair.

"Oh, you're friends with Juno?" she asked.

I offered a clipped nod, which made her fidget on the hard wooden chair. Forcing her smile wider than what looked natural, Stephanie focused on Juno. "Did Eric tell you we hoped you'd come? To the wedding, that is."

"You're kidding me," West said with an incredulous laugh.

Fingertips pressed to her temples, Juno rubbed small circles as if massaging away a headache.

Needing to find a better solution to her discomfort, I sorted through the causes while taking in the mostly empty table, minus the four drinks and an empty water glass. Angling back to look behind Juno, I hitched my chin at West to get his attention.

"Food?" He shook his head. "We need to feed her before we leave."

"I'm right here, listening to you," Juno huffed with zero frustration in her wiry tone. "And saying it like that makes me feel like a pet."

"We're here to take care of all your needs, pet." I shot her a cocky smirk, which she returned with an exasperated headshake.

"Yes," Eric called out, forcing our attention back on him, just how he liked it. "Steph and I want *you* there, Juno." The way he emphasized the word had West and me both chuffing. Like that would happen.

"When and where is this joyous occasion happening?" Juno exhaled. She picked up the highball glass filled with amber liquid and crinkled her cute nose.

"Care for something different?" West asked, leaning in close.

"Yeah, would you mind? This isn't even on my radar of drinks I like."

"No duck farts," I ordered.

"Agreed, no shots," she said through a fake gag.

West pushed back from the table. "I'll grab you something from the bar. Vodka and Sprite with a lime is your usual, right?" At her slow nod, as if shocked he had noticed it was her go-to drink, West shot her a small smile before hitching his chin my way. "Plus, I'll order some food." He scanned the table. "To go. I have a feeling we'll be leaving soon."

When he turned for the bar, I watched her eyes follow him as he walked away, gaze locked on his firm ass.

"See something you like, shortcake?" I murmured.

Juno narrowed her eyes my way and stuck out her tongue.

"Remember what I said. I'll put that to good use if you—"

"Next weekend," Eric blurted, once again pulling our focus back to him. Fuck, couldn't the asshole take a hint and go drown in the bay? "The wedding is next weekend."

Juno's head whipped around fast, jaw slack. I frowned, not understanding why that was such a big deal. Maybe she felt it was too soon?

"I can't wait to marry the love of my life." Keeping his gaze locked on Juno, Eric lifted Stephanie's hand and kissed her knuckles. "She makes me happy, not as much work as past relationships."

"Please let me kill him," I muttered under my breath.

"Where?" The word was more of a pushed breath; I barely heard it over the boisterous conversations around us.

A calculating grin spread across Eric's face, which meant that whatever he said next would hurt Juno. "Saint Mary's back home, of course."

It looked like someone had hit the pause button on Juno; she didn't even blink, face completely frozen. Hell, I worried if she was even breathing.

"You're fucking with me," she rasped. "You're not only getting married the same weekend but at the same damn church that we had planned for *our* wedding?"

"It was already paid for, Juno," Stephanie admonished. "Please come. We want you there." She turned a small smile to Eric. "We both need you there, your blessing of sorts."

"Also, if I'm there, supporting you two, then everyone at home will think I approve, and so will they. I have to hand it to you, Eric. Your scheming ways to keep your public image intact are impressive."

Eric scoffed. "I don't know what you mean. You being there would be for us, June Bug."

"She said to stop calling her that. Don't make her repeat herself," I stated. I lightly grasped Juno's chin and turned her attention to me. "If you want to go, we all go. But if you don't, then we don't." But I'd love to leave town for a few days and get her away from whatever the fuck danger was drawing closer and closer to us daily. "It's your call."

A full glass of clear carbonated liquid thumped to the tabletop. Juno's hand shook as she wrapped her fingers around it and raised the thin straw to her lips.

"What did I miss?" West asked as he resumed his seat.

"They invited us to the wedding next weekend," I said, watching Juno attempt to down the drink in one go. Clicking my tongue, I grabbed the glass from her hand and set it down in front of me. "You need to eat first."

Her pout was as infuriating as it was cute.

"I love weddings." West leaned forward, resting his forearms on the table. "What was your answer, sweet cheeks? Do I get to show you off, spin you around the dance floor, feed you cake, and then take you back to the hotel to give you a night the bride and groom only wish they could imagine?"

"That sounds tempting," I murmured. Clasping the back of her neck, I gently massaged around her hairline with my thumb, attempting to ease some of the tension while studying her features for any sign of distress.

"It would mean a lot to me," Stephanie begged.

Before Juno could respond, two plastic bags stuffed with to-go containers were plopped in the center of the table. Ches wiped both palms down the front of a grease-stained apron, gaze locked on Stephanie. For half a second, an expression I couldn't read settled on his face, but when I tried to study it more closely, he grunted and turned, heading back toward the swinging kitchen door.

What the fuck was that about? It was almost the same type of malevolent expression her fiancé would give.

"I need to think about my answer," Juno stated, slumping back against the chair. Using my hold on the back of her neck, I gently turned her to face me. "Can we go?" she implored, voice quivering.

That was all the approval I needed. Boot heels to the worn hardwood floor, I pushed back from the table and stood.

"We're done here. Juno will let you know her answer when she's ready, and not a damn second before that. I'm sure she knows how to reach both of you," I stated, grabbing the bags off the table with one hand.

West stood from his chair and held out a hand to Juno, helping her out of the seat.

"Uh, we're here for a couple of days," Stephanie stammered as if shocked by our abrupt departure. "We thought we could all hang out or something, since it's been so long."

"Yeah, that's a hard pass," Juno huffed, but I saw the indecision on her face.

"You're staying at The Nest, right?" I asked.

Eric sat up straighter and looped an arm around

Stephanie's shoulders. "Yes. Only the best for my Stephanie."

Juno rolled her eyes so hard I was surprised it didn't make a sound. There was the sass I was drawn to the last few months, each day needing another hit of the woman's alluring attitude.

"Come on," West said, tugging on Juno's hand. "Let's get you home."

Gaze scanning every face of the thinning crowd, I followed Juno as West led her to the front door, but no one stood out as a threat or unfamiliar. After the incident at Calista and Hudson's, the urgency to keep my family safe was an insistent itch under my skin I couldn't scratch.

I needed to be more alert than ever. Which meant keeping the two most important people in my life close.

Though neither of them understood to what extent that meant just yet. I couldn't help the growing smirk as I imagined Juno's reaction once she realized what keeping her safe would entail.

There was no doubt she would push back at the extremes I was about to go to, and I couldn't fucking wait.

18

WEST

The crinkle of plastic sounded over the hum of the tires as the full bags shifted on my lap with every bump and turn on our way home. Langston drove—control freak, that one—with one hand gripping the wheel, the other constantly fidgeting with his cap, a sign he was more wound up than he let on. I couldn't blame him, though, because so was I. Between being so turned on that I worried I'd be hard for the rest of my life mixed with the searing anger that pumped through my veins from how Eric treated Juno right in front of us and not being able to do anything about it, I had never been on edge like this before.

I shifted on the seat, the movement drawing Langston's attention; our eyes met in the rearview mirror. The dark shade of his green eyes said it all. He felt the same way I did, half needing to comfort her, the other half wanting to fuck her until she forgot all about that douche's words.

Once we were home, we needed to tread carefully, following Juno's lead. Today was an ongoing emotional roller coaster for her, and as much as I was desperate to soothe her frayed nerves with a few orgasms, neither

Langston nor I would make the first move. But if she needed a night to forget the day, sandwiched between two men who wanted nothing more than to worship her perfect body, well, then we would give her everything she wanted and needed until the sun broke over the horizon.

The distressed woman up front hadn't uttered a word since Langston had literally buckled her into the passenger seat. Recalling the deadpan glare she gave him as the metal latch clicked into place had me chuckling again. Fuck, we would have our hands full with her, and I couldn't wait. I knew she would revolt against every protective instinct Langston had, and I had my work cut out for me as well to convince Juno that she was nothing like what Eric made her believe about herself and instead everything I longed for in a lifetime partner.

I winced to myself. Maybe I would keep the lifetime part out of it until she was more comfortable and the term wouldn't spook her.

As we rode in silence, worry crept in at how quiet she was, no doubt processing it all in that brilliant mind of hers. She'd done that alone, with no one to talk to, for so long, even when she was in a relationship with that douche nozzle, that I wondered if she even knew how to ask for help. It would take time; her letting her walls down wouldn't happen in a twenty-four-hour period, even though I wished it would. I had known Juno was ours before either of them would admit it even to themselves, but hell, it was only last night that I finally made our intentions obvious.

Gravel crunched beneath the SUV's tires as Langston pulled into the small parking lot those of us with personal cars in the community used. After cutting the engine, he turned in his seat and eyed Juno, then me, his attention falling to the stack of containers in my lap.

"Think you got enough food?"

I lifted my shoulders in a slight shrug. "I hope six orders of elk nachos is enough; if it's not, then either you or I can run down to the general store. You know Amy and Carl always have those healthy ready-made meals handy." I studied the side of Juno's face. "So, where are we eating?"

"Our place," Langston answered before she could speak up. Her lips pressed in a tight line. "It's safer, more guns—"

"Guns in general," Juno added.

"You don't have a weapon?" Langston growled, leaning forward against the center console.

"I figured if I did, I would be arming the bad guy since I wouldn't use it," she said with a nonchalant shrug.

"You don't know how to shoot?" I asked, growing slightly worried about Langston's blood pressure at the fluttering of the thick vein along his neck.

"Of course I do. I grew up in Alaska. I just don't like to, and I don't think I could ever use one."

"You need a gun," Langston demanded.

"You need to back off," Juno responded.

"So, our place," I said with a clap to end their argument. Before either of them could restart it, I shoved open the door and exited the SUV, hoping like hell they would follow. The setting sun's glare burned into my eyes, making me squint as I waited. "I don't like the nearly twenty-four-hour dark in the winter, but I sure as hell don't like the sun being out this bright at eight."

"What will people think if I don't go to the wedding?" Juno asked after slamming the door shut.

Gathering the bags in one hand, I draped an arm over her shoulders and sealed her to my side as we walked toward our cabin.

"Who cares what people think? You choose what's best

for Juno Jones, not anyone else, and we'll support you in that decision. Also, remember that just because they asked doesn't mean you have to go."

"But it feels like I do. It'll look like I'm jealous and bitter if I say no." Her loud, frustrated groan filled the air as she tipped her face up to the sky. "Or still have feelings for Eric and am too upset at them being together to attend."

"All we care about is what you want to do, what's best for you. If you want to go to show off your two hot boyfriends—"

"Friends who are boys," Juno corrected.

Langston smacked her ass, making her gasp and whirl around to him. "I am not a boy, and what I want to do to you is anything but friendly, shortcake."

"Or if you want to stay home with enough ice cream to last the weekend and hole up with Langston watching Hallmark movies, then we'll do that." I dodged Langston's punch with a barked curse, moving to the other side of Juno.

Grumbling about having two brats to keep in line now, Langston bounded up the porch steps, keys already in hand. He unlocked the first deadbolt, then the other. Juno arched a questioning brow and inclined her head toward the multiple locks, and I shrugged in return. That was Langston being Langston. I'd put my foot down after the second one or there would've been more.

"That sounds like fun." Juno went in after Langston, me hot on her heels. "Please tell me he cries at the end."

My boots thumped against the floor as I made my way to the kitchen. Setting the bags down, I reached into the cabinet for three plates.

"Oh yeah, but he calls it 'allergies.'"

"You two are the worst," Langston grumbled, coming to

lean against the counter beside me. "And it is allergies, you asshat."

"Allergies that kick in at the end when they finally kiss."

Grabbing a dish towel off the counter, he gripped both ends and whipped one toward my ass. The popping sound was worse than the sting, but still I yelped, rounding the island to take shelter behind Juno for protection. Her full, genuine laugh echoed through the cabin.

"Save me, Juno," I fake pleaded.

She scanned the counter, a smirk pulling at her lips upon spotting another dish towel. Swiping it off the top, she twirled it around before snapping one end right toward Langston's crotch. He sprang back with a high-pitched yelp, barely missing the hit that would've decommissioned him for several minutes.

Seeing she had the upper hand, Juno advanced on Langston, chasing after him when he darted around the island, putting it between them. Their smiles were so wide and carefree, it made my heart fucking ache with the swelling joy.

"Is this how it always is around here?" Juno asked, not taking her eyes off Langston as she twirled the towel around and around, preparing for her next attack. "All fun and games?"

"Never," I said honestly, voice rough with emotion. "Never once until you walked through that door."

She froze, cutting her eyes my way. "Really?"

I offered a nonchalant shrug in response, not knowing what else to say.

"Don't make it sound like we're boring," Langston grumbled, clearly offended.

"Aren't we?" I joked. "All we do is work out, work, and go

to Anchorage to...." I trailed off, not wanting to finish that thought, but Juno did it for me.

"To meet women," she said with an arched brow.

I felt my face warm, and Langston avoided eye contact with both of us, finding something interesting on the floor in front of the oven.

She laughed. "Come on, guys. It's not like it's a secret around here. Most of the guys do. Well, until they find their lobster. Or lobsters, in this community's case."

I raised my hand high in the air, which she questioned but still slapped with hers. "Nice *Friends* reference."

"Thank you."

"Though not really the case lately," Langston muttered under his breath.

Juno spun around to face him. "What do you mean by that?"

I cleared my throat, drawing her attention. "He means we haven't gone to Anchorage for that in a while. Well, I actually know the exact date." I pointed at her. "Since you arrived."

"What?" Her voice was high-pitched in utter disbelief. Langdon's broad shoulders rose and fell. "Why? Why would my coming to Anchor Bay have anything to do with your"— she waved her hand around—"extracurricular activities?" She pointed at Langston. "You've hated me since the day I arrived."

"Considered you a potential threat, not hated," he corrected.

She swung her finger my way, tapping the center of my chest. "And you never once made it clear or even gave me a hint until the last forty-eight hours that you would want something more with me than just being friends. Honestly, if I didn't know that you guys were into girls too, I would've thought you two were happy together."

Langston and I exchanged a look and winced.

"That is definitely not the case. West and I sometimes...." He trailed off and looked at me for help.

"You can say the word *fuck*, Langston."

He groaned and adjusted his ball cap while staring at the ceiling.

"Exactly. We're not *together*, together. I love the asshole like a brother. And sometimes things just happen."

He looked at me, and I held up both hands in surrender.

"No, keep going. You're doing great." He launched the dish towel at my face. "Langston and I don't know what we are," I said, crossing my arms. "Which works for us; neither of us needs a label. I've always swung both ways, if you will."

"And I have not," Langston said, "until I met West."

Juno's eyebrows rose. "Oh."

"And now," I hedged, "we hope that you're okay with knowing that I'm attracted to Langston and I'm attracted to you. I want you, and I want to be with Langston too, but not in the same way," I said. "If that makes sense."

"Not really," she said, looking utterly confused.

"It's not romantic," Langston clarified. "Is that a good way to explain it?"

My loud clap rang through the room. "Exactly that. It's just fucking. When tensions are high and we both need that release, sometimes it just happens."

Juno rubbed her temples. "This is a little confusing."

"It doesn't have to be," I said. "It just is what it is."

"And we want you in the middle of that. Hopefully, we have made that very clear and not confusing." Langston rounded the island and grabbed her hand, drawing her toward the stack of plates. "Come on. Let's eat. Get some much-needed food in our stomachs, more drinks, and go from there."

Juno sagged against the counter. "Yes, please. I'm starving, and those few sips before you stole my drink"—she shot an accusing glare at Langston—"were not enough to dull this crazy night. Tonight's been one I'll always remember but want to forget, that's for sure," she muttered under her breath with an eye roll.

The responding gleam in Langston's gaze told me he took that as a personal challenge, which had a grin spreading across my face.

Good.

Hopefully, we could turn the night around so it became one she would never want to forget for all the best reasons.

THANKFULLY, we had enough food and extras for later if we wanted them during our cozy night in. The day started great, went to shit, got better, then went to even more shit, and now it was the best night ever.

Understanding that she was at max capacity and needed to decompress, we had her change here instead of going home. She swam in my sweats, even after rolling them up a few times, and the way Langston's shirt hung off her was almost comical but completely adorable too. After she was comfortable, we set her on the couch with our softest blanket—thank you, Mattie—and tossed her the remote to choose what we were watching first.

She melted into the couch, as if an actual weight had been lifted off her. It was then that I understood what Baylee and Aspen tried to explain a few days ago—most women were tired of having to ask for what they needed instead of their partner, or partners in this case, seeing their exhaustion and just taking care of it without having to be told.

It wasn't difficult, but it required energy and time to watch, learn, and act. Maybe that was the hard part for men in today's culture. They think it's all about them, their girl needing to adapt to their lives instead of seeing the weight she carried daily and doing whatever they could to ease some of it.

"What are you thinking hard about?" I tracked her finger until it pressed between my brows. "You have a line there you're focusing so hard."

"Oh, you know—just gender roles, relationships, and how to establish true partnerships," I rattled off.

Juno chuckled. "So, just a bit of light thinking. Come up with anything solid that you'd like to share with the rest of us?"

"No, I'm enjoying this. I'll save the heavy stuff for later."

She just nodded and leaned her head on my shoulder, attention going back to the Hallmark Christmas movie that Langston chose for us to watch. They were just about to fall victim to miscommunication when Juno shifted to place her head on my lap, aqua eyes gazing up at me.

"West," she whispered.

"Yes, Juno?" I followed the tip of her tongue as it traced her lower lip.

"I can't stop thinking about everything." She paused, and I didn't move, barely breathing as I waited for what I hoped her next words would be. "Can you help me?" Her gaze slid to Langston. "Both of you? Just for tonight, I want to not feel so heavy."

The couch groaned beneath Langston's weight as he shifted, moving closer, having heard every word. "Are you asking for a distraction, shortcake?"

"Yes," she breathed. "But it doesn't mean anything."

"It means you're attracted to us," I offered. "And feel safe with us. What do you need, Juno?"

"More of last night?" Her cheeks bloomed red. "But this time, more?"

"How much more?" Langston asked, scooting even closer until our thighs touched. He reached down, brushing the tip of a single finger along her lips.

"A little more?"

He chuckled. "There is nothing little about either of us, Juno."

The stain on her cheeks deepened to an almost burnt red. "Can I just let the two of you decide?" she whispered. "I don't want to make any decisions; I just want to get lost."

"On one condition." Langston slid his hand lower to collar her neck. I swallowed a groan at the sight. "You tell us to stop if it's too far or too much. I have to trust that you'll be honest with us or nothing happens. Understood?"

"Yes." His fingers flexed in warning. "Yes, sir."

"Good girl. Now, Westly, kiss our girl until all she can think about is us."

"Not your—"

I silenced her with my lips pressed to hers, cupping her cheek to keep her in place. The couch creaked when Langston stood, coming around to the other side where Juno was stretched out along the cushions.

Her soft moan had me hardening, my cock pressing uncomfortably against the zipper of my jeans and the back of her head. The feel of her lips against mine, teasing her tongue with my own for her to envision how it would feel deep in her pussy, only made me want more.

At her gasp, I peeked one eye open, smirking at finding Langston kissing along her stomach where he had rolled the shirt she was wearing up to just under her breasts. Peeking through his lashes, his green eyes met mine, making the heat blazing through my veins burn even hotter.

"You like his mouth on you?" I murmured, our lips barely brushing with each word.

"Yes, a lot," Juno breathed.

"How about if he goes higher?" Her lids fluttered open, glassy eyes meeting mine. At her nod, I slid my gaze down to Langston. "You heard her."

His brow quirked at my command since he was usually the one doing it, but he slid her top up all the way to her neck just the same. For a few moments, neither Langston nor I moved, too caught up in staring at the way her full breasts pushed against the black lace bra. With a quick flick of his fingers to the front snap, the two scraps of lace fell to the side.

We groaned in unison, his lips going to one breast and my fingers to the other. I was mesmerized by the way the nipple pebbled beneath my soft touch, the stiff peak begging for my lips.

I studied the way Langston's wide hand wrapped around her, squeezing the soft flesh between his fingers as he massaged. Juno gasped, eyes wide open as she squirmed on the couch.

I took her lips with mine once again, nipping as I pulled back. "Are you ready for more, sweet cheeks?"

"Yes, please," she whined. "I need more."

Langston's dark chuckle had my cock twitching beneath my jeans, no doubt leaving a wet stain of precum from how hard and ready I was.

"Tell us what you want, Juno," he rasped, swirling his tongue around the pebbled nipple while he gazed up at her.

Fucking hell, it was hot. "Tell me exactly what you want me to do to your pretty pussy."

"I don't know. I just need.... Please, Langston. Please, please, please," she begged.

He clicked his tongue but sat back, fingers going to the hem of her borrowed sweats. He inched them down little by little until the top of the matching black lace panties appeared. Lower and lower he dragged them down her thighs before ripping the gray cotton off her feet and tossing them to the floor.

He stared at where the lace glistened, showing us exactly how needy she was. Langston swiped a finger along the delicate material and held it close to Juno's face. Without warning, he slid her desire along her lower lip before thrusting the slick finger into her mouth.

Her guttural groan mixed with my own sounded through the cabin.

"Let's get her on your lap, and then you spread her open wide with your thighs."

Gently gripping beneath her arms, Langston lifted her off the couch and set her ass right on top of my throbbing cock. At my grunt, he laughed, the bastard knowing exactly what kind of torture he was putting me through.

He draped her legs over mine and pushed my knees out wide. Kneeling before the both of us, Langston watched us, green eyes almost black with desire.

"I can't wait to do this when his cock is buried deep inside you," he murmured.

"Yes," Juno and I said in unison.

"But not tonight. No, that's only for good girls who let us call them ours." Juno whimpered. "I hope you're not fond of these panties."

"What—"

The sound of elastic snapping and material ripping cut her off.

Sitting back on his heels, Langston held up the ruined underwear before pressing the soaked area to his nose and inhaling deeply. Juno's back shifted with each of her rapid breaths.

"Until it's his dick, we'll both have to settle for his fingers."

Not needing direction, I dipped my good hand between her thighs, fingers gliding along her slit before drawing teasing circles around her drenched entrance. A sharp breath whistled through my clenched teeth when I sank a single finger inside, her walls clenching down tight.

"But I don't want to miss out on all the fun while I suck that needy nub until you squirt all over my face," he added.

"Fuck, Langston," I hissed. "Are you trying to get me to come in my fucking pants?"

He just arched a brow while lifting his hand to her core, sliding a single finger inside beside mine. Juno gasped, shifting on my lap at the added pressure. We moved in unison, curling our fingers as we thrust in and out.

Keeping his gaze locked on me, Langston pitched forward and sealed his mouth around her clit. Juno cried out and pressed back hard, as if attempting to escape the new sensation. My harsh breaths brushed along her hair, making it float with every exhale.

It only took a few seconds of Langston's mouth on her before she cried out, back arching as her chest and neck flushed red. He didn't stop, though; instead, he added another finger, stuffing her full as we quickened our pace. This time when she fell apart, her voice cracked on a broken scream before she slumped back against me.

I squeezed my lids shut and bit down on my tongue hard

to keep from exploding in my jeans. The built-up pressure was past a pleasureful pain and hurt like fucking hell.

But it was worth it. I'd live like this every day, every second, if that meant she was as happy and content as she was now.

Langston sat back, pulling his fingers free and taking mine with him, raising our combined fingers to his lips. I shook my head, knowing it would be too much—not that the bastard cared.

When he slipped our glistening fingers past his lips and sucked hard to clean her orgasm off our skin, I shuddered, head dropping back against the couch.

Fucking hell, the man was trying to kill me.

19

JUNO

"Up." My lids fluttered open at Langston's command. His hooded gaze wasn't on me, though. It was directed just over my shoulder. When his green eyes slid my way, his features softened. "Better?"

"Yes," I whispered, shifting on West's lap. His hiss of pain and the dick poking me in the ass told me he wasn't, and by the way Langston's pants were tented, neither was he. "But you two... I should—"

"You shouldn't do anything," West said in my ear. I shivered at the feel of his breath against my skin, but he must have thought I was cold. "Let's get you dressed and warm."

After grabbing the sweats off the floor, Langston helped me into them before securing my bra and pulling the too-large shirt down, but not before planting a sweet kiss on my stomach.

"You relax a minute while I take care of our situation," Langston said, helping me down to the couch. I gaped at him while he carefully draped a blanket over me. "West, my room, fucking now."

West popped off the couch like someone had lit his ass

on fire. Langston smirked, gaze following West as he hurried to obey.

Elbows pressed into the soft leather, I pushed up, brow furrowed. "What are you doing?"

His hand dipped into the front of his jeans, lids slamming shut as he gripped himself. "Just need to take some of the pressure off, and I know he does too." My lips parted to tell him I would help, but he cut me off. "Not yet, shortcake. Tonight, it was about you, but if West and I don't want to die from blue balls, we need to take care of this. Feeling you, taking your sweet taste, and hearing your sounds—fuck, I've never been so hard."

The desire from earlier roared back to life, making my lower belly flip and twist.

"Can I—" I licked my lips. "Can I watch?"

There was nothing warm about the cruel smile that pulled at his lips. "I think we'll save that show for when you admit to yourself, and us, that you're all ours." He started toward his bedroom but paused. "Don't you fucking dare touch yourself, no matter what you hear. You understand me?"

"Yes," I whispered.

"Yes, what?"

"Yes, sir."

"That's my good girl."

Fucking hell. With no underwear, there was no doubt a wet spot growing in the crotch of my borrowed sweats. Thank fuck they were black; hopefully that would hide the evidence of how turned on I was at the thought of them together and hearing Langston's small praise.

The bedroom door slammed shut, making me jump. I stared at the solid wood, hand itching to slide beneath the blanket and slip between my thighs as images of them together came to life. Then the sounds started. West's groaned curses, the sound of masculine grunts followed by the slapping of skin, and Langston's barked commands for West to take all of him had me shivering with overwhelming desire.

A small orgasm raced through me when they both shouted their climax, something either slamming against the wall or falling on the floor startling me. Breaths coming in quick pants, I watched the door, wishing like hell I was in there too.

Soon.

AFTER THE BOYS cleaned up and came out of Langston's room, both relaxed and smiling, I let them convince me to stay for another movie, not ready to go home alone. It was nice to be so comfortable around them that I could let my walls down and be me for a little while. Especially after the emotionally stressful night at Dave's. It was almost as if by simply being in the same room with them, I was absorbing their strength.

By the time the credits started rolling, my lids were so heavy that each blink was more of a few seconds nap than anything. Blissfully peaceful in that magical space where you're partly asleep and awake, the couch cushions shifted, jostling me. Knowing it was time for me to head home, I pressed both hands to the smooth leather and pushed to sit up. Jaw wide with an open-mouthed yawn, I stretched both arms overhead, hoping that would wake me up enough to walk from their place to mine.

"That," I said with a sleepy smile, "was a great night, but my bed is calling my name." I emphasized my point with another wide yawn. "Which one of you is walking me home, because I know you won't let me...." Even with my sleepy brain, I caught the strange look the two men exchanged. "What am I missing?"

"We discussed it, and neither of us will walk you home," West said cautiously, flicking a worried glance at Langston as he ran a hand over his short hair.

The sting of rejection made me flinch. It was probably because of earlier; I wasn't what they'd expected, and they were seeing what I'd meant by being broken. Why else would they suddenly not care about my safety?

"Oh, well, um, that's...." I shook my head, trying to get my brain to work. "Totally fine. I get it, and I tried to tell you two that I wasn't good at that stuff. I guess you believe me now."

Feeling completely used and really, really sad, I pushed off the couch, biting my lower lip to keep my chin from quivering while fighting off the stinging tears threatening to fall. Nose hot from the unshed tears, I whirled around with an accusing finger aimed at both of them. "I cannot believe I trusted all the bullshit tonight. Everything you said, how you defended me with Eric, I really believed—" Cutting myself off, I wiped at a stray tear with the back of my head. "Screw you both and your cat too." I paused. "Actually, I take that back. I like your cat better than you two right now."

The long sweats tripped me, catching beneath my feet as I stomped to the front door, very ready for a quick exit so I could die from the hurt and embarrassment in my bed. With a bottle of wine and a tub of ice cream.

Too focused on escaping, I didn't notice anyone coming after me until a thick, tattooed arm wrapped around my waist, yanking me back against a hard chest.

"You're killing me, shortcake," Langston rasped in my

ear. "Do you really think so little of us that at the first misunderstanding, you think we're anything like that dipshit ex of yours?"

I swallowed down the unshed tears. "It's all I know, Langston, and West said—"

"That we aren't walking you home because you're not going. I want you here, with us, and so does he. Next to us, in our bed, not alone in yours."

I blinked at the dark-stained door as if it held the answers to my confusion. "So, you aren't disappointed in me from earlier or for being lame and wanting a chill night in—"

"Tonight was the best night I've had in what feels like a lifetime, Juno, because you were here with us. You didn't make the night anything but perfect."

Warm tears broke free and trickled down my face. "I'm sorry I thought...."

He gently spun me around and tipped my face up to his. "I'm sorry that we didn't think our phrasing through. We were worried you'd push back; that was the hesitation you heard in West. Neither of us wants you to go."

"Why?"

"The main reason is that a part of me is afraid you'll go back to your place and never come back. And two, I haven't gone into detail about what happened tonight, but I need you here where it's safe."

The finality in his tone had me backing up a step. "And if I say no?" Which I had no intention of doing, because I'd accepted that this between us was real, or at least genuine enough that I should give them a chance. If they wanted me to be their girl, undesirable pieces and all, then why not let them?

The sharp smile that curved at his lips was my only

warning that I would pay for my words. A surprised shriek escaped, bouncing off the cabin walls as I was hauled into the air and tossed over his broad shoulder.

"This is becoming a habit, shortcake." His chuckle was deep and full of mirth. "Can't say I hate it either."

My hair swung from side to side with each long stride. Curling my hands into fists, I punched his firm ass, hurting myself more than him no doubt, pretending to hate it while biting back my growing smile. One large, calloused palm wrapped around mine, stopping me.

"Careful or you'll hurt yourself, and we can't have an injured hostage. That would look bad."

"You two are ridiculous," I chided, but there was no truth to it. Because if I was finally ready to be theirs, then it was time to be truly honest with myself. I loved their over-protective, caveman sides when it came to me.

Free hand pressed to Langston's firm ass, I pushed off for leverage, angling my face toward West. Blowing the hair out of my eyes, I shot him a wry smile. "I'm sorry I thought the worst about you two."

"And yourself?" I huffed and shook my head. "But I get it; I would too if I went through what you did." He looked over Langston's shoulder once we entered his room, West's smirk growing to a conspiring grin. "Hold on."

"What—" The word was cut off when I was tossed into the air. All those drinks and nachos rolled in my stomach as I free-fell. The air rushed from my lungs when my butt and then back landed on a soft mattress, the pillows around my head bouncing from the impact.

Elbows pressed into the thick quilt, I started to say something snarky, but the words, and all thoughts at all, dried up.

Both men were stripping off their clothes, shirts already removed and piled on the floor. The front of Langston's jeans was undone, hanging open precariously low on his hips as he helped a sheepish looking West unfasten his.

"And you say you're not romantic," I whispered. "That right there is."

"That's functional and helping a friend, not romantic," West said, removing his glasses and tossing them on top of the dresser.

Their jeans removed and added to the growing pile of clothes, both men were clad only in tight boxer briefs. I wiped at my lips to remove any drool. Holy hell, they were mouthwateringly sexy. West with his full back tattoo and others along both ribs, plus his lean and muscular frame, was so picture-perfect that I wondered if he'd ever considered modeling. Then there was Langston, with his full sleeves that bled onto his defined pecs, bad attitude, and constant scowl. He looked deadly, in the hottest way possible.

Langston paused on one side of the bed, West on the other. With a lot of shifting and wiggling, I scooted under the thick quilts, allowing them to slide into the sheets beside me.

Held breath burning in my lungs, I waited for the touching to begin, for one of them to grab my boob or stick their hand down my pants. The weight of sexual expectations felt like an elephant was sitting on my chest. Not that I didn't want to per se—everything that happened on the couch earlier was great—but the expectancy of sex when in bed together was so drilled into me that I dreaded going to bed, knowing I would have to do that before I could sleep.

I stayed stiff, completely still, like I always would with Eric, hoping I'd get a pass on the obligation. Which was so fucking dumb because I actually wanted the two men beside me, but my head was a complicated, messed-up mess.

"Why are you so tense right now?" Langston asked, turning on his side to face me. I felt the heat of his stare on my cheek. When I didn't respond, he sighed. "Juno, talk to us. We can't help if we don't know what's going on in that mind of yours."

Swiping my tongue over my lips, I tried to swallow to ease my suddenly dry throat. "I told y'all I was broken," I whispered. "And you didn't believe me."

"If anyone is broken in this bed, it's me, Juno, so please don't say that again," West rasped. "Talk to us."

My hair scraped against the pillow when I turned to face him. "How would you be broken? You're perfect. I was just thinking that when you were getting undressed. Sexy, good with your hands, kind—you're all the things, West."

His sad smile broke my heart a little. "My past is dark and full of monsters who took advantage of any situation they could, sweet cheeks. But we're not focusing on my triggers right now," he said with a deprecating chuckle. "What's going on in that brilliant mind of yours?"

The weight of my silence hung heavily in the dark room, the quiet only interrupted by the pitter-patter of tiny paws on the hardwood floor before a weight landed at the foot of the bed. Padding across the quilt, GG moved up toward us, doing a few circles before finding a snug spot between me and Langston. Pulling a hand free from beneath the covers, I stroked her soft head, debating how to answer them.

"There was always the expectation of sex," I blurted. "With Eric—"

"I really don't enjoy hearing another man's name, especially his, when you're in my bed." Langston pouted, making me smile despite the heavy memories filling my thoughts.

"It was always the focus, the expectation or obligation, I guess. For example, when we went on vacation or went away for a weekend, he would talk about how he couldn't wait to have sex at least three times a day. It wasn't about spending time away with me or being away from work so we could focus on each other, just sex. It made it this heavy expectation that I dreaded. Sex began to be something I resented because it was an obligation. It was all he wanted from the relationship, not the intimacy or a partnership, just sex. That was his need from me and the only thing he ever focused on as a measure of how our relationship was going. It felt very transactional, like if he got what he wanted, then we had a good time; if he didn't, then, well, I would hear about how cold I was, that he wasn't getting what he needed, blah blah blah. Listen, I get that men need sex. It's part of how they feel connected—"

"That's a fucked-up statement, Juno," Langston interrupted. "You're making it sound like all we want is sex and not the relationship side of it. Maybe that's true with some men, but how empty is that if you don't have the connection with your partner to go with it? That's like treating your partner, the person you say you love, like a fucking cum dumpster."

"Ew," I laughed. "That's a disgusting visual."

"But an accurate one," West added. "So, us crawling into bed with you triggered the thought that we expected sex because we're in bed with you?"

"Well, yeah. Don't you?" I asked.

"If you jumped on me naked, I wouldn't say no." Langston shifted on the bed, disturbing GG. A heavy arm dropped across my chest as he sealed himself to my side. "But I'm getting everything I need knowing you're here and safe, and in my bed beside me. I feel like I won the damn lottery right now."

"And the two people I care about the most have finally admitted they're fucking obsessed with each other; they just show it in their own strange ways." I smacked West on the chest, making all three of us laugh. "And you're here beside me." He shifted so he was pressed against my other side, drawing an arm around my waist just below Langston's. "And in my arms. But this means nothing if you're not comfortable or not getting what you need, Juno. Tell us, talk to us. Don't just expect the worst because that's how it was before."

This time, the silence in the large room was freeing.

"Okay." I slid my arm back under the blankets. "So, you're both okay just going to sleep right now?"

"Is that what you want?"

"Yes. I'm sorry I'm not feeling up for—"

"Careful, Juno," Langston growled, his voice rumbling through the room. "Do not finish that sentence if you want to sit tomorrow."

I swallowed hard and nodded. "I'm exhausted."

"I'm almost asleep now. You're like a weighted blanket. I don't know if I've ever felt this relaxed in the dark."

I wanted to ask West what he meant by that, but his deep breathing told me he truly was asleep.

"Thank you," Langston whispered, pressing a kiss to my shoulder.

"For what?"

"Giving him peace so he can do that. His demons torment him at night. I don't think he's ever had a full night's sleep, ever. Maybe you're the one to change that. Good night, Juno. Don't worry about anything; I've got you both."

Within a minute, his breaths turned soft and even, like West's. GG padded up toward our heads and curled up next to Langston's on his pillow. I smiled up at the ceiling like a crazy person.

For the first time in a long time, I inhaled deeply, the weight of having to handle my safety and their expectations lifted.

As I drifted off to sleep, I wondered if I'd ever felt so utterly safe before as I did in that moment in both their arms.

***

VIBRATIONS against my ribs stirred me awake, my heart racing at the unfamiliar feeling. Head slowly lifting off the pillow, I gazed down at my side and a breath caught in my throat. GG lay curled against me, her fluffy tail laid over her nose so she looked more like a random puff ball than an actual cat.

Relaxing back with a slow, calming breath, I blinked a few times to clear my fuzzy vision. Sunlight poured through the blinds, but that didn't tell me anything, considering we were at the time of the year when it was daylight most of the day.

Gentle breathing to my left had me sliding my attention from the ceiling to the man sprawled out beside me. As West lay on his stomach with the sheet draped low on his hips, I nearly choked on my spit at how utterly gorgeous he looked. Features relaxed, lips slightly parted, and with his arms up by his head, the defined lines of his back muscles were on full display.

Pulling my hand free of the covers, I ghosted my fingertips over the intricate design, careful not to touch and risk waking him. Langston's admission from the night before fluttered to the front of my mind, making my heart clench.

What had the amazing, kind, and gentle man been through in his life that made him unable to sleep soundly? I knew little about his background, nothing at all really. My lips turned down in a frown. That needed to change. They had pulled so much information and excavated all kinds of memories from me; it was only fair to do the same to them. Plus, I was excited to learn more about them. Know where they came from, what they loved about being here, where they saw themselves in the future.

I wanted it all.

But first, coffee.

With him on one side and GG on the other, I made the tough decision to disrupt the cat instead of the sexy sleeping man, one she did not appreciate based on the side-eye and sassy flick of her tail as she jumped down. Careful not to shift the bed too much, I slid out from under the thick blankets, noting that the sheets on Langston's side were cold, meaning he'd been up for a while. I started for the door, goose bumps pebbling on my arms, only to pause outside Langston's bathroom, remembering that last night, due to my utter exhaustion and slight kidnapping, I didn't brush my teeth.

After taking care of that with a bit of toothpaste on my finger and using the restroom, I resumed my search for Captain Asshole, who wasn't so much of an asshole anymore.

The smell of coffee wafted up my nose with a deep inhale, the scent alone taking a bit of the edge off my brain, knowing the goodness was close. But before I could round the island to the full coffee carafe, movement outside the open back door had me redirecting to the small concrete stoop just on the other side of the threshold.

Shoulder against the doorframe, I smiled down at Langston. His bare back shifted as he lifted the coffee mug to his lips, making the inked designs dance and move. Without a word, he lifted his free hand and stretched behind him, reaching for me. Placing my hand in his, I allowed him to guide me around him, pausing between his spread knees. With a gentle tug, he urged me to sit on the step below him.

A chill from the concrete seeped through the borrowed sweatpants, making my shoulders shake with an unexpected shiver. A strong inked arm wrapped around my shoulders and eased me back until my head rested against his chest. Tipping my head, I smiled up at Langston, who was already doing the same, green eyes locked on me.

"Good morning," he said, voice deep and raspy. "Coffee?"

With an eager nod, I accepted the offered mug and took a sip. The moment the flavor hit my tongue, my eyes widened and I whirled around, gaping at Langston. It was exactly how I made mine; it tasted so similar I would've thought I made it.

His shoulders rose and fell. "I pay attention."

I should give him a blow job or something for that, right? I mean, who the fuck paid that much attention to a woman they weren't dating or planned to date?

"Full of surprises, aren't you," I murmured, taking another drink.

"Oh, shortcake, you do not know how many more I have for you." He leaned in close and nipped at my earlobe. "All good, I promise."

"Okay," I whispered, because what else was there to say.

Screaming "show me now" seemed desperate. I swallowed hard to keep those exact words to myself and took another sip of coffee, settling back against him to gaze out at the gorgeous mountain view.

"I love this view in the morning," he stated. "I come out here to soak it up before the stress of the day starts. It makes it all bearable."

"Protecting everyone here doesn't fall just on your shoulders, you know that, right?"

The vibrations of his heart thumping in his chest reverberated against the back of my head.

"If only it were that easy. But once you've failed someone you love once, it's hard to rationalize with that fear."

"What fear?"

"Of failing someone again, of them not being able to recover from it like Mattie did. There are some things we just can't come back from." My heart ached at the pain in his tone. "Brandon called an all-Uplift community meeting in a few hours. That will give us time to go to your place and grab your things."

I choked on a sip of the delicious liquid. Shifting on the cold concrete, I whirled around and pointed at Langston's chest. His very hard chest. Very defined and sexy chest.

Fuck, stay on topic, Juno.

"What the what? I thought I heard you say we'd grab my things." He nodded, looking pleased with himself. Which looked good on him because it was this cute smile that made him appear years younger. "Why?"

His brows pulled in tight. "Because it's safer here. We discussed this last night."

"No, we discussed you kidnapping me for my safety for one night. *One* night."

He shook his head. "Nope, this is a permanent thing for the foreseeable future until it's safe."

"You cannot be serious right now," I blurted, completely caught off guard by his fucking audacity. That I would move in with them because some sicko was out there hurting single women and had apparently come into our community and.... I froze.

His damn smirk told me he knew I had realized he was right.

Fucker.

Sexy fucker.

"I'll just move in with Finley," I said with a wince. That sounded terrible for so many reasons. I loved the girl, but she was not the cleanest person.

"Right," Langston huffed. "Why would you do that when we can protect you better?"

"Because she's scared." I jumped a little at West's voice, not having noticed him looming in the doorway. "And don't tell me I'm wrong."

I blew a raspberry and tossed up the hand not holding the coffee mug. "Fine, okay. It makes this"—I gestured between the three of us—"feel serious, and I *just* decided that I was okay with it all. Now moving in together—"

"I'm pretty serious about us now. Aren't you, West," Langston asked, not taking his green eyes off me.

"Yep," he said, popping the *p*.

"Okay, both of you slow down. This is way too soon, plus you'll get frustrated with me because—"

"Careful what you say next, Juno," Langston growled, "or that meeting will feel even longer when you're sitting there with a sore ass."

I looked between the two men—the two ridiculously

attractive men. Yes, this was moving fast, but there *was* that danger hanging over all our heads, so staying with them instead of alone was smart. It was a terrible idea but, at the same time, the most logical.

What was the worst that could happen?

20

LANGSTON

O ur normal space for Uplift meetings was not meant to hold the number of people who were currently stuffed inside. Every rickety chair was taken, with several of the guys standing or leaning against the wall behind their partners. Scanning the room, I paused at Finley before flicking my gaze to Dax at the opposite end of the room. Finley's expression was blank as she stared at a spot on the long table while Dax shifted from side to side, fidgety as hell.

I rolled my eyes. Those two needed to figure their shit out before it was too late. Not that I was one to talk. I'd almost missed my chance, but thank fuck I'd wised up in time.

As I pulled out a chair for Juno, Aiden tracked the move with a knowing grin.

"Will you look at that? Langston finally pulled his head out of his ass," he sang with a wide smile. "Halle-fucking-lujah." He pushed off the wall he was leaning against and clapped his hands loudly. "Okay, who put their money on them getting together before six months? There's a big pot to claim." He shot me a dramatic frown. "I chose six weeks, but I should've known it would be longer. You're a stubborn fucker."

"And you're a fucking asshole," West laughed. Grabbing a pen from the table, he launched it at Aiden, who dodged easily.

Aiden pointed at West and turned to the deputy sheriff. "Oliver, did you see that? I'd like to file an assault charge."

Oliver rolled his eyes and mumbled a reply before turning his attention back to the papers in front of him.

At the end sat Aspen, with Miles standing like a sentry behind her. I scoffed at myself when I realized I was doing the same thing. Hitching my chin at Miles in greeting, I did the same to Liam and Memphis. I scanned the floor for the dogs but came up empty. Guess they left the large Bernese mountain dog and yellow lab back at their respective homes, either to keep their cabins protected or because they knew there wouldn't be room for their large bodies today.

Juno spun around in the metal chair and tipped her face up to me. For a second, I lost all thoughts, the enormity of the last couple of days hitting me square in the chest. I'd denied my true feelings for the woman for so long, and now I didn't have to. She was mine.

And she was finally open to admitting she was ours.

"For now," she'd said, but I'd do everything to ensure it was permanent.

"Hey," she said, just loud enough for me to hear over the multiple conversations filling the small space. "So, this morning, I realized I don't know a lot about you. Or you." She shifted her gaze over to West, who hadn't taken his eyes off her since we left the cabin. "And I was hoping maybe we could change that. You know, since we're roommates and all now." She tried but failed to suppress a grin.

"What did you have in mind?" Whatever she wanted to do, I was down for it. Hope filled my chest at her wanting to get to know me better. Not that it was all sunshine and fucking rainbows, but I'd love to tell her about some of my past, and Mattie.

"Do you have any clients today?"

I shook my head. "Not today, but I'm booked up tomorrow, though." I felt my lips pull down into a frown. That would mean I'd have to leave her, but the best part of this multi-partner relationship meant she wouldn't be alone. West, even with one good hand, was lethal and would protect her with his life.

"A little more information for that booking add-on I'm creating would be great, and I want to see you in your natural habitat." I chuckled and nodded. "So, maybe we go fishing today?" She swiveled to face West. "Can you come too?"

He scanned my face before slowly shaking his head. "I think I'll stay behind today, but you two go. You and I can hang out tomorrow while he has to work."

Fuck, I loved that man. He never thought of himself first, which made him a great best friend—and, it seemed, partner in this relationship. But sometimes I hated it. It was almost like he felt like he didn't deserve to be thought of first.

Or at all.

"Everyone, listen up." Brandon's deep, commanding voice vibrated through the cramped space, making everyone go silent at his serious tone. "As most of you know, there was a break-in at Hudson and Calista's place yesterday. Nothing was stolen, but something was left behind, suggesting it was from the same psycho asshole who's behind the missing women."

Juno stiffened in her seat. Without even realizing I was doing it, I squeezed her shoulder before sliding my hand to palm the back of her neck in a comforting hold.

"We thought the threat was out there on the trail," Brandon went on, "but it seems our continued investigation has brought that danger to our doorstep. That doesn't mean we're stopping, though, or backing down."

"The opposite, in fact," Hudson cut in. "I reached out to a friend in the FBI, a talented-as-hell medical examiner, and she's agreed to help. She needs all the autopsy findings, photos, and evidence shipped down to her in Dallas for the profiling team to review. Rain also had me go to Anchorage to meet with a local FBI agent about the missing women cases while I was there talking to the coroner. He seemed surprised by what's going on here and said he needs to look into a few things before getting back to me on his suspicions, whatever the hell that means."

Oliver stepped up to the table, arms crossed over his chest. "While Hudson was gone, Ethan called me, saying he found something on the trail around the area he thinks that female hiker we found a week or so back would've camped." He looked at Ethan. "I can't go into too much detail about the evidence we found, but we're hopeful it will give us an idea of how she ended up so far away."

"And dead," Ethan muttered.

"Until we catch this bastard, I don't want anyone going anywhere alone, especially you ladies. I know we were being cautious when on or near the trail, but we need to be just as vigilant here too. No more unlocked doors." Calista grimaced and tightened her hold on Sam, who squirmed on her mom's lap. "No more morning runs." Baylee leaned back in her chair with a huff. "And you need to find a roommate for a while." His pointed look was aimed right at Juno.

"Now, wait a second," she protested.

"Already taken care of, boss," I cut in before she could finish. "She's moving her stuff over to our place after this."

"Bossy asshole," Juno grumbled under her breath.

"What about her?" We all turned our attention to Dax, who was aiming a death glare at Finley. "Finley lives alone, so why aren't you demanding she find a roommate? She needs to be safe too."

Brandon massaged the back of his neck, looking uncharacteristically uncomfortable.

"That won't be necessary because she won't be here."

"What?" the room basically gasped in unison.

"With the chopper being out of commission and us only needing one pilot for a while, Finley has decided to take some time off." I chanced a glance down the table. Dax's expression said he was as shocked as us about this news, and utterly heartbroken. "She's leaving soon to stay with family in San Diego for a few weeks—"

"When?" Dax asked, voice cracking before he cleared his throat. "When are you coming back?"

Brandon looked at Finley, who just nodded.

"The vacation is open-ended." Before Dax could ask for more details, Brandon continued. "We will keep everyone updated as the case develops, but remember to be extra vigilant wherever you go. If you see something strange, let Oliver, Hudson, or the sheriff know."

"Like he'll do anything," Liam stated. "I'm wondering if he's mixed up in this somehow. Why else would he block this investigation at every damn turn?"

"While I don't think my dad has ties to the cases, I do agree that him pushing back has hindered the investigation, which is why I've asked him to step down." I felt my jaw go slack in utter shock at Oliver's words. "Yeah, I know, he was just as surprised by my balls to confront him." He took off his hat and tossed it onto the table. "While he hasn't agreed to retire, I've at least set the stage and informed him that I will take the official lead on these cases from now on. No more going through him or having to wait; it's all on me now."

"Damn," West murmured. "Fucking finally. Maybe now something will actually get done. I heard he was pushing back because he was pissed Brandon brought in Hudson."

I nodded in agreement. That was what I'd heard too, but it didn't make sense unless the sheriff was really that much of an asshole that he believed help meant he was failing somehow. There had to be more to it.

"Everyone has their schedule for the week," Brandon said, "so that's it for now. Stay safe out there."

The room was noticeably quieter than it had been before the start of the meeting. A shoulder slammed into my side, pushing me against the wall as Dax made a path wide enough to get between me and Juno.

"What the hell?" I snapped, not that he heard me. His full attention was locked on the door where Finley had disappeared the second Brandon stopped talking.

"I need to talk to her," Juno said, more to herself than me or West, before she stood and followed Dax.

I turned to West, who shrugged. "No clue what's going on there. I'm just as in the dark as you are. Come on, let's go do what you do best."

"What's that?" I grumbled, following him as we made our way to the door.

"Stalk Juno from the shadows while she talks with her friend." I shoved his shoulder hard, making him stumble forward. "Just saying, you've had a lot of practice lately.

While we watch and wait, we can make a plan for your day date."

That sounded good to me. This was one date I couldn't afford to fuck up.

"Ugh," Juno groaned. "How do I keep getting this tangled?"

My boots dug into the rocky bank when I turned from my line, brow furrowed. A laugh escaped at the pitiful and dramatic pout on her face as she messed with the knotted fishing line. Her aqua eyes cut my way, making me fight my smile. Apparently, she didn't find it as adorable and funny as I did.

Setting down my pole, I gently took hers to inspect the damage.

"This pole hates me," she grumbled.

"And the last two?" I chuckled.

"They're all ganging up on me."

"It's okay that you're not good at fishing, you know. That's not a requirement for this." I gestured between us. Setting the rod down beside the other two to fix later, I pulled her into my chest, wrapping both arms around her.

"I know, but you love it, so I'd at least like to be not terrible at it."

But she was. She really was. Staring out over the crystal-clear water, I couldn't help the smile that pulled at my lips.

"I think West packed us some food." I inclined my head to the stuffed backpack near the rest of the fishing gear. "How about you take a break—"

"Oh, snacks," Juno exclaimed like I'd just told her something exciting. Which I guess snacks were by her response. Stepping out of my hold, she moved around me to the pack and squatted low to rummage through the contents. "I'll eat, you fish and talk."

"Talk," I grumbled, bending over to pick up my discarded rod. "About what?"

"Life, you, Mattie, your nephew, anything. I want to know more about you."

I arched a brow as I flung the line back into the water. "We have plenty of time for that, shortcake. West and I, we aren't going anywhere."

"Oh, chips. Yum." The rustle of the bag had me shaking my head. Fuck, she was adorable. "Speaking of you and West, how will all this work? If we do this, that is."

"Oh, we're doing it," I chuckled. "And I don't know what you mean by that. What specifically are you asking?"

"Well," she drawled. "After last night, I guess I'm just wondering if you two will do your own thing, or if it will always be the three of us." I started to respond, but she kept going. "Does that mean that we can't do anything one-on-one? Does it always have to be group activities? If so, that will get really hard to coordinate, I think."

"The way I see others make this work is that there aren't any set rules on who can be with who and when. Like any relationship, sometimes things just happen, and not everyone can be around when it does. So you and me can have alone time like we are now, and you and West can too. There isn't room for jealousy or favorites in this kind of relationship. But to answer your question about me and West, I don't see us needing that now that you're with us."

"You did last night." She popped a chip into her mouth before handing me one.

"Yeah, well, that was more of... incentive," I said with a chuckle. "And after eating your tasty cunt and feeling you squeeze the fuck out of my fingers, I needed him."

"Not me?" she asked, munching on the edge of another chip.

"The way I felt last night, Juno, it was best for me to take all that out on West. He likes it, don't worry, and so do I. Plus, last night, neither he nor I wanted to make you feel obligated."

"I wouldn't have," she protested, only for her to cringe at my side-eye. "Fine, I would have. But just because—"

"We know, Juno, which is why last night happened the way it did. Are you upset at how it turned out?"

Her face flushed red. "Not at all. Hearing you two was hot as hell." She peeked up through her lashes. "I'd like to watch instead of just listen one day."

I hummed a noncommittal response. "I have a feeling you'll not only be watching but participating too. I can't tell you how many times I've fucked my hand thinking of us three together." Her eyes went wide as the chip in her hand fluttered to the smooth stones at her feet. "My favorite one is West buried balls-deep in your tight cunt while I fuck him into you."

Her throat worked with a hard swallow. "Wow, okay... that's...." She cleared her throat and jerked her gaze out over the water. "Holy hell, that is hot." She shifted side to side, rubbing her thighs together.

Tossing the rod to the side, I looped an arm around her waist and pulled her to me, sealing her back to my chest. Head against my sternum, she looked back at me. Cheeks flushed, eyes glassy, and lips slightly parted, she looked as turned on as I felt.

"Juno," I muttered, dipping my hand beneath her shirt.

"Langston," she breathed. Her soft gasp as my fingers traced along the waistband of her jeans had my dick twitching beneath my own. "Aren't you supposed to be fishing?"

My chuckle was dark and humorless. "Why would I want to waste my time with that when I have you, so fucking needy for me, in my arms?"

"Am I?" Her lids fluttered shut when I popped the top button and slowly lowered the zipper.

"Let's see how drenched you are from the thought of me fucking my best friend into you." Dipping my fingers beneath her panties, a guttural groan rumbled in my chest when I felt how soaked her pussy was.

"Langston," Juno pleaded. "I need more."

"More than what?"

"More than your fingers." She shifted to press her ass against my steel-hard cock and grinded. "I need you, Langston. Please. I want you, here, right now."

A sharp hiss whistled through my teeth when I sucked in a short breath. "You want the first time I take your perfect cunt to be out here, right now? Not something romantic or some shit?"

I nearly swallowed my tongue when Juno added her hand to mine, guiding my fingers to her opening. "I don't need romantic." Rolling her head, she looked up at me. "I just need real, passion, imperfect."

"Well, then you're in luck, shortcake. Because I am all that." Pulling my hand free, I spun her around and lifted her in the air, then smacked her ass hard, making her squeak. I scanned the empty rocky bank for somewhere somewhat comfortable for me to take my girl, gaze pausing on a downed tree. The thick trunk was the perfect height for what I had planned.

Arm around her waist, I carried Juno in that direction, her lips brushing along my throat and jaw, making my steps falter. Heart hammering in my chest, I paused beside the fallen tree and slowly lowered her to the ground.

She twisted, brow furrowing when she looked down.

"I really don't want bark scratches on my ass," she muttered.

"That wasn't the plan, but good to know." Stepping back, I crossed both arms over my chest and hitched my chin to her top. "Strip."

Surprising the hell out of me, Juno didn't push back; instead, she instantly ripped her long-sleeve shirt over her head. A groan caught in my throat at her full breasts spilling out of the top of her sports bra. When her hands went to her jeans, I clicked my tongue, making her freeze.

"That too. I want to see all of you." For a second, she hesitated, gaze snapping one way and then the other. "No one comes out here, so don't worry about that. You trust me to take care of you?"

"Yes," she breathed.

"Trust me to not let anyone see what's mine and West's, and if they do, then they lose both eyes?"

"This just got dark," Juno said with a slight shiver.

My smile sharpened as I watched her nipples turn to hard peaks beneath her sports bra. "I think you like it. It turns you on thinking about me being so fucking possessive over you that I'd kill someone just for looking at what's mine. Now, strip."

"What about you?" she asked, gripping the bra band and tugging. Her tits bounced free, and I didn't stop myself from reaching out to palm both. Her moan and my guttural groan mixed as I pinched her peaked tips. Carefully watching her features, I applied more pressure, waiting until her lids popped open and a gasp brushed past her lips. "Why does that hurt but feel so damn good at the same time?"

"It's a fine line, one that we'll explore together—a lot," I murmured. Reaching down, I grabbed my rock-hard cock and squeezed, hoping to ease the throbbing pain. "Are you on birth control?"

Juno stilled. "No, shoot. I'm sorry, I didn't—"

With a feral growl, I gripped the back of her neck in a commanding hold and yanked her to me, our lips colliding together in a violent kiss. I devoured her words, nipping at her lips and tongue in punishment for even thinking she should apologize.

"Your body, your choice," I said and nipped at her lower lip again. "But for even thinking you needed to apologize... turn around and put your hands on the tree trunk." When she didn't move, I pinched her nipple hard enough to make her gasp. "Now, Juno."

Eyeing me with suspicion, she did as I asked. When both palms were sealed to the rough bark, I gripped the hem of her jeans and ripped them down her thighs, taking her soaked panties with them. The scent of her desire wafted in the faint breeze, making me bite my lip to keep from diving between her thighs and licking her clean like I did the night before.

No. I had other plans.

Popping the top button of my jeans, I released a sigh at the instant relief from the pressure on my throbbing cock. Looking over her shoulder, Juno's eyes went wide at finding me palming my cock with one hand as I worked my jeans down my thighs.

"Langston, that's...."

"Going in your soaked pussy very soon."

"I don't know how I'll take all of you," she whispered, sounding both a little horrified and in awe.

"Oh, you can and will." Searching the back pocket of my

jeans, I pulled a condom free and smiled. "I was a Boy Scout. Always be prepared." Ripping it open with my teeth, I slowly rolled the condom over my cock and tossed the trash to the side to pick up later. "Now for that punishment."

"But I—"

I smacked her bare ass before she could finish, watching in fascination as her fair skin bloomed pink in a perfect handprint. *My* handprint. Wanting the other side to match, I smacked her other cheek this time, her groan filling the air around us.

"Fuck, seeing my handprint on your ass drives me fucking crazy." I grabbed my dick and squeezed tight. At this rate, I wouldn't last two seconds inside her. "Are you sure you want this now?" The words rasped from my throat, every muscle tight with restraint to keep me from slamming into her before she was ready.

"Yes, please. And Langston." She turned, dark curly hair obscuring half her face. "I'll try to make it good for you too, because I know—"

Nope. Hell fucking nope. This woman was perfect, and I was determined to make her see that too, in a way that benefited both of us.

Reaching between her legs, I thrust two fingers deep into her soaked cunt. When I pulled them free, her whimper of disappointment had a smirk pulling at my lips.

"Hold on as best you can, shortcake. I've never been a gentle man, and after that comment, I really won't be." Fisting her hair, I gave a slight tug, making her back arch and ass stick out. "Your pussy is ready for me. Are you?"

I needed to hear it one more time, one more confirmation so I knew for certain this wasn't me so desperate to make my fantasies come to life that I misunderstood what she needed and wanted from me. Fuck what I needed—this was about her. Always, now and forever.

"Fucking hell, Langston," she snapped. "Fuck me, now. Don't make me beg."

My brows shot up at that. Begging would be fun, but not now. She was too keyed up from hearing my own dirty dreams to make her wait.

Guiding my cock between her legs, both knees shook, and my thighs trembled at the way I easily slid between her folds. Our combined gasps filled the deserted area when I pushed inside, her tight cunt resisting my size at first.

"Relax for me," I murmured. Reaching around her, I palmed one large breast and pinched her pebbled nipple.

Her whole body tensed before relaxing, allowing me to slide in an inch. Sweat beaded along my forehead and dripped down my spine. Heat and desire like I'd never felt before shot through my veins, filling every cell until all I could focus on was Juno.

Little by little, I pushed inside, the position not ideal for her taking all of me. Both hips in my tight grip, I pulled out until the tip barely crested her opening before thrusting back inside.

Juno cried out, making me still, worried I'd hurt her.

"If you don't keep fucking moving, Langston Allen, I will do this myself."

The passion and frustration in her tone was exactly how I felt.

"Yes, ma'am," I murmured before repeating the motion, again and again.

In and out, I pistoned into her as deep as the position would allow me, my rhythm picking up with every thrust. Knuckles white, I flexed my fingers, hoping to keep from leaving bruises on her delicate skin but also loving the idea of marking her any way I could.

Juno's gasps and moans, combined with the way her cunt squeezed my cock so tight that it was difficult to pull out, had a familiar tingle racing down my spine.

Releasing one hip, I snaked a hand around the front of her and dipped between her thighs. The first flick of her swollen clit had her crying out for more. *Fucking gladly.* Keeping a perfect rhythm, I pounded into her while playing with her nub. Within seconds, Juno's back arched just as her piercing cry of ecstasy sliced through the air and her pussy clamped around me, sending me falling over the edge into erotic bliss with her.

I slammed inside her as deep as possible, grumbling curses as her pussy milked every drop from my cock. When her knees gave out, I caught her with an arm curled around her waist, lifting her limp body until her sweat-slick back was sealed to my chest.

Still inside her, the movement sent a body-trembling tingle through me, making me hold her even tighter. For several seconds, we stood like that, catching our combined breaths.

"If you were that worked up just thinking about me and West together—" I swallowed a curse when her cunt tightened around me at my words. "—just imagine what it will be like when you actually are watching me own his ass, and him loving every fucking second."

Juno whimpered and shifted against me, squeezing her thighs tight, increasing the stranglehold she had around my still-hard cock.

"You need more, shortcake?"

"I don't know how, but... yes, I think. Fuck, what is happening to me?"

My dark chuckles brushed along her neck as I kissed her soft skin.

"Nothing, Juno. Like I said, you're perfect. Now, stay just like this, and we'll both get what we need."

Palming both her breasts, I tipped my face up to the cloudy sky and muttered a thank-you to whatever made the gorgeous woman in my arms as I slowly pumped my hips, the slight movement making Juno moan and plead for more.

Best damn fishing trip ever.

I HADN'T SMILED as much in my entire life as I had in the last four hours standing along the riverbank with Juno. It wasn't even that we talked a lot or laughed the entire time; I couldn't stop the damn goofy grin on my face from just being around her. Her presence alone made me happier than I had been in a long time—though the few orgasms I wrung from her, and her me, helped my mood too.

A metal clang disturbed the peaceful afternoon when I set the poles and tackle box into the truck bed. I could've used my SUV, but this was the truck I used for the land-based fishing trips scheduled through Uplift, and it already had everything we could've needed.

"I think we need to hire Aspen to take some photos of the areas where you take clients fishing, maybe even for the other adventures Uplift offers too. It would be cool to add some to the page, give clients a brief look into what they're signing up for."

Head down, she almost clipped the lowered tailgate, too focused on whatever she was typing on her phone. Snaking an arm around her waist, I gave a slight tug to redirect her trajectory, keeping her safe from a nasty bruise. Juno stumbled to the side, coming to a stop right between my legs where I leaned against the warmed metal.

Her dark eyelashes fluttered as she stared up at me in confusion.

"You almost ran right into the edge of the tailgate." I inclined my head toward the spot.

"Ah. And where I ended up?" She arched a brow and gave a pointed look to where our lower halves were pressed together.

"Lucky coincidence?" I said with a raised brow. She huffed a laugh with a wide smile while shaking her head. "Did you have fun today?"

"Fun? What I had today was beyond fun. It was peaceful and adventurous and with you, so a perfect day, really. And the other part was perfect too." She wrapped her arms around my waist and buried her pink face against my chest. "I loved getting to hear stories about you and Mattie growing up, the crazy stuff you and West have gotten into, and why you love fishing so much. I just wish I was better at it for you, though I know it's okay that I'm not. But even so, the peace that comes from being out here alone, along the water—it's cathartic."

"When I come out here early in the morning by myself, it has a spiritual feel to it." Juno bit down on her lower lip to stop a growing grin. "What?"

"Who would've thought Captain Asshole himself would be so... enlightened."

It was the way her face was tipped up to mine, her smile that reached her eyes, and the combination of the amazing day that had me leaning down and pressing my lips to hers. There was still one more story that I hadn't told her. One that weighed on my chest daily, a dark memory that would never leave me.

"Remember how I mentioned how Mattie and I grew up?"

Pulling back, Juno gazed up at me and nodded.

"Our mom always had new boyfriends coming in and out of the apartment, and there was this one who treated me and Mattie like his own kids. He would take us to dinner even when Mom was working, brought us small gifts, hell, he even paid the electric bill one time so we didn't die of heat exhaustion in our own apartment." I sealed my lids shut and blew out a slow breath. "One day, he came over when Mom was at work, which was normal for him, and offered to take me and Mattie to get some candy, but he had a business call to take first. At our disappointed faces, he offered to give me the money so I could run down to the corner store and get it myself, and said that since it was so hot, Mattie could just stay in the cool apartment and wait for me.

"All I could think about was that fucking candy," I growled, curling both hands into tight fists and pressing them into the tops of my thighs. "So I took his money and left my little sister with a practical stranger. She was eight years old, and I just left her with him, alone."

"Langston," Juno whispered. "You were just a kid yourself. You didn't know."

"But I'm her older brother. My job is to protect her, and I fucking failed."

Her small hands cupped my face and pulled until I was gazing down at her. "You were just a kid. Does Mattie hold you responsible for whatever happened next?" I shook my head. "Then why do you?"

"It was the first time I failed someone I loved and they

were hurt. She was left with memories that gave her fucking nightmares for months after."

Her brows flew up her forehead. "That's why you try to protect everyone you love now, why you're hypervigilant and suspect everyone."

I nodded, waiting for the pity or anger to appear, but neither did. Instead, something like understanding had her features softening.

"Thank you for telling me. It helps me understand"—she gestured up and down my frame—"this."

"You just pointed to all of me," I grumbled with a smirk, remembering a similar conversation just a few days ago with West.

"Exactly. That incident made you who you are today, and I like this man, who you are, how protective you are of your friends and family. Look at it as a lesson, one that made you this amazing man today, instead of a failure."

Gathering her in my arms, I held her close and rested my chin on top of her head.

A lesson instead of a failure. That would be a hard shift. But maybe with her help, one day, I could.

21

WEST

"Are you sure you don't mind all my computer stuff in here?"

Her lips were curved downward as she scanned the now-cluttered corner of my bedroom. We had worked for the last half hour getting all her computers and monitors set up on the small desk we brought from her place. Every inch of the compact surface was covered with some type of electronic, the nearby outlet nearly maxed out.

"I'm positive." Unable to stop myself, I wrapped an arm around her waist, sealing her to my side. "Seeing all this here, in my room no less, not only means you're here safe but that all this is real and not some cruel dream I'll wake up from. Plus, being sidelined because of the hand means I have a lot of downtime, and with Langston working a lot, I'm looking forward to the company." I inclined my head toward the bed. "Maybe I'll lie around all day and watch you work."

She turned to wrap her arms around my waist. "If you do that, then I won't get anything done."

A soft vibration brought my focus to her phone

humming along the top of the dresser. Juno tensed but didn't say a word or make a move to answer the incoming call.

"I think we should set up my gaming system next." She angled her head toward the living room only to tense again at another round of continuous vibrations against the solid wood. "That is definitely high priority. I'm legit having withdrawals, and I need to keep my hands in prime gaming shape."

Eyeing her phone, then her, I pressed a kiss to the tip of her nose. "Juno." She hummed a response. "Why are you avoiding your phone?"

"I don't know what you're talking about," she defended while attempting to wiggle out of my grasp. I only tightened my arms, holding her even closer. "West, come on, let's get the rest of this set up so we can chill when Langston gets back." Her gaze dropped to the floor, and she worried at her lip. "Did you see the group he took out today?"

"Yeah," I hedged, not sure where she was going with that question or if it was just a way to distract me from whoever kept calling her over and over.

"The women were really pretty and seemed to know what they were doing with all the fishing gear."

"Okay, not sure what you're getting at, Juno. Now, who keeps calling you—"

"Do you think he'll like them more than me?" she blurted, eyes going wide like she did not intend to say that out loud.

"What? Who?" Her words made absolutely no sense.

"Langston," she muttered. "They were so pretty, and did you see all their cool gear? I bet they fish all the time and are fantastic at it. Not like me yesterday, who got the line caught in a tree branch twice, which Langston had to untangle and—"

I couldn't help it. The moment I understood what she was worried about, a chuckle escaped that turned into a full-on laughing fit.

"It's not that funny," she grumbled and again tried to break out of my hold.

I wiped at the tears leaking from the corners of both eyes. "It is, because it's so impossible that the idea of it is hilarious."

She glared up at me. "Well, I didn't think it was possible that the man who asked me to marry him would cheat on me either."

That sobered me right the fuck up.

"Juno." I hugged her tight. "I'm sorry. I didn't... fuck, I didn't think about it that way. The thought of Langston betraying anyone is so far-fetched that it didn't even cross my mind as an option, but doing it to you...." I pulled her back enough to angle her face up to mine. "He'd rather cut off his own balls than do something like that to you. That man is loyal down to his core for his family and friends, and you're in that group now, sweet cheeks."

"As family or friend?" she questioned, arching a brow.

The corners of my lips curled upward as I gazed down at her. "As someone who is quickly rising to the very top of all his relationship lists."

Once again, the phone shimmied along the dresser. "Now, either tell me who keeps calling you or I'll go check myself."

Head tossed back, Juno let out a loud, dramatic groan that had me chuckling. Feet dragging like she was walking to certain death, she trudged to the other side of the room, snatched the phone off the dark wood surface, and dramatically tossed herself onto my bed.

"Who do you think I would avoid like the worst computer virus known to technology? My sister and the asshat wanted to hang out today before they leave tomorrow, and I'm avoiding them instead of telling them I'd rather pluck out my eyelashes than see them."

Loose fist hovering over my lips, hiding my smile, a humor-filled chuckle rumbled in my chest. "Right." The bed dipped beneath my weight when I perched on the edge of the mattress beside her. Interlacing our fingers, I gave them a gentle squeeze.

"And they want my answer about attending the wedding." Rolling to the side, she curled up, facing me with a hand tucked under her cheek. "I don't know what I want to do."

"Do you want to hear my opinion?" After tossing my glasses onto the bedside table, I lay down next to her, mirroring her position.

"Sure."

"If you're up for it, I think we should go to the wedding." Both eyebrows flew up her forehead, clearly surprised by my answer. "We being the three of us. It would be good to get away from here for a few days, plus I want to show you off. Rub it in everyone's faces that we won the damn lottery because you chose us."

Stroking a single finger along the back of my hand, she stared at where we touched. "People aren't as open-minded as they are here. Me bringing two men will have them all talking, and someone might say something. There are a lot of judgmental, small-town jerks there who won't be afraid to confront us about their version of right and wrong."

I studied each stroke of her fingers. "It wouldn't be

anything I haven't heard before, believe me. I'd never fit in, been accepted for who I am, until I moved here."

Warmth bloomed along the side of my face from her studying stare. Ever so slowly, I dragged my gaze up to meet hers, knowing what she was about to ask before her lips even moved. "Where were you before coming to Uplift? I don't think I've ever heard you mention where you grew up. Langston told me yesterday about his childhood in Vegas with Mattie, so now it's your turn."

Her wide smile at the innocent question had a lead weight dropping in my stomach.

Blowing out a controlled breath between pursed lips, I flipped to my back to level my blank stare at the ceiling. "That's a dark story with even darker parts spread out through the years. And while I'd love for you to get to know me better, I'm not sure I'm ready to taint your view of me just yet."

"How would how you grew up taint how I see you? You haven't seen me differently or thought less of me after I told you about my messed-up family and drama-filled life."

"This is different, Juno."

The mattress moved as she pressed herself against my side, draping an arm over my chest. It was her touch, that comforting hold, that gave me the strength to let some of my sad story slip.

"I don't have anyone but Langston and the few friends here. I have no family who misses me, no mom or dad who are either proud or disappointed in who I became. I don't have a family, Juno, good or bad; it's just me, and that's how it's always been."

A grunt whooshed past my lips, the air forced from my lungs when she plopped down on my chest, knees on either side of my ribs. She studied me with a combination of frustration and worry, a deep line between her furrowed brows. With her loose hair hanging down like curtains around her face, the compassion radiating off her, and the fierce, tight line of her lips, another part of me melted for her.

The way I craved her attention and time made me wonder how I had survived without her all these years.

"That's okay, West. You're enough for me, for anyone. Just you. Family or no family, that doesn't matter to me. How you treat me, your friends, strangers on the street—that's what matters. Not your past, but I do wish you'd share a little with me to help me understand you better. I want to know you, West. All of you—the good, the bad, and the ugly. I've shown you mine; now I'd love it if you could show me a peek of yours."

It was the pleading in her tone, the hopeful expression that did it. Squeezing my lids shut, I rubbed at my eyes, wishing it would erase the visuals flashing behind them of those worst moments as a kid.

"All I can remember are children's homes and foster homes, never a place of my own. I was a scrawny kid, so I got picked on a lot, and was shy on top of all that." I reached up and grabbed her hips, needing the comfort of holding her to keep going. "Knowing what I know now, after a lot of research on the subject, my being isolated and shy made me a perfect target for predators to groom. The first time, I was so excited. I thought the old man running the foster home really thought I was special, that his extra attention meant I was important to someone." A humorless laugh escaped. "And I was... only not the way I wanted to be."

"West." The heartbreak in her voice had me slowly opening my eyes. Tears rimmed her lower eyelids, threatening to spill over.

"It was the first time I learned that being used like that

came with a mixed bag of emotions. Shame, disgust, but also longing, because even with the pain and other emotions, at least someone wanted me around, had picked me. That started an entire cycle of abuse, different houses, different types, until I ran away from that final foster home." A cruel smile curled at my lips. "He was a mean mother-fucker who hit the boys on a daily basis, which we could take, but the night he turned his fist on Cindy, a foster girl who was already terrified and years younger than me, I lost it. I never checked to see if he had died from the injuries." I lifted a single shoulder, truly not caring. "But I knew the cops would come for me either way, so I ran. With nowhere to go, I ended up living on the streets of Portland until I turned eighteen, then walked into an Army recruitment center and signed my life away.

"Boot camp was hell. I was so weak and malnourished from barely keeping myself alive. But I made it, and after a while, my commanding officers noticed I was decent with fixing things around base and anything with an engine, so they put me in the mechanics division, where I finally found my niche. After I served my time and had gained a whole lot of useful experience, I moved to Alaska, wanting a fresh start and to put as much distance between me and my past as possible. I worked at different shops as a mechanic but missed the community I had in the Army. That's when I learned about Uplift. I dropped everything to travel here, interviewed with Brandon, and was hired that day. The rest is history, I guess."

"That is a lot of traumas in a few sentences," she whispered, eyes wide. "West, how are you here and so... *you* after all that?"

"So me?"

"Kind, thoughtful, funny, happy, generous, sexy...." She

said the last one with a wink. "But seriously, you should be angry at the world and blaming everything on what was done to you, so yeah, how are you so *you* after all that?"

"I have my bad days; you'll find that out soon enough. But a while back, I decided I wouldn't allow my past to dictate who I turned out to be. So instead of focusing on what happened to me, which I can't change, I focus on the good, and on seeing the good in people." My lips curved into a slow smile. "I think that's why I'm basically Langston's only friend."

Juno barked a laugh and wiped the few tears that had escaped off her cheek.

"He can be a major asshole, but when you really see him, see who he is—"

"It's confusing as hell," she mumbled. "So contradictory, those two sides of him. But I understand what you're saying. The person he shows everyone differs from who he actually is."

"Exactly. So that's the sad summary of my childhood and as deep as I can go today."

Pitching forward, she placed a chaste kiss on my lips. "Thank you for sharing that with me. I'm here no matter what, West. I don't know what the future holds for the three of us, but I will always be here for you. Always."

I moved my good hand from her hip to wrap around her waist. "Thank you." I cleared my throat and forced a smile, hoping it would help lift the somber mood. "So, the wedding. What will it be? Are we going or staying here with an unknown threat lurking around?" I waggled my brows, letting her know that last part was to lighten the conversation.

She blew a raspberry, face tipped to the ceiling. "As

apprehensive as I am at seeing my stepfather and everyone else I left behind, I feel like I need to go."

"Need to go or want to go?"

"Need," she clarified. "For closure on that part of my life. I want Stephanie and Eric to see I'm not happy for them. I'm not upset or jealous about it either. That part of me that felt like a gaping hole the last several months doesn't hurt like it did. I'm finally healing, and maybe letting everyone back home see that can give me the closure I need."

"So we go." I slid my gaze to my very empty closet. "We might need to go a day early, stop in Anchorage. I'm not sure about you, but I have nothing appropriate to wear to a wedding."

She grimaced, making me bark a laugh at the disgust on her face. "I have nothing to wear either, but I really hate shopping. What about Langston?"

"When he visits Mattie and his nephew, she always takes him shopping around Vegas to update his wardrobe. I can say for certain that I will need to find something. I only have a few pieces of clothing. Old habits die hard—less stuff in the black trash bag the next time you have to move houses."

She crossed her arms and gave me a pointed look. "But you have a home here now, a real one. You're surrounded by people who love you and aren't going anywhere. Maybe it's time to buy a little more than what's absolutely necessary?"

"That's what I've been trying to tell him."

Juno's head whipped around, sending her hair flying to the side, at Langston's deep voice. He stood in the doorway, green eyes focused on us. "Hey, you're back. How was today?"

The slight vibration in her shaky tone gave away her uncertainty and vulnerability. Langston had no idea the impact his answer would hold. Intervention was needed before he innocently said the wrong thing, not knowing her worries about him and the female clients.

"Juno was worried you would want one of those women from the group today over her."

A surprised squeak escaped her and she tried to slap a palm over my mouth, but I smacked her hand away, gripping it in a tight hold at her side.

"She thinks they were prettier than her and had cool gear, which meant they were good at fishing and you would want them because of it."

Her chest rose and fell in deep breaths as she glared down at me.

"Traitor," she whispered, sticking out her tongue.

"Is that so?" Langston stepped into the room, pausing beside the bed. Wrapping his fingers around her chin, he tipped her face up to his. "You think so little of me, shortcake?"

"No, it's just...." She shrugged, not finishing the thought.

"You've been betrayed before, so you're cautious of it happening again?" He looked down at me. "What do you think, West? Should I punish her for thinking that she's not perfect for us, or that I'd even think about fucking up the best thing that has ever happened to me?"

"Yes," Juno and I said in unison.

Langston's smile grew, making faint lines spread out from the corners of both eyes. My heart slammed in my chest. It was rare to see that genuine, carefree, truly joyful smile, and every damn time, it took my breath away.

"You think you deserve to be punished?" He released his hold on her chin to cross both arms over his chest. "Why?"

"Because I'm mad at myself for even thinking it. Maybe it will help disrupt that automatic suspicion. I hate it, but even when I try to reassure myself, that sinking feeling in my stomach won't go away." She blinked up at Langston with an imploring expression. "Please."

Without a word, Langston moved over to my side table and yanked open the drawer, pulling out the box of condoms I kept there and tossing them onto the bed beside my head. He had told me after his date with Juno that she wasn't on birth control, which was fine by me; it was her choice to be on it or not. If condoms were needed to be with her, then I'd buy a lifetime's supply. Hell, I'd do, wear, and buy anything to be with Juno.

When she tried to climb off me, Langston stopped her with a quick slap to the ass.

"Stay where you are." He slid his gaze down to me. "Both of you. I think West here needs to be reminded of his worth too."

"Fine by me," I said, winking at Juno. "Looks like we'll both be having fun."

"Fun?" Langston chuckled, the sound dark and humorless, making my smile drop. "We'll see how much fun you're having shortly."

Stepping behind Juno, he gripped the waistband of her yoga pants and worked them over her hips, then down her creamy thighs, carefully helping her maneuver out of them. When he pulled the large T-shirt over her head, she helped, raising both arms in the air until it was tugged free.

"Fuck, you have the best tits," Langston murmured before flicking the front clasp of her bra, allowing her full breasts to burst free. After tossing the bra over his shoulder, he palmed one, the soft skin spilling between his thick fingers. With a wicked glint in his eye, he pressed between Juno's shoulder blades while guiding her peaked tip toward my lips.

A full-body shiver had me twitching on the bed as he

dragged it along my lips, teasing us both. Unable to hold back, my tongue slid out to flick her pebbled nipple, desperate to suck it between my lips. Juno's gasp had my hips bucking off the bed, my steel-hard cock throbbing beneath my jeans. Langston noted the movement with an arched brow.

"Having fun yet?" he chuckled before pushing her nipple between my lips. "Suck her hard like you do me." Juno's and my groaned curses filled the bedroom, followed by Langston's laugh. "Oh, we're just getting started. Remember, you asked for this, shortcake." He snaked a hand between us and popped the top button of my jeans. "And you egged it on."

Best decision ever.

After loosening my pants, he wrapped the waistband and top of my boxer briefs in a firm hold and tugged. Heels digging into the mattress, I lifted my hips, helping him work them down my thighs, maneuvering Juno's legs as he went. When he pulled them free, he tossed them aside, adding them to the growing pile of clothes.

Langston brushed the tip of his thumb along his lower lip as he stared at us, neither Juno nor I moving except for our heaving chests from each ragged breath. The scrape of the cardboard flap opening followed by the crinkle of the condom wrappers had my dick jumping against my stomach. Juno's head fell forward, forehead resting on my sternum with her ass high in the air.

"See something you like?" Langston asked around the condom wrapper between his teeth. He ripped it open and tossed the trash to the floor, reaching between us. I hissed when his fingers wrapped around me, my lids slamming shut as I bucked into his firm grip. "Why don't you help me,

Juno? I know West would love to have your hands on him too."

She shimmied down to sit her bare ass on top of my thighs, and a guttural groan rumbled in my chest when her spread thighs gave me a perfect view of her dripping pussy. I slid my good hand up her thigh, fingers brushing her soft skin, and dipped into her folds. Juno's breath hitched only for it to turn into a whimper when Langston swatted my hand away.

"Not yet." He paused, lips curling in a smile as if he'd just thought of something sinister.

Tossing the condom to the quilt, Langston stepped behind Juno and gripped her hips. Guiding her higher until her core hovered over my cock, he slid his hands down both legs, gripping her knees and spreading her wide. With a gasp, Juno dropped low, her drenched cunt landing right on top of my dick.

Grip back on her hips, Langston shifted her up and down, gliding her along my shaft. Hands curled in the quilt, I squeezed both lids shut in an effort to not shift, adjusting my angle to slip inside her.

Juno tossed her head back, her curly brown hair cascading down her back. Fisting the thick curls, Langston guided her mouth to his. Their combined moans filled my ears, my already-simmering desire now boiling.

"Langston," I gritted out. "You've made your point. Please let me fuck her."

With his hold on her hair, Langston kept her still, breaking their kiss to stare down at me.

"Please."

I was on the verge of exploding all over her stomach and my own, but I wanted to be inside her, feel her snug pussy tighten around me.

"Lift your hips, Juno," Langston ordered and picked up the discarded condom. Keeping his dark gaze locked on me, he gripped my cock in a firm hold and rolled the condom down my shaft. The mattress molded around the back of my head where I pressed it back hard, full focus on not coming from his touch and anticipation of what was to come.

With one hand holding me and the other gripping Juno's hip, Langston helped her lower down onto me. The feel of my head slipping past her opening had a garbled string of curses escaping while Juno whimpered. My lids flew open, worried I'd somehow hurt her, but the look of ecstasy on her face told me differently.

Slowly, Langston worked her lower until she'd taken all of me, every inch inside her hot core. When she tried to move, he held her down, keeping her in place.

"You still need your punishment, Juno, and this will add to West's too. Now, keep his dick stuffed inside you, but raise that fine ass."

Her hooded gaze met mine as she did as instructed, the slight shift making me hiss at the sensation.

When nothing happened, I peered around Juno's shoulder. Langston stood behind her, pants around his hips and hard cock in his hand as he stared at her ass. I licked my lips and reached around her, fingers skimming down her soft skin until I found her back entrance. Langston's eyes met mine while Juno's breathing picked up. I worried I'd pushed her too far, but instead of stopping me, she shifted back, causing the very tip of my finger to dip into her.

"Fuck, I can't wait to feel West's dick in your cunt while mine is stuffed in your ass." Langston's hand worked faster up and down his shaft, his knuckles white from the strangling hold.

Knowing he needed relief, I looked up at Juno, finding her already staring down at me.

"How about you take us both now?" I rasped.

Her eyes went wide. "I'll need a little bit of prep for that or you two will rip me in half."

My lips curled in a smile as I shifted just enough to make us groan in unison.

"Not that way. We'll definitely need to work up to that dirty fantasy. I'm thinking while I fuck your tight pussy, Langston can be doing the same to your throat."

Juno's head fell forward. Langston ran a hand along her spine in a comforting stroke.

"I don't need—"

"Yes," she rasped. "I want that." Looking over her shoulder, she licked her lips, gaze locked on his swollen cock. "I want that a lot. You two aren't the only ones who've had dreams about us three together."

"You sure?" I asked, squeezing her ass cheek for emphasis. "There's no pressure to—"

"I know there's not." Her features softened as she gazed down at me. "And that's why I want to—no, I *need* to. I want you both. Please."

"You heard our girl." Gripping her waist, Langston easily twisted her around so she faced him and I was now blessed with the view of her perfect ass. I palmed one globe, loving the way the flesh molded between my fingers.

Helping her lower, I muttered a string of curses at the new angle and feel of her clenching around me. Movement in the mirror on the wall caught my attention, freezing me in place. As if watching the best porno ever, I studied their reflections as Langston's cock disappeared past Juno's parted lips.

His head fell back as a hiss escaped his clenched teeth,

his hand coming up to wrap around her throat. In and out he slid his thick cock, pulling out until just his head breached her lips before thrusting back in.

My heart slammed in my chest, each breath like glass against my dry throat. Juno lifted and lowered, the movements small, mimicking Langston's as he fucked her mouth. Rising off the bed, I slammed into her with every dip of her hips, making us both cry out. Only our ragged breaths and moans sounded over the slapping of skin. A pleasure-filled tingle started at my balls and shot up, my orgasm fast and almost painful as I slammed deep inside her, holding her in place with a bruising grip as I spilled into the condom.

Juno's garbled cry, her walls clenching tight, had another smaller orgasm ripping through me. I cried out, my own combining with Langston's as he cursed through his own release.

Slumping back against the bed, I blinked up at the ceiling.

How was this real, her with us, absolutely perfect in every way?

Now we just had to figure out a way to keep her, to make our Juno see that this wasn't something as simple as obsession or love. No, this went deeper than that.

This between us three was forever.

22

"I can't believe this is actually happening," I rasped, voice thick with emotion as I tried to keep the building tears from falling. "Anchor Bay won't be the same without you. *I* won't be the same without you."

Face pinched in a mix of a grimace and a frown, Finley appeared highly uncomfortable as she reached out and patted my shoulder. "There, there. All will be fine, I promise."

A snort escaped, and I rolled my watery eyes. "So comforting, Finley. Thanks."

Her slim shoulders rose and fell in an exaggerated shrug. "I'll give you a kidney in a heartbeat, but a hug? You're better off trying to take an organ that I don't have a duplicate of." Twisting around, she glanced over her shoulder to where Langston and West stood a ways away, allowing us some space to talk without their protective hovering. "And I think you'll be too busy with those two to miss me. I'm happy for you, you know that, right?"

I nodded with a tight smile.

"Good. And I'm happy for me, because I chose the over

on the bet we had going on which means I won some decent cash." She wobbled on her feet at my playful shove. "But seriously, you're not mad, are you, at my leaving? You understand why I have to do this, right, for me?"

When I'd cornered her last week after the meeting, she was vague about her reasons for leaving, but today she opened up during the trip from Anchor Bay to Anchorage. Her flight left in a couple of hours to Portland, where she would catch another flight to California. It worked perfectly since we had planned to stop over in Anchorage for some wedding shopping, so she hitched a ride with us.

"I get needing space—believe me, that's how I ended up in Anchor Bay. But I still don't understand why you need it from Dax, your best friend?"

Adjusting her grip around the thick canvas handle of her duffel, she shifted to toss it over her shoulder, staring at the busy dock at my back. "The mess between Dax and me is complicated. He doesn't know what he wants from me, and until he figures that out, I can't stick around, allowing him to confuse me in the process. We've been friends for so long that I'm just one of the guys to him, but I'm not. Until I'm gone, he won't see me for what I am."

"And what's that?" I asked, chafing my hands up and down my arms to chase away the chill from the wind whipping off the water.

"I might be tough, can hold my own in a fight, outfly him, and burp the alphabet—"

"Ew," I laughed.

"—but I'm still a woman who wants to be soft every now and then. To be smothered with comfort and protected so I can, at least for a short amount of time, let my defenses down. I want flowers, damnit. And chocolate and a bubble bath with candles lit along the edge, not another invite to come over for beers and watching the game. I love that stuff, don't get me wrong, but I also want a chance at the other side of me too." She blew out a slow breath. "I need a break from all this, from him, to figure out what I want next. And to get laid without the whole damn town knowing about it."

We shared a conspiring smile and laugh, knowing that was the truth. Small towns were both a blessing and a curse.

"Just call me and let me know how you're doing, please. I need to know my friend is okay."

Finley's chuckle was deep and mischievous. "Oh, Juno, I'm headed to Coronado Island where I can watch the SEALs play from my brother's back porch. If I'm lucky, a riptide will sweep me out to sea one morning when a group is running by, and they can all jump in and save me, then give me mouth-to-mouth one by one."

"So you've thought a lot about this, clearly."

Without giving her a second to react, I wrapped my arms around her waist in a tight hug. Her standing utterly stiff, barely breathing in my hold, only made my smile grow wider. A fake, almost pained grin was plastered on her face when I pulled back.

After several more goodbyes and promises to keep each other updated, Finley started toward the bus stop, where she would wait for her ride to the airport. As I wiped at my wet cheeks, unable to look away, a heavy arm draped over my shoulders, drawing my attention from the corner where she'd disappeared. I gazed up at Langston.

"She'll be good. Finley needs time away from that idiot. Maybe it will help him pull his head out of his ass."

"Maybe," I murmured. "She said something that made me see her differently, and I think maybe it would do Dax good to know. Maybe help him see what she's afraid to admit."

"What's that?" West questioned, coming to stand at my other side, interlacing our fingers and raising them to his lips to kiss each knuckle. I smiled at our joined hands, loving his open display of affection and claiming.

"That a strong woman like Finley, tough and brave and one of the guys, still longs to be treated and protected the way a woman deserves. Finley can handle herself, yes, but she wants to be with someone where she knows she doesn't have to. That when she's with her person, she can be soft and carefree."

Langston rubbed his jaw. "You got all that from her saying she needed distance from Dax?"

I bit my lip to stifle my smile. "She said more than that, but yeah, that's a summary." I stared back down the sidewalk. "I just hope she comes back."

"She will," West said with a confirming nod. "Now, she might bring someone with her, which will be a whole different shit show, but I think she'll be back sooner than we expect."

A gust of chilled air rolled off the sea behind us, making me shiver. Langston grumbled something about me not bringing warm enough clothes as he shrugged off his jacket and wrapped it around my shoulders.

Pushing up to my tiptoes, I pressed a soft kiss to the underside of his jaw.

"My hero. Thank you. Now, to the hotel, then shopping?"

"Hotel, bar, then shopping," West corrected as we started down the sidewalk. "I'll need some liquid courage to shop for myself. Langston is damn lucky he has Mattie."

"When do I get to meet this Mattie?" I asked, glancing up at Langston.

"We can FaceTime whenever you want. You can meet my nephew then too, but she's not planning a trip up here soon. She's never been to Anchor Bay; we normally meet in Anchorage if she comes for a visit, but mostly I go to Vegas for a couple of days. It's easier for me since I don't have a kid."

"She stopped by to see me in the hospital," West added. "I think she'd just gotten off a cruise or something like that."

"Yeah, my nephew was with his dad for a week, and she needed a distraction, so she booked a last-minute Alaskan cruise. She had wanted me to come too but knew she needed the downtime. Things are constant in her life, plus the divorce, so it was good for her to go alone."

My stomach churned thinking about meeting the amazing woman. She sounded confident, was a great mom, talented, and based on the pictures Langston had shown me on his phone, was also absolutely gorgeous. The way Langston and West both talked about her, it was clear she was a big part of Langston's life, which meant if she didn't like me, then all this could crumble, leaving me alone again.

West tightened his fingers around mine, drawing my attention.

"Whatever you're thinking, stop, sweet cheeks. Not only will she love you, but she'll see how happy you make her brother, and she'll love you even more."

I forced a smile. His words eased some of the worry but doubts still lingered. Because everything good in my life spoiled, and I just knew if it happened this time with them, it would be the one I didn't survive.

"I NOW UNDERSTAND people's obsession with online shopping," West grumbled beside me as we walked side by side down the sidewalk, hands swinging between us.

My cheeks hurt from smiling all day, and it was the best ache. I never wanted it to fade.

"It was two stores and four outfits for you, and the rest were for me. It wasn't that terrible of an experience to push you into only reclusive shopping." I bumped my shoulder against his side, making him stagger a little before righting himself.

"You two quit whining. I'm the one who has to carry all the shit." To emphasize his point, Langston held up the shopping bags in each hand and rolled his eyes, but the smile he fought back told a different story. All day there was that small smile pulling at his lips, and I even heard him laugh a few times when West and I joked around in different stores. Apparently, we turned into mischievous toddlers when shopping together.

"How much farther is this bar?" I asked while looping my arm around West's, pulling him closer to my side. There was a woman a few feet ahead of us putting something up on a wooden telephone pole, and I didn't want him to accidentally bump into her. As thin as she looked, one tap would send her flying into the street.

The stranger's exhausted gaze followed us with a helpless expression as we hurried by. I offered her a tight smile, attention sliding to the paper in her hand that flapped in the strong breeze. A single word, the letters large and bold, written across the top made me slow, coming to a complete stop a couple of feet after we passed her.

Langston and West went into full protection mode, squeezing in tight with their heads on a swivel like we were about to be attacked.

"What is it?" Langston murmured.

Without a word, I squeezed out from between the two men and turned, cautiously walking back to the woman.

Short, tight, black pleather skirt, torn tights, high heels, and a top that barely covered her boobs—I had a hunch at what she did for a living, but that didn't matter, nor was it why I stopped.

I kept my gaze trained on the flyer in her hand, locked on the word in bold print.

MISSING

"Who is she?" I asked, not looking up from the young woman's blurred picture.

"My friend Sabel," she rasped. "The cops aren't doing shit about it, just like the others, and—"

"Others?" Langston asked at my back. His hand wrapped around my waist almost like he needed the reassurance that I was close and safe.

The woman eyed Langston, then West, who stood at my side. She arched a brow at me. "Both of them?" I snorted and nodded. "Damn, girl, leave some for the rest of us. Don't be so fucking greedy."

I shrugged. "They came as a package deal, a two-for-one-special type of thing."

She smiled for just a second before it faded when she looked down at the flyer she'd clearly made and had taken on the duty of posting around Anchorage.

"Cops said she's not missing, that it hasn't been long enough. But Sabel always comes home, always, and last night she didn't."

"You said others?" Langston prodded with a gentleness in his tone that I knew was a conscious decision. Such a good guy, my Captain Asshole.

"Yeah, the others. They're one second doing"—she jerked her gaze to the cracked concrete—"jobs, then boom, gone, never to be seen again. The cops don't take it seriously, though, because of what we do." The corner of her lip curled upward. "Some of us even went to this FBI guy, found his information online, and he didn't give a shit either."

"How long has this been going on, the women going missing?" I asked. My stomach churned, all the happy and excitement from the day now replaced with worry and dread.

"I don't know... a year, maybe longer. Though it's not the first time."

"What do you mean?" West asked.

"Some of the older girls said there were a bunch of missing women back when they were just starting, but then one day it just stopped." She rubbed at her arms and glanced up and down the street as if expecting the one responsible to jump out from the shadows. "Now it's happening again. I just want to find my friend. She's all I have."

I carefully slid the paper free from her tight hold. "Can I have this copy? We might know someone who could help." And maybe tell us why the hell women were turning up missing here in Anchorage too.

"Sure, I made a lot of copies to put up." She held up the small stack of flyers.

"Want some help?" West asked. He turned to me and Langston. "You two head to the bar. I'll help her put up the rest of the flyers and then meet you there."

I looped my arms around his neck and pulled him down for a quick kiss. "You're a good man, West, you know that?"

"I have to be to have any hope of deserving someone like you, Juno."

My heart clenched at his words. "We deserve each other."

After one last quick kiss, I waved at the woman and

allowed Langston to guide me down the sidewalk toward our original destination.

"Are you thinking what I'm thinking?" I murmured, gaze locked on my shoes. "It can't be a coincidence, right?"

"I don't know. Anchor Bay is best accessible by boat, and that's an hour's trip. That would be a lot of fucking effort, for what?"

"For what?" I parroted. "That's the big question if they are linked. Why at home and why here?"

"And let's not forget the type of person missing are opposites there and here. On the trail, it's healthy, adventurous young women, and here, it's—" He cringed. "—the opposite."

"Yeah." I held up the flyer and studied the woman's picture, loving her fire-red dyed hair. "I just can't shake the feeling that it's connected somehow. And what she said about it happening before, isn't that what Jasper said to Liam and Memphis that day in the street? Caroline was trying to connect disappearances from years ago to what's happening now. Something to do with her mom, I think."

My brows pulled in tight as I tried to remember what the guys had mentioned about that run-in with Jasper Cain weeks ago. That was before he turned up murdered. But how could someone be connected to the missing women from two decades ago and now? That part didn't make sense.

With a resigned sigh, knowing there was nothing I could do now, I folded up the flyer and stuck it into my back pocket. "I can't believe we're headed to my hometown tomorrow. And then the big shit show—I mean wedding— the next day. Did I tell you Stephanie wants me to come to her bridal shower tomorrow if we arrive in time?"

"Will you?" Langston opened a heavy wooden door and

guided me through with a gentle hand pressed against my lower back.

The mixed aromas of stale beer, fried foods, and smoke permeated the air, reminding me of Dave's back home. My heart swelled at that thought. Yes, Anchor Bay was my home now. More of a home than I'd ever had before, filled with people who truly cared about me, and it wasn't just about Langston and West. It felt like a loving family, everyone checking in on you when you were down, stopping by when you were sick, considering you when making community plans or changes.

Yes, Anchor Bay was my home.

"What are you smiling about?" Langston asked as he helped me onto the high-top barstool before taking a seat beside me.

"Just happy. But to answer your question, I don't know if I'll go. It'll be a game-time decision. The only thing we're committed to going to is the wedding, and I like it that way. This will give us plenty of free time for me to show you around the three-block town without having to rush to get somewhere."

"Sounds like a plan to me. The less time I'm around that asshole, the better—for his sake, anyway." He looked over his shoulder to the bar and then back at me with a small frown. "I have to order over there."

I shrugged. "I'll be fine on my own, here in the middle of a crowded bar while you're twenty feet away with a clear line of sight to where I'm sitting."

He grumbled something under his breath about me needing the sass spanked out of me and stood. After promising several times that I wouldn't move, he turned, making his way to the bar.

Blowing out a slow breath, I relaxed against the hardwood chair back and allowed my gaze to wander around the dive bar. Most of the tables were full of what seemed to be friends or coworkers all enjoying a drink after work, laughing and talking loudly with one another.

A couple sitting at a high-top table similar to ours caught my attention. It was like a flashback to how Eric and I used to be when we went out alone. The guy nursed a beer, several empty pint glasses littering the table in front of him, as he played on his phone while the woman stared off into space, acting like him ignoring her was okay. They both looked miserable.

Never again would I allow that, to feel so invisible and alone while sitting right next to my partner. All the hard work and active healing I'd done since moving to Anchor Bay had shown me I was a pretty amazing person. I'd started my own company doing website design and system programming for small businesses, took up self-defense classes with Oliver, and put myself out there with the women in the Uplift community, who welcomed me with open arms. For years I was coerced to push aside who I really was and what I wanted, but that was in the past.

One part of my new life that I absolutely didn't expect but now cherished were the women in the Uplift community who quickly became friends I never wanted to live without. They didn't give me the option to be a loner; instead, they showed up one day with wine and cookies. Now book club, where we drank more than read, was a night I looked forward to the moment the previous one ended.

"It's less about my feelings toward Stephanie," I mused when Langston returned with our drinks—beer for him, vodka soda with a lime for me, "and more that I'm done wasting time on things because it's 'what you're supposed to do.' Fuck that, right? Why should I be forced to spend hours of my life stuck in a room with a bunch of women who I don't like, playing nice and acting like a give a fuck if Stephanie got the china she registered for?"

"People still do that shit?" Langston asked, taking a sip of his beer.

"Yeah, all to put it in a special cabinet, only to be brought out when the queen comes."

"Gotta love a good *Friends* reference." I whirled around with a wide smile to face West. "I'm so glad I'm obsessed with a woman who can quote movies and shows with me."

"Obsessed, huh?"

He kissed me on the cheek and sat down, grabbing Langston's beer right out of his hand and taking a drink.

I took a drink to hide my laugh at the disgusted expression Langston shot him. "You two are adorable."

They both turned to me with unamused expressions.

"We're not adorable," West said, giving Langston back his drink. "We're...."

"About to kill that motherfucker at the bar if he doesn't stop eyeing our girl," Langston grumbled.

A serious expression replaced West's dimpled smile. "Which one?"

"Stop it, you two," I cut in. "He's probably trying to figure out our dynamic, not looking at just me."

"He wants what's ours," Langston muttered as he took another sip of his beer while death glaring across the bar.

"Or wants to join in?" I said with as straight a face as I could muster. "How do you two feel about adding to our group?"

Both heads whipped my way with raised brows. I couldn't hold back a second longer; the laugh that was desperate to escape erupted, making the table next to us turn our way. I slapped a hand over my mouth, attempting to quiet myself.

West sagged in his chair. "Funny, sweet cheeks. Very funny. You had me there for a second."

"Like I need more," I chuckled. "I already have two slightly obsessed—"

"Remove the slightly," Langston added.

"Protective—"

"Add in over-the-top," West chimed in.

"And practically perfect in every way men."

"While I don't agree with your *Mary Poppins*-coined description of us, I do agree that we're all you need."

"Forever," Langston said before downing the last of his drink and watching me over the glass rim. The heat in his eyes made my breath catch and stomach flip. "We're all she'll ever need. We'll make sure of that."

Holy hell, who knew being claimed by someone like these two would be so fucking hot instead of suffocating and terrifying? Forever seemed like a long time, except when it was referring to the three of us together, just like this.

Then it didn't feel nearly long enough.

23

LANGSTON

"Why the fuck are you sharpening your knife?"

I dragged my stare from the dangerously sharp blade to West before returning to the monotonous task. It was the only thing I could think to do to lower my blood pressure and calm my pulse since Juno left for the bridal shower.

"Never know when you'll need to use it, so I might as well keep it in pristine condition."

West snorted, shaking his head before turning to face out the window again. He had stood sentry there for the last thirty minutes, watching out the glass panes for Juno to return. Our little hotel room was less of a room and more of a shoebox with a queen-size bed. I eyed it for the hundredth time, wondering how in the hell we'd all fit on the thing later.

"She should've been back by now," West complained, crossing and uncrossing his arms in his clear agitation. "The thing ended at four so everyone could leave to get ready for the rehearsal dinner." He turned and tossed his hands in the air. "We should've gone with her."

"To a women-only bridal shower?" I arched a brow and shook my head. "You're the one who told me to cool it with the overbearing shit."

"We could've waited outside or something. Fuck, you could've done your stalking shit and just hid in the shadows."

The blade clicked into the hilt. West was worked up, that was for fucking sure. I watched him pace from one window to the other. He continued to rant under his breath about us being lazy with her safety and how we should go after her. It was when he started talking bad about himself that I knew it was time to end the toxic shit.

Pushing out of the armchair that had creaked when I sat down, a warning that it could break under my solid weight, I marched over to my friend and stepped into his path. He stumbled to a stop to keep from smacking into my chest. Running a hand over his short hair, he attempted to sidestep me to continue pacing, but I mirrored him, keeping him from passing.

"Langston," he gritted out. "I'm not in the mood for games. She's in danger."

"Is she now?"

"Yes, and you're doing nothing about it. Do you even care about what happens—"

Forearm to his throat, I shoved him against the wall and pinned him there with my weight. He snarled, bucking in my hold, attempting to break free. Not that I let him.

"First of all, I do fucking care. I care so fucking much that I'm taking your advice and trying not to smother her when I know she can take care of herself. If she needs us, she'll call." I slid my phone free and held it up so he could see the blank screen. "She hasn't reached out, so she's fine."

His eyes narrowed. "You're way too calm. What did you do?"

My responding smile was sharp. "Nothing."

"Langston," he demanded—well, as best as he could with my forearm still pressed against his throat.

"I might have installed a tracking app on her phone so I know where she is at all times."

A colorful string of curses left his lips, drawing my focus there. Not resisting, I leaned in and bit the lower one hard enough to leave an indentation but not draw blood. His chest rose and fell with his deep breaths. Gazes locked, I tossed my phone onto the bed and reached between us.

His breath caught when I yanked open his jeans and ripped down the zipper. Dipping into his boxer briefs, we hissed in unison when my fingers brushed against his hard cock. Wrapping around him, I squeezed hard, making him gasp.

But I didn't move, just stayed perfectly still, waiting.

It took only a few seconds before the sound of heels echoed down the hall outside the room. A slow smile tugged at my lips, making his brows pull in tight, not understanding.

But he would. In just a few quick seconds.

The sound of the key tapping against the door before sliding into place and disengaging the lock had an almost evil chuckle vibrating in my chest. I knew the second she came into the room, took us in, and understood what was going on.

Her steps were light on the thin rug as she drew closer, pausing at my side.

"He's worked up about you not being back when he thought you should be," I explained. Keeping my eyes on West, I slowly ran my palm up and down his shaft. His perfect lips parted with an explosive exhale. "Want to watch or participate, shortcake?" I cut my gaze over to her.

Cheeks pink, lips parted, pupils dilated, my Juno was turned on at seeing me dominating West. Good. Very good. I wasn't sure which answer I wanted from her—both would be perfect, because it would be the three of us together.

"Both," Juno rasped. "I want to watch you two then participate."

I hitched my chin to the bed. "Get comfortable, short-cake, and watch how I make our boy beg."

Then it would be her turn.

Best fucking day ever.

I wiped the sweat from my forehead unable to smother the cocky smile aimed at the two completely wiped lying beside me. I had no idea it could be that mind-blowing, but I guess it only was when you were with the right people.

"Great, now I need another shower before tonight," Juno rasped, chest still heaving. "Not that I'm complaining because... wow."

Not understanding, I leaned up to gaze down at her, brushing a rogue lock of light brown hair off her sweaty forehead. "Tonight?"

She winced. "Yeah, so, about that. I was a little later than expected because Stephanie cornered me after the shower and begged me to come tonight and bring you two." She looked between me and West. "To the rehearsal dinner."

"Please tell me you said no," West whined. "I don't know if Lang and I can take any more time with that asshole. Plus, that would mean his family would be there too, and I bet they're just as douchey as he is."

"They are," she replied. "And they will be." Rolling over, Juno climbed on top of West, thighs straddling his ribs. "But I promise to make it worth your while."

"While I love that gesture and would take you anytime you were offering, I'll go if you want to go and simply ask. No need for a sexual incentive tied to my going or not, sweet cheeks."

Her lower eyelids filled with unshed tears. "I'm so fucked up in the head."

"You're not." He wrapped his hands around her waist. "We just have to work to change your conditioning, that's it. It's not fucked in the head when you're responding in a way that was expected or needed before. That was adapting."

"And now we all need to un-adapt in different ways," I added.

"I don't think that's a word," she said, shooting me a soft smile.

"I'll make it a fucking word, just for the three of us."

"Un-adapt," West mused. "Not sexy at all, but I like it." He slid his grip down to her bare ass and squeezed. "Now, about the rehearsal dinner. What do you want to do, Juno? That's what we'll do."

With a sigh, she lay down, resting her cheek on his chest to face me. "I think I want to go. If anything, to get the awkwardness of us three together over with. Apparently, Eric mentioned our unique relationship to his mom, who told everyone."

Her squeal reverberated around the room when both of West's palms slapped her round ass.

"Then that settles it. We're going to this rehearsal dinner and will gladly let you show us off, so everyone knows we're proud as hell to be your dates."

She shifted to press her chin on his sternum and smiled up at him. "Same."

My heart stuttered at the sight of them lying there, smiling at each other, completely and utterly happy. I always had the need to protect those who I loved, but this was different. It was more—way fucking more.

Prison more.

Death more.

Anything to keep these two protected, safe, and together.

24

JUNO

A light breeze ruffled my styled hair, sending rogue pieces to flutter in front of me, distorting my view of the glowing restaurant sign. One of their hands wrapped around each of my own, offering silent comfort and support as I gazed at the humming orange light, building up my courage and patience to walk through the door. A sense of relief washed over me knowing this could've been me, this exact restaurant on this exact day, but instead of being twenty-four hours from sealing my life to a baby narcissist, I was free, living a life I actually enjoyed and didn't dread every morning.

Nostalgia swirled as I looked through the painted glass to the party going on inside. I had chosen this place because it was where I first met Eric. On the short walk from the hotel, I'd prepared myself for the grief to hit me full force standing here, that the pain that nearly killed me when I first left would come roaring back.

But instead, I felt nothing but weight-lifting liberation.

Sensing his stare burning into the side of my face, I shifted my attention up to Langston. He studied me like he was actually concerned about how this affected me, and not because of how it would reflect on him, but because he cared about me, my feelings, my emotions. Turning to West, a giggle escaped at him fighting with the collar of his shirt, pulling it away from his neck like it was tightening by the second.

It was then that the relief vanished and I was overwhelmed by utter gratitude and love for the two men at my side. *Love* might be too strong a word considering things were new between us, but then again, they actually weren't. This, between the three of us, had been building, almost to the boiling point, since I arrived in Anchor Bay.

Nostrils flaring with a deep inhale through my nose, I forced my feet forward up to the glass front door, the guys matching me step for step at my sides. For a second, I wondered what it would be like to do this alone, to face the crowd without any support. There was no doubt in my mind that I wouldn't have come. But with West and Langston at my sides, I could not only handle whatever the night brought but maybe anything.

With a white-knuckled grip, Langston pulled the door open, guiding me through first with a firm hand pressed against my lower back. The moment I stepped across the threshold, all the laughter and loud, excited chatter stopped. It was as if all noise of any kind was sucked from the room as every face turned our way, gazes flicking between me and the guys with mixed expressions of disgust and curiosity.

I felt the heat build along my cheeks and down my neck under all the critical stares of the twenty-plus people attending the rehearsal dinner.

"The entire time you were at that shower, Langston was sharpening his knife," West murmured in my ear. "So if you want anyone taken out, I know a guy."

Just like that, his words plus the humor lacing them had all the tension draining from my taut muscles. I huffed a laugh, shaking my head in fake exasperation, but shot him a smile full of gratitude as I forced myself deeper into the viper's nest.

Pushing through the still-silent crowd, the happy couple approached us both with wide, fake smiles on their faces. I noted Eric's too-tight hold on Stephanie's waist; it seemed more controlling than romantic or protective. Her rigid posture was obvious, making her movements stiff as she leaned in for a hug, constricting her arms around me so tight that I almost couldn't breathe. Her hold felt desperate; I half expected her to whisper, "Help me," in my ear.

"I'm so glad you could make it, Juno, and... friends." Eric's words were as stiff as his posture as he glared at Stephanie's back. "All right, that's enough of that. You just saw her this afternoon. Release my June Bug."

When the words registered, I narrowed my eyes at Eric, lips parting to correct him, but I should've known Langston would beat me to it.

"Not yours," he practically growled, then gestured to West. "Ours. If you try to claim her like that again, I will see it as a challenge. And she fucking hates that nickname, so don't use it again."

"Whatever, it was just a wording mistake," Eric said condescendingly. "I have the best girl here tonight, so why would I want to claim her?"

"Fucking hell, you're trying to die tonight, aren't you," West bit out, his fingers tightening around mine. "Stop being an asshole, Evan. You know exactly what you're doing, and it is disrespectful to all of us, including your future bride."

"It's Eric," he snapped. Based on the curving of West's

lips, he was quite enjoying pissing the asshole off. "You two weren't even—"

"It's fine, it's fine," Stephanie said in a rush, hands up in a placating move as her frantic gaze bounced between all of us. She grabbed Eric's arm and sealed her side against his. "No need to get upset over mistaken wording." Her little nose scrunched in her attempt to make a silly face to ease the thrumming tension.

Damn, how many times had I done that, forced a distraction to keep things from escalating because Eric was a self-centered tool who loved to provoke?

She beckoned me forward. "Come on, let's find Dad. I told him you were coming, and he said he couldn't wait to see you."

Somehow, I doubted that, unless he was eager to rehash how big a disappointment I was, which was probably the case.

Yay, me.

West's fingers slipped through mine as Stephanie dragged me toward the back of the large room. With a quick glance over my shoulder, I swallowed a laugh at both men standing shoulder to shoulder, their heavy glares leveled at Eric as he talked, hands waving in excitement as he no doubt attempted to win them over to Team Eric.

Maybe it made me a bad person, or at the very least petty as fuck, but knowing they saw through his "good guy" mask made me immensely happy. Most people saw the version of him that he wanted them to see, not the one he truly was inside. It was one of the reasons I'd stayed, because for the longest time, I believed his mask too. That his anger and control issues were just stress-induced or a fluke, not who he truly was. Plus, I didn't want to be the bad guy, which leaving him ultimately made me become to everyone in town.

"Dad."

At Stephanie's voice, he turned. I didn't even attempt to force a smile, not wanting to waste the energy on him. The genuine smile he wore from the conversation he'd been in with the three older gentlemen slipped into a disapproving, tight-lipped frown when his gaze fell on me.

"I told you she would come." Stephanie beamed at him, seemingly oblivious to the animosity between us.

"So she returns," he muttered before tipping back the remaining clear liquid in his highball glass. He thrust the empty tumbler at Stephanie, sending the ice clinking against the sides, and hitched his chin in the direction of the open bar. "Grab me another while I catch up with your sister."

Who knew that word could sound so disgusting?

Without waiting for her response, he turned to face me straight on while adjusting the cuffs of his shirt beneath the navy blazer. "I cannot believe you actually showed your face here after the shit show you left us high and dry with when you ran away."

The normal apology or overexplaining myself didn't spill from my lips as he stared at me, waiting for my response. I simply blinked at the man I used to be so intimidated by. Whose words I believed too much—that I was too geeky, too quiet, too everything he thought wasn't normal.

Now, standing in front of him, I didn't feel apprehensive at all. Instead, hot, boiling anger filled my chest at him and myself for believing all those lies. For *allowing* the weak man to make me feel so fucking small when I wasn't.

"Earth to Juno." He huffed and shook his head. "Do you even know how to act normal in social situations?"

"I do, I just had nothing to say to your comment."

He arched a brow, surprised by my backbone. "Well, I hope you're not here to try and win him back. He lucked out with your poor decision, falling for Stephanie after the weeks of comfort she offered him after you left."

I snorted. Sure she did. I almost gagged thinking about the "comfort" she gave him.

"I'm glad Eric found someone who will make him happy, who'll focus on him first like a good wife should," he continued. "A woman who will make the sacrifices needed to ensure he's taken care of."

"Right," I drawled, hating myself a little more, knowing I once believed the bullshit that came from his mouth. "What about what Stephanie needs and wants?"

"She has him, someone who can provide. That's all a woman really wants anyway."

I just mouthed, "Wow." It was all I could come up with.

"At least a normal woman." His gaze shifted over my shoulder. "I can't believe you brought that fucking sideshow act with you. Have some damn respect for your mother's reputation."

"My dead mother's reputation?" I tilted my head. "Or do you really mean yours?"

"Fuck, you're a brat. Always were, though. I'm sure they'll get tired of you too, just like Eric."

His words hit right where he wanted them to. I tried to keep my features neutral despite my stomach dropping so fast I felt nauseous, but the evil grin that crept up his cheeks told me I had failed miserably.

"Oh yeah, he told me all about how selfish you were, all the shit you did to him. Let's be honest, Juno, you've never been the type to make anyone happy or give them what they need. You're just—" He gestured toward me. "—you.

Though good job on losing some of that weight. I'm sure those two appreciate it."

I swallowed hard to keep the bile creeping up my throat at bay.

"Just don't ruin this for your sister," he said with a disappointed huff. "Keep your bullshit in the background while you're here, then take it with you when you leave."

Someone approached, slapping him hard on the back—our old neighbor, maybe—yanking his glare off me. He should win a damn Oscar for how fast his face morphed into a wide, easygoing smile as he greeted the man with a laugh and hug.

Thankful for the interruption, I mumbled an excuse and bolted. With no destination in mind, I wove through the familiar faces eyeing me with disgust and pity, anxious for a reprieve. It was too much, the boisterous voices, bursts of laughter, plus the slightly too loud background music. The combination grated on my nerves, making me desperate for a quiet moment, any space to fucking breathe and get my emotions back under control.

Hair shifting side to side from my frantic search, I swallowed a whimper when I caught the glowing red Exit sign in the back. Already moving, I beelined toward the restaurant's back door. Not breaking stride, I slapped both palms to the metal release bar and shoved, sending the door flying open. The cool evening air brushed against my heated cheeks, instantly soothing the fire burning beneath my skin. After making sure I was alone, I staggered to the side and slumped back against the brick building, almost too exhausted to keep standing.

I was so mad at myself, so angry that I allowed his words to hit the way he intended. The last few months, I thought I'd grown stronger, healed in ways I'd never imagined, and then bam, he said a few lies and it was like I was still that same, small woman they'd turned me into.

At least now I knew they were lies, but the words zeroed in on my vulnerabilities and struck deep all the same. Me being introverted and slightly socially awkward was an easy defect of mine for them to target. They made me feel unlovable and weird because of it. So what if I wasn't the social party girl who everyone loved instantly? Was that so fucking terrible? Did being reserved and needing quiet space to recharge make me boring and undesirable?

My hair snagged on the rough brick as I rolled the back of my head to stare up into the cloudy sky.

Why in the hell did I feel the need to come tonight, or even tomorrow? I'd done so much healing, and now it felt minuscule compared to how far I still had to go. Maybe this thing with Langston and West was too soon. I needed to figure my shit out on my own before I could be what they needed.

I wanted them, yes, but was I ready to be in a relationship?

"What are you doing out here?"

I startled at the voice, too lost in thought to hear the door crack open. A concerned-looking Eric stepped out into the alley, carefully shutting the door behind him with a soft click. Brows pinched tight, lips in a thin line, he actually seemed worried about me. But the moment his blue eyes locked with mine, I saw the show for what it was.

"What are you doing out here?" he repeated. "I didn't see you inside and got worried."

Defenses up, I dipped my chin in a slow nod as I pushed off the brick and started inching toward the door, hoping to make a quick exit.

"One second you were talking to your dad—"

"Stepdad," I grumbled.

His head tilted to the side. "The only dad you've ever known, right? Don't be too hard on him. He's a man who tried to be a good dad. He didn't know how to relate to girls."

My nose wrinkled at that. *What the fuck is that bullshit about?*

"But yeah, he can be a bit of a hard-ass," he said with a chuckle. I swallowed a curse when he leaned a shoulder against the wall, placing himself between me and the door. Both hands shoved into the pockets of his pressed slacks, he gave me a slow once-over. "I guess I understand you needing a break from all this. I'm sure being here, seeing me and Steph, is hard for you. I know it is for me." When I didn't respond to his ridiculous assumption, he continued on. "You're different, you know. From when you left me."

"How?" I asked, very curious to hear his observations. It would probably end up being hilarious.

Again, he slowly slid his assessing gaze up and down. A repulsed shiver raced up my spine at the desire that flamed in his gaze when he met mine. "Well, your figure is back, that's for sure." Leaning forward, he brushed a single digit along my thigh, but it was there and gone before I could say anything. "And I have to guess if you're keeping two guys happy, then you've realized what men need from their girlfriends. That was always such a hard spot for us." I pressed my lips shut before a frustrated scream escaped. "You just never wanted me like I needed; it was hard getting rejected all the time by you. That's why I cheated, to finally be with someone who was as into me as I was her."

"You're blaming me," I deadpanned. "For you cheating on me."

He sighed and reached out to touch my cheek, but I jerked away. Lips in a tight line, he scanned my face. "Well, yeah. If I would've been taken care of by the woman I was engaged to, then I wouldn't have needed to find release somewhere else. Men need sex, and you just didn't want to be who I wanted you to be. And of course, there's the whole...." He winced. "No one really likes you. They think you're cold and not fun, which was hard to be around when everyone loves me."

My jaw went slack.

He had to be kidding right now.

Pushing off the wall, he came to stand directly in front of me, his loafers touching the toes of my wedge boots. "But I think you see the error, how you needed to change to be better. You understand what it means to be good in your role."

"My role," I whispered, barely able to get the words out around the angry tears that clogged my throat.

"Yeah, as a girlfriend, fiancée, wife. Which is why I wanted you to know I'd do it."

"Do what?"

His condescending smile made my stomach churn. "Take you back."

"You're getting married tomorrow." The disbelief in my tone could've been heard three towns over.

"Yeah, but that doesn't mean we can't still see each other. I love you, Juno, but you just weren't who I needed you to be. But now maybe you could be. Can't you see what I'm doing here?"

"Talking nonsense?"

He pressed his hands to the brick on either side of my head. My heart leapt into my throat, feeling caged in. Panic filled my veins, making sweat slick the back of my neck, the need for escape clawing at me from the inside.

"I need you to step back," I rasped. Palms to his chest, I shoved, but he barely shifted.

"I'm giving you another chance." Inch by inch, he leaned closer. My spine sealed to the wall in my desperate attempt to put more distance between me and his approaching lips. "You should be grateful."

I froze.

Grateful?

He wanted me to be grateful to be his sidepiece while he was married to my sister?

I'll give him something to be grateful for.

All those self-defense training sessions had my body moving like it was second nature. Hands to his shoulders, I sidestepped just enough to get the right angle and sent my knee straight to his balls. His eyes went wide, mouth open on a silent yell as he stumbled back, clutching his crushed manhood.

I didn't give him a second to recover, just like Oliver taught me. I cocked my fist back and swung it straight at his nose. The crunch of bone and gush of blood had an evil smile pulling at my lips before it turned into a wince at the pain.

Damn, that fucking hurt.

Cursing under my breath, I shook out my hand but kept my guard up in case he recovered and came after me. But before that could happen, the metal door swung open, allowing the noise from inside to pour out into the alley.

"What are you two doing out here?" Stephanie's accusing tone echoed around us.

With a gasp, she rushed to Eric's side. He was still bent over with one hand clutching his balls and the other around his nose to stop the blood from streaming out. Stroking a comforting hand up and down his spine, Stephanie turned a hateful glare on me. "What the hell is wrong with you?"

"*Me?*" I pointed at myself, shocked at the disdain dripping from her tone. "He's the one who—"

"I don't want to hear it, Juno. I don't want to hear your lies," she shouted. Face flushed, eyes a little wild, she stepped toward me, making me flinch back. Crazy Stephanie was slightly scary. "I should've known that you'd ruin this for me, for me and Eric." She pushed my shoulder hard, sending me stumbling backward. My back collided with the brick, making me wince from the hard impact. "I cannot believe you."

"Steph," I rasped. "It's not what you think."

"You want to know what I think? I think you saw how happy I was and just couldn't take it, so you lured him out here to try to get him back."

My mouth hung open. "That is 100 percent not the case. I came out here to get some air—"

"I just wanted to make sure she was okay," Eric said, words muffled. You know, from his probably broken nose. I smothered a grin knowing I did that. "And then she attacked me."

"What the fuck?" I screeched. "You lying motherfucker. You offered for me to be your sidepiece." I raised both brows at Stephanie while pointing at Eric. "He said—"

"Juno, I know there is no way he said that, because I know what he likes and needs, and you're not that. He told me what a prude you are, so really, Juno, can you blame him for cheating on you?"

I opened my mouth, but no words came out. Thankfully, the back door swung open once again, and this time it was a face I wanted to see.

Langston took in the scene before stepping to my side

and pulling me against him. I buried my face in his chest while his hand cupped the back of my head, holding me gently.

"Did you do that damage, shortcake?"

My lips rubbed against his shirt as my smile grew. "I did."

"Such a good girl." His deep voice vibrated in his chest, helping soothe some of the pressure in mine. "If he touched you, I'll finish the job." Shifting back, I tilted my face up to his, finding green eyes focused only on me. "You just say the word. It's why I made sure my knife was in perfect condition today."

"You're a psychopath," Stephanie breathed. "Juno, you're not safe with him." The door opened again, and West stepped out. "Neither of them."

Turning, I leaned back against Langston and shook my head. "No, Stephanie, I'm not safe here. And you know what? That's okay, because I have no plans to ever return. I wanted to warn you about the miserable life you're signing yourself up for, to offer a way out, but you know what?" I looked between her and Eric, sadness welling in my heart. "You two deserve each other. Good luck with all that, and do not ever contact me again."

Stepping out of Langston's hold, I flipped them both the bird and stormed down the alley, headed toward the street.

It was time to leave Banks and never return.

25

WEST

We were both worried about her. Giving her a little space, Langston and I walked side by side, just a few steps behind Juno as she stomped down the empty sidewalk. I looked over my shoulder, hoping that asshole Eric would chase after her so we could finish what she'd started.

The image of his swollen, bleeding nose had my lips curving upward. Our girl was a badass. I just hoped she knew that too.

She hadn't given us the rundown of what happened in the alley, despite Langston champing at the bit, ready to demand answers. Probably so he could feel justified in killing the son of a bitch. My friend no doubt felt responsible that she had to defend herself alone while we were being held hostage inside by three older women very interested in our lifestyle.

One realized she wasn't our type and started showing us pictures of her grandkids. That was why we didn't initially notice Juno wasn't in the room, and neither were dipshit and his bride. Langston realized it first, cutting off mid-sentence while scanning the room, then storming off. I apologized for his abrupt departure and raced to catch up with him. It took him all of two seconds, and looking at the tracking app on his phone, to realize she was there but not.

Even if we didn't know the full story, we had her back no matter what. But the way she wouldn't look at us made me wonder if something Eric or someone else at the dinner said had hit home, making her question us or even herself.

Hand shoved into the pocket of the uncomfortable-as-hell slacks, I pulled out my phone, going straight to the train schedule, hoping like hell we weren't too late to catch the last one out of this hellhole.

"It looks like the last train tonight to Anchorage leaves in thirty minutes," I stated, already tapping on the purchase button for three tickets. "We can make it if we pack up fast."

"Juno," Langston called out, making her stop and spin around. The yellow glow of a nearby streetlamp highlighted the wet streaks marking her face.

My heart clenched at the sight, desperate to hold her. Not even trying to stop myself, I closed the distance between us and wrapped her in a tight hug. "Based on what just happened, I'm assuming our invite to the wedding tomorrow is revoked." Juno and I both huffed out a laugh. "Do you want to leave tonight?"

Her cheek moved along my chest with a slow nod. "Yes, I want to get out of here now. Like *now*, now."

"We can stop by the hotel, grab our things, and get to the train station in time. That puts us in Anchorage late, so we can get a hotel there and—"

"I want to go home," she said, her voice cracking. "Can we leave for Anchor Bay tonight?" She chewed on her lower lip and looked to the concrete, shifting on her feet. "Would that be dangerous since it would be late?"

Langston scoffed and pulled her to him. "I'll be the one

behind the wheel, remember, so we'll be fine. It's not ideal, but I can make it work. I *will* make it work to get you home if that's what you want."

"It is."

The hesitation in her voice had me turning her face up to mine. "What is it? I sense that something was said or happened that's making you... question."

Fresh tears leaked from the corners of her eyes, confirming my suspicion. "I thought I was healing, that I could be here and be okay. I'm such an idiot—"

"Watch how you talk about our girl there, Juno. That train ride will suck with a sore ass."

She rolled her eyes at Langston before continuing. "It took just a few sentences from my stepfather to undo all the progress I'd made these last few months. I was outside by myself getting some air, and I just thought that maybe this is too soon. If I let his words affect me when I *know* they aren't true, then maybe I need to keep doing the healing... alone."

With the side of my thumb, I brushed away her tears.

"I agree that you still have healing to do, but not alone. Please don't push us away because some asshat knew exactly what to say to weaken your defenses. You still feeling the sting of his words doesn't mean you haven't been healing, nor does it negate the hard work you've put in; it just shows you that there's more to do. It will take time and talking through your feelings and reservations. Remember, Juno, you don't have to do this alone. Not anymore."

Her wet eyelashes fanned up and down. I could almost see the war going on behind her gorgeous eyes. She wanted to believe me but had done it alone for so long that it was hard to ask for help. If she was like me, the fear wasn't in asking for help but in opening yourself up for disappointment. Exposing your weaknesses only to be turned away by the person who said they would be there for you.

"We're here, Juno," Langston said, coming to stand on her other side. "No matter what. But don't let some asshole diminish everything you've done to this point to survive and move on. He doesn't get that power over you; no one does."

She sucked in a tight breath. "You're both right. It was just a lot tonight, and I went right back to how I would always handle high-stress situations—alone." Wiping her cheeks, she stood up straighter, a soft smile on her lips. "Let's go home. I'm over this place. For good."

Interlacing her fingers with mine, I guided us toward the hotel. If we wanted to make that final train, then we couldn't waste any time. Plus, I wanted to get as far away from the rehearsal dinner as possible. It was taking everything I had not to turn around and find that stepdad of hers. No wonder Juno had confidence issues; all the men she grew up around were toxic as shit. It's a wonder she ever got the courage to break free.

"Just promise you'll wear that dress we picked out one night soon for only me and Langston. I was looking forward to showing you off at the wedding and then taking you back to the hotel to rip the flimsy material off you."

A wide smile split her face as she shook her head and leaned against my bicep. Already it seemed she felt lighter, more centered than just minutes before.

It was this whole damn town that brought her down, which meant we needed to get the fuck out of Dodge. I picked up our pace, eager to get our stuff packed up, board the train, and head home.

My shoulders dropped as some of the thrumming tension eased at that thought.

Home.

Yes, it was time for the three of us to go home.

* * *

THE COARSE ROPE scraped over my hands as I helped Langston ready the boat for our trip back to Anchor Bay. The docks were eerily quiet, most of the fishermen long gone; only the hum of cars passing on a nearby busy street filled the air.

After dusting off my hands, I turned to Juno, who stood a couple of feet away, giving us space to work. "You know, the house arrest still stands," I commented. "We've only been gone a couple of days. The threat is still there until we catch the asshole."

She wrapped both arms around herself and turned to look out over the dark water. It was that time of night during the summer months when the sun had finally set, the elusive nighttime gracing us with its cool presence. Above us, brilliant stars sparkled in the sky, occasionally covered up by the fast-moving dark clouds that seemed to promise rain at some point. The bright sun would reappear on the horizon in just a few brief hours, unlike closer to the Arctic Circle, where they had almost twenty-four hours of daylight.

"She doesn't seem that upset about it," Langston said, a bit of pride in his tone.

"I'm not," Juno commented over her shoulder while sticking out her tongue at him. "I've gotten used to my two jailers."

He and I shared an amused look before going back to the task at hand. After untying the last rope, I hopped on board, Langston following right after me. As we trudged slowly through the dock area, waves slammed threateningly against the hull, making a seed of worry bury itself in my gut. Fully dark now, not a peek of the glorious sun to light our way, I didn't know how Langston knew where to go, but he'd made this trip so many times that he could probably do it blindfolded.

With us in expert hands, I plopped down next to Juno and draped an arm around her, pulling her in close. After a contented sigh, she rested her head on my shoulder. Her hair tickled my lips as I placed a kiss on top of her head while twirling a light brown curl between two fingers.

"I love this color on you," I murmured loud enough to be heard over the roaring engine. "It looks like you."

She shifted so she stayed leaning against me but could angle her face up toward mine. "I like it too. It'll be even better when my real hair grows out and it's my natural color, not something out of a box." She bit down on her lower lip, and I waited patiently, knowing she had something on her mind. "It felt good tonight, standing up for myself and kicking Eric's ass." I barked out a laugh at her genuine grin. "I felt strong. Does that make me a bad person? I enjoyed hitting him—really, *really* enjoyed it. But no one told me how much it would hurt."

Hand stretched out in front of us, she flexed her fingers. I grabbed it in my own and held it close, inspecting each digit for injury.

"Enjoying it doesn't make you a bad person at all, Juno. He put you in a critical situation, and you stood up for yourself. If he hadn't done it, you wouldn't have."

"I want to keep working out with Oliver." She cut her eyes to Langston. "Do you think he'll let me?"

"Let you?" I scoffed. "You have that entire man wrapped around your finger. You tell him what you want to do, and he'll be the one bending over backward to make it happen.

Plus, it adds another level of safety for the times when we're not around."

Wrapping both arms around me, she snuggled in close and sighed. "I'm so ready to see GG." Juno popped up as if a random thought just hit her. "Who takes care of her when you're both gone?"

A slow smile crept up my lips at her concern for the grumpy cat. "Baylee. She won't let us pay her either, says she gets her payment in kitty snuggles. GG loves her."

"I think all animals do. It's what makes her an amazing vet." She settled back against me. "Okay, good. I just thought about her being home alone and sad, and that made me sad."

Chuckling to myself, I kissed the corner of her dramatic frown. "You're the sweetest to think about GG and—"

"What the hell?" The confusion in Langston's muttered words cut me off, drawing both Juno's and my attention to where he stood at the front of the boat.

Slipping my arm from around her shoulders, I slowly stood, using the side of the boat to steady myself. Stance wide for balance, I made my way to Langston's side at the wheel. Without uttering a word, he pointed to the right of the boat before dropping that hand to the throttle, slowing the engine.

Neither opening my eyes wide nor squinting them helped me see whatever Langston saw. As far as I was concerned, it was black water everywhere, except for a few slivers of moonlight that shimmered on the surface. Brow furrowed, I parted my lips, ready to ask him what he thought he'd seen, when our boat shifted with an enormous wave, adjusting our angle. That was when I saw it—a flicker or shadow of something not too far from us on the water.

Palm to the side of the boat, I pitched forward, watching,

but as the moon slipped behind the clouds, the area outside of our running lights went into utter darkness.

"I think I saw something, but no clue what." I stood straight and twisted to face Langston.

Powerful waves rocked the boat from side to side, the spray misting my face as we idled in the middle of the black water. He nodded, letting me know he heard me, but didn't take his focus off the area where he'd pointed.

"It looked like the outline of a boat to me, but that makes little sense. It would have running lights like we have to alert other boats and for them to see what they're doing."

"True. What if they lost power and are stranded?" I mused.

"Good point. Let's see if they're reaching out for help on the radio." Twisting the knob, Langston clicked through the various channels, his frown growing by the second when there were no calls for help or SOS signals.

"If they were stranded, they would either be on the radio or sending some type of signal to us that they need help. There's no way someone doesn't see us with our lights on." Never breaking his stare out over the dark water, Langston reached into a side cabinet, withdrew a nine-millimeter, and placed it on the dash. "Just in case things aren't on the up-and-up. Something doesn't feel right."

I nodded, fully agreeing with him; this felt off. I studied my friend and sighed. "You want to check it out, see what's going on, don't you?" I glanced over my shoulder at Juno, giving her a tight smile. "You know, I would normally be all in, but our girl is on board with us. Wouldn't that be putting her in a potentially dangerous situation?"

Langston grunted in agreement, twisting around to check on Juno, who was already coming closer. Brows pulled in tight, gaze locked on us, she made her way from the back of the boat to where we stood.

"What's going on?" she asked, studying us, no doubt sensing our tension. "What is that look?" She pointed to Langston's face and then mine. "You'd think we were in danger or something." Her nervous laugh faded when we didn't respond. "Wait, are we? Is it something to do with the boat?"

"There's nothing wrong with the boat, but we're not sure what's going on," Langston stated. With a hand on each shoulder, he turned her toward the mystery spot and pointed like he had with me. "Out there. It was there and gone, so I'm not positive, but I thought I saw a boat stranded."

"We're assuming stranded," I mumbled.

"It makes the most sense," Langston replied, pulling Juno against him, sealing her back to his chest.

"Or," I drawled, "the boat is fine, and whatever they're doing, they don't want anyone to know about it. What if we just interrupted something illegal, Lang? They would no doubt have more guns than your single nine-millimeter. It's not smart to—"

"But what if they *are* in trouble and need our help?" Juno interrupted, placing a hand on my forearm. "We have a weapon just in case, right?"

Langston inclined his head to the gun on the dash, and of course, he had his knife stashed somewhere too.

She nodded. "Then I think we should check it out, make sure they're okay. If they are doing something illegal...." She paused, chewing on her lip as she stared at her feet. "I mean, like, it's already happening. So on the super-odd chance they are, then we can figure out what to do from there. But again, I highly doubt it." She gestured around us. "We're in

Alaska, in the middle of the water, at night. Who would it be, the Russians?"

I huffed out a laugh while Langston smiled and shook his head.

"Russians," he joked. "This isn't a Bond or *Mission Impossible* movie."

Juno slapped his bicep. "See, you *are* into action films, not just cheesy romance."

"I agree that it's a long shot that they're a danger to us, but you're here with us. I don't want to potentially put you in harm's way," I stated, extracting her from Langston's hold and pulling her into my arms.

"And we have more than one gun." He reached into the cabinet again and pulled out another nine-millimeter. He looked between it and my bandaged hand. "How good of a shot are you with your nondominant hand?"

"Guess we'll find out," I said with a resigned sigh. After taking it from him, I cursed under my breath and handed it back to him. "I can't rack the slide. Can you put one in the chamber for me?"

His responding cocky grin proved he was the ultimate jackass for reveling in my current limitations. *Asshole.*

The click of the slide slamming into place cut through the night, making Juno jump. Taking her hand, Langston guided her to his seat, made sure she was secure, and shot me a glance over his shoulder. At my reluctant but confirming nod, he gripped the throttle and pushed, making the engines roar to life. The boat quickly picked up speed, gliding over the water in the direction of our unknown fate.

"I don't want to run into the fucking thing," Langston grumbled under his breath before hitching his chin toward the back of the boat. "Grab the spotlight from one of the storage compartments. That will help us see farther."

With a clipped nod, I went in search of the light. There were only life jackets and spare ropes in the first hold, but I found it in the second with other miscellaneous equipment. Careful not to move too fast so I didn't lose my balance and fly overboard, I stumbled up to Langston's side and plugged in the power cord.

A blinding stream of light cut through the dark, highlighting just how far away from land—hell, anyone—we were out in the middle of the large bay. Sweeping the light from side to side, my frown deepened. Nothing but water, more water, and wavy water. I shared a confused look with Langston, who shrugged.

"Maybe we were seeing things?" I suggested, though the doubt was clear in my tone.

"Keep searching, widen the scope. If the engines are off, it would have drifted with these choppy waves," Langston stated.

On my third, much wider scan over the water, the light glinted off metal. There it was—a ship, not a boat like ours, utterly dark and quiet as if abandoned.

"Even with it drifting, there's no way it made it all the way over there unless...." He trailed off, sounding bewildered as he slowed the boat, maintaining a comfortable distance between us and the ship. "Why would they try to evade us if they need help?"

"Maybe you just have a shitty sense of direction," I joked, knowing it was a lie, but hoping it would help lighten the tense situation we'd found ourselves in. My stomach tightened with nerves as we all watched the dark ship. "I don't have a good feeling about this, Langston."

"Same." Flexing his fingers, he adjusted his white-knuckled grip on the wheel as we idled, the waves pushing us closer. Too fucking close. "It's too late to turn around and hope they didn't see us, though, not with that spotlight." Grabbing the end of the light, he adjusted the angle, sweeping it along the hull. "I'm trying to tell what kind of ship it is. It looks to be a midsize commercial fishing boat, but it's old. I don't see any fishing gear stacked on the deck, which is odd. And where the hell is the IMO number?"

He continued to direct the light where he needed it as he scanned for the number that identified the boat.

Breathing in deeply through my nose and slowly out through pursed lips, I worked to slow my racing pulse. Blood pounded in my ears as my brain and body sounded every damn alarm, telling me something was wrong, and that we were, in fact, sitting fucking ducks. But Langston was right; it was too late to act like we didn't see anything, not with our light shining on a ship that they obviously wanted to remain hidden in the darkness.

Swallowing hard, I peered around Langston's wide frame. With a stilted smile and rigid posture, Juno shot me two thumbs-up. I snorted at her attempt to act nonchalant about this increasingly terrible situation we'd put ourselves in.

"Lang," I started, my voice trembling with nerves. We had to leave, no matter if they saw us. We were a smaller boat, so surely we would be faster and could make a clean getaway. But I never had time to finish my plea.

From somewhere near the boat, a masculine, garbled yell cut through the lapping waves, making all of us jump at the sound. Was that fucking Russian or some other Eastern European language, or was it just too far away to sound like English?

Before I could process that, a terrified feminine scream sliced through the air, followed by a splash, as if someone or something had fallen overboard.

Still in shock, trying to figure out what the hell we just "witnessed," Langston's hand wrapped around my wrist, guiding the light a few feet to the side.

"Is that another fucking boat tied to the fishing ship?" he murmured more to himself than to me or Juno. "And did anyone else hear that guy yelling in fucking Russian?"

I didn't respond because I didn't have a fucking clue.

"Maybe we are in a Bond movie after all," Juno chuckled. "Does that mean I'm a Bond—"

A flash caught my eye first before the resulting boom of the shot, followed by the tearing of metal as the bullet ripped through some part of the boat. Langston yelled a warlike battle cry for us all to get down just as another shot rang out, then another, and another.

Under heavy gunfire from high-powered weapons, Langston and I shared a distressed look, crouched behind the steering column. Juno was down, curled in a little ball, making herself as small as possible.

"They can't hit something they can't see," I shouted.

Langston didn't bother responding; instead, he reached up and started flicking off the running lights while I yanked the power cord out, instantly killing the spotlight.

Chest heaving with my rapid breaths, I palmed the gun's grip, sweat already slicking my skin and making it slide in my hand. Langston had been in dangerous situations before, but not me. I was the fucking mechanic, not part of the infantry.

The roar of massive engines had us both stilling. I started to speak, but Langston held up a finger, stopping me, and tapped his ear. Straining to hear whatever he did, I shifted to angle my ear in that direction. It was there in the background: a second, smaller, high-pitched engine that was almost drowned out by the ship's larger ones.

Lights flickered to life, giving us our first decent look at the commercial fishing ship as it trudged forward. More shots rang out, making both Langston and me duck with a curse, but this time, none of the shots hit their mark.

Peering around the corner, I searched for the smaller boat, but it was already gone, or making its getaway with no lights, while the ship moved farther and farther away.

For several minutes, we were frozen, all of us trying to piece together what the hell had just happened.

"I don't know what the fuck that was," I rasped, "but we survived it. You all right, Juno?"

Silence. My heart stopped at the quiet.

Langston flipped on the lights, the small bulbs blinking awake. He rushed forward and knelt beside her, hand hovering over her still form as if afraid to touch her.

"Juno," he called out. "You okay, shortcake?"

Still no answer.

Heart slamming in my chest, I yelled her name, the desperation clear in my voice.

"Answer us, Juno," I pleaded. "Please be okay. Please be okay."

If she was hurt, or worse....

I shook my head.

No, I couldn't think that way, not only for myself, but especially for Langston. He'd just accepted her role in his life, allowed her past his defenses, and if something happened to her, we were all in trouble. He would burn the world down in his grief and rage.

No one would be safe, especially him.

My entire body throbbed, especially my knees and elbows, which took the brunt of the fall when I dove from the chair to avoid the bullet spray and landed hard on the unforgiving deck. Sweat soaked my palms, coating my ears where they were sealed tight as I continuously swallowed to keep my stomach contents down. The panic and terror filled every cell, making my heart race so fast that I almost couldn't breathe and locking my muscles so tight with tension that they quivered, almost a full-body shiver in my tight ball, like it was below freezing out here.

My sluggish thoughts tried to process what the hell had just happened. The ship clearly wasn't stranded and had actually been doing something they didn't want anyone to know about. Then came us, the damn cavalry, thinking we would help them. But they didn't need rescuing. So what did they do? They fucking *shot* at us. Not just once but dozens of times, as if trying to actually hit us, not just scare us away. West's theory of the boat and its crew taking part in illegal activities didn't seem so far-fetched now.

A squeak forced its way through my tight throat when a

firm grip clamped around my shoulders and easily hauled me into the air. Smothered against a solid chest, I breathed in West's cedar and spice scent, allowing it to calm my frayed nerves enough to peel my lids open. Blinking several times to clear my vision, I gazed up into his worried face.

"Fuck, you scared the shit out of us." The obvious relief in West's trembling voice had me tilting my head, not understanding why. "Why weren't you answering me or Langston?"

Even now, blood pounded in my ears, making his words distorted, but I could still decipher what he was trying to say. "I couldn't hear through my hands and—where is Langston?"

I sagged against West when Langston popped up from where he hung over the side of the boat, no doubt inspecting the hull for damage. Bullet hole damage, because we were just shot at. My knees shook, followed by my thighs. Patting behind me, I found the seat I'd occupied pre-gun battle and fell into it before I took another tumble to the deck.

"Anyone have any idea what the hell all that was about? If I didn't hear the bullets hitting the boat, I would have thought someone was punking us."

West moved in close, pressing his body against mine. "We're just as in the dark as you. All I know is we need a plan to get the fuck out of here."

"I'm working on that." Langston's deep voice soothed a sliver of the anxiety still thrumming through my veins. "I'm just checking the hull, seeing what the damage is and making sure she's seaworthy."

Resting my head against West, we waited in silence while Langston did what he needed to do. Arms wrapped around his narrow waist, I tightened my hold on West. I needed the reassurance that he was okay. Langston too, but I didn't want to interrupt him. As I waited, chewing on my lower lip, the urge to touch him, to feel the safety of his embrace, finally became too much.

"Langston?" I said, just barely over a whisper, but he paused what he was doing and turned to me. "Can you... I mean, when you have a second." The confusion on his features made me realize I was being unreasonable. I shouldn't have interrupted him. "Never mind."

Furrowing his brow, he strode toward me, gripped my chin in a soft but controlling hold, and angled my face up to his.

"What do you need, Juno?"

"It's stupid. I'm fine—"

"If you need something from me, it's not stupid, but I can't help unless I know how."

"A hug," I rasped. "Can I have a hug to know you're okay and—"

He hauled me against him, arms banded around my back as he clutched me to his chest. My legs went around his waist, arms looping around his neck. Just like with West, I inhaled his unique, all-masculine scent, allowing it to ease more of the tension pulsing through every inch of my body.

For several seconds, we just held each other before another body stepped up behind me and pressed against my back.

And just like that, the last bit of worry and fear drained out of me. Between these two, I was safe, always, from anything attempting to do me harm. How did I even consider breaking it off with them? They were everything I needed, now and maybe even forever.

"I was so scared," I whispered against Langston's neck, his hold on me tightening. "I was afraid I wouldn't get to tell you, tell you both, that this is so much more than I've ever felt for anyone. I'm safe with you two, from others and sometimes even from myself. I know I'm a work in progress, but I need you to know." I swallowed hard, the next words clogging my throat. "I think I'm falling in love with you both."

My heart hammered in my chest, a mix of relief at finally admitting my feelings and fear that they would reject me. But I was tired of playing it safe to protect myself, expecting the worst. It was time to be honest, both with myself and with them. The worst that could happen was we didn't work out; the best would be the best life I never could have imagined.

"Thank fuck," Langston mumbled in my hair, making me smile. "The depth of what I feel for you, shortcake, should be alarming to you." A snorted laugh escaped. "For me, I know what I want, and it's you and West, all three of us together. I was terrified tonight for the first time in a long time, because my life was here on the boat with me in the center of the danger. I was afraid we wouldn't get a chance." Fingers in my hair, he pulled my face off his neck so I could look up at him. "A chance for our own cheesy-romance happy ending." He sealed his lips to mine in a demanding kiss before pulling back. "There is no falling for you. I'm already there, deeply submerged, obsessively in love with you."

Happy tears leaked down my cheeks, which West wiped away for me. After one more kiss, where I could feel Langston's love pouring off him, West extracted me from his arms and pulled me into his.

Even with his healing hand, he supported my weight, tucking a forearm beneath my ass to keep me wrapped around him. His dark eyes searched my face, all the worry and tension from earlier gone.

"You really mean it?" he rasped.

"I do, West. I feel so much for you, it's like I might explode with it."

"Even though you know it won't be easy loving me, Juno? I have my bad days where I'm very hard to love, and I don't think I could survive you leaving me if it gets too difficult."

I nodded. "I have the same fear, West, but I can't stop this. And you know what? I don't want to. I want to build a life where I matter, where the people who love me do that with respect, patience, and a lot of effort. That's what I want to give too, to both you and Langston. I want time to figure all this out so that someday we can look back and realize how going through the hard times together made us that much stronger, together."

His warm forehead pressed to mine, lids closed as he released a relieved breath.

"You do not know how long I've waited for this." He pulled back and met my gaze. "I love you with all the twisted, shattered pieces of my heart. I am constantly amazed by you and want to be there for you every day, to cherish you the way you're meant to be and support you like a true partner in life should."

Cupping his face between my palms, I pulled his mouth to mine. My lids fluttered closed as I parted my lips, pouring all the hope and love I had for the man into him with a passionate kiss that had my stomach twisting as desire pumped through my veins. When a soft moan escaped, I felt fingers thread through my hair. A gentle tug pulled me from West's lips, turning me to meet bright green eyes.

"None of that here, shortcake. We're not out of the

woods yet. I think they're gone, but we need to get the hell out of here." He slapped my ass hard. "We can play at home."

I pushed my lower lip out in a full pout, making him chuckle.

"Fine," West sighed. "Be the responsible one, thinking of our safety."

Langston grinned, but it fell just as fast. "I have no damn clue where that smaller boat went, and that has me on edge."

"Another boat?" With a quick peck on West's cheek, I wiggled out of his hold and fell into Langston's captain's chair. "That doesn't make sense," I said, totally bewildered. "Unless we broke up some kind of drug deal or something."

"Or something," Langston muttered to himself. "West, keep your gun close. We need to stay on alert until we're back home, safe at the docks."

He stared off into the night, studying the area where we'd last seen the ship—and the extra boat, it seemed. "I want to do a quick pass by where they were. See if they left anything behind that would tell us what the hell we just interrupted." The cushions molded beneath my palms when I pushed off the seat to stand, but Langston shook his head. "You stay right there for now, where I know you're safe." He kissed the top of my head before gripping the wheel with one hand and the throttle with the other.

I wrapped both arms around his waist and squeezed. "Same."

West plugged in the spotlight, directing the blinding beam over the dark water. I scanned the waves, not noticing anything floating among the whitecaps. A few moments later, West jerked the light, moving back a few feet.

"Did you two see that?" he muttered. "Get closer to where I'm spotlighting. I think I saw something floating."

"What was it?" Langston asked, already turning the wheel to do as West asked. The engines roared to life, pushing the boat through the water.

"It was orange, I think. The color of those cheap life preservers."

I sat forward, palms on the seat to keep me steady.

"Remember that scream and splash? Could be that someone fell in," I suggested.

"There," West exclaimed and jutted out his index finger, cutting through the light to help isolate where he pointed. "You see it?"

I sat up, holding on to the edge as I leaned forward, but I still couldn't see a damn thing.

Langston grunted something and pushed on the throttle, clearly seeing whatever West did. Frustrated, I doubled my effort, straining to see whatever it was.

The boat shifted; the waves had calmed for a split second. A surprised gasp escaped and my hand flew up to cover my parted lips when I finally saw it.

I wish I hadn't.

"Is that...?" I couldn't finish, too focused on keeping my breathing steady so I didn't pass out. Turning, I buried my face in Langston's side, not wanting to see the floating life vest and person attached to it as we drew closer.

The two men whispered over my head, their tones low to keep me from hearing the conversation. If only it worked.

"What the fuck should we do?" The panic in West's tight voice made me want to hug him.

"We can't leave the body out there. Not only is it cruel to the deceased, but it's evidence of what went down tonight."

Langston's deep voice vibrated in his chest, tickling my cheek.

"Evidence of what?"

"Fuck if I know. Fuck if I fucking know."

West's radiating body heat vanished from my back as he went to... I didn't want to know.

Yet I did.

His shirt clutched in my tight grip, I shifted to peek around Langston's ribs to where I heard West's steps fading.

"You got it with your bum hand?" Langston asked.

"I'll figure it out. You've got Juno; that's most important."

My cheeks bunched with a small smile at West's sweet response. I watched him lean over the side, my heart racing with worry that he would fall overboard. His grunt rang through the night as he hauled something out of the water. "I'm good. Even waterlogged she's not that heavy."

"Sh-she?" I stuttered, pushing away from Langston to face where West tugged the limp body of a woman over the side.

Langston grumbled something about me not needing to see this and pulled me back to his chest, but not before I got a good look at the body splayed out on the boat deck. Brow furrowed, I racked my memories. There was something about it, either the face or frame, that felt familiar.

That was crazy, right? How in the world could a dead woman floating in the water, caught up in the middle of some kind of drug deal or whatever was going on, be familiar?

Then it hit me like a punch to the gut. I sucked in a sharp breath and pushed off Langston's chest to stare up at him.

"I think it's her," I whispered.

"Her who?" Langston cupped my face, his worried gaze scanning mine.

"That missing woman from Anchorage, the one on the flyer. It looks like her."

His features softened. "Juno, the body is soaking wet, and it's dark out here even with the lights. How—"

"Holy shit," West shouted, cutting Langston off. "I think she's right. The hair."

I nodded. "She had fire-red dyed hair in the picture. It looks darker wet, but... I mean, what are the odds?"

Langston's lips pressed into a tight line. "Looks like home will have to wait several hours, Juno," he said, sounding utterly exhausted.

Hell, we all were. It had already been a long night and just got longer.

Turning to West, he hitched his chin toward the opposite side of the boat. "There should be a tarp tucked in one of those storage holds. Wrap her up in it; it's our best option to preserve whatever evidence is on her that hasn't been washed away in the water. And...." He paused, brows pulling in tight as if he was thinking hard. "Fuck." Langston's curse rang through the dark night. Turning around, he ripped off his ball cap and threw it down on the ground.

"What?" I asked, hugging myself. A chill had wrapped its icy fingers around me as I came down from the adrenaline high and refused to release its hold.

He turned and stared at me, clearly torn about responding.

"What, Langston? What were you just thinking about?" I asked again, adding force to my tone.

With a resigned sigh, he tipped his face up to the cloudy sky.

"I think I know what's happening to all the women."

THE FLAMES in the fireplace flickered, the bright orange and glowing reds pulling me into an almost hypnotic state. The cup of coffee I held between my palms had lost its warmth long ago, but still I clutched the mug like it was a lifeline.

Three days had passed since that horrible night. In stunned and horrified silence, we'd escorted the body to Anchorage and notified the coroner. We also stayed to speak to the FBI agent Hudson wanted us to meet with after we told him about the incident. Almost six hours later, our boat coasted into Anchor Bay, with Langston and West worried and on alert, and me exhausted, traumatized, and terrified.

The crackle of the flames licking across the wood was what I focused on instead of the conversation happening behind the couch between Langston, West, Hudson, and Oliver. I didn't want to hear the details of what everyone now suspected was actually happening to the missing women in Anchorage and here.

Human trafficking.

Those two words ran on a loop, ringing in my ears, following me in my sleep since Langston had uttered them that night on the boat. It was terrifying and disgusting, but it made the most sense. It was why we hadn't found most of the missing women, and why their male hiking partners ended up dead.

I pressed a fist to my stomach as it rolled. It hadn't been settled since that night, and I wondered if it ever would be. Tears sprang to my eyes, turning the flickering flames watery in my vision as my thoughts once again shifted to those poor women who we'd all assumed were dead. Now we knew they probably weren't, though they likely wished that they were. I swallowed hard to keep the bile from creeping up my throat.

So much had happened in the last several days, it was almost too much to process. Too much for me, at least. The guys were better at compartmentalizing everything. Amy had been by to check on me, but what was there to say?

"I agree that it seems suspicious," Oliver whispered as he paced the room, judging by the sound of his voice moving away from behind the couch. "But that woman went missing from Anchorage, not Anchor Bay. We have nothing to tie the cases there to what's going on here."

"That's bullshit, and you know it," West spat, clearly worked up.

Blinking several times to force away the unshed tears, I swiveled on the couch, the leather groaning beneath me, to face the four men.

Oliver held up his hands in surrender. "I agree it's bullshit, but we need evidence, something to link those missing women to the ones here. Until we can do that, they're separate incidents. The FBI is handling the Anchorage cases as top priority with everything that happened on the boat, but they are *only* investigating those cases as potential human trafficking."

"Then what are your thoughts on the unsolved cases here?" I asked.

Everyone turned to me, concern and worry clear on their faces as I stood, setting the mug down and hugging the blanket wrapped around my shoulders. "Where are the missing women? Where is Caroline? Nothing about this made sense before. Now this, human trafficking, does."

West shifted around the couch to stand beside me, pulling me against his chest in a comforting hold.

"We don't know," Hudson answered after a few seconds

of awkward silence. "What we thought Ethan found along the trail belonging to the deceased female hiker was a dead end. On that case, at least, but possibly something else unrelated." He and Oliver shared a strange look that had me stiffening. *Fuck, what else is going on in this town?* "Ethan is back out there searching for anything that could be helpful."

I studied his face as he spoke, the concern for my friend's husband mounting. Dark circles had formed beneath both eyes. His face, normally slightly tan, was now pale, the whites of his eyes bloodshot.

"When was the last time you slept?" I asked, hitching my chin at Hudson so he knew I was talking to him.

The corners of his lips curled in a forced smile, but it came off more like a grimace. "I don't know, maybe before that bastard broke into my home and threatened my family?"

I gaped at him. "You can't be serious."

He shrugged his broad shoulders. "A few hours here and there are enough until we catch this fucker."

My loose hair shifted over my shoulders as I shook my head. Stepping out of West's arms, I walked right up to Hudson. "No." His brows flew up his forehead, his gaze sliding over my head to Langston and West. "Don't look at them. Look at me. You need proper sleep to be at your best, and right now, Hudson, that's exactly what we need." I turned to Oliver. "No offense."

He scoffed. "None taken. I'm a deputy sheriff of a small town where poaching was our biggest problem before all this. Hudson is the big-shot detective who's closed tons of murder and serial cases back in LA."

"What are you getting at, Juno?" Langston asked. His familiar scent wrapped around me as he curled an arm around my waist.

I twisted to point at him and then to West. "I'm volunteering one of you to go to Hudson's place with him and watch over his family while he gets some much-needed sleep." They all started to protest, but I sliced a hand through the air. "That's it, right? That's why you're not sleeping, because then your family will be vulnerable."

"Juno, I—"

I cut West off with a hard look.

"You don't think I've noticed that one of you is always awake?" He and Langston both quickly avoided eye contact, proving I was right. "Hudson doesn't have that. So one of you will go with him to watch over the house while he sleeps."

"I don't need a babysitter," Hudson grumbled, sounding very pouty.

"No, you need a friend who will watch over your family like you would so you can get the sleep you desperately need."

"Juno," Langston sighed.

Stepping out of his hold, I crossed both arms over my chest and gave him my best "don't fuck with me" expression.

"Okay." He clapped his hands together. "You heard her. West, let's draw straws to see who gets to play guard dog while the princess here sleeps."

Hudson flipped him the bird and rolled his eyes. "I'd threaten to kick your ass for that, but I'm too fucking tired."

Langston's brows pulled in as he studied Hudson before nodding. "No straws. I'm coming with you."

While he and Hudson figured all that out, Oliver came over to me, rubbing the back of his neck. "Thank you for that. I don't think anyone else has noticed how exhausted he is besides me and Calista." He reached out and grabbed my hand, holding it up to inspect my knuckles. "I heard you popped that douchecanoe ex of yours." A small smile formed on his lips. "How did it feel?"

"Fantastic," I replied, a wide smile pulling at my cheeks.

"Good. And it looks like your fist form was perfect, nothing broken and no heavy bruising."

"I had an excellent teacher." He shook his head and dropped my hand, but I grabbed his before he stepped away. "I'm serious, Oliver. Thank you. I felt strong in that moment. I knew what I could do, and I did it. I haven't felt that powerful in a long, long time."

"I hate that you felt weak before coming to me, but I'm so damn proud of you for where you are now."

Langston stepped up beside us, glaring at Oliver like he wanted to test his punching skills on his face.

"You're going to make some woman beyond happy one day," I said to Oliver while wrapping both arms around Langston's waist. "I wonder what she'll be like."

He waved me off with a grin and turned to follow Hudson out the front door.

"I'll be back later tonight." Gripping my chin, Langston held me in place as he pressed a hard kiss to my lips.

My heart raced, heat filling my veins as desire had my lower belly flipping. A pitiful whimper escaped when he broke it off, pulling back just enough that our lips brushed.

A cocky smile curved his lips. "Tonight, we'll finish this." A deep chuckle escaped him at my dramatic pout. "And no playing together while I'm gone. I want to be here to watch it all when I get home."

A hard chest pressed against my back, a hand sneaking around to dip beneath my shirt and rest on my bare skin. I sucked in a tight breath as West's fingers brushed along the seam of my low-rise sweatpants.

"We'll be waiting," he said, nipping at my earlobe.

Cursing under his breath about sleep being dumb and asshole friends, Langston stormed out the front door, slamming it shut behind him.

With a wide smile, I shifted to look up and behind me. "That wasn't very nice," I admonished West.

With a quick kiss to the end of my nose, he stepped back and shrugged. "Keying him up now will make tonight more fun for all of us." He waggled both eyebrows suggestively as he pushed his thick frames up his nose. I loved those glasses on him and had almost asked him to stop wearing contacts altogether so they would be a permanent accessory. "Don't worry, I'll ask him to take all that pent-up frustration out on me."

I slapped his arm with a laugh, his wide grin making his dimples pop.

After grabbing the dirty mug off the coffee table, I started for the kitchen, unable to stop grinning from ear to ear. Placing it in the sink to wash later, I leaned back against the counter, taking in the small cabin. The living room looked different from that first visit, a little more disorganized with all my gaming systems around the TV, my shoes by the front door, and the several throw blankets I couldn't live without lying in piles on the couch and floor. It looked warm, lived-in, and the warmth filling the space had nothing to do with the fire I'd begged the boys to start earlier to help distract me from all the dark thoughts racing through my head.

This was what a happy *home* felt like.

This was what being loved for who you were, true partnership and friendship, was meant to be.

I worried my lower lip. Maybe, just maybe, this time the good wouldn't fade away or end.

With Langston and West, us three, we were the real

thing.

What we had was beyond love. It was a beautiful, perfect mixture of love, trust, and respect that we would never let slip away.

This kind of life, truly living out loud, was everything I'd always wanted and finally had.

I loved them with all that I was. Every cell in my body, every beat of my heart was theirs. And it wasn't because of the orgasms or pretty words or fickle feelings. They loved me for me, saw my quirky and irritable and introverted sides and still loved me. Neither wanted me to change for them or hide parts of myself.

And maybe now, with their help, I could finally figure out how to love myself too.

27

LANGSTON

Beads of sweat dripped down my spine as I raised the axe over my shoulder before swinging it down with a grunt. The sharp edge landed in the middle of the log, splitting it in two. Dropping the heavy tool, I grabbed both pieces and added them to the firewood stack. Gripping the rag stuffed in my back jeans pocket, I wiped the sweat about to drip into my eyes.

Loud laughter poured from the open windows of the cabin, and a genuine smile pulled at my lips at the sound. Juno and West were inside having a *Friends* marathon, which I'd opted out of so I could get some work done that only someone with two good hands could do. We needed the extra firewood since Juno requested a fire almost every morning despite the nice weather we'd been blessed with the last few days.

It made it hotter than Satan's asshole inside, but the fire made her happy, and West and I loved seeing her happy. I also think she secretly enjoyed seeing us walk around the house in nothing but our boxer briefs all day in our desperate attempt to not die of heat exhaustion.

Chuckling to myself, I reached for the axe handle, ready to continue, when movement out of the corner of my eye had me reaching for my pistol instead. Pointing the barrel at the people coming toward me, I cursed and slowly lowered the weapon when I recognized who it was.

"You trying to get shot, assholes?" I grumbled to Oliver and Ethan.

When they didn't respond, I froze, studying their rigid body language and grim expressions.

"What happened?"

The two men exchanged unreadable looks before turning back to me.

"As you know, I've been out on the trail, scouring every inch to find anything that could link back to the woman we found a few weeks ago," Ethan said.

I nodded, having known this already.

"Well, yesterday I took my search farther off the trail. I hadn't gone far, and I swear I'd searched that area before, but...." He trailed off with a sigh.

"What?" I demanded. "What the fuck did you find?"

"A body?" He said it more like a question, as if he was unsure.

"How are you not sure what you found?" I huffed. "Are you saying it wasn't human?"

Ethan looked to Oliver for help, which made my impatience rise.

Oliver was the one who responded. "What Ethan is trying to get at, in a strange way, is that yes, it was human, but it was badly decayed."

Ethan grimaced. "It looked like a damn mummy. Something out of those history shows Oliver likes so much."

The man in question shoved Ethan hard. "The hell, man. Stay on topic."

"Just saying, you have a strange fascination with the History Channel."

My brows pulled in tight as I listened to the two go back and forth, trying to piece together the information. "That means the body had been in the elements a while, so it could be one of the missing female hikers and they really did go off the path?"

They exchanged another look, pissing me off. There was something going on between those two, but I wasn't in the mood to figure it out. Later, when I wasn't about to bash their heads together, hoping that would speed up the conversation so I could finish chopping wood and get inside to finish what we'd started earlier.

"Get the fuck on with it," I snapped, instantly stopping their strange silent conversation.

"It was near the base of a large rock formation, a place where Caroline would go on her own sometimes."

Hearing our missing friend's name froze me in place. "You don't think...."

Oliver's responding nod had me sucking in a breath. "Even though the skin was wrinkled and dried out, we made out a few tattoos along the body's forearms." He took a deep breath, blowing it out roughly through his nose. "The body Ethan found yesterday evening, which is on its way to the Anchorage coroner now, is Caroline."

I stumbled back as if someone had landed a blow right to my stomach. "But how...?" I rasped, my mind running through a thousand thoughts a second. I shook my head. "There's no way. We searched all her normal places and found nothing, not a scrap of evidence saying she'd been there recently, much less a fucking body. And that's not even counting the hours Miles and Aiden put in searching. There's no way we or they missed her."

My heart raced with the unanswered questions, big fucking red flags waving wildly, telling me this was wrong. Something wasn't adding up. Just like the entirety of the missing women cases, nothing made sense.

Ethan shook his head, running a hand through his thick hair. "I don't know, Langston. I don't fucking know. It's like it appeared out of nowhere, but the condition of the body says it was there the whole damn time."

I scoffed, dropping my head forward with a slow shake. "So, either we're all idiots and are terrible at the rescue and recovery part of our jobs, or...." I looked at the two men, hoping they had something to offer.

"Someone moved her body," Oliver stated, his tone solemn. "That's the only thing that makes sense to me. And I can only think of one reason someone would do that."

Dipping my chin in agreement, I released a slow breath. "To throw us off."

Ethan stepped closer. "Because we're getting too close."

Fucking hell. Too close to what? All I knew was that the danger that had felt far away, removed from our community, was circling, putting us all in the crosshairs.

Our friend was dead.

Her body had been moved.

What the hell was going on in Anchor Bay... and how the fuck could we stop it?

Keep reading for the conclusion of Langston, Juno, and West's story.

SEVEN MONTHS LATER

"You have to understand, I'm glad you did that, but I'm just not at a place where I'm ready to see you yet. Maybe one day, but not now. Everything is still too fresh." I watched Juno pace in front of the stone fireplace, the flames flickering and adding much-needed warmth to the cold cabin. Phone pressed to her ear, she nodded along to whatever the other person said. "Again, I'm happy for you, but give me time, okay? You too. Bye."

With an exaggerated groan, she tossed her phone onto Langston's chair, disturbing GG's nap, and stomped over to the couch, falling down beside me.

I chuckled at her dramatics. "That bad?"

Sticking out her lower lip in a full pout, Juno laid her head on my lap and turned to stare up at me. "That was my sister." Lifting a curly lock, I twisted it around my finger. "They didn't have the wedding that weekend, which we figured, since they didn't want his two black eyes in the pictures." Her slow smirk turned into a wide smile. "But it turns out, it never happened at all. I honestly hadn't even thought to follow up with everything that happened here and our big news."

"Shut the front door," I exclaimed. What could I say? Her terms had rubbed off on me these past few months.

Juno nodded. "She wants to see me, but it's too soon for me. The way she believed that asshole in the alley isn't something I can just get over. It will take more time than what's passed for me to be ready to see her again."

"And that douchecanoe?"

"Didn't ask, don't care," she responded with a small shrug.

We both turned to the front door when it swung open, snow billowing inside as Langston stormed in. He slammed it shut, dusting off the thin layer of flakes that had settled on his thick coat.

"How did it go?" Juno asked. "Is Brandon good with the cabin design?"

After removing his coat, he turned with an arched brow. "Do you think I'd actually let him say no to something you want?"

She looked at me with a wide grin, making my own lips pull upward.

"Told you." I pitched forward and planted a soft kiss on her lips. Without even realizing it, my hand settled on her lower belly, dipping beneath her thick sweatshirt. She shivered as I drew lazy circles around her belly button. "Like he'd ever let you or this little guy—"

"Or girl," she cut in.

"If it's a girl"—Langston's knees popped as he squatted beside the couch, brushing his lips against hers—"I'm going to need more guns."

"Either way," I laughed. "No way would Langston let him or her not have the very best."

Just thinking about being a dad had my heart rate picking up. There was equal amounts of fear and excitement that constantly flowed through me after Juno told us she was pregnant. I didn't have a father figure to look up to, but I sure as hell had several I knew I never wanted to be anything like.

Same with Langston.

The grump had always been high-strung, but he'd been a thousand times worse since finding out about the baby.

Hell, all the men in the community had. It was a fucking baby boom, to the point that Carl was debating adding a school to the building list on top of all the three-bedroom cabins. Ours being one of them.

"I know one thing he or she will have the best of," Juno said, her lids fluttering closed as if already halfway asleep.

"The best dads. Loving, protective, fun." I brushed some hair off her forehead, my heart swelling to the point that it ached. "They are already so lucky to have something none of us did."

"A family," I whispered. "A real, happy, loving family."

"A home," Langston added. "Safe, secure, warm."

Her soft snores filled the small space, barely audible over the crackle of the fire.

I couldn't stop watching her, in utter awe of how my life had turned out. It took living through hell and barely crawling out of it for me to be here, with her, with Langston, beyond happy and unconditionally loved. I'd always thought that someone like me didn't deserve a perfect life like this, my past too tarnished, but now that I had this life, I would cherish every moment, each second, forever.

I just wished forever was a little bit longer.

. . .

Want to know what happens next with the missing women cases? Preorder Anchor Bay book 4, Keeping Ours, today! Throuple reveal coming soon!

Interested in reading Hudson and Calista's story? Download a copy of Mind to Shelter for FREE with Kindle Unlimited!

Read Rain, Jameson and Slade's story before seeing them in Anchor Bay book 4! Mine to Share is available now and free to read with KU!

ALSO BY KENNEDY L. MITCHELL

Anchor Bay: An Alaskan small town suspense, MFM, interconnected standalone series.

Our Chance - Anchor Bay prequel

Forever Theirs - Aiden, Miles, & Aspen

Claiming Ours - Liam, Memphis, & Baylee

Only Theirs - Langston, Juno, & West

Keeping Ours

Book 5

In Clear Sight: A Small Town, WITSEC Interconnected Standalone Series

Safe Haven - FREE Prequel

Guarded by the Marshal*

Cherished by the Agent*

Saved by the Officers *

Hidden by the Doctor *

*Now available in Audio!

Protection Series: A Dark Romantic Thriller Interconnected Standalone Series

Mine to Protect *

Mine to Save *

Mine to Guard *

Mine to Keep *

Mine to Hold *

Mine to Love *

Mine to Share *

Mine to Shelter

Mine to Shield

*Now available in audio!

SEALs and CIA Series: A Navy SEAL Interconnected Standalone Series

Covert Affair

Covert Vengeance

More Than a Threat Series: A Connected Bodyguard Romantic Suspense Series

More Than a Threat

More Than a Risk

More Than a Hope

More Than a Threat Series Boxset: Complete Series

Power Play Series: A Protector Romantic Suspense Connected Series

Power Games

Power Twist

Power Switch

Power Surge

Power Term

Standalones:

Finding Fate - Dark, Captive Romantic Suspense

Memories of Us - Contemporary, Small Town Romance

ABOUT THE AUTHOR

Kennedy L. Mitchell lives outside Dallas with her son, goldendoodle, and giant puppy. She began writing in 2016 and has no plans of stopping.

She would love to hear from you via any of the platforms below or her website www.kennedylmitchell.com You can also stay up to date on future releases through her newsletter or by joining her Facebook readers group - Kennedy's Book Boyfriend Support Group.

Thank you for reading.

ACKNOWLEDGMENTS

I hope you enjoyed Juno's healing journey and if you're going through something similar, it made you feel seen. No relationship is perfect but that doesn't mean that how you're being treated is right.

For those of you close to me you know how much writing this story meant to me. Thank you to Chris, Emily, Kristin and Darlene for being there when I needed you most. You listened to me vent, process through my grief, and help me understand that while I blamed myself for everything that wasn't exactly the case.

And of course to my two amazing editors and proofreader who turn my crazy mess of words into something readable!

I have so much more I want say about this book and my own healing journey but not yet. Maybe in some future acknowledgements I'll sneak something in, but until then I just want everyone to know that you're amazing. And if you're hovering in the deep, pitch black hole of grief that you can't seem to crawl yourself out of I get it. I was there and with the help of amazing friends, family and a lot of therapy I finally made my way out of it. I wish the same for you. If you don't have anyone to vent to, email me. I'm here, I'll listen.

Until next time friends.

Stay amazing.

I hope every book you read between now and when we're together again are all five star reads!

www.ingramcontent.com/pod-product-compliance
Lightning Source LLC
Chambersburg PA
CBHW032142050726
47591CB00001B/54